Songbird

WALTER ZACHARIUS

Songbird

A Novel

ATRIA BOOKS

New York   London   Toronto   Sydney

ATRIA BOOKS
1230 Avenue of the Americas
New York, NY 10020

ISBN: 0-7434-8211-5

First Atria Books hardcover edition September 2004

10 9 8 7 6 5 4 3 2 1

ATRIA BOOKS is a trademark of Simon & Schuster, Inc.

Manufactured in the United States of America

For information regarding special discounts for bulk purchases, please contact
Simon & Schuster Special Sales at 1-800-456-6798 or business@simonandschuster.com

Roberta Grossman

My former publishing partner who challenged me to write this novel sixteen years ago. She died almost twelve years ago at the age of forty-six and never had a chance to read the final version. If it wasn't for her inspiration, I would never have challenged myself to write *Songbird.*

Steven Zacharius

My publishing partner for the last eleven years. It is interesting to have a son working with you. It's not always easy, but I think we got to know each other much better.

Judy Zacharius

My adventurous daughter, who has traveled throughout the world and is living many of my dreams. Maybe someday she will write her own book. I hope to read it.

Cori Zacharius
Adam Zacharius

My grandchildren . . . may they never live through the horrors in this book.

Jonathan Teicher
Mary Stanton
Richard Marek

Without you I don't think this book would have come together. I would still be lost in the wilderness.

Owen Laster

From the William Morris Agency, who had the courage to take me on as his client and gave me the confidence to move ahead.

MICHAELA HAMILTON

Editor in chief of Kensington Publishing Corp. She gave me a quick course in the do's and don'ts of writing. She made me realize that being an author is far more difficult than being a publisher.

DOROTHY TARALLO

My assistant for many years. She retyped so much of this manuscript over and over again that she knows the story by heart.

ERENA TOPCHIEVA

My piano teacher for the last ten years and the only piano teacher I ever had. She not only taught me the piano, but also her love of music. She helped me select the music in this book and encouraged me to keep going.

EMILY BESTLER

Vice president, executive editorial director at Atria Books, a division of Simon & Schuster, and the editor of my book. She made me rethink many parts of this book. I always believe a great editor is behind a great book. She personifies what is important in book publishing.

TO MY ENTIRE STAFF AT KENSINGTON PUBLISHING CORP.

Your words of wisdom and encouragement were a great help.

ALICE ZACHARIUS

The most important person in my life. She has shared my dreams for over fifty years. She encouraged me and walked hand in hand with me throughout many difficult periods of my publishing career. Without her help and encouragement I would never have come this far . . . and we still have many miles to travel.

Songbird

Prologue

1975

In the twilight, the grove of cypress on the Lebanese border looks like a small army, poised for attack. This is not too fanciful, for the kibbutz next to my tiny farm has been subjected to periodic shelling, and if an invasion comes there is little to distinguish me from the kibbutzim, though unlike them I have no weapons with which to fight back.

The shelling has been going on for over a year now—sometimes weekly, sometimes three or four times a week; idle entertainment for the Arab troops—but most days I feel safe. The grove that separates my fertile land from the brown, untended fields on the Lebanese side is a place of shelter, my refuge from horrors.

Although the night is quiet, I feel intoxicated. Tomorrow I am to be visited by a man I once loved, and the prospect is at once so exciting and so chilling that I cannot be still: I pace in front of my house, looking at the verdant trees, smelling the sweet air, listening to the sounds of the birds singing, and remembering his touch, his taste, though I have not touched or tasted him for almost thirty years.

Oh, I can't wait. My flesh comes alive again even without him here, even at the thought of him. The sense memory is so strong I find I must take deep breaths to slow my heart, and when I do I am able to go back inside and pick up the letter announcing his arrival.

Dear Mia,

I saw your picture last week in a TV news report about the border tension—and there you were—working the fields (you a farmer?) as lovely and heartbreakingly beautiful as ever. I knew immediately that I must see you. I realized how much I missed you and with a bit of detective work I found your address.

You can't stop me. By the time you get this I'll be on the plane to Israel, arriving at your house on the twenty-seventh, and besides, you don't know my address. I've moved since we last saw each other in America.

What will it be like, our meeting? You can kick me out, or choose to say nothing, or you can greet me with a hug and we can fill in our years apart. But most of all, of course, we can remember.

Your Vinnie

Remember him, true. But by doing so, I remember all the other things as well. That's why I'm chilled. That's why I'm afraid. His letter has ripped open the scab, and I sit here bleeding for both of us.

Maybe if I force myself to remember it all before he comes, the sight of him will bring comfort and I can begin to love again.

Or maybe not.

BOOK I

Confined against my will. Trapped. *Imprisoned.* That's my memory of the summer of 1939. It was, of course, long before I'd seen a real prison or been locked away.

We were vacationing that summer in Krzemieniec, "the Polish Athens," an ugly, provincial little artists' colony where we had stayed the past ten summers and which, until this year, I had adored. Now adolescent hormones had taken hold, spiraling me alternatively into giddiness and despair, and keeping me in a near rage at my parents, who had brought me to this hellhole while my classmates were spending their holidays at chic Riviera hotels and Loire Valley chateaux. Jews had always made up a sizeable minority of the resort's seasonal population, and this year was no exception. The Polish families, like ours, mingled with the guests from Germany and France.

The Café Tarnopol, once the poet Slowacki's salon, seemed old-fashioned now, dusty and boring, just like our hotel, and the bourgeoisie who rented the same rooms year after year filled the café with their mediocrity. They no longer spoke of Slowacki, or Pushkin, or even Baudelaire. On no. Conversations this season focused on "Jew this" and "Jewish that" till I thought I'd go mad.

It was impossible to concentrate on my music. In previous years, I'd played Chopin's *Fantaisie Impromtu* or Nocturne, Op. 72, but this year the non-Jews insisted on Wagner, Hitler's favorite composer, and the Jews didn't dare object. Aryan music had become high culture because of Adolph Hitler, and also because of him my parents, obsessed with our safety, returned to Krzemiemiec from our home in Lodz, rather than go to Switzerland, which my father could at long last afford. It was too cruel. I gave up playing anything at all in public, refused to sing, and moped about the hotel, looking vainly for someone to share my misery. Jozef, my brother, was working on his doctoral dissertation in Kraków, all the other guests were as old as my parents, and the local girls shunned me and called me names.

My mother scolded me for being too dramatic and too impatient. "When it rains Mia gets wet," she told my father, "even if we're inside."

The miserable summer of 1939 dragged on. Once, after a wasted afternoon of failing to practice my scales on the hotel's piano, I escaped to my room and flopped across the massive four-poster. Catching my reflection in the full-length mirror as I landed, I jumped up, startled, to examine the mysterious creature who seemed to have taken over my body—a young woman with high, taut cheekbones, dark skin, jet-black hair, and green eyes rimmed with amber.

"You have Jewish eyes," I told the stranger. "You have big sensuous Jewish lips, a succulent Jewish neck, and big Jewish breasts." But my height and long waist were gifts from my mother. Although my hair was black and curly, my hands were tapered with the long fingers of a pianist, and my legs were thin and shapely, my feet small. Maybe I'm only half-Jewish, I told myself, and I should be grateful. I could pass.

Jozef, I realized, did not look Jewish either. With his tall, muscular build and blond hair (where had *that* come from?) he could have passed for a Nordic prince. Back home in Lodz when I walked beside him with my hair tied back with a silk scarf, he made me look like his gypsy bride. How I missed him!

I stared at my profile, trying to imagine one of those repulsive Jewish armbands with the Star of David set against my skin. Just before term's end, a classmate had brought me one from Berlin. My father told me that if I had gone to the Salzberg conservatory instead of the Lycée in Paris, I'd be wearing one.

A wave of rage engulfed me, and I yanked off the carved ivory barrettes I wore in my hair and released the two long braids, which Mama had painstakingly, and painfully, wound around my head. The long curls bounced back wildly and spilled onto my shoulders. I was well past sixteen, yet Mama insisted on treating me like a child. She kept me in plain cotton slips like some wretched Heidi and forbade me to use lipstick.

There was a sharp rap on the door. "Schatzie?"

My father. I raced to the latch and locked it.

"Are you in there?"

"Yes, Papa." I sighed, leaning against the door.

"Have tea with us in the gazebo. I have a surprise."

Father's surprises were usually disappointing. "I'm not ready."

"You've got five minutes," he said. Then, perhaps regretting his harshness: "Is anything wrong?"

Wrong! I felt tears gathering in the corners of my eyes. How could I make him understand that *everything* was wrong? This place, my clothes, a summer among Jews without Jozef. Even Bach seemed boring. Mozart. Schoenberg. The Café Tarnopol. Mama and Papa themselves. Boring, boring, *boring!*

"I'll be right down," I shouted and began pinning my hair up, rebelliously allowing a few stray wisps to float about my ears and neck.

Papa's surprise was sitting beside Mama in the gazebo—a trim, immaculate man of about fifty, dressed in a three-piece suit utterly out of place in a resort, who was tugging on his long mustache.

"Here you are!" my mother exclaimed, looking angrily at my messy hair. "Pappie and I have been waiting for you to—"

"Never mind," my father whispered in Yiddish. Then, in French, "Mia, this is professor Jules Stern. He is a lecturer in philosophy at the Sorbonne, and a great lover of opera. And this, Professor Stern, this is my little songbird."

Songbird! All my triumph at my mother's distress dissolved, leaving me stranded between humiliation and fury.

"Enchanté," Professor Stern said, rising to kiss my hand. His eyes roamed over me. "And may I call you—"

"Marisa, Monsieur . . . Mia," I managed.

He flashed a toothy grin beneath his mustache, and I felt the intensity of his eyes. Removing my hand from his sweaty grip, I scurried toward a chair next to my mother's.

Papa intercepted me, grabbing my waist playfully and swinging me onto his lap as if I were a child.

"Dr. Levy has told me of your accomplishments, Mia." The professor smiled. "A singer and a pianist both! Perhaps you'll perform for me."

"Of course she will," Papa exclaimed, sending me on my way with a stinging love-spank. "My daughter is a prodigy. Why, in Paris she performed Schoenberg's *Erwartung.*"

I refused to look at either of them. Was this some sort of slave market at which I was to be auctioned off?

"As you can imagine," Papa rattled on, "it was a hard decision—denying her the Mozartium. But the way things have gone for poor Austria. . . ." His voice trailed off.

My mother poured tea, passed around a platter heaped with Sacher torte. "Our son, Jozef, is also accomplished," she offered. "A celebrated German scholar at the university in Kraków."

Stern ignored her. He was staring at me. "Do you know Stravinsky's work?" he asked me. "Nobody is more talked about in Paris. I sincerely hope, Benjamin, that you and your family will be able to see his *Oedipus Rex* at L'Opera this fall."

Papa sighed. "I'm afraid I won't be able to get away from Warsaw. I will be extremely busy at my medical clinic. But Mia will be back in Paris by then. She has another year at the Lycée."

The professor practically salivated. "I shall be delighted to accompany you myself, Ma'amselle. That is, of course, with your parents' consent." He took a bite of his Sacher torte.

I snapped my head up as though I had been slapped by an invisible hand. I thought Stravinsky far inferior to Schoenberg so wouldn't even have gone on my own. But with this man. . . .

My father was looking at me expectantly. "Of course, Monsieur. I would be honored," I heard myself mumble.

A piece of pastry from my plate tumbled down onto the pale violet napkin on my thighs. Blushing crimson with embarrassment, I seized the corners of the napkin, flung it on the table, pushed my chair back, bolted down the gazebo steps, and fled down the gravel path to the safety of the gatehouse at the bottom of the hill. The tears that had been building all summer began to spill.

Embarrassment for my parents filled me with shame. Wasn't there condescension in the way the other guests hailed them? Did the Parisians and Berliners think of them as "those boors from Warsaw"? Were they the brunt of those hideous Jewish jokes?

My parents wanted me to attend the best schools because education was very important to them. I began studying the piano in Lodz when I was six and for many years had dreams of being a concert pianist. I also loved to sing. The lycée in Paris seemed to be the best school for me to attend. My father was a successful doctor, and he wanted my brother and me to benefit from his success.

Two years before, in September, Papa insisted on driving me to the lycée, taking a route through Austria and Switzerland, and touring the French countryside on the way to Paris.

In Vienna, Mama's Yiddish—she knew no German—embarrassed her. The hotel maids and bellboys ignored her or pretended not to understand what she was saying. In Switzerland, she regained some of her composure, but in the peaceful heart of the Loire Valley, the innkeepers made fun of her French and behind our backs pointed us out as *les Juifs* to the other guests.

When we reached Paris, Papa registered us at the Hotel Steinfeld, a place Jews preferred, where at last my mother was comfortable. I insisted that we go immediately to the lycée LaCourbe-Jasson, and after interminable introductions and instructions, the headmistress at last directed me toward my room in a building across the courtyard.

I ran away from them, my mother, who seemed somehow tainted, and my father, who was unable to protect her. I ran without looking back, carrying my heavy suitcase, and stumbled up the steps of my home-to-be. I paused at the door of my room on the second floor long enough to catch my breath and pull my sweaty cotton under-shirt away from my skin. There was light coming from the transom and I could hear girls laughing within. My roommate hosting a first-day party, I imagined. I knocked.

The door opened and a round face peered out. "Who's there?"

"It's me. Marisa Levy."

"Levy did you say?"

"Yes."

"Okay, Marisa," the face said, and the doors flung open, leaving me revealed to six sets of inquisitive eyes.

At my appearance, the room exploded with laughter. Somebody said the words "new Jewess," and the hilarity increased. I thought of my mother at the Viennese hotel and understood that I was experi-encing now what she had—and that I always would.

For the next weeks, my classmates made fun of my textbook French, my braids, my homemade school dresses. And so I retreated into music, the piano keys my dearest companions, their sounds the balm to my soul. I played for my teachers and loved to talk to them, but with the other girls I was silent. Meanwhile, I set about building a wardrobe, mastering French, going alone to cabarets or concert halls.

A clarinetist named Benny Goodman came to Paris to perform with his band, and through the lycée I was able to buy a ticket to hear them. What music they made! It was new to me, melodic, rhythmic, filled with a sensuality I experienced throughout my body, the notes flying from the instruments like wild birds, diving and soaring around my head. Some in the audience began an impromptu dance, and I ached to dance with them, but when a young man came up beside me and asked me to join in, I shook my head and remained seated. When I'm older, I told myself. Then I will dance.

Undaunted, he sat beside me and introduced himself as Jean-Phillipe Cadoux, who had arrived in Paris from Lille two years before, now lived in the 9th arrondissement, and was working as a postal worker to support himself as an architecture student at the École des Beaux Arts. We could talk easily together, once I found that his aggressive approach masked an innate shyness, and we became friends. Just friends so far, but it was to him that I poured out my loneliness and alienation and I knew that when the time came—when it was right—we would become closer. At the end of term we parted, promising to see each other again, and as soon as I returned to Paris he contacted me and we resumed our relationship.

Back in Lodz that summer, more sophisticated and snobbish than all of my classmates combined, I was restless and unhappy. My sweet, pompous father irritated me, and I despised my well-meaning mother for being such a fear-ridden shrew. I scorned them for a lack of elegance and savoir faire, and pitied them, too.

But at that moment, at the hotel gate in Krzemieniec in the summer of 1939, I would have given anything to be Papa's little girl again. When I looked up and saw him coming toward me along the gravel path, I gave a little scream of pleasure and ran to him, crumpling onto his broad shoulder.

"Eh, what's this, Mia?" he asked, stroking my hair.

"It's that man," I said. "Professor Stern. He—"

A loudspeaker began to blare from the top of a black panel wagon approaching the hotel. Papa held up his hand, signaling me to listen. "President Mos´cicki," he said.

"Fellow citizens! Last night, our age-old enemy, Germany, began hostilities against the Polish State. I place on record before God and history that our noble Poland will never be vanquished, that our gallant army will fight to the last man before. . . ."

My father grabbed my hand, and we ran up the hill to the hotel. Guests were fanning out in a dozen different directions. There was pushing and shoving. Young children screamed for their mothers. My own crisis was pushed aside. Life was reduced to motion.

By the time we'd fought our way back to the hotel suite, Mama was already packing. "I thought it would be best," she told Papa.

"You were right not to wait." They spoke in a fearful staccato. Papa paused in the middle of the sitting room, chewing on a fingernail. He was working on our dilemma as if it were a chemical equation.

I ran around Mama and darted toward my room. She raised her head, for once oblivious to my disheveled appearance. "Don't fuss over the packing," she called. "We must be ready to leave at once."

With quick, mechanical motions I transferred piles of clothing from drawers to an open suitcase. Everything fell into a kind of rhythm. Throughout the resort village, the Volhynian Mountains, perhaps all of Eastern Europe, life rushed toward a frenetic crescendo.

I carried my suitcase back to my parents' suite. My father had picked up the phone, his hand covering the receiver. "I'm trying to get through to Jozef, darling. Yes, right this very moment. I . . . wait. Operator? I'm calling Kraków. . . . No. Kraków . . . Yes, Madame, I fully understand . . . yes, of course. . . . But if you would only nonetheless try. . . ." After a while he hung up with a sigh.

An hour later we were standing outside the hotel, huddled next to a mountain of traveling bags, in the midst of a long line of people shoving one another in their attempts to commandeer cars, trucks, wagons—any transportation that would take them home.

Finally we were permitted our turn. A hay cart driven by a drunken peasant rolled up. "Please, sir," Papa called out in his elegant, educated Polish, "we would like to hire your services to take my wife and daughter, plus myself and the luggage as far as Dubow."

"You hear that?" the driver whispered conspiratorially into the horse's ear. "As far as Dubow." He patted the horse's neck with affection then spat on the ground. "How much money you got?"

I could feel Papa fighting an impulse to thrash the farmer for his insolence. "Enough to pay for a cart ride to Dubow."

The peasant raised a questioning eyebrow. "What then?"

"Then?" Papa shook his head as if the question had not occurred to him. "We decide once we arrive. Maybe the train to Lemberg. Or Ostrog. Eventually, Lodz."

"In that case, the price is five hundred zloty."

"Unheard of! In Lodz, we could hire a Daimler to drive us to Krzemieniec and back for that."

"Then do it, Mister. I was offering you a bargain only because you've got such a pretty daughter. I thought she might want to sit in front with me, to keep me warm. Otherwise, my price would be a thou—"

"How dare you!" Papa bellowed in Yiddish, leaping at the driver's throat. With his free hand, the driver drew back his whip and lashed out.

My father fell to the ground, blood streaming from his cheek. His face was a dangerous vermilion.

"His heart," Mama hissed, kneeling to open his collar.

"Filthy Jew bastard," the peasant snarled, lashing out again at the empty air. "You're not fit to lick my horse's asshole." He turned to the people in line. "Next."

A crowd gathered around Papa. Hands stretched out to help him up. The peasant, finding no takers, drove off cursing. "We are not all like that," a woman in the line said. "You and your family will take the next vehicle, whatever it is."

My father, still stunned, looked at her gratefully. My mother began to cry. And I—I thought my heart would never heal.

"Grand Hotel Dubow," our driver called out. Papa climbed out of the back of the oxcart and, with stiff, dignified gestures, brushed the dirt off his suit and handed a wad of zloty notes to the driver. "For a new breeding bull," he explained to the astonished boy. "To replace the one you told me was lost."

Papa helped me and Mama down, removing bits of mud and straw from our hair and shoulders. All about us, an endless stream of travelers passed to and from the train station, evidently seeing nothing unusual in a middle-class family debarking from the rear of an oxcart.

At the reception desk my father introduced himself and asked for rooms.

"Any news?" asked the graying hotel bell captain, clapping his hands to produce a crew of help in red uniforms.

Papa shook his head. "I'm afraid I know nothing. I had hoped that perhaps on the radio. . . ."

The bell captain shrugged. "It must be the same everywhere. Yesterday, there was fighting in Poznan´. They said the Germans also attacked farther down the western border."

Mamma blanched. "Kraków?"

"Madame, the accursed Germans will never reach Kraków. I hear they've been beaten back at Katowice. They're simply no match for the Polish Army. I shouldn't worry. This so-called war may be over before lunch. Now, how may I be of service? Would the doctor care for a suite of rooms or regular connecting rooms? Normally, we're too heavily booked for guests without reservations, but. . . ."

I stared down Main Street. From all directions, people were spilling out onto the road. Dubow had become a town of windup toys gone berserk.

Papa reserved a suite, then reviewed his thinking for us as we sat on the horsehair settee. He thought it would be wise to stay here while the rest of Poland thrashed about. "In a few days the Polish Army might prevail," he mused, "and the Nazi threat could be silenced forever. If not, we would of course be vulnerable in Dubow, so perhaps staying here is not a good idea. For one thing, unlike the artists' colony of Krzemieniec, Dubow is not a town that welcomes Jews." A frown crossed his face. "The bell captain would probably betray us instantly if it meant his own survival."

He paced, examining our options.

"Ostrog is inhospitable, but just beyond it is the Soviet frontier. If the Nazis prevail, from there we could flee to Kiev. Or head south toward Bucharest. But getting to Ostrog would not be easy—"

Mamma interrupted him. "I will not leave Poland until Jozef has joined us."

Papa took her hand and looked into her eyes. "If bad comes to worse, then, we could make our way to Chelm or Lublin, where we have friends. That, of course, would be more difficult than going to Lemburg and taking an express train to Lodz. But surely the Germans will bomb the main railroad tracks, so that way almost surely means exhausting delays if not outright failure." He resumed his pacing. "We could get to the capital from Lublin as well, using a roundabout route, that is, if the Nazis have not bombed the tracks there as well—but that's far less likely—and in Warsaw, we could stop off to see your sister Esther, if she has not fled to Ostrog with David and the children. . . ."

My father's thinking grew more and more convoluted until at last my mother and I could only stare at him helplessly. "Lunch," he said at last, as though he knew what to do, "but first a bath. You women will be able to think more clearly then. Meanwhile, I'll try to call Jozef."

He could not get through, and it was mother, frantic, who persuaded him to go to Lodz via Lublin and Warsaw. For if Jozef had left Kraków, he would surely make his way to our home. There we would welcome him with hugs and kisses, and all would be well.

CHAPTER 2

"*Halt.*"

A surge of humanity carried me across the Lodz station, where I struggled to catch a glimpse of my parents. It had taken us days to travel from Dubow to Lublin, with a stop in Warsaw, on our way home. Although the fighting continued we knew that Poland would finally fall and we had to make provision for the future. In the train, we'd agreed that we had a better chance of avoiding the station guard's suspicion if we detrained separately, since we were smuggling goods my aunt Esther had given us in case the Lodz grocery shops were empty. Suddenly, though, I was not so sure.

"*YOU!*" the same voice thundered. I froze.

My breasts and hips were enhanced by packets of wheat, flour, oats, and ground millet. I literally waddled attempting to navigate through the crowd.

A young soldier stepped in front of me. "Name?" he thundered.

Beneath his clumsy German I detected a Polish accent; he was a *Volkdeutscher,* a German Pole proud to be more Aryan than his Nazi counterparts. His military cap was balanced jauntily on his straw-blond curls, and his glance was insolent. I turned away.

He snatched my coat collar and raised it, forcing me to look at him. "I said give me your name!"

"Let go of me," I ordered him in Polish. How dare he take such liberties? I was a free citizen and he was a pimply faced parody of a soldier. I dropped my suitcase and stared at him defiantly.

"You little cunt," he roared, tearing my coat open. "I'll teach you to defy me." He pushed me to the ground, straddled me, and pried my legs apart. I felt no fear; only anger. A crowd formed around us. Surely they would protect me. Yet they made no move, and their gasps and cries seemed to come from far away. The guard explored my thighs, my breasts. I screamed and flailed at him.

"What seems to be the problem, soldier?" an authoritarian voice snapped above us.

The *Volkdeutscher* leapt to attention, brushing dust off his sleeves. His cap was askew and his ruddy face shone with sweat.

"She's a gypsy smuggler, lieutenant."

The officer shook his head. He was no fool. All around him were overstuffed coats, weighted suitcases, baby strollers without babies. Smuggling in wartime might be a capital offense, but people had to keep from starving. "Is it true?" he asked me. "Are you a gypsy?"

I stood, straightened my clothes and looked at him squarely. He was about my height, barrel-chested with a bulldog face. "No, sir."

"She's lying," the soldier insisted. "Just look at her. Bulges every-where. She's a gypsy smuggler and—"

"Shut up," the officer snarled, slapping the boy's face. The soldier recoiled. The crowd murmured. Instantly, I knew that the lieutenant regretted his impulse and that I would pay for it. I wanted to run, but the crowd had us pinned in.

"This girl denies being a gypsy," the lieutenant said.

"Whatever. She's still smuggling food under her dress."

Now the officer was trapped. Faced with a formal accusation, he couldn't ignore it. "Are you a smuggler, young lady?"

"No, sir." My voice was weak.

"Then you wouldn't mind a search."

The *Volkdeutscher* grinned and took a step toward me.

"I'll take care of this," the officer growled. "Lift up your skirt."

Men in the crowd pressed forward. Women looked away. I stood still, my face afire with humiliation.

"Lift it," the officer repeated, "or I'll do it for you."

I scanned the crowd, hoping that miraculously father or Jozef would rescue me. But of course they were not there. Shame overwhelmed me and I began to cry.

The officer stood in front of me. I raised my head to look at him, seeing—what?—some sort of odd pleasure in his eyes? Deliberately, he caught the hem of my skirt with his riding crop and raised it over my hips. He ran his free hand up and down the inside of each of my thighs, then let the skirt drop.

"Everything's in order," he barked hoarsely, turned on his heel, and parted the crowd just as Moses had parted the Red Sea.

I arrived home to a commotion. The entry doors to our house on Kowalska Street were wide open and a horse-drawn cart was backed up to the porch. Papa, who had evidently arrived moments before me, raced across our lawn where the horse was tearing up mouthfuls of grass.

"What's going on?" he demanded of the driver seated on top of the cab. "Remove this cart immediately!"

"I was hired for this," the driver said. "Who the hell do you think you are?"

"Who am I? I *own* this property, that's who I am. You have exactly two minutes to leave these grounds before I—"

"*Put that down!*" a familiar voice bellowed.

Papa ran into the house where Stasik, our butler, was brandishing a kitchen cleaver above the head of Maria, the maid. "There's the doctor now," he shrieked. "You'll drop it now, all right!"

"What the devil's happening?" my father demanded. "Why is that cart on my lawn, and what's Maria doing?"

"She's stealing Mrs. Levy's silver," Stasik wailed, tugging at the box under Maria's arm. "Drop it, I say."

"Let go," Maria shrieked, digging her nails into his hand. Abruptly, the box sprang open, and silver scattered over the hall floor. "Don't come near me." Maria shrank from my father's approach. From the looks of him, he could have killed her.

Papa seized her wrist and dragged her outside to the rear of the cart, where a half dozen chairs and several paintings had been hastily stacked. "You mean to rob us, Maria? In the name of God, why?"

"Let go of me!" The girl kicked at his shins. "Let go or I'll report you to the authorities." Maria looked at my mother. "For rape."

"But that's disgusting. Absurd. Mrs. Levy and I just this minute arrived."

"Who'll believe you?" Maria's voice was filled with contempt. "Who'll believe a Christ-killer? A lousy stinking Jew?"

A loud roar like an ocean in turmoil filled my ears, and I flew past my father and clawed at her eyes. "You bitch!" I shrieked. "You bitch, you bitch, you bitch!" I flung her to the ground, kicking her as hard as I could.

It was my mother who rescued her. With a strength neither Papa nor I could have imagined, she pulled me off the maid and held me until I stopped shaking. Maria lay curled at our feet, whimpering, and it took an enormous effort to keep me from kicking her again. At last I became aware that my mother was kissing my head, and I heard my father's calm voice reassuring someone that everything was under control.

"It's taken care of, officer," he said, producing a wad of zlotys for the policeman by his side. "A disagreement with the help, that's all."

The policeman extended a hand. "Let me know if you need me," he said, evidently anxious to be off. "This is a peaceful neighborhood, and I wouldn't want it disturbed."

"Thank you." Papa escorted him out the gate then returned to his reclaimed possessions, a trembling Stasik, and Momma clinging to me as if I might erupt again. But my fury was spent.

My father lifted Maria up and placed her gently in the back of the cart. He handed the driver some money. "For a doctor," he explained, "not for you. Understand?" He slapped the horse's rear to get him moving. We stood and watched it go, too numb to say anything. My mother released me but kept kissing my hair. My father put his arms around both of us.

"We shall never discuss this moment again," he said, leading us to the front steps.

The facade of our house on Kowalska Street had always seemed beautiful to me, but now, in the twilight, it was forbidding, and I was loath to cross the threshold, afraid of what we'd find inside. I had been born in this house, grown up in this house, endured my father's tantrums, my brother's teasing, my mother's scolding—and experienced their love. Now as we entered it motes of dust flew around our head like flies and the air smelled musty. The joy each of us felt at being reunited— imagine that, joy because we all made it home from the train station!—was replaced by intense melancholy. Even Stasik, who had preceded us inside, was somber, not at all pleased to see us again.

"The piano," I gasped as mama and I entered the drawing room. "Where's the piano?" It was where I had spent my happiest hours.

Behind me, Mama reeled as if my words had physically struck her. "And the Monet?" she shrieked.

"Maria stole them," Stasik said. "And the silver candlesticks. Her family came and took them yesterday. I pleaded with her, Mrs. Levy. Begged her not to take them. But the girl wouldn't listen and I couldn't stop her. She said if I tried, she'd report me to the authorities." He lowered his lead. "At least I kept the silver menorah."

"You did your best, I'm sure," Mama said. "Dr. Levy and I are very grateful."

"I've worked for the doctor's family for fifty-two years. I started out in Mr. Levy Senior's stables. . . ."

"We appreciate that," Mama said, exhaustion etching her face. She turned to climb the stairs.

The old man wrung his hands. "I watched Jozef and Mademoiselle Mia grow up. I know every nick and swirl of the banister there. I've polished the door knocker so many times that—"

Mama turned to face him. "We appreciate it all," she said warmly. "And in view of the difficulties, I'm sure you earned a vacation. Perhaps you'd like to visit your brother in Zakopane."

"A vacation?" Stasik dropped into one of the chairs at the foot of the landing and began to sob. "After so many years, something more should be said. Surely Dr. Levy's father would have wanted a lifetime employee to. . . ."

"What's the problem?" my father asked, appearing at the top of the stairs.

"Dr. Levy. This house. It's the only life I know. My wife, Bertha, died under this roof. And now, to be sent away without any ceremony. It doesn't seem right."

"Who said anything about sending you away?" Mama seemed to be struggling to understand. "I offered you a vacation."

"But what else could you mean?" Stasik stared at her as if she'd gone mad. "Is it possible that Madame and the Doctor have not read the notices? The ordinances?"

"Of course not," Papa said. "We just arrived."

The old man shook his head. "The new German governor of the Wartheland says it's illegal for Jews to employ *Volkdeutschers* or Poles. If I stay, they'll take everything from you. You are not even allowed to say the name of the Fuhrer or you could be shot."

I watched blood drain from my father's face and felt a strange tug at my heart, as though someone were trying to dislodge it from its steady beat. My mother gave a little cry and ran upstairs to embrace her husband. They seemed suddenly old, older even than Stasik, and the trap I thought I'd escaped by leaving Krzemieniec now seemed to close so tightly around me that I could barely breathe. Selfishly, all I could think of was Paris and the Lycée and Jean-Phillipe and my music. In Paris, I could play and sing. There was no music left in Lodz.

The Nazis conquered Poland in October 1939. Lodz now became a German capital. Street signs were changed, so that Pomorska Boulevard became Fredericusstrasse, and Kowalska Street was now Sophienstrasse. German officers strutted the streets, resplendent in black uniforms and hats, as though they, not we, were its citizens. We learned to keep our voices low, our eyes downcast, our gait measured. We were a defeated people, the Jews most of all.

There was no word from Jozef. Papa finally got through to his school in Kraków, but he had left. No one knew where he had gone. The telegram I was expecting from the lycée telling me when school was to reopen never arrived, and when I called, I was told someone would return my call, but no one did. I knew that without the school's acceptance letter I would not be allowed to leave Poland. Jews were obliged to stay where they were unless they had proof of need to travel. I was a Jew; I had no proof.

Stasik stayed, no longer as our butler but as our guest. Papa gave him two thousand zloty to buy clothes and to use as spending money. He now dressed as one of us but rarely went out. He lived in constant fear he would be discovered, interrogated, and forced to betray us, so he kept to the guest room on the second floor, a silent presence in a silent house.

My father was not allowed to return to his clinic, so he commandeered the laundry room as an office and saw patients—Jewish patients—without having access to adequate medicines. He too left the house rarely, and then usually to go to the Kehillah, the council of prominent Jews who met each week to discuss concerns of their community, which daily became more secularized and isolated.

After every session he would return, have a drink, and report to us: The government in Berlin was encouraging able-bodied Jewish men to enlist in the German Army, but the local government was grabbing Jewish boys off the streets and sending them to labor camps. There seemed to be a choice of one or the other.

There was to be no marrying among Hebrews until further notice.

Groups of vandals had been breaking into Jewish-owned shops and homes, looting at will, the police doing nothing to stop them.

Jews were banned from jobs in all sensitive industries, including military and industrial and biotechnical research. Jewish professors at schools and universities were summarily dismissed, and of course no Jews were allowed to hold government positions. This last applied not only to Jews but also to all but a few select Poles, their places being taken by *Volksdeutscher,* many of them wholly without experience.

Papa would explain all this in a monotone, his eyes dull, his movements slow and awkward, and we, equally inert, would take in his words but not their full implications. During the day, I would go shopping for food, exercise as best I could, and go to a friend's house where I would practice on her piano. But I played without enthusiasm. The works of Bach and Beethoven seemed without meaning, as though they had been written for a different time, a different place, a different people. I was no longer the girl who had returned to Lodz a few months ago, wearing a fine dress, a fancy hat, "the latest" shoes, and full of scorn for those not shaped by Paris, the City of Light. In fact, I could barely remember her.

Winter would be coming soon, and with it the darkness and cold. But it was already dark and prematurely cold in the Levy house on Sophienstrasse.

CHAPTER 3

*O*ne day in October Papa left for the council at nine in the morning and had not returned by three in the afternoon. Mama tortured herself with visions of him lying in a gutter, shot, or beaten. In her agony, she obsessed, too, about Jozef, certain that he had been conscripted into the German Army and was now in a field of battle, awaiting death. Her mood infected mine, and though she was hysterical and needed my comfort, I could not stay in the house or she would have driven me crazy.

"I'm going to get us coal and find us something for supper," I announced, not sure she heard me.

When I returned, Papa still wasn't home, and I watched with a combination of sympathy and irritation, my stomach a tin pit, as Mama cried and cried. Finally, there were footsteps, and she flew to the front door and pulled it open. Papa stood in front of her, shivering.

"I stood for two hours at the coal merchant's, Pappie," I said, coming up to him. "They didn't have any fuel for us."

"Krevlin Brothers?" He turned an anguished glance on me. "That's impossible. We've done business with them since I was a boy. My grandfather used to walk to the synagogue with Rev Krevlin every Sabbath."

"There's a *Volksdeutscher* in charge now," I told him. "Appointed by the Nazi High Command."

He rubbed his neck wearily and let Mama lead him into the sitting room. "Ah. The war against the Jews."

"I had to wait at the butcher, too. Then, though there were steaks and chops, all Mr. Goldberg would let me have was a chicken. I convinced him to sell us some potatoes, even though he swore the Germans had forbidden it. And we also have some cabbage and—"

"Where's Stasik?" Papa interrupted. "I don't see him. He should join us."

My mother cleared her throat. "He heard about the new law preventing Jews from withdrawing more than two hundred zloty without written permission from the Kehillah—"

"So he went to his relatives in the Carpathians," I finished. "He knew what the Kehillah would—"

"It's the Judenrat now," Papa snapped. "The Kehillah doesn't exist any more. Only me and Applebaum and a few others remain. A third were slaughtered when the Aryans took over. Another third fled to Warsaw. Our New Masters have appointed Chaim Rumkowski Eldest of the Jews."

"Rumkowski?" Mama's face twisted in disgust. "But he's a nebbish. Ignorant as dirt. Surely the professional class will refuse to—"

"If by 'professional class' you mean me," Papa said, "then I'll tell you we'll refuse nothing. Chaim's in charge of who gets to trade with the Germans and who gets sent to the labor camps. That's all that gets decided now. Our agenda means nothing, it's even dangerous to bring it up. Our neighborhood will be safe this week because we've paid dearly for peace. Tomorrow morning, Rumkowski will hand over a list of names for a labor crew. And, Nora, when he runs out of poor Jews and his personal enemies, the professional class comes next. Men and women both. You and me and Mia."

"Stop it!" I screamed. "For God's sake, no more." His words were a virus and I was infected with fear. Yet what could we do? Run away? How far could we get, with Aryans prepared to turn us in as soon as they discovered us? And even if they didn't, how could we move when it meant leaving Jozef behind? No, we were all trapped, not just me, and I felt a loathing for my Jewishness, for the Jews themselves, for my mother and father, more Jews, who should have converted when it was still possible. They had stolen my life just as Maria had stolen my piano, and with it my music. A blackness settled over me, stifling and impenetrable.

My father pulled me to him. "Come," he said, "it's time for our delicious-smelling supper. I have my beautiful wife and my exquisite daughter. Jozef is on his way home, he must be. Let's thank God for what we have today and not worry about what we might not have tomorrow. It's only a matter of time before England and France drive the Master Race back to Germany, and sooner than you know it, you'll be in Paris again with your precious Jean-Phillipe." His smile made my heart rise. "That's a promise. I'm buying diamonds as a kind of insurance. They'll pay for a trip to Paris. Pay for all of us."

Mama went to the kitchen and brought out the chicken, potatoes, and cabbage. Papa briefly disappeared, and when he came back he was bearing a dusty green bottle, which he displayed with a flourish. "A toast," he cried, staring at the label. "To our brother Monsieur Rothschild in honor of the Levys past, the Levys present, and the Levys to come!"

"Go, Mia," Mama said, her voice high with excitement. "Get the crystal goblets."

I found them, and when I returned the room was steeped in candlelight. I could see Mama's hand moving hesitantly over my father's as though she were reading Braille.

Papa poured and held his glass above a glowing taper. "*L'chaim*," he said, and we echoed "*L'chaim.*" (Was I imagining it, or had my mother and father smiled at each other as they raised their glasses?)

I started to giggle, but the nervous tremor was cut short by the dry white Bordeaux rolling gently over my tongue. I took another, longer sip, savoring the taste and its effect. Then I dove hungrily into our modest feast, pausing frequently to sip the wine and look over the rim of my glass. On the other side of the table, my parents seemed to be trading special understandings in silence. The moment thrilled me and yet infused me with a curious jealousy. I longed for Jean-Phillipe, closing my eyes at the thought of him.

Life, I thought. And it seemed to me so infinitely precious that tears came to my eyes. My body, my brain, my soul—all were alive, I embodied life, I was life itself. If Jean-Phillipe were here now, I would give myself to him fully, fuse his spirit with mine, and together we would know pleasure beyond happiness.

There was a pounding on the door; a loud voice called, "Dr. Levy! Open the door!"

My father pushed Mama back to the kitchen and motioned for me to follow her. We watched him march to the door, pull it open. "What in hell's the meaning of this?" he said sternly. "Why are you disturbing innocent citizens at this time of . . ."

The words died in his mouth. I caught a glimpse of a man who stepped aside, and then a tall silhouette with blond hair stumbled through the doorway and crumpled into my father's arms.

"Jozef!" my mother screamed, rushing forward.

"Quiet," the man said, taking my brother from my father's grip and carrying him into the sitting room where he laid him gently on the floor.

My mother bent over him, wailing. "Nora, no," Papa whispered, clamping a hand over her mouth.

"Do you want the cats to find out where we've taken their mouse?" the man asked. "I risked my neck getting him out of that alley. Such a fine, beautiful young man. And so Aryan-looking. If only they hadn't asked for his ID card. But don't worry. He'll be okay. They beat him pretty badly, but I don't think anything's broken."

My father, kneeling, ran his fingers gently over Jozef's battered face, then carefully along his arms and legs. "Yes, nothing broken. He'll be all right." He turned to the man. "Now, my friend, to whom do I owe—"

"I'd rather not give my name," the man said. "It might not be good for you if they came looking for me here and you knew it. And you owe me nothing. I just thank God that I recognized your boy and knew where to take him. I sat beside him once while you were addressing the Kehillah."

Papa grasped the man's hand. "All the same, we must give you something. I and my family are very grateful. Please. A glass of wine. There's no chicken left, but I'm sure Mrs. Levy could . . ."

Jozef's savior waved his hand. "I must be getting home. My wife will be crazy with worry. But if you have a little bread, I'd be most grateful. Forgive this begging, but we haven't had much to eat."

"Begging? When you saved my only son? Mia, wrap up a loaf, please, and if there's cheese, that too. And a bottle of schnapps. Toast to your good health tonight, my friend."

I raced to the kitchen and did as instructed. Returning, I handed him the package, which he carefully hid under his heavy wool coat. "God bless you," he said, "and grant your boy a quick healing."

He gravely shook Papa's hand, and reached for mine. But I threw myself against him, kissing his face, and hugged him with all my force. He pried me loose and with a bow retreated to the door.

Only my mother, kneeling beside Jozef while she stroked his hair, did not say good-bye.

Chapter 4

Effective immediately, the Levy family dwelling is transferred to 21 Adolf Hitlerstrasse within the Jewish Zone, in the area formerly known as the Baluty.

Papa read the letter from the Judenrat with a trembling voice, though his face showed no emotion.

In accordance with the regulations established by Regierungs President Matthias Ubelhoes, passed by the Council of Jews and signed into law by the Praesidium, you will be reimbursed on a par value for your house and possessions by a special fund of the Jewish Treasury designated for this purpose. Until you are established at your new address, the Jewish Treasury will maintain an escrow account for all monies receivable in your name, to be converted into legal deutsch marks.

As recent events have demonstrated, dawdlers and smugglers do grievous harm to the Jewish community. Those who fail to follow the orders contained herein are subject to full prosecution in the Jewish courts, with a maximum penalty of five years' imprisonment at hard labor, a fine of 10,000 zloty, or both.

All questions should be addressed to the Jewish Ministry
of Housing, c/o Judenrat, 20 Munsenstrasse (formerly
Sworske Street).

The letter was unsigned, but was stamped in bold letters **C.
RUMKOWSKI, ELDEST OF THE JEWS.**

"Traitor," Papa hissed while my mother sat in stunned silence and
I mentally began cataloging our possessions. Jozef retreated to his
room, the sound of a slamming door behind him the only sign of his
fury.

Establishment of a Jewish Zone had been inevitable. And now it
had come.

Perhaps, I thought, it might be for the best. Acts of violence
against Jews had increased. SS troops developed a careful pattern of
spot checks and shakedowns. Forced recruitment into the army or
banishment to labor camps continued. Night attacks by bands of
Aryan Poles were commonplace throughout Lodz. The German
regime was behind this newly announced segregation, but maybe
Jews would be subject to less harassment if we were banded together
in one area. But I knew this was skewed reasoning. Nothing the government decided was ever for our benefit.

The order was issued in February, but not all acquiesced to it.
Thousands filed exemption requests with the Judenrat. By early
March, however, German soldiers gunned down more than two hundred Jews in the streets, underscoring the need for cooperation. The
relocations, including our own, began in earnest.

The day before we left, we were visited by an apple-cheeked rabbi
whom I immediately loathed.

"We're saving you the best location we can," the young man
declared, helping himself to a slice of rationed bread Mama had
offered him. "Of course, it might be possible to upgrade your status
by speaking to the right people."

When Papa ignored his awkward hint for a bribe, he looked with
pity at my brother, as if to ask, how could you do this to him? "I as-

sure you, doctor, you'll have sanitary facilities as befits your status, but your rooms will be small unless you can make other arrangements."

"We'll take what's given us," Papa said, ushering the rabbi out.

Papa stood motionless, staring at his ruined garden. I knew what he was thinking: last summer, when we had a chance, we should have gone to Kiev, somehow leaving a message for Jozef so he could follow. But all the foreign borders were closed now, and we would soon be sealed in with no access to news or non-Jews. Possession of even a radio was punishable by death, and the new law would prevent my father from ever researching or teaching in his chosen field, or even treating an Aryan patient again. The life we'd known had reached its end.

I couldn't stand to watch the pain of Papa's face and went to look in on Jozef. He was lying on his bed listening to Beethoven's Seventh Symphony on his phonograph. I sat beside him, listening to the music.

"Don't you understand what is happening? How can you just lie here—we must do something. We could lose everything: The lovely glass solarium our grandfather had designed, the elaborately turned balusters, the newel posts of the magnificent staircase, the rugs, the furniture, the garden, the library. Everything. Our family has spent generations erecting this house and filling it with beauty."

"Mia, you know I love you and mother and father, but I don't have any hope. At the university I tried to pretend that I wasn't Jewish, but the other students wouldn't let me forget. All the things you mention can be replaced, but we must find a way to survive. Life is more important."

"But, how could this have happened? Our ancestry is German. Our house has always been staunchly Germanic—more Viennese, actually, than Polish. Our father and his parents waved from the front steps of our house when Emperor Franz Jozef of Austria arrived in Lodz, insisting when he came to our neighborhood, on riding behind the Jewish Elders and their holy scrolls. Papa told us a thousand times how in temple Franz Jozef had kissed the Torah and called it the mother of his own religion."

"It's a different world—you can't look back. We must now look to the future and find a way to survive. We are the hopes of our people."

Jozef fell asleep. I ran my hand over his brow and kissed his hair. The strains of Beethoven wove in and out of the noises of the emigration outside. I left his room and joined my parents.

"Mia," my father said, resolution in his bearing, "go out and get a cart and driver. We'll need provisions, as much as we can get. We must move now, and we must move quickly."

"But she can't," Mama gasped. "Ben, you don't realize what it's like out there, how dangerous. It's bad enough that you send her in the daytime to get bread, but—"

My father glared at her. "A pretty young woman is far more likely to rent a cart and driver than I am. Half the time when I go out for food, I return empty-handed. And this is an emergency. We have to survive. If we're to get to Warsaw, all of us must be strong. Remember, Warsaw is a big city and we have many non-Jewish friends there who can hide us until this craziness is over."

Warsaw! I knew he had dreamed of moving there ever since the occupation had become stifling, but it seemed to me only a fantasy, like going to America. The trip would entail constant danger, constant suspense. It was approximately 130 kilometers away, yet because we were Jews there seemed little hope of making such a journey. We were, in effect, jailed. But evidently my parents had talked of it before. His announcement did not seem to shock her.

Instead, she was horrified. Papa disregarded the fury in her eyes. Jozef would be well soon, he explained, and then we could travel. Without food and warm clothing we'd freeze to death on the journey. "And meanwhile, we're going to hold out in Adolf Hitlerstrasse until we can travel."

"Then don't send Mia. Go to the black market."

My father walked past her toward the parlor. Stopping in the doorway, he pressed both hands against the molding with all his diminished might. But he was no Samson. The great house did not fall.

He turned back to my mother. "Don't you understand?" he said. "They depend on us stalling. Paying for every second of freedom with our savings. Buying on the black market to ward off hunger, to stay warm. You heard that baby-faced rabbi. He recommended bribes for better housing, for security, for preferential treatment."

"But that's human nature," my mother said. "What do you hope to prove by refusing us what everyone else is begging for, particularly since we can afford it?"

"It's not human nature," Papa roared. "And I hope not your nature or Mia's or Jozef's. We have no right to put ourselves above the others, at least not anymore."

My mother's voice was cold. "So you intend for us to starve before we even set out for Warsaw?"

"No. I intend to resist them. Every cent of bribery paid to the Judenrat ends up in the hand of the Nazis. It's like digging our own graves and waiting politely to be thrown in. What they can't get by confiscating, we're delivering to them."

"Then how long do you intend to hold out? Until Jozef dies? Or me? Or Mia?"

"Until I'm convinced there's no other way."

I could not understand him. He was willing to sacrifice us for some ideal! He was willing to let us die. For the first time in my life, I stood against him in league with my mother, and he knew it.

He gripped my arm. "Find a cart, Mia. Fill it with what you can find. Nora, it's time to pack. I'll be upstairs straightening out a few things for the new tenants. We wouldn't want them to think us poor housekeepers, now would we? "

I ran out in a fury, not daring to speak to Papa for fear of what I might say. It was not like me, I always allowed my anger to explode, but today it seemed dangerous, capable of inflicting mortal wounds.

Trucks, pushcarts, and wagons rolled over the cobblestone streets, a parade of woebegone vehicles, most of them carrying the few possessions families could salvage.

"You see that house?" a Polish man remarked to his companion. "We're moving in tomorrow night."

"Very nice," his friend said, whistling in awe. "How'd you manage to land something so grand?"

"My brother-in-law works for the SS."

It was our house that he pointed to. An old woman, showing her toothless gums beneath a bleached babushka, passed by me. With all her strength, she pressed against the strap on her forehead, which supported the load of her belongings tied to her back in a cardboard carton.

I recognized her. She was one of the Jewish peasant women who used to paw through the pushcarts for scraps as the merchants shut down for the Sabbath. The ones who haggled with the dry goods merchants over a few groszy. Women like her would now be our neighbors. Papa was right. It would be intolerable.

I looked around at the stupefied expressions of the human packhorses pulling their carts laden with trunks and boxes and felt a wave of nausea. These were supposed to be my brothers and sisters in the land of Abraham. The people that Papa said were our fellow creatures were beasts of burden, hideous to behold, misshapen humanity.

No! I was not one of them. I belonged to Paris, to music, to opera houses and concert halls. To Jean-Phillipe. I leaned against a lamppost, feeling my stomach lurch in an attempt to give up a meal I had stood in line for three hours to get.

Nearby, I knew, was the Café Astoria, where Jozef and I had spent many evenings, sipping port and listening to Viennese waltzes on the Wurlitzer. Perhaps it was still open. I would go there now and order a grenadine and soda to calm my stomach. I could warm myself there against the fender of the coal stove as I used to do with Jozef and his friends.

I started down the street, veering through the oncoming traffic.

"What have we got here?" a voice boomed in German. "Walking in the wrong direction. A thief? A gypsy saboteur?"

I spun around. An SS soldier stood at ease in front of me.

"*Nein, mein Herr,*" I said, my voice quavering. "I was going to the Astoria Café."

His eyes wandered casually over me. "So you're Jewish then?"

I struggled for air. "Yes, sir. My father sent me out to find a cart, to help us relocate to the Jewish quarter. But all the carts are already taken. I'm cold, so I thought at the Astoria—"

"Do you have any identification?"

"Just my school card." I fumbled in my handbag and produced it. "I attend the lycée in Paris, so it's in French. But here, you see, it says my age and name, Marisa Levy. I swear to you I was only going to get a cart. Honest. My brother's home sick, recovering from—"

"Calm down," he said, and I did. Perhaps the man would not put me in prison. He put his meaty fingers on my shoulder and I froze. Worse than prison!

The German soldier looked so big in his uniform at first I was frightened, but when I saw his soft blue eyes and he spoke, I relaxed. "You're a pretty girl," he said. "I've a daughter of my own. Annaliese." He pulled a wallet from his pocket and showed me a picture. "She's four years old, a charmer. That's my wife next to her." The picture was torn at the edges; a crack ran down its center. Evidently he had looked at it often. He shook his head. "This war. It drives us all crazy. Here I am, showing off my family to some Hebrew, as if she were my niece. Now listen, I'll escort you to Wolnosci Plaza. This area is no place for you—it's filled with scum. Times have changed at the Astoria Café. When you told me you were heading there, I thought . . . Well, the girls are . . . Understand?"

Heat flooded my face. I nodded.

"Good. So let me escort you out of this neighborhood. I'll walk two paces behind you. Keeping company with a Jew—even a pretty one like you—is forbidden in the SS. Now, let's find you a cart before it gets any darker."

He pointed down a narrow alley, and I led the way. I could feel his eyes roaming over my back, my hips, my legs, and I almost bolted. Images of my humiliation at the train station plagued me, and here there was no crowd to protect me, even as silent witnesses. I forced my legs forward in rapid, even steps, dreading his touch, the feel of his breath on my back.

We emerged into Wolnosci Plaza. He stepped past me and commandeered a cart drawn by two burly boys, tossing aside the protests of the family walking beside it. "Hurry up and take your things or I'll give you a hard kick," he growled. "Jewish swine."

My heart grieved. My father would never have taken the cart that belonged to another family; he would have searched until he found one not in use. But the search might have been fruitless, I told myself. Everyone needed carts, everyone was moving. It was cold. We had little time. I still had to get as much food and coal as I could. It shames me to admit that after grief came relief, and that as the family unloaded their belongings, I willed them to be quick about it.

"Take this girl where she wants to go," my benefactor snarled at the drivers. "If I find you've overcharged her family, I'll have you sent to the labor camps." He winked at me and handed me a bar of chocolate. *"Auf wiedersehen."*

"Auf wiedersehen," I murmured. *"Danke schoen."*

The boys helped me onto the cart, and we set off to find provisions that I would take back to my family for our last night in our home.

Chapter 5

My father's dream of going to Warsaw did not happen. We were forced to move to the Baluty, a large industrial area the Germans created so we Jews could help the Nazi war machine. My assignment was to sew buttons on German uniforms six days a week, ten hours a day. (In an "act of friendship," the authorities let us have the Sabbath off.) We worked in a hot, airless room on the second floor of a warehouse. In the summer it became so oppressive many of the girls fainted. I was able to withstand the heat, but my skin turned a dull yellow.

The Baluty was cold, dirty, and disease ridden. It had been a slum even before the Germans came. The buildings were old and crumbling; many of the streets had never been paved. As fall approached, the Nazis cut off our water supply and stopped all refuse collection. The result was a typhus epidemic, which cut our population nearly in half. We were hungry all the time. Hungry people get angry easily, and we fought over trifles. I celebrated my eighteenth birthday by having an apple all to myself.

In November, fuel was rationed, and when there was nothing left to burn a mob demolished a wooden shed on Brzezinska Street for firewood. An old woman was crushed to death in an attempt to collect some of it.

Nate Kolleck, Jozef's schoolmate who, like him, had made his way back to Lodz, said we were becoming like the legendary golem: the soulless walking dead. I despised the comparison, but it was obvious he was right. I knew I could look forward to my sallow skin turning corpse-gray.

Nate lived in our tenement. I knew him from Lodz. He wasn't much older than I, although he always seemed so much more mature. Maybe it was because he was so thin and had lost some of his hair. He was always interested in people, and I thought that someday he would become a psychologist.

Each family was allotted one room, no matter how many members there were. Nate was "lucky," for he lived alone, even though it was in a closet. He had no brothers or sisters, and his father, David, had been beaten to death at the Astoria Café on the first day of the occupation for attempting to stop the rape of a waitress. His mother had later leapt out of her third-story window rather than watch the *volksdeutscher* take her home. The Jewish Ministry of Finance seized all their valuables.

Nate, like the rest of us, was reimbursed in "rumkes," currency engraved with "King Chaim" Rumkowski's profile. Rumkes were the only legal tender in the Baluty and useless outside of it. Marks, zlotys, even American dollars, all had to be surrendered. The smuggling trade died overnight, and with it our contact with the outside world.

And then the rumkes became useless as well. Eventually there was nothing left to buy. In Chaim's ghetto the rule was "work or starve." Every man, woman, and child was harnessed to a factory as part of Rumkowski's plan to make us indispensable to the new masters.

From his apartment in the Summer Palace Fronic just inside the far walls of the Baluty, Chaim ordered the diversion of the railroad tracks of Litzmannstadt onto a special line, which terminated inside the ghetto. There, raw materials—scrap leather, confiscated furs, quilts, down comforters, and pillows—were off-loaded at the Umschlagplatz, where a transport picked up reconditioned winter uniforms and reclaimed steel and aluminum from our salvage plants. There was work to do, and the inhabitants of the Baluty were grateful.

But when the German war effort started to bog down, life in the Baluty also began to collapse. Work *and* starve was what we ultimately did. Rations for bread, meat, and dairy products were cut in half, then halved again. Whether one's share was a pound a week or a ton, it mattered little. There was no meat to buy. Even those on double rations—the Judenrat families, members of the Jewish police, doctors, those who collected human refuse in the pushcarts—all were slowly starving together.

Mama and Papa fell into a torpor that made me feel I was living with mechanical toys robots. Listlessly, my mother cooked the meager meals and my father tended an ever-growing list of patients with similar complaints: dysentery, rickets, anemia—starvation. Jozef, on the other hand, was in a perpetual rage, inveighing against the gods and the Germans with an energy that seemed boundless, as though he were the sea crashing endlessly on an unyielding shore.

As for me, I disappeared into a world of fantasies lit by chandeliers from L'Opera, where I starred as Sophie or Suzanna, depending on whether I was in the mood for Strauss or Mozart. Jean-Phillipe attended every performance, always picking me up backstage after the performance and taking me to Maxim's, where we would get dizzy on wine before going back to his flat or mine to make languorous love amid a landscape of pillows. These visions sustained me. When, because of a scream, a collision, a fight, an accident, I was forced to open my eyes to reality, I would cry until the music in my brain would once again bring comfort.

Thousands of Jews died of starvation during the winter of 1940, and the survivors quickly began to succumb to typhus, doubling my father's already inhuman workload. Even as the epidemic spread, however, the Baluty's factories continued running nonstop. Work crews kept improving the roadways and installing new trolley lines, and we developed a halfhearted respect for Rumkowski: at least he was keeping us busy in jobs that held some hope for the future of our enclave. Working for him, Jozef said, was better than being sent to the camps.

When a worker was needed for a special job, Nate Kolleck volunteered. For each job, summer or winter, he would arrive wearing a heavy wool coat, which concealed his ancient Rolleiflex camera. With it he recorded every atrocity he saw on film he'd been hoarding for months before the ghetto was established. Old men with long sideburns and beards, their black wool coats dragging in the mud; women with screaming babies trying to suckle milkless nipples; swaggering young Jewish militiamen stalking the ghetto; corpses poking out from beneath newspapers as they lay in the gutter awaiting the refuse collectors. In the corners, in doorways, the living also waited, their legs swollen, their stomachs distended, too sick to move.

Every night Nate developed his negatives with chemicals he'd hidden away. The film was carefully sealed in tin cans and hidden behind the bricks of the converted closet where he slept. Sometimes I walked the streets with him after sunset. Once we saw two naked children shoveling handfuls of offal into their mouths. I turned away. Nate grabbed me roughly by the arm.

"No, Mia, you must look," he urged, pressing the shutter lever. Click. The child's image was preserved.

Next a sanitation cart rolled up the unpaved street, pulled by human horses with stringy sinews bulging from their skeletal frames. It moved along the twisting alley; even the naked boys ran from its stench. People darted in and out of their doorways to empty their bedpans and chamber pots into its bed. A few clicks, and everything was recorded.

Nate looked satisfied as he concealed his camera under his coat. It infuriated me. "How can you bear it?" I asked. "It's as if you enjoy watching their misery."

He shrugged. "I'm not the cause of it."

"But it's wrong to take their pictures. You could let them hide their shame instead of documenting every bedpan and bloated belly in this hellhole."

"Someone has to do it," he said urgently.

"Why?"

"Because we're sealed off. With the smugglers gone, nothing enters from the outside and we are kept in. If we have no idea of what's beyond the barriers, what do you think they know about us? Take a look.

Tens of thousands of people are walking around like they're already dead. Skulls are crushed over a piece of bread, families live twenty to a room, children eat shit. Now tell me, without photographs who would ever believe what the Germans have done to us?"

I shook my head.

"Do you remember how I used to devote my time to painting?" he asked.

"Of course. Jozef said you had tremendous talent."

"Will that talent get me a piece of beef fat to throw into the ditch water they serve us for soup in the factories? No. The paintbrush made me too romantic. The camera, even if I'm the only one to see the pictures, keeps me honest."

It wasn't that simple, I thought. *It couldn't be.* Once a person gave up romance, beauty, music, color, and light, his soul atrophied and he might as well be dead. I started to tell this to Nate but held my tongue. The changes the ghetto had forged in him made him unapproachable, though I believed he wanted to be approached by me. I think he might even have been a little in love with me. If photographs of the demonic allowed him to escape the demons, so be it. But he frightened me.

"Listen to your father," Mama begged, staring into Jozef's rage-filled eyes.

He shrugged off her hand. "I'm fine without a lecture."

"You'll listen," she said sternly. "You're physically well at last, which means you've got to be all the more careful. That temper of yours isn't healthy. Especially with the militia patrolling the streets. And the informers—your friends and neighbors."

Jozef blazed like a flare. "Who wouldn't be angry, with Führer Rumkowski marching around his summer palace in jackboots? And his announcements—in Polish, yet—'my Jews' this and 'my Jews' that. The bastard's a disgrace to the Jewish race."

"There's no such thing as the Jewish race," Papa said wearily. "There are only Jewish people, and we have real problems here. People are dying every day. The Mieckiewicz State Hospital is overflowing. We need doctors, disinfectant, drugs."

"And you expect to get that from King Chaim?"

"He's our only hope."

"He's an ignorant swine. It's the dregs of humanity like him who give the rest of us a bad name."

"No more!" Papa thundered, and I was glad to see he had passion left. "Don't you understand? If the Jews weren't brothers before, the Master Race has made us indistinguishable. Do you think only the uneducated starve, or that typhus will spare you just because you're gifted?"

"Don't tell me that I have anything to do with the rabble over on Miehlstrasse. They're animals! Half of them can barely speak Polish, let alone German. And even their Yiddish—"

"That's precisely why I'm going to the Summer Palace to see Chaim alone," Papa interrupted.

"Why? So he can walk all over you? Show how much he hates educated Jews?"

"To ask him to save his fellow Jews in this rotten ghetto. I'll kiss his feet. Get down on my knees and beg, dance naked through the streets if I have to. One life saved on the Miehlstrasse is worth more than all the pride in the universe."

Jozef applauded. "Bravo. In the meantime, I'll go and commune with my fellow Jews at the button factory, where I'll listen to their ignorant prattle for six hours, then stand in line and pray for some carrot leaves or a bit of mealy potato to flavor my soup. Give my regards to the Summer Palace."

But Jozef's words were wasted. I watched Papa leave, back straight with a new resolve, and prayed he would succeed.

A depressed and discouraged man returned. For a long time, he sat slumped at the kitchen table, head resting on his folded arms, saying nothing; I could not tell if he was weeping. At last Mama persuaded him to take a glass of tea, and its warmth seemed to revive him, for he was able to look at us now, shame and sorrow in his expression, and tell us what had happened.

"They made me wait a long time in the outer office," he said. "I could hear him yelling about a postage stamp. Seems Berlin had refused to issue one in his honor—said no Jewish face could be pasted next to an Aryan one—and he was furious, even though the stamp would only be issued in the Baluty. It would have been farcical, only I worried that he'd take out his bad mood on me.

"Finally, I was allowed in. Chaim was standing at the window, his back to me, muttering to himself. There was a massive desk in his office cluttered with papers, and at the side of the room a table on which lay a bowl of fruit—apples, pears, oranges. My darlings, how I wanted to ask for that fruit! To be able to bring it home to you, to let us share for even one day God's bounty—"

He clutched his stomach and his eyes filled with tears. "Go on," I said softly, knowing that I could offer no comfort.

"Chaim turned and greeted me. He's grown fat—fat, while the rest of us starve! His chins hung over his collar like udders, and it was hard to see his eyes above his cheeks. I told him he was looking well, and he told me he exercised every day—yes, I thought, by chewing. 'Can you imagine,' he told me, 'yesterday a bum on the street tried to attack me.' I sympathized. 'It's always the Bundists, the rabble. Hiding like rabbits. Thinking I don't know where their lairs are and who's sneaking out at night to scrawl on our factory walls: OPEN THE GATES. KILL CHAIM. But I know everything that goes on with my Jews. These thankless ones—the labor camps are too good for them. Instead of working, they spread rumors, lies. Don't they realize what I'm doing for them? The new trolley lines, the road improvements, a brand-new railroad depot. Do they think these things are easy for the Eldest? Don't they realize I'm keeping them alive?'

"I coughed, otherwise he'd have gone on for another five minutes. 'Ah yes, Levy. What's so urgent that it necessitates a personal interview?' "

It was a wicked imitation, and I laughed. My mother glared at me, as though I had made a joke in temple.

" 'It's the typhus, Eldest,' I said. 'We are facing an epidemic.'

" 'Don't you doctors have a treatment?' he snarled.

" 'Yes, but we can only do so much without medicine. Sanitation has to be improved. The dead have to be buried immediately. We need more supplies. And staff. A handful of doctors and nurses can't stop the disease from reaching overwhelming proportions.'

"Every word I said infuriated him. He walked up to me and put his face not a foot from mine. I could smell his garlic breath. 'What do you expect me to do?' " he shouted. 'Do you imagine your Eldest is a magician? That he can pass his hands over a top hat and produce supplies? Our community is spared from catastrophe only because I've made us indispensable to the war effort. How can you ask me to divert doctors and nurses from that? Or medicine? It would be insane, like signing a death warrant.'

" 'What about the work crews?' I pleaded. 'Do you suppose we need modernized streets more than clean water, or trolley lines transporting workers for a few lousy blocks, when the men are needed to pick up the dead?'

"This produced a tirade. 'Do you presume to question the judgment of the Eldest of the Jews?' he screamed. 'You who know nothing of the inner working of Berlin? I'm sick and tired of you sniveling Polish Jews. Think you're smart and know nothing.'

"He raised his fist and I was sure he would hit me. God pity me, I became just the sniveling Jew he had described. 'Forgive me,' I said. 'I meant no offense. I only wanted to help you save the Jews.'

"Chaim lowered his fist and now looked at me with what I can only call disgust. Evidently, I was too much a toad for him to scrape his knuckles on. I knew I had failed, that there was no way to change this monster's heart. I turned to go—then froze. On the corner of

Chaim's desk lay a hand-lettered map of the Baluty. I missed it when I came in because I was so concentrated on the fruit. On it, the transport to the Umschlagplatz, the valves for shutting off the water supply, and the ghetto power plant were clearly marked. Around the perimeter, spirals indicated existing barbed wire around the walls, and places where a second ring would be installed. The main streets had been renamed: Ghetto Nord Strasse Ein, Ghetto Nord Strasse Zwei. It was obvious what all this meant. The Germans were going to seal us in, let us all die, and then use the Baluty as their own transportation center. Chaim hadn't improved the roads or put in the trolley lines to help us. He was doing it for the Germans! He was perfectly willing to let his fellow Jews die if it meant saving his own skin."

All Papa's energy seemed to seep away. He laid his head back down on the table and remained motionless, though his shoulders seemed to relax beneath Mama's consoling touch. I watched the scene like an outsider; theirs was an intimacy I could only dream about, and it seemed that for me, that was all it would ever be. A dream.

Then, with a shake of his body like a bear coming out of hibernation, my father roused himself and rushed to the little room he used as an office. From there he returned, carrying a box full of medical instruments—scalpels with wooden handles, stethoscopes, devices I had never seen and did not know the purpose of. He laid them out on the table with great pride, a magician about to perform his greatest trick, and with a flourish unscrewed the tops and turned them upside down over the table.

Mama gasped. Jozef was shocked. And I simply stared at the cascade of diamonds that fell to the table—there must have been ten in all—and glittered at us like friendly eyes.

"There is an administrator at the hospital," Papa said solemnly. "A non-Jew, sent by the government to make sure we doctors behave. He's a good man, horrified by our condition, and over the months I have come to trust him." He sighed. "I told him about the diamonds. He says if I give them to him, he will be able to get us on a train, get us documents. They'll allow us to travel, even though"—he spat the words in imitation of his German masters—"we're Jews. And there are more diamonds, hidden in the basement of our old house, ones he doesn't know about. Once the war is over, we'll reclaim them and have enough to start a new life."

Mama covered her mouth to stifle a cry. "But he can just take these diamonds and never come back."

"True."

"Then don't do it!" Jozef said.

My father waved his hand to indicate our room, our street, our ghetto, our life. "What choice do we have?"

CHAPTER 6

"*But* I'll tell them, Nate," I assured him. "As soon as I get to Paris. I'll make them understand."

"They'll never believe you. Never." Angrily he shifted the lens of the battered Rolleiflex until my inverted profile slid into focus, silhouetted by the Baluty skyscape. Then he snapped the photo and motioned me to move away from the window. We were in my family's flat. It was the day before we were to leave.

"Without the photographs, there is no proof," he said. "You must take them with you."

I ran my fingers through my hair. "It's not possible."

"I'll put the negatives in a sealed envelope with a Baluty stamp on it. Nobody will ask you to open it. I'll make it look like a love letter. I'll write 'I love you' on the back." He looked wistful.

"What if I'm caught?"

"You won't be. And if you are, what can they say? A few negatives of factory workers, sanitation workers? Chaim's Summer Palace? That's all." He took my hand and stared at me with the intensity of a lover. "It's worth the risk. It would open the eyes of the world."

"*My* risk. What if they shoot me?"

"For what? Carrying a few snapshots of your family and showing the places where they work?"

"For sedition. Espionage. Crimes against the state. Take your pick." I turned back to the widow to watch the glowing smokestacks, wishing that it were already tomorrow morning and we were on the train.

What would the Germans do if they caught me carrying Nate Kolleck's precious documentation? Treat it as an innocent child's blunder? I didn't think so. The first guard to see the scrawny, starving figures, the sanitation carts loaded with corpses, the children with distended bodies gulping offal, would take me straight to the Gestapo. My family, too, would be hauled off the train. And they wouldn't be shot immediately, like me. They'd be tortured, made to tell where I got the pictures. No, it was too awful. I couldn't take the chance.

I cringed when his chilled fingers reached out to touch me. "Please, Mia. You must do this. My work is everything and I need your help."

"It would jeopardize my family."

He didn't seem to hear me. "Who else can do it? Who else will tell the world the truth?"

He was right, I knew. "Maybe you can come with us," I said. "On the same train. You could be my cousin, my half brother."

"My place is here, taking photographs. I'll stay in the Baluty until they catch me and kill me. And I'll find others to take out the pictures. I only thought that you—"

He's a hero, I thought. And I, a coward. "Oh, Nate . . ."

He forced his lips on me. They were cracked and dry, like field grass after a killing frost. Instinctively, I moved my head away, and his kisses scratched along my throat and down to my shoulders. His blue fingers clutched at my arms, ran up and down my hips, and reached upward to cup my breasts. I just stood there, motionless, doing nothing to stop him and nothing to lead him on.

It was like being trapped inside a bottle of poison, a skull and crossbones clutching at me. I felt sobs wracking his body; it drained heat from mine. Gooseflesh ran up my spine, and I bit my lower lip hard, trying to will numbness. I felt Nate slipping down against my body, his head against my stomach, but to let him do this would be too much, too much, so I merely stepped back and he embraced thin air before collapsing. I walked stiffly out the door, down the stairs, and into the street, just as the golem do.

We were allowed on the train, but not in any of the compartments. Instead, we found places in a boxcar, surrounded by at least forty other people—had they sold their diamonds, too, for a trip to Warsaw?

For it was toward Warsaw we were heading, sitting in the dark in icy air, wrapped in our coats, clutching those few belongings we could carry with us, hoping that from the vast, anonymous city we could make our way out of Poland and optimally to France.

"Couldn't your diamonds buy us a seat?" Jozef asked. "Or a cushion?" His voice was loud in the hush of the car.

"Lower your voice," Papa commanded. "Don't utter another word of German or Yiddish. You are to speak only in French. That's an order—for you, too, Mia. If they hear you, they'll—"

"What?" Jozef growled. "These people can barely understand anything. That's why they're in a cattle car. Because they're stupid Jews. Like you, Papa, but not like me."

The sound of the slap was as shocking as a gunshot. Jozef recoiled, and I stared at Papa in bewilderment. Never once had he hit any of us. My mother's "Benjamin!" spoke of her anguish.

I was anguished, too. In this miserable, smelly moving carton, feeling filthy in my wool dress and heavy shoes, hungry and thirsty, uncomfortable and frightened, only the thought of Nate, of his defiance against his German Masters, kept me from complaining as bitterly as Jozef. I tried to picture Paris and Jean-Phillipe, but the lights had dimmed even in my fantasy. Guilt at leaving without Nate's pictures forced me to deny even the image of pleasure.

My father vomited. Just like that. Without warning.

"He was sick last night," Mama said. "Oh my God."

"It's nothing," Father said. "Just too much excitement, too much stress." But I could see he was shivering and I took off my coat and put it over his shoulders. He was too weak to resist, though he managed a "No, Mia, not needed," and now it was I who shivered, as much from fear as from the cold.

The train seemed to be inching along. At this rate, it would take days to get to Warsaw, and in the interval who knew what might happen? It was only a matter of time, I thought, before Jozef turned against him, against all of us, and when that moment arrived, Mama and I would have to decide what to do.

I woke up on the worn wooden planking of the boxcar. Icy winds nipped through my dress. I felt an insect crawl along my scalp; then it disappeared. Was my mind going? There goes breakfast, I thought wryly, and realized that if nothing came to ease my hunger, my thought would no longer be a joke.

The train was going at a fairly good rate now; soon we would be out of this hellhole. I looked for Jozef in the blackness. There he was, a sleeping knot of bony arms and legs. I longed to run my fingers through his hair until the pomade made it stick straight up, just as I had when we were kids, and I'd run away squealing, with him chasing me as he used to do. But there was no place to run, and Jozef's mood of the night before made any teasing seem like a bad idea.

My parents were sleeping nearby, their arms around each other, as though they were one form. I started to crawl over to them, wanting their warmth to enclose me, too, when I struck something on the floor. A body!

"Sorry," I said, but there was something wrong. I had hit the body hard, but it hadn't moved. I looked down. Two eyes stared up at me in the dim light coming through the slats in the sliding doors of the car. A woman's eyes. Eyes that did not blink. Sleepless eyes. *Dead eyes.* I had crawled next to a corpse!

I screamed. My father sat up. "What is it, Mia?"

I couldn't answer. Rather, I scurried like a rodent away from the body toward the far end of the car. There, two German soldiers sat facing each other, a small cooking lamp between them on which they had placed a kettle for tea. Should I tell them of the dead woman? Dare I speak to a German soldier at all?

"Let the corpses wait," one of the soldiers said, sighing. "Let's have some tea before we throw them out."

I stopped breathing, strained to hear more.

"You throw them," the other soldier—the younger one—said. "-I've no stomach for it."

"Better get used to it," his companion replied. "There are corpses on every train, and we're supposed to get rid of them before we reach Treblinka."

"What then?"

"We dump this load, turn around and go back for the next."

"More Jews?"

"Sure. There's an inexhaustible supply. Raw material for the work camps."

"Lousy duty," the young soldier said.

"It beats the front. At least here your life's not in danger."

Work camps! A place called Treblinka, which I'd never heard of. We were going there. The final stop. We Jews, we "raw material," were doomed. As quietly as possible, careful to avoid the bodies (alive or dead?) now more easily visible in the early morning light, I made my way back to my parents.

My father was sitting up, clutching his stomach. He smiled when he saw me. "We must be almost there," he said.

I told him what I had overheard, watched comprehension creep into his eyes. "Betrayed," he whispered. "The administrator fucked us."

He had never before said *fuck* in front of me, and his use of the word was in its way as frightening as the conversation between the two Germans. "We must act," he said, shaking Mama awake. "Do you know where Jozef is?"

"Yes." I pointed.

"Get him, tell him to join us as quietly as possible. Tell him I don't give a shit how angry he is at me, that he must come now and that he must listen."

My father's resoluteness comforted me. He was brilliant, Papa, and strong. He would save us. I did as he commanded; Jozef, perhaps struck by my urgency, followed me obediently, and we sat in a little group, waiting for my father to speak. All around us people were waking up. Groans, complaints, screams, whispers filled the air. At the far end of the car, one of the soldiers stood, the better to watch us. He gripped a rifle with both hands.

'We're in trouble," Papa said. "Bad, bad trouble. This train is going not to Warsaw, but to Treblinka, which is where they've sent many of the Lodz Jews. I've heard that not everyone survives, that the work is harsh and there is no chance of leaving. Your mama, my Nora, would have a hard time there."

"And you, Benjamin," my mother said. "You've not been well—"

"So we must not go there," Papa went on, as if he hadn't heard her. He lowered his voice. "We must escape."

Jozef snorted. "How? Do we fly away?"

His contempt angered me, but I shared his worry. I felt nauseated by hunger and fear. We were trapped in this car. There was no escape.

"We jump," Papa said, disregarding Josef's tone. "We make our way to the doors. The soldiers open them from time to time to give themselves some air, so I know they're not locked. We'll simply walk to them, single file. You, Jozef, will pull them open, so you'll go first but jump out last. Mia, you'll go second. I third, and Mama will hold on to me when I jump. From where we are, it can't be more than ten or twelve large steps to the doors. We'll wait until the train slows down, then chance it. Don't run, but walk quickly, steadily, as though on an important mission. We'll stand now, but not all at once. Try to make it seem as if we're not part of one family. Stay close enough to me so you can hear me whisper. I'll count to three. Then we'll go. And for God's sake, don't hesitate."

Mama and I were so used to following Papa's orders that we didn't argue. If he said this was the right plan, then it was. But Jozef had questions.

"Assuming we survive the fall, what can the four of us do in the middle of nowhere, without money or food, without passports? We'll be caught within days, if we're lucky to last that long, and then God knows what will happen to us."

Papa looked at him emotionlessly. "If you don't want to come with us, that's your choice. We will need you, though, to slide the doors open, for you are the only one strong enough to do it. You might be better off at Treblinka. I don't think the rest of us would be."

My mother began to cry. Papa put his arm around her waist, and she looked at him with shining eyes. "Trust me," he whispered, and she nodded.

"Very well," he said. "Stand, Mia." I did. "Now you, Jozef. Don't look at her."

Jozef obeyed without protest. His expression was grave, and I could see he was frightened. I reacted mechanically, though grotesquely, a snatch of the melody accompanying Konstanze and Belmonte's escape from Osmin's house in Die Entfuhrung aus den Sereil sprang up in my head.

Papa stood and Mama with him. They held hands. "One," Papa said. "Two. *Three!*"

As best we could we walked toward the door, avoiding the others, stepping past those still sleeping—or dead—on the floor.

"Halt!" The soldier had noticed us. I tried not to look, but out of the corner of my eye I saw him raise his gun. "What are you doing?"

Jozef was at the door. With a mighty pull, he slid it open, just a crack, just enough for a person to jump through.

"Stop or I'll shoot!"

I felt my father's hands on my back, heard him grunt as he pushed me as hard as he could. There was the sound of a shot, the sensation of falling a long distance, searing agony—and blackness.

CHAPTER 7

I awoke to a blazing, blinding searchlight. As my panic-stricken eyes moved from left to right, excruciating pain ricocheted through my skull and I feared I'd lose consciousness again. Slowly I realized it was no searchlight. The searing beam was the noontime sun.

Brown leaves darted and swirled above me. When I tried to move my head, pain ripped down my spine. I was drenched in sweat. My cheeks burned, yet my back and legs were numb. I forced myself into a sitting position—at least my back wasn't broken!—and looked around. To the left, a scraggly field with a few trees. To the right, two brilliant fireballs glowed like the smelting ovens of the Baluty. The sun again. With great concentration I brought the orbs together, as if focusing on an image through one of Nate Kolleck's cameras. The orbs merged, flew apart, then came together as my ears hummed with a high, insistent buzz. I shook my head to clear the noise. Nausea overwhelmed me.

Lost. Alone. Hurt. I rested on my hands and knees, allowing my head to hang limp until the nausea subsided. My coat was torn. I could see bruises on my arms and legs.

I dragged myself onto an embankment. Railroad tracks. Oh, God! I remembered.

What had happened to Papa? He was directly behind me, shoved me out, then the shot. Was he killed? Had the Germans murdered them all, Papa and Mama and Jozef? Or were they on their way to

Treblinka, no escape possible, and there a fate no one could foretell? I began to sob. There was a thicket some fifty feet from where I was lying, and I crawled to it. I would make my way to Treblinka, I decided, to see if I could somehow rescue my family—buy them out, perhaps, with money I made en route, or at least signal them that help was coming so they would not lose hope. Even as I had these thoughts I knew they were fantasies, yet I let them sustain me. I lay in a thicket and closed my eyes, picturing the house on Kowalska Street when I was young.

I fell asleep, and when I awoke, dawn was creeping over the fields. For a moment, I felt refreshed, the long rest having dulled my body's aches, but then I remembered where I was and what had happened, and anguish returned. I was glad of one thing: I had not taken Nate's photographs, and so if I was stopped on my travels—to where? In what direction?—I could not be accused of spying. Indeed, no one would know I came from Lodz or, more important, that I was Jewish. It was a strange feeling; I could be whoever I wanted, create my own past, make up any story to explain my circumstances, even—no, I would keep my first name. It was my gift from Mama and Papa.

With great care, I got to my feet and walked back to the embankment, pain shooting through my left hip where the bone had shifted in its socket. There I examined my injuries, as if Marisa Levy was some laboratory animal for study. My feet were swollen, my legs were scratched and cut, the bruises had darkened in the night. My ribs were badly bruised and my coat shredded beyond repair. Beneath my cardigan sweater, my cotton dress was ripped, and my underwear showed through. I would have to do something about that, but had no idea what. The dress was stuck to my body in a dozen places where my bloody wounds had dried.

I crossed the tracks, dragging my left leg through fallen stalks of meadow grass. The sun, out fully now, was blessedly warm, and I realized I was ravenous. In the distance, I could make out a farm cottage; on the edge of its harrowed field, the blue-black surface of a pond glittered in the sunshine. I would decide later whether to approach the cottage; what was incontestable was that I needed the pond. I pulled up a handful of winter-spared field grass and chewed the stalks, my parched tongue taking in the moisture.

Soon enough I'd have water. I'd drink from that pond and take a bath in it too. Clear, clean water. Then I'd find food—at the cottage if I dared, or somewhere along the road. That I had no money, no direction, no plan did not trouble me. I was about to have water.

Tossing aside my useless coat, I took one tentative step, then another, crouching low in the grass and moving with careful precision, fighting to keep my balance, alert for approaching footsteps or the whine of hunting dogs.

At the pond's edge I dropped to my knees and let the icy water bite into my mouth. Then I thrust my head down and pierced the shimmering reflection of my face. The shock of the cold thrilled me. I was alive!

A moment later, I was naked, washing the dirt, grime and all the sickness off me. I slid down in the water again and again, gasping at the effects of the cold. Thrashing back to shore, I collapsed onto the brittle, scratchy grass and smiled up at the sun.

"Marta?" A woman's voice, calling from across the field. Her lumbering figure came closer. She was maybe eighty years old.

I slipped back into my filthy rags. The old woman was nearly at the pond. There was nothing to do but try to make a break for it. I stood up, clutching my shoes, but my left leg gave out, and I crumpled with an involuntary cry of pain.

The old woman came closer, peering at me in confusion. "Marta? Are you all right?" Her dark eyes were sunken and they rested on me, then moved past. Blind!

She held her arms out in front like antennae, spreading her fingers in an effort to grasp something solid. "Who's there?" she cried in alarm. "Marta, why won't you answer? Why won't you tell me who's there?"

My teeth began to chatter; the old woman stumbled backward. "I know someone's there," she moaned. "Please don't harm me. I'm a defenseless old woman. The Germans have already taken all the wheat and potatoes. Even the milk cow is gone. I swear to you I have nothing. Please just let an old woman—"

Oblivious in her fear, she moved forward, her senses focused on my unseen presence. "I know someone's there," she wailed, tottering for a moment. Then, swinging her arms wildly, she toppled into the water.

I plunged in after her, heedless of my own safety or the consequences. She had fallen in headfirst and was sputtering in an effort to keep her head above water. I grabbed her arm and pulled her to the bank.

"Don't worry," I said, "I won't harm you. You're safe. I promise."

She peered at me from cataractous eyes. "But why didn't you answer when I—"

"I was afraid," I answered quickly. "But it's all right now. It's the war. It makes us all fearful. Is that your farmhouse on the rise? Come, I'll take you home."

She let me hold her arm and walk her back to the cabin. The feel of her comforted me, and I was glad to give her comfort in return. "I thought you were my daughter Marta," she said. "She hasn't been here since dawn. She went to Vishna to trade for bread, and she's been gone all day. Marta never let the fire go out before. It must be dusk."

"No," I said quietly, "it's still morning. Marta will be home soon, I'm sure." I felt myself starting to black out. I hadn't eaten in twenty-four hours, and now my legs couldn't support my own weight, let alone the woman's. My field of vision narrowed until I saw the cottage as a tiny model at the end of a long tunnel. I fought to keep my feet moving. With each step the cottage came closer, then receded. Marta had gone for bread. Oh, if the old woman could give me some! "I'll get the fire going," I assured her, "and—"

And what? I'd heard too many stories of Jews being betrayed by Polish peasants to expect any kindness from Marta. If not from hatred, then out of fear of German reprisals Marta would turn me in. I would have to leave as soon as I got the old woman settled. If she had no food, then maybe a cup of tea, and I'd be gone.

"Why didn't you answer me by the pond?" the old woman asked again. "You know, you should have said something, you gave me such a fright. I thought perhaps you . . . Now tell me the truth. You're not a gypsy, are you?"

I marveled at the irony. "Of course not, grandma."

The old woman retreated. "I'm sorry. It's just that ever since the invasion, you hear all the time how—"

We were almost at the house. "I know."

"When Marta comes back from the shops, it's all she talks about. The war. The soldiers. They carry on in broad daylight with the young girls, though not Marta, of course. She wouldn't let them touch her. But some of the loose girls, they have husbands even. Bands of gypsies roaming the countryside. Renegade Jews. It's disgusting how they let their women—"

I shivered.

"You're cold," she said. "Why. You're so thin you're almost a stick. I can feel your rib cage. And where's your coat? Don't your parents feed and clothe you, poor thing? Or is it your husband?" We reached the steps to the house and began to climb them, though it was difficult to say who was supporting whom. "I shouldn't ask so many questions," the woman prattled on. "I'm just a prying old woman. But there's a fine borscht left over from last night. You can heat some for us if you're hungry. What did you say your name was, dear?"

Mia. "Saskia," I said.

We went across the porch and entered the kitchen. In fact, Marta had made a fire this morning, and I knelt by the dying embers, tossed in a log, and blew into the hearth until it ignited. A pot of soup was suspended over the fire, and it quickly heated until the air was thick with its sweet pungency and I nearly fainted in anticipation.

I took up a poker resting by the fireplace and poked at the log, glancing from the iron rod to the old woman's head, then back to my white knuckles. I could do it! I thought, horrified by my own fantasy. If Marta came and realized who I was—a Jew without clothes, without food—I could murder them both. My father had been betrayed by a "friendly" Pole and then had bought my freedom dearly, perhaps with his own life. It was my duty to survive. Papa had set in motion the events that had brought me to this cottage full of warmth and steaming food and danger. Surely he—and perhaps even God—had a reason for sparing me.

The old woman fussed with the chairs, the place setting, and the bowls until I thought I'd go mad. Finally, she let me ladle out the soup, and we sat facing each other at the table. I swallowed my first steaming spoonful, not caring that it burned my tongue and seared my throat. Nothing had ever tasted so delicious. Tears filled my eyes; my thoughts of murder were too horrible, too cruel. I lifted the bowl and poured nourishment into me. Thank God the woman was blind.

When we had finished eating, the old woman went to a different room and returned carrying a soft flannel robe. "Wear this," she said. "You'll want to hang your clothes by the fire to dry."

"Yes." I shook my head as if wakening from a dream. The old woman could not imagine what lay behind my clipped responses, the joy and the anguish, the rapture and the terror all colliding in my mind.

I prayed with all my might that Marta would never return.

CHAPTER 8

Marta never did come back. Perhaps she had died long before my arrival; perhaps she had run off, eloped; perhaps she had been killed that very day. Whatever, the peasant woman sometimes thought I was she, sometimes that I was her schoolmate, but most of the time she knew I was a stranger. She did not seem unhappy that Marta was missing. The vicissitudes of war seemed to have inured her to tragedy. She was simply living out her years as best she could.

In truth, the old woman was very kind. She fed and clothed me and treated me like her own. In turn, I helped with the chores and even went shopping for her—terror-filled trips to the village, where I was sure I would be found out, but nobody seemed to care about me, if they even noticed.

Yet I had come to mistrust kindness, and I was wary of anyone placed between me and my imprisoned family. Once I learned that the farm was less than one hundred kilometers from Warsaw, I determined to go there. My Aunt Esther and Uncle David lived in Warsaw. I could find a home with them, earn some money, figure out a way to free my family (by now I was convinced my father had lived and was with Mama and Jozef at the work camp), and at least live safely till the war was over.

I wasn't sure what I would find in Warsaw, but I thought it must be better then Lodz. There had also been rumors about Warsaw, but I still felt my only hope was to get to my aunt and uncle.

So exactly one week after I came upon the farmhouse—a week of incessant nightmares and the growing terror that I might be discovered— I left it, my feet swimming in a pair of Marta's boots. The old woman would be left alone, I knew, but I was curiously unmoved by her fate. She was a good soul, but my family was my concern. Maybe I was wrong, but I also considered her a *Volksdeutscher,* otherwise she would not be alive, and I had no pity for any Pole who sided with the Nazis.

I left on a cool, sunlit morning, the first taste of spring in the air. I wore one of Marta's dresses, carried one of Marta's coats, sported Marta's knapsack with additional clothing on my back. Without compunction, I had taken a loaf of bread from the kitchen; I would need it later in the day.

For twelve hours, I kept moving. I avoided the main highway to Warsaw but rather walked down country roads, attempting to look nonchalant as occasional troop transports stopped and soldiers tried to coax me into the back with them. Eventually, the knee of my bad leg gave way, and I was forced to sit down. There, in the twilight, terrors filled my mind.

What would happen when the old woman discovered Marta's clothes were missing, I wondered? Would she call the police? The Gestapo would find I was a Jew and had escaped the transport. They would charge me with robbing a Polish citizen and sentence me to death. I would die without my family knowing about it. Nobody would know. Jean-Phillipe would find another girlfriend—he probably already had—and I would be placed in an anonymous grave, since no one would know my name.

My body ached and tears poured out of my eyes as if they had a will of their own. Sometimes laughter also came unbidden and I began to fear that I was going mad. I slept that night in a grove of elm trees that provided me with shelter from the wind.

The next morning, I resumed my journey, ignoring the pain in my leg by counting the number of steps I took—when the number reached a million, I figured, I would reach Warsaw.

It took two more days, and by the time I arrived I had, of course, lost count of my steps, but no matter, I was here. Just before the country turned to city, I changed into another of Marta's dresses, scrubbed the mud off Marta's boots, groomed myself with Marta's comb and, quite the self-possessed and pretty Polish girl, set out to find Aunt Esther. As in Lodz, all the street signs were now in German, but at Eisenstrasse, I recognized the corner bakery and knew that I was close to Esther's home.

At the next corner I froze. A massive wooden barricade, ten feet high and flanked by double walls of tightly strung barbed wire had been erected. The area behind it was divided into two districts connected by a high bridge. On either side, streams of pedestrians scurried to and fro like schools of fish.

A work gang came toward me carrying shovels, pickaxes, hammers, and chisels. Behind them, human workhorses dragged loads of bricks, the hods balanced across their shoulders by steel rods. I stared at their beards and shaven heads, their blue Star of David headbands. They turned right at the barricade, evidently looking for a way around it so they could enter the cordoned-off area. The Jews on the other side of the wall ignored them.

A Baluty? In Warsaw? More than half a million Jews, not counting the millions whose ancestors had "jumped the fence" to become Christians, lived in Warsaw; it was one of the reasons Esther and David felt comfortable there. Yet now they had obviously been penned up, just as we had been in Lodz. If this could happen in the Polish capital, was there anywhere else to go?

All through the days of living at the farm, I'd dreamed of Warsaw, of the happy reunion with David and Esther. A number of upper-class Jews had fled here just before the establishment of the Lodz ghetto, and it was not surprising to any of us that they had not sent word back. After all, what news was there? Only rumors of the impending collapse of the Allies and the continuing success of the German Army.

My mother used to say just because no one mentions the sea, is that any reason to suppose it has boiled away?

I moved closer to the barbed wire, pressing my face against it until the cold metal scratched my forehead. On the other side of the wall, Jews were going about their business, performing all the ordinary acts of normal street life. They did not seem as poor and miserable as those in the Lodz ghetto, but they soon would be, I guessed, if the patterns were repeated. I wound my way along the fence, following the workers to an entrance on Kaiserstrasse, formerly Zlota Street, I remembered.

At a respectful distance, crowds of curious Poles watched the German sentries screening all the Jews entering the compound. On the other side of the wall, police with Star of David armbands were doing the same thing to anyone who wanted to leave. Off in an alleyway, a group of Polish children screamed obscenities while others threw stones and bottles over the barrier.

At the entrance, I watched men—there were few women—produce their photo identity cards for the sentry. Did everyone carry them? Who could tell? All I knew was that I didn't have one. And if Warsaw was like the Baluty, the penalty for not having one was death.

All of a sudden I realized how ridiculous I looked in Marta's oversize clothing and shoes. Not a pretty Polish girl at all. A Jew without ID. A refugee. An escapee from the train to Treblinka.

I felt the sensation of being watched and tried to move deeper into the crowd at the entrance. As the German soldiers began to pummel an old man returning to the ghetto, the crowd pressed in closer. My eyes were riveted on the helpless figure as he cried out for help.

One of the guards turned to me, opening his mouth as if to say something, perhaps to accuse me. My heart began to pound.

"Out of my way, you stinking Christ killer," I screamed at the pathetic old man, driving the toe of Marta's shoe fiercely up into his soft stomach. Following my lead, the crowd joined in. By the time the guards pushed them back, the old man lay unconscious in the street, and I had shoved my way out of the mob.

My dreams of safety had come to nothing. Hunger, exhaustion, even common sense told me I was in a hopeless position. How could I get inside the wall to find Aunt Esther and Uncle David without being arrested? Without getting them arrested? Deep in Aryan Warsaw, I wandered through the maze of buses, trams, cars, and uniforms along the newly christened Bahnhofstrasse, dazed, numb, and shaking. I did not know where I would spend the night. Without an identity card, how could I avoid the SS?

Would it have been better to stay on the train? I wondered. Or to surrender to the authorities near the old lady's farm? To have given up without a fight and pleaded for mercy? Maybe I would have been assigned to farm labor out in the country. Perhaps I would have been reunited with my family in Treblinka, to suffer the same fate with them, but at least have their love to sustain me.

Or maybe it would have been better to remain in the Baluty with Nate Kolleck—or at least to have smuggled out his negatives. Then all this misery—maybe even my death—might mean something.

I was in the heart of the city, everything familiar from our many visits to my relatives, so that I registered the streets under their Polish names without looking at the signs. Tripping over cobblestones in my oversize boots, I hurried past the former Municipal building on Konopnicka, now a soldiers' barracks, and into the Plaza at Three Crosses Square and limped past the marble steps of the great Byzantine cathedral of St. Aleksander, where my beloved Chopin's heart sits in a little black box on the altar. Looming before me were the massive brick and steel walls of the Vienna modern girls' high school, and it was there that fear finally overwhelmed me.

Soldiers were everywhere, strolling across the plaza, leaning against railings and lampposts. Their voices were low and threatening, like thunder. The only other sounds were bursts of clamoring boys and toddlers chasing after them, begging, pleading, and cajoling the soldiers.

"C'mon, officer. What do ya say?"

"Hey, I was here first. Look at these cigarettes, officer. Egyptians. I swear it."

"Out of my way, you son-of-a-whore Polack," the soldier shouted, cuffing the second boy, and the sound of the slap reached into my soul and made me move away from the school doors.

A sensation of being followed unnerved me as I wandered across the square again. Abruptly, I stopped and listened. Did that shuffling noise mean someone was behind me, or did it come from discarded newspapers in the wind? I started up again, walking faster toward nowhere. The sound drew nearer. I stared at my shadow, waiting for another shadow to appear.

Finally I spun on my heel and faced only the sun dropping behind the glowing dome of the cathedral. Peals of laughter echoed across the almost deserted plaza.

"Please, miss. A zloty. Fifty groszy. Anything," a voice whimpered. A boy wrapped in a woman's tattered fur coat was begging at my knees. "I'm so hungry."

"I wish I could," I said, listening intently to his accent. It had been so long since I'd heard the singsong rhythm of the Jews north of Lodz that I couldn't be certain. Yet . . .

"Haven't you got anything? A crust of bread? C'mon lady, give me something. Those boys stole my cigarettes. I got nothing to sell now."

He had a round face with cheeks rubbed raw by the wind and enormous brown eyes. His feet were blue and swollen. Seven or eight years old, I thought, although it was hard to tell. I found myself drawn to him. "I haven't a zloty to my name. Honest. Not even a place to sleep."

The news seemed to cheer him—here was someone less fortunate than he. "You can stay with me. I've got my own den. You'll see."

"Den?" I asked, intrigued.

"Yeah. You know. Out past Poniatowski Bridge. In Saska Kepa. It's dry there. Or I have a better idea. You might be able to stay on Krucza Street. Would you like that?"

The names meant nothing to me, but dry sounded wonderful. "How do I find—" I began, but he had perked up his ears and was listening intently. There was a whistle. He answered it with a shrill blast of his own. Then he sped off across the plaza, clutching the string around his coat to keep it from falling open.

Night descended like an executioner's hood over Warsaw. Gas and electric lights were scarce in the occupied city, giving it a gloomy, haunted feeling, but I welcomed the dark; it might let me pass undetected.

Now I understood there were different kinds of terror. Against a German officer it was a hot, burning fear, the knowledge that with one small provocation he might blow your head off. But out on the street, there was no face to the enemy. It might be some peasant woman, or a beggar, or a bounty hunter. Even another refugee or stray dog could give you away. As a child, I had never been allowed to go out alone in Warsaw. What would Aunt Esther think if she caught sight of her prim and proper niece now?

I tried to comfort myself with the melody of the cooing pigeons as they circled the square. All other music had disappeared from my brain.

"Hi there," a voice called out, and a man with a cap in his hand touched my shoulder. I jumped back, startled. There was another man behind him. I thought they were going to attack me—but then I saw they were not men, they were boys.

The first, the older one, was wearing a clean shirt and new woolen trousers, but his pointy black shoes were full of gashes.

"Nich' verstehn, nich' verstehn," I said shrugging, edging away from them.

"It's okay," he muttered in Polish. "Please don't be scared. Paulus said you needed a place for the night, and now that I see you, I think you look familiar." He shifted uneasily on his feet. "I used to work at the Café Tarnopol," he said. "Didn't you sometimes sing and play the piano there?"

I dug my fingernails into my palm. The second boy, with carrot red hair and freckles, was perhaps ten or eleven. It was possible, just possible, that he had Jewish blood. But this one? He made Jozef look like a rabbi. Still, mention of the Café Tarnopol was like waving a Star of David.

"You must be mistaken," I said, afraid to take the chance. "I've never heard of the Café Tarnopol. I have to go home now. I'm sure that my father will be—"

I turned. He leapt forward to stop me. "Don't you understand that we're all in the same fix? We're risking our necks out here for you."

I wanted to believe, was desperate for someone to help me, even a boy. But, "I have no idea what you're talking about," I said.

"We seek one another out," he whispered. "Trust us. There's no other way."

"I don't know what you want from me," I said coldly.

"I'm Amchu." I watched as tears formed in the corners of his eyes. *"Ich bin ein Yid."*

I hesitated, struggled out of his grasp. "Please. Leave me alone."

He finally gave up. "Okay, go then," he growled. "But I saw you at the ghetto wall, and I know. There are more of us, many of us. We stick together. We're smart and we survive. Come by thirty-seven Krucza Street. It's an alley so tiny the Germans haven't bothered to change the name. Tell the woman there that Wolf sent you. You'll met him later. Knock twice, wait, then again three times." He turned to the other boy who was watching open-mouthed. "Let's get out of here quick," he said. And then: "She'll come or not as she pleases."

I debated for an hour, walking aimlessly though feigning a sense of purpose. My brief forays into the surrounding lanes and alleyways yielded nothing. I didn't even know what I was looking for.

Arriving at anyone's doorstep without an identity card would be asking for an invitation to Gestapo headquarters, and to remain on the street much longer was suicidal. I gathered my nerve and asked a pedestrian for directions to Krucza Street; she waved toward the railroad station just visible behind the barracks, and I set off. I knew I might be walking toward capture and death, but I had no alternative.

As I approached Krucza, a boy of about nine crossed the street and walked directly in front of me. "You are to come with me," he said without turning his head. "Wolf thinks you might have been followed, so you don't know me, and it's too dangerous to go to Krucza Street. Stay half a block behind; we'll come to a bar. It's always crowded this time of night. No one will bother you. Go inside, wait five minutes, then come out again. If you see me, follow me. If you don't—good luck."

I did as instructed, and when I went out, there he was at the end of the street. I don't think I've ever been happier to see anyone. If the boys had wanted to turn me in, there was no need for this game.

Walking behind him, I doubled back through side streets until we reached the banks of the Bug River. The boy slackened his pace as we approached the Wermacht boathouses, then motioned me to catch up. My throbbing hip joint slowed me down.

"Hurry up," the boy whispered. "This is a bad stretch—it's crawling with Germans. If anyone tries to stop us, don't say a word. Most of them are *schmalzers.*"

He looked at me to make sure his message had sunk in. My obvious bewilderment annoyed him. "Don't you know what a *schmalzer* is? For every one of us there are ten of those creeps. They make you pay to keep them from squawking, then they catch you the next time and ask you for more. That's what happened to our pal Hymie. We all chipped in to pay—three hundred zloty. Then Hymie disappeared anyway."

He kicked at the broken pavement. "You've just got to be smart, that's all. Stick with me and I'll keep you from the *schmalzers.*"

I stared with something like love at this waif, who seemed so old and wary. We drew apart again and he led me across the New Bridge into Saska Kepa. Without my realizing it, we'd come almost full circle. I scrambled down an embankment and through a strand of trees. The boy was waiting impatiently, tossing stones at the bridge footing. The moment I appeared he set off again, and I followed him along the railroad tracks until we plunged back into a copse of elm trees.

There I caught up to him. He held up a hand for silence. "Paulus," he whispered. "Hey, it's me, Winky. C'mon out. I've brought some bread. And a visitor."

"Bread?" The moon-faced boy in the fur popped his head out from the mouth of a cave hidden by an elaborate system of bushes and briars. "Hi, lady." He grinned. "Thought you'd show up. See? This is my den."

"What are you waiting for?" Winky growled, nudging me forward. "Go on in. You get to share the den with my brother, here."

I crawled in between the mud walls and found myself sitting in a tiny limestone cave. Paulus set out a straw pallet and covered it with a threadbare blanket. Next to it an oil lamp glowed reassuringly, and I realized how bone tired I was. That bed looked more comfortable than my own four-poster in Kowalska Street. All I wanted to do was lie down and sleep.

But first, bread. Winky divided the loaf into three sections and gave one to each of us. "Stolen from the finest bakery in Warsaw," he said proudly, and indeed it was more delicious than anything I'd eaten in Paris. For the moment, all my questions and fears were forgotten. Talk, I'd learned, was what you did when there wasn't any food.

Winky divided up the crumbs then reached into his pocket and pulled out a roll of zloty. "Here's a hundred for the week," he said, handing the bills to Paulus. "It better last till next Tuesday or you won't get any more. Understand? The rest of us are leaving at dawn. Meeting with Wolf."

"I can bring her there. I know the way by heart," Paulus offered.

"Sorry. You've got to stay here a few days. Wolf's orders. Things in the square are heating up, and it's the older boys he wants to meet with." He reached over and turned down the lamp wick. "Sorry," he repeated, tousled his brother's hair, and disappeared into the night.

Paulus began to cry. He let me put my arms around him. We lay down together on the pallet. "Good night," I whispered. "Sleep well."

Still sniffling, he curled up in my arms. I could imagine him in the days before the invasion, strolling with his papa, neatly scrubbed, his wavy brown hair brushed back on his forehead. He rolled over, curling his arms around thin air, as though hugging an invisible teddy bear. He whimpered, and I again put my arms around him, recognizing my own pattern of recurring nightmares.

Did Paulus also wake to his own sobbing, as I so often did? Did faces appear at the window for him—the helmeted soldiers with their machine guns? "It's okay," I said and softly sang him Brahms's lullaby, my voice and the beauty of the melody sounding profoundly poignant to me in the quiet of the cave.

He smiled at me in his drowsiness. Then his left hand balled into a fist and rose in the air as if to strike an attacker. My God, what he must have seen, must have experienced! I went on singing, and finally the little man surrendered to the sound and fell into a deep sleep, his only movement the in and out of his lips as he sucked his thumb.

Despite my exhaustion and the warmth and stillness of the cave, it took me a long time to join him in sleep. Visions of my family crowded my mind. I imagined my father dead, or wounded, or beaten by the guards for his act of defiance, and I saw Jozef beaten too for coming to his aid. My mother—my poor mother—would be left alone, and she would not survive. Oh, I should not have left them! Even if it meant death, I should be at their side.

The lullaby kept repeating itself in my head, and I began to weep. Yes, I could comfort a small boy with it, but who would comfort me?

CHAPTER 9

"Cigarettes, soldier?"

"What have you got? Lint-packed stinkweeds?"

"Of course not!" I said. "Look at the label—and the Reich stamp."

"Stamp my ass. No French smokes?"

I shrugged and turned away. The soldier followed belligerently. He was drunk, and it was drunks I feared most. Quickly I scanned Three Crosses Square for my comrades. But Winky and Freckles were gone, and Paulus was sulking alone on the steps of the Church of St. Alexander. Where was Wolf, the supplier of the cigarettes? Winky told me he would always be on hand, ready to intervene in case of trouble.

"Cigarettes, Kommandant?" I called to a stocky figure heading toward the church. I hoped his rank might deter the drunk who had grabbed my arms and suggested he pay for a fuck rather than the cigarettes.

"At ease, soldier," the officer barked, noticing what was happening. "You've got ten seconds to disappear."

The drunk shoved a hand into his pocket, but by the time he had found his knife, the officer's Luger was drawing a bead between his eyes.

"I could kill you for threatening an officer," he growled. "Now drop the weapon, back off, and keep you hands behind your back. What's your name?"

The solider sobered quickly. "Schwitters. Two-forty-two Panzer Division, sir."

"Because I'm in a generous mood, Schwitters, I'll let you go. But I don't want to see you in Three Crosses Square again. Understand?"

"Yes, Kommandant. Thank you, sir." He was sweating profusely. "Forgive me for—"

"Shut up and apologize to the young lady."

The soldier's eyes filled with hate. He glared at me. "Forgive me, you little—"

"Very good, Schwitters. That'll do."

"Yes, Kommandant."

"Schwitters, you would do well to learn the difference between street women and ladies. This is a lady under my personal protection. Molest her again and you'll face a firing squad."

"Heil Hitler." The soldier saluted and turned away.

The *kommandant*'s hands glided over my arm to straighten out the sweater where the soldier had grabbed it. It was a friendly touch, not at all suggestive, and I smiled at him gratefully.

"A girl like you should be more careful," he said. "It's not safe out here at dusk. What's your name?"

"Marisa. And thank you, Herr Kommandant. You are very kind."

His look was pleasant, paternal. "Where do you live?"

"In Saska Kepa." In a cave on a pallet with an eight-year-old boy.

He held out his hand. "I'm Egon Hildebrand. Please call me Egon."

"If that's what the *kommandant* wants."

"That's exactly what he wants. I need a smoke, too. What have you to offer this evening, Marisa?"

"All kinds, Egon. Would you like some Seagulls, home-rolled Swojak? Or maybe Egyptians? All of them authentic, no substitutes."

His eyes lit up. "I know that. And from now on I'll buy my cigarettes only from you. The others will sell me field grass for thirty-five zloty and call it a bargain. They think they can fool me. But I know the difference between brass and gold, and I can tell you sell gold. Tonight I take four packs. No, make it five. Seagulls."

I stared at him. "But Komm—Egon. That's a hundred and seventy-five zloty."

"What else should a lonely soldier do with his money? It's this or drink or buy a diseased whore. Indulge me. I'll feel better knowing that you won't be standing here late tonight waiting to be molested."

He slipped two hundred zloty into my hand and opened a pack of the cigarettes. "Would you care for one, my dear?"

"No, thank you. I don't smoke."

"Well, it's a pleasure to share your company, Fraülein, and I look forward to seeing you again. I can tell that your upbringing was far different from the others' on the street. Someday you must tell me how you came to be in these circumstances."

"If it pleases you to think so, then I'm delighted." Would he be delighted, I wondered, if he knew I was Jewish? The thought sent a shiver across the back of my neck.

"It pleases me very much. Perhaps next Friday I can persuade you to walk along the banks of the Bug with me."

What would Winky think? Or Wolf? Me walking with a German officer. Yet to refuse him—"I'm not sure," I said. "Friday evening is always very busy."

"At least consider it. You don't have to answer now. I'll come by next week about this time, and by then you can make your decision." Again he held out his hand.

"Very well." I shook his hand and released it to fumble through my pockets. "Wait a minute, Egon. You're forgetting your change."

"Keep it for now," he said. "We'll settle up next weekend."

His chunky figure marched stiffly toward the barracks. I blew on my stack of zloty notes for good luck, then buried them in the waistband of my dress. Two hundred zloty! A miracle! I could turn in for the night.

For a while, I knew, I would be able to fend Egon off and still keep him spending his zlotys. If he got too anxious to take me out—well, there were plenty of German officers in that barracks across the square. I knew that I had to survive at any cost, and I would do anything to see my family again.

Though only 18, Wolf Rydecki was a man. Fearsome in size, muscular like a weight lifter, tough as an ironworker, he nevertheless exuded a gentleness to his friends that bespoke a kind heart.

Nothing seemed to faze him. Danger brought a smile, pain a laugh. He was fearless but prudent, and he watched over his small gang of thieves and sneaks like a benign Robin Hood, stealing from the goyim to feed the Jews.

I liked him from the moment I met him, which was two days after I had taken up residence in Paulus's den. Winky brought me to him at the dosshouse on Krucza Street where he held court like a prince, doling out the day's assignments, plotting escape routes should we be threatened, inventing the lies we would use in case we were interrogated. He told me how to dress so that I would look most sympathetically sexy, and how to modulate my voice both to lure a customer and to hold him off if he got too frisky. Within a week, my income in Three Crosses Square was the equal of any of my comrades'.

We thought of ourselves not as thieves and sneaks, but as Jewish freedom fighters, and called ourselves the Zydowska Organizacja Bojowa—the ZOB. I often wondered if it was sheer good fortune that Paulus found me in that square, or if he had been recruiting for Wolf. Whatever, I was now a minor member of a Jewish band of underage soldiers, and I had real friends who could look after me. It never seemed surprising to me that I, the oldest of the band, was the most in need of care, for it was not years but experience that matured us. To the Germans we looked no different from the thousands of other ragged, hungry refugees who had fled the countryside for the relative safety of Warsaw. But in our hearts, we had more to fear.

From the first, I wondered how Wolf could afford his room on Krucza Street, the good clothes he wore (he was fond of blindingly white shirts and sailor pants), and the money he meted out to his minions from time to time; surely we were the best-fed beggars in Warsaw. And then, one day, the answer came.

I was coming up Krucza Street in order to give Wolf the day's receipts (we pooled all our income, with Wolf the chief financial officer as well as president and secretary of the group) when I saw a man arriving carrying a bulging burlap bag. He kept looking around furtively—he had none of the sang froid of us ZOBs—and as soon as he knocked on the door, Wolf himself opened it and took the bag, a transaction that could not have taken fifteen seconds. The man darted off, but Wolf had noticed me and now came out to greet me, having stowed the bag safely behind him.

"Let's walk," he said. "Hold my hand. We'll play boyfriend and girlfriend so I can whisper in your ear."

Actually, I wouldn't have minded being Wolf's girlfriend, but any sort of fraternization was strictly forbidden, and so I merely let him put his arm around my waist and leaned my head into his shoulder.

"Guns!" he said. "That bag contains guns. Tonight, we'll smuggle them into the ghetto. I'll want you to help with the smuggling."

I gasped. "But—"

"It'll be easy for a girl. You'll just walk in through the sentries, carrying a pistol under your jacket, and you'll be met on the other side."

A hundred questions sprang to my mind. "Who are the guns for?"

"The Jewish army. They're forming one inside, an army of resistance, so that one day they will rise up against their Nazi tormenters, fighting like lions instead of dying like sheep."

He was usually calm, but now there was electricity in his voice. In the dusk, I could see his eyes blaze.

"When will that be?"

"I don't know. When they have enough weapons. My job—our job—is to give them as many as possible."

"Who supplies them to you?"

He shook his head. "I can't tell you. The man who brought them tonight, he's just a messenger. The man who sent him—well, I know his name, but no one else in the ZOB does. You see, if you're caught the Gestapo might torture it out of you."

Torture! And he wanted me to be a smuggler. No. It was too terrifying, too dangerous, too—

He was looking at me strangely. "You don't have to help, but if you don't you must leave the ZOB and promise on pain of death not to tell anyone about us."

Amazingly, his words were a comfort. There was no way I could leave the ZOB, and his threat, put so baldly, removed any ambiguity from my mind. Of course I would stay with my friends. I put my arm around him. "I have no identification papers. How will I get past the guards?"

He took a paper from his pocket and handed it to me with a smile. "Presto magic. You're Mira Luxenberg, allowed to go in and out of the ghetto to work at the army hospital."

I took it with fear and gratitude. There was my picture (I remembered Winky taking it a few days ago—"as a keepsake," he'd said), and an official-looking stamp. "Now I can see Aunt Esther," I exclaimed.

His expression grew dark. "Don't go near them! There are German spies in the ghetto, for all I know hundreds of them. If they follow you, you'll put yourself and your aunt and uncle in danger."

He was right, of course, but the realization was acutely painful. I was cut off from all family and for a moment imagined that I would never see any of them again. That I would be caught smuggling pistols; that Esther and David had been driven out of their home; that Mama and Papa were dead in Treblinka and Jozef in prison for arguing with an SS man.

Wolf turned and we headed back toward Krucza Street. "I must leave you here," he said as we neared it. "I know I've given you a perilous assignment, but all of us must share the risks. Winky and Freckles are also supplying guns. Freckles and even little Paulus are smuggling in vials of potassium, benzine, and hydrochloric acid. And there are many more—Peter and Ariel, Kivi and Halinka—it's time for you to meet them all. Whether you know it or not, you were on trial. But I trust you now, you're one of us. And don't be frightened about the smuggling. The guards are bored and stupid. Franklin Roosevelt could get past them in his wheelchair. You won't have any trouble."

He trusted me! This valiant young hero, this champion of the Jews. My fear eased, and in its place—pride.

A few evenings later, I sat with Wolf in the Café Hirschfeld, a well-known hangout for Jewish war profiteers allowed to socialize inside the ghetto, watching him press tea leaves against the edge of his cup. Hirschfeld must have had pull with the Warsaw Judenrat. Nobody bothered him, and we were free to meet here, as long as we spent a little money. Wolf used it as an occasional gathering place for the ZOB. He would reward those who had done exceptionally good work on the streets with a decent meal, "to keep up their strength," even though he only drank tea.

"Why not order another?" I asked. "There's nothing left in those leaves."

He frowned. "That would be wasteful. And we need to hold on to every zloty we can. Deportations are starting. Gypsies are being rounded up across Warsaw. This morning Peter told me there's a death camp near Auschwitz where prisoners are being gassed as soon as they arrive. Trainloads of them. Soon the Nazis will fall on the ghetto like falcons claiming mice. That's why our work is so urgent, and money so important. Those in the ghetto must be able to resist."

"But what chance do they have?" I asked. "The Germans have tanks, machine guns, bombs. They'll be slaughtered."

He straightened in his chair. "At least they'll fight for their lives instead of marching off to the gas chambers. At least they'll die with glory."

I could tell that he foresaw his own death, fighting with his comrades, but my own heart resisted. There was nothing glorious in death. "What about the Americans? Surely they'll join the war and will save us."

He looked at me with pity. "It won't happen. Even though they hate the Nazis, they don't give a fuck about the Jews. Even if they decide to fight, it'll be on the battlefield, not in the ghetto. Are they telling the world what our situation is here? No. They remain silent. The Russian treaty sealed our doom."

It frightened me to hear him talk like that. His mood was all darkness. I started to ask a question, but he gestured for me to keep silent as Amchu and a few others came in and filled our table. Wolf introduced me to Ariel, Peter, Halinka, Walter—all of them children or teenagers, their zeal their only common bond. Their eyes were hard.

The waiter appeared with plates filled with pickled beets and cabbage. I had been living on bread and an occasional apple but did not share in this feast. Yes, I had begun my new career and had transported five pistols into the ghetto, but that was nothing especially heroic, and I did not feel I deserved special rations. Wolf noticed my abstinence, smiled, and said nothing.

The café began to fill up. The patrons were mostly rich Poles, and the atmosphere was lively. I wondered how much Wolf had to bribe Hirschfeld to be allowed his table. Ariel motioned toward the door, and we all turned to watch as a plump man in his sixties entered with a girl on his arm. She was fifteen, maybe younger, and she tossed her long blond hair as if she were a thoroughbred. "Meltzer the profiteer," Ariel explained in a whisper. "The girl is part of the profit."

"Halinka," Wolf asked suddenly, "how are we doing with the medical supplies?"

"Half bad, half good," she replied nervously. "We're pretty much on schedule, but it's been hard to meet the quota on surgical knives. And I haven't been able to locate a sterilizer. I think one or two of the doctors suspect me. I suppose we just have to rely on them to keep silent."

"We have no choice." I followed his eyes to a platter of stuffed roast duckling and heaps of kasha, its aroma tantalizing in the smoky air. Up onstage, a comedian was telling Hitler jokes and laughter erupted from the surrounding tables. The ZOB members kept silent. It was one of our rules: never take Hitler lightly.

I recognized a heavyset, middle-aged man at the next table: Henry Keller of Cohen and Keller whose picture was plastered on the trolleys they owned, which were used to transport those too ill to walk across the ghetto. Sooner or later, everyone would ride in them, I thought. Cohen and Keller also held the concession on rickshaws, "ambulances," and the only burial carts in the ghetto.

Keller noticed my glance and winked at me provocatively. My eyes dropped to my hands, which fidgeted with the sash of my threadbare dress. Wolf stared at me and I blushed. Had I let him down in some other test of loyalty?

"Don't be embarrassed," he said. "It's perfectly natural that Keller finds you attractive. Or Kommandant Hildebrand, for that matter."

So he knew about Egon. The officer had approached me several times, but I had been able to collect his money without agreeing to walk with him. I felt stung by Wolf's words.

"It's not my fault," I said.

Wolf laughed. "Well, really, it is. If you weren't so pretty . . ." He rested his hand lightly on mine, but I pulled it away. Around the table, the comrades pretended not to notice. It was times like these that their fanatical loyalty to Wolf stirred my doubts and made me feel like screaming. They called themselves the ZOB, but beneath their bravado and allegiance to Wolf, they were just children playing at revolution, too young to realize the possible consequences of what they were doing. It was exciting to plan armed resistance, thrilling to be smuggling guns or bombs or medical supplies. But who among them would be able to pull a trigger or throw a bomb? Ariel with her acne? Freckles with his squeaky voice? Halinka who wagged her tail like a lovesick puppy every time she caught Wolf's eye? Eight-year-old Paulus?

"Does Hildebrand have an interest in you?" Wolf had pulled his chair close to mine and was talking so the others couldn't hear.

"I suppose so. What if he does? I really don't understand why you need to keep bringing it up."

"Because it's important for all of us. *You must accept that date.*"

"Never!" I knew what Wolf meant, but he was asking too much. "You must be out of your mind."

The couple at the next table clapped for the maître d'. He bent down to listen to them over the peels of laughter the comedian evoked. A moment later a pastry cart appeared, laden with cookies and pies and cakes, distracting our young comrades.

"He won't be content just to walk along the river."

"You're not a child," he growled.

"And you're not a fool. You realize what's at stake? Or don't you care, Wolf? To him I'm just one more—"

"We'll be there to keep an eye on you."

A meaningless promise. I hated him for it. "And what if he decides he wants to be alone? Takes me to some hotel or private room?"

Wolf leaned back. "As a matter of fact, we're counting on it. You'll do as he says. And we'll arrange a little diversion to keep him from—"

"From what? Raping me? And only a little diversion? Is that the idea?"

"Do you think if a man touches you, you'll die?" Halinka said. "At least you could say you'd given something to the cause."

Damn it! She had overheard us. I wanted to scratch out her eyes. "Oh, so you all agree to give me up. Is that the idea? Well, sorry. The bait wants nothing to do with it. Why don't you take my place?"

"Keep your voice down." Wolf was his authoritative self. He turned to me. "First of all, we're not giving you up. You're not going to lose your precious virginity, I promise you. Second, I think Hildebrand's the man responsible for Hymie's disappearance. And I'd rather like to see him paid back. To do that, we need to get him alone." He stared at me with a ferocity I had never witnessed in him. "You're elected, and here's what you must do."

Halinka reached for my hand in an attempt to comfort me. "You see," she explained, "Hymie was Wolf's brother."

"It's been a lovely evening, hasn't it?" Egon Hildebrand asked.

It was easy to agree. Far from being the sexual predator Wolf portrayed, the German was a model gentleman, solicitous of me and my feelings.

The balmy spring night had gone well. We strolled along the banks of the Bug for a mile or so, then stopped at a candlelit Polish restaurant for dinner, far from the Four Seasons, where most of the officers went to dine. Egon was fresh-faced and fresh-voiced, maybe in his early twenties. He told me of his Bavarian childhood, of his love of skiing and the poems of Goethe and Schiller, of his parents, who wanted only the finest education for him, a hope thwarted when he was inducted into the army. He was proud, he said, of graduating Officers' Training School and hoped someday he would be sent to the front to fight for his country. He told me all this without seeming to realize I was his "enemy," perhaps because of my perfect German or because for these hours he was able to fantasize that I was a Bavarian girl, one of his at-home sweethearts.

I found myself in a strange situation. I was sworn to hate him. Not only was he responsible for the disappearance of Wolf's brother (just how Wolf never explained), but he was also an Aryan, one of the tribe that sent my family to Treblinka and forced me to live in a den and smuggle guns to the ghetto to earn my keep. But I liked him. He was a sweet boy, openly romantic, enjoying himself and wanting me to have a good time, too.

"You would like a nightcap perhaps?" he said as we walked back to Three Crosses Square after dinner.

"I'm afraid not, Egon," I said automatically, forgetting my assignment.

"Yes, of course. I meant no insult . . ."

With a shock, I remembered Wolf's instructions and the task ahead of me. Backing out was not an option. "I didn't take it as such."

"I was too forward. Maybe in time, as we get to know each other better—"

I took his hand. "No, really. I was just momentarily tired." I let his arm brush against my breast. "There's a hotel," I said. "Some of my girlfriends go there with their sweethearts. I thought maybe it would be a good place for us."

"Very well," he said with such eagerness that I knew he had thought it all out beforehand, had pictured himself stripping me, kissing me, making love to me all night. "We wouldn't have to do anything—that is, if you don't want to. We could just be together a little longer. Maybe sleep side by side." He was so embarrassed he couldn't look at me. "It's just that it's been so long since I've been with a girl who wasn't a whore. A nice girl like you."

A nice girl who was leading him into Wolf's trap. "Yes," I said. "That is, if we just sleep side by side."

His gratitude was painful. I put my arm around his waist and led him off the riverbank toward a dingy building on a side street that declared itself the Ritz Hotel.

I looked around. No sign of Wolf or of any of the ZOB. It was not late, but the street was deserted, and only a few lights shone from the windows of the surrounding buildings. If Wolf didn't show up, I wondered if Egon would be true to his word, if he would be content only to sleep by my side. But surely Wolf would be there. He had promised, and the fact I couldn't see him merely meant he had chosen a good hiding place.

As Egon and I came up to the hotel, I felt afraid, but there was an excitement stirring in the depths of me that had nothing to do with rescue or betrayal. Egon was a handsome man, a dear man. If I could forget for one night that he was a German and I a Jew, then maybe . . . We mounted the steps leading to the lobby.

"I don't understand you, Marisa," Egon said, his cheeks on fire. "One moment you say no to a nightcap, and the next you're dragging me up the stairs. What a strange girl you are."

So strange that at the moment I wasn't Marisa at all, rather Mira, the name Wolf put on my identity papers, and I looked at my prey as though from a great height, cold and removed and ruthless. "I might change my mind again," I suggested coyly, then added hurriedly, "but only if it would please you. Don't think I don't want to please you."

"You will please me and I will please you." He was practically singing.

I stood stiffly, tension wrapped around me like a vise. The desk clerk hesitated, looking guiltily from side to side before slipping Egon a room key on a crude leather thong. "Two seventeen," he hissed, accepting Egon's cash in advance without checking our papers.

We climbed three flights of stairs, walked down a dusty corridor accompanied by the sound of whispers, staccato laughter, moans, and the telltale rasp of bedsprings, and found our room. Egon had trouble opening the door—his hands were shaking—but at last we were inside and his arms were around my waist.

Whatever sexual anticipation I might have felt before had drained away, and I stood with my arms at my sides like a schoolgirl awaiting punishment.

He kissed my forehead while I tried to remember Wolf's lessons. Tonight would be just as we'd rehearsed it, I told myself. Train yourself not to feel anything. This man is your enemy. Wolf's enemy. The enemy of the Jews. I stepped to the gas lamp and turned the wick all the way up, the signal for Wolf to come.

"It's too bright," Egon said and came up behind me to dim it. In the moment of light, I saw a tiny, unadorned room with peeling wallpaper and plaster falling from the ceiling. There was a queen-size bed with a tattered cotton bedspread, a washstand in the corner, and a cheap, scarred vanity table at the other side of the room. There was a skylight in the ceiling—we were on the top floor—so dusty that even in daytime, I was sure, no light could get through.

And no wardrobe! This was a hotel for prostitutes! What was Wolf thinking? What must Egon be thinking? What else could he think except that I was just another whore, perhaps prettier and better spoken, but a whore all the same? He probably regretted the money spent on dinner; he could have bought me without it. I froze, waiting for his next move.

It was gentle. If he was disappointed in me he gave no sign of it but rather swung the door shut and stood behind me. We were all alone. There was no place for Wolf to hide.

Egon's eyes met mine in the mirror on the vanity. "Don't be afraid, Marisa," he whispered. "I'll be kind."

Did he not think I was a prostitute? Was his own fantasy so great that he did not notice our surroundings? "The mirror doesn't do you justice," he whispered, removing the pins from my hair and running his fingers over the strands like a blind man as he painstakingly began to unbraid them. "There now. Look at yourself." His soft hands brought my head back to my reflection. Long waves of black hair framed my face; it was the way I wore it for Jean-Phillipe. How dare Egon see me like this!

"How beautiful you are," he said. "I've dreamed of a woman like you every night since my wife, Elsa, died of pneumonia. Ah, don't shake your head. What would be the point in lying to you?"

"I shouldn't have come here with you," I moaned, feeling his hands glide over my bare arms. He brushed my neck, my shoulder with his lips and began to undo the buttons in the back of my dress.

"You are my reward," he said, not heeding my protest. "All miracles have their cost. Elsa was taken from me. Don't think for a moment that I haven't suffered for Germany. She was young and beautiful and gifted, but you are more beautiful still and all the love I had for her I want to pour into you."

He dropped to his knees, turned me to face him, and crawled into my arms, his head against my breasts, pulling me close. I felt his suffocating heat, his overwhelming need. With a stifled shriek, I moved away, looking frantically around for a way to escape.

"Please," he said, his voice hoarse, "let me love you."

Love? To him, love was some fairy tale laced with chamber music and passionate sonnets. Perhaps, in another life, in Paris, it would have meant the same to me. But here in Warsaw, love meant shelter over your head, a shared crust of bread, a partnership of survival.

Egon moved to the vanity stool, holding me before him like a mannequin, admiring me as I stood staring into our reflection—the back of his head, my terrified eyes. He stood and kissed my throat and shoulders. I made no effort to stop him.

"Yes," he murmured, "yes." He ran his hands lightly along my sides and down onto my hips, all the while nuzzling his head against my breasts. This time I did not pull away. Emboldened, he unbuttoned my dress, then eased the thin shoulder straps down until I saw my breasts straining against the soft white fabric of my camisole.

"So very beautiful." Egon pressed his lips greedily against the camisole, pulling down its straps with one hand while the other passed lightly over my nipples, which trembled and grew hard. No one had ever touched my naked breasts before, though Jean-Phillipe's hand over my clothing often made me dream of it. Despite my fear I felt a nameless pleasure and closed my eyes.

Glass shattered above our heads. A figure dropped through the skylight and flew across the room. Wolf's arm brought a hammer down on Egon's skull with a low, cracking thud. I screamed and pulled at my camisole. Wolf was regarding me strangely, as though for the first time realizing that I was a woman, then he stared down at the dead soldier at his feet and began to cry—long, anguished sobs that contorted his body.

I finished dressing, slipped on my shoes, and stumbled to the door, tossing my key in Wolf's direction. Perhaps it was Wolf's first time as well.

CHAPTER 10

The ghetto became my second home. It was a city where almost 500,000 people lived. To go in and out of the checkpoint I would wait until the local police took over guard duty from the SS because they didn't seem to care who went through.

Before long we became so brazen that we moved through the checkpoints without a tremor and conducted "legitimate" business on either side of the barriers.

As often as twice a week, I wrote to my family at Treblinka, using Krucza Street as the return address. And one day—miracle of miracles!—an answer came. Wolf handed it to me as we strolled with our wares in a busy shopping district.

Treblinka, 17 April, 1941

And so our beloved daughter and sister,

At last we are given the opportunity to write from here at the work camp. We cannot say conditions are at all bad. I, Benjamin, work in the fields, but it is easy work, and since I am old our bosses do not push me as hard as the others. Nora works in the kitchen where she helps prepare the sparse but wholesome meals for the camp. And Jozef, well he is the best off of all, for he has become the star of the camp boxing team.

I write to ask if you would send us some woolen blankets, and perhaps some leather boots and down pillows. I hate to

beg this of you, but the days are still cold here and despite
their best efforts, the men and women who run the camp
have been unable to procure enough supplies from Berlin.
Also, any extra gold will be faithfully delivered to us by our
camp commander and used to acquire some of the necessities,
like soap and razor blades.

Give our love to Esther and David, and also to our beloved
Uncle Horowitz. Tell him he is with us always in our
thoughts.

With all our love

I handed the letter to Wolf.

"Is that your father's handwriting?" he asked.

"Yes. It seems feeble, though, as if he didn't have much strength."
I couldn't contain my joy. "But he's alive!"

"One wonders for how long," Wolf said somberly.

A noose of fear constricted my chest. "What do you mean?"

"The letter is all lies. Surely you can see that." He snorted.
" 'Uncle Horowitz is with us always.' That's the name we Jews gave to
Hitler when we joked about him before the war. He's telling you
Hitler made him write the letter—or at least Hitler's minions."

I knew about "Uncle Horowitz" but did not register my father's
use of it, so thrilled was I to read the letter. "Then the easy work in
the field, the good food, Jozef's team . . ."

"All lies."

I refused to believe it. "But what's the point?"

"Obviously they need supplies—the blankets and leather for the
troops, the gold for themselves. So they made your father write what
they told him to say. I'll bet the same letter's gone to thousands of
families across Poland." He shook his head. "It's sheer sadism. My
God, how they can think of ways to torture us!"

I knew he was right. Instead of balm, the letter was poison. "What
can we do?" I asked, feeling as helpless as I had in the old woman's
house.

"Fight on!" His words were spirited, but I could tell how depressed and tired he was. I glanced anxiously down the street at a group of Death's Head soldiers staggering out of a Germans-only café at Three Crosses Square. I moved toward them. "Cigarettes for the officers?"

They bought ten packs among them, accompanied by the suggestive remarks I was by now accustomed to. Wolf seemed to vaporize as they bargained with me but returned when they had left the square.

The square became my place of business. I marveled at its transformation. Before the Germans arrived it must have been beautiful with the Byzantine cathedral and modern high school—now it was a place for prostitutes and cigarette sellers.

The April sun had not yet warmed the ghetto, and Wolf wore a bulky cloth jacket over corduroy pants and a long-sleeved coat. "You don't have to worry about the soldiers anymore," he told me. "I have a way to protect you."

His announcement did not cheer me. By now I was sure I could take care of myself. "What's that?"

He pulled open his jacket. Stuck in his belt was a German Luger. "Anyone tries to harm you, I'll blow his head off."

"Egon's!" I gasped.

He grinned. "Precisely."

"Oh my God." The horror of that night in the hotel room came flooding back. In my distraught mind Wolf seemed the aggressor, Egon the victim.

He stood smiling before me, expecting congratulations. Instead, tears pouring from my eyes, I slapped him so hard my hand tingled.

"Assassin," I said. "You didn't have to kill him."

"Mia, he was not only a fucking Nazi," I heard him say. "He already killed my brother. He was gathering information on all our people and in a few weeks we would all be dead. The gun was my prize. Isn't it better that he's dead so that we can fight on?"

I headed back toward Three Crosses Square, carefully skirting the German army barracks. Egon's death precipitated an influx of Gestapo looking for clues, and I feared I would give myself away if I was stopped. Every now and then I slid over into the shadows, imagining I saw Egon's silhouette approaching.

In the next few days, fear took over. The freedom I'd enjoyed slipping into and out of the ghetto was severely compromised. The local police were clamping down at all official crossing points. Barbed wire was being installed on the top of the newly completed brick sections of the wall. Guards were detailed everywhere. Then there was the Gestapo. In their pressed uniforms and polished shoes, they looked like machines of war, and they were terrifying.

And always there were Polish youths skulking in the shadows, ready to blackmail, steal, or bludgeon their victims and leave them lying bloody and senseless on the pavement for the Germans to finish off.

"Mia," Paulus cried across the cobblestones. "Hey, Mia, wait. It's me. I've got to tell you something."

Paulus, trouble incarnate, raced toward me, his moon face shining with the importance of his message.

Whatever news it was, it could wait. "Beat it," I growled at the astonished boy, then spun around and quickly strode away.

"But wait, Mia," he bawled. "You've got to hear this. The *schmalzers* are looking for a mouse. A mouse who lured a fat German cat to a hotel room, but he never came out alive. Better watch out, Mia! The Germans are setting a mousetrap for you."

I could no longer stay in Warsaw. If I stayed inside the ghetto, I'd have to compromise Aunt Esther and Uncle David, for there'd be no other place to go. Sooner or later, there'd be no way out except the camps. But if I stayed on the Aryan side, I'd inevitably be questioned by the Gestapo, and then the way out was death. Besides, being seen with me was too dangerous for the others.

I walked, trying to think of a plan, my mind numb and body exhausted. At Chlodna I mounted the elevated sidewalk, which had been built so the trolly lines could run through the work area. People from outside used the cars to go to their jobs. The area was guarded so Jews could not escape. I climbed up onto the Polish Corridor, which joined the two halves of the ghetto. All along the railings, sightseers and children were throwing stones down at the Hassidim. Below me, scurrying figures in armbands moved about like bees in a hive, busily looking for "traitors" among a population so beaten down their movements seemed those of pack animals—or, more accurately, beetles with their frail shoulders hunched forward to protect themselves from bottles and rocks.

The ghetto seemed impenetrable, but I knew that the best time to move in and out was when the Germans changed guards. The smokestacks of the Toebbens factory glowed red, and I thought of the Baluty, where similar smokestacks promised similar misery. Hard work hadn't saved us in Lodz. Here, greed kept the corridor open for the goods manufactured by Warsovian Jews, enabling them to achieve a standard of poverty for which King Chaim's subjects would have killed.

But very soon, the Germans would have taken all they could from the bodies and hearts of the Jews of the Warsaw ghetto. And what would become of its inhabitants then? Typhus, cholera, spotted fever, starvation? The few arms we had smuggled in now seemed to me no more potent than toys. All right, so a few Germans would be killed, but a rebellion meant certain torture and death. How many other ghettos were scattered through the German empire? Did each provincial capital have its own?

I pictured Nate Kolleck's sickly face as he squinted before his camera, focusing on the death carts, as prevalent here as there. It had seemed far-fetched back then that the agony could last, impossible that so many cities and ten of thousands of Jews could suffer like this while life elsewhere went on. In Paris, the girls at my lycée were surely planning a foray to the boutiques of St. Germain. They had laughed at me, called me Jew, treated me like a lower species of animal. Well, perhaps they were right. The evidence below me, stark in its clarity, seemed to prove them right.

When Hitler's juggernaut reached Paris, Rouen, Liege, Amsterdam, London—who could withstand it? Was that what it would take before the rest of the world listened to the cries from Poland? I knew that my father had a brother in America. Martin Levy and his wife, Ceena, lived in a place called Brooklyn, evidently a part of New York City. My parents did not speak of them much, perhaps because when they had had a chance to emigrate with them, they decided to stay in Lodz because, as Papa put it, he had an obligation to his people. Ha! A lot of good he did them, or his family.

When I got the chance, I would write to my American uncle, and to Jean-Phillipe, and if necessary to the whole world to tell them of the sights I saw below me and the work camps, the rations, the rats, even the profiteering and collaboration. About the typhus and the starvation and the crazy woman who roamed the streets every night singing Yiddish songs at the top of her lungs.

The Songbird of the Ghetto, the Germans called her. A songbird, just like me. But I swore to myself I would never sing for the Germans, never work in the camps, never be tortured. There was no place to go, and hopelessness descended on my soul. I gripped the railing. It was at least eighty feet to the ground. No one could survive such a fall. The comfort of death lay before me.

A Polish policeman tapped me on the shoulder. "Identity card."

Shaking my head to clear it, I handed the card to him. He studied it while my knees grew weak with terror. It was the first time I had been stopped since Egon's murder.

"Mira Luxenberg," he read. "Yes, you're the one."

"The one what?"

He exploded. "You slut, you know damn well what for. I'm tired of you *Volksdeutsch* girls, thinking you can get away with insolence."

He paused to suck in a breath of air, his neck turning red beneath a crop of wavy blond hair. "I'll have you singing our national anthem before we're done with you."

He slapped my ear then dragged me by my hair down from the bridge to a waiting black Daimler amid the hoots and cheers of the Polish onlookers.

I wished I had jumped.

The familiar smell of rich upholstered leather and saddle soap inside the car flooded me with memories. Hundreds of times I'd closed my eyes in my father's old Daimler and opened them to find myself magically transported to the countryside. Now when I opened them, I saw only my captor by my side, and the uniformed German officer driving us. Why an officer? I wondered briefly but was too frightened to give it more thought.

I had been prepared to jump. Yes. Then he seized me and dragged me down. His eyes were crystal blue, icy. His mustache was like a pale blond pencil line across his face.

The ride took less than five minutes. The soldier pulled me from the car and pushed me into a nondescript house, through its corridor, and into a tiny, windowless room at the back. A torture chamber!

I felt a wave of nausea. My ear throbbed where he had slapped it, and my scalp was on fire from his hold on my hair. Had I revealed anything? I wondered. Called out for Wolf, whose new Luger would be no help to me now? If only I'd jumped in time!

We sat at either end of a small wooden table. The only other furniture in the room was a standing lamp, its naked bulb emitting a sickly light. There would be others coming, I was sure, to take me to an even worse place, with instruments of torture. Resist, I told myself. Don't betray your comrades. But I didn't know if I'd have the strength.

"Don't be afraid, little sister," the soldier offered in clumsy Yiddish. His tone was kind. A trap.

"German is my native tongue sir, if you please."

"Mine, too. We'll speak German." He held out his hand across the table. "My name is Peter, and I've been working with the cigarette sellers through Wolf."

"Wolf? Is that a Christian name, sir?"

He laughed. "You're every bit as delightful as Wolf said, and a great deal more clever. My congratulations."

If it was a trap, it was seductive. I longed to trust him, but dared not. "Is that a fact?"

"I like the feisty ones. I can see we'll get along fine."

"*We?*"

"The National Committee. I thought Wolf would have explained to you. You are in great danger, my dear. Wolf only calls on our services in times like these. I was sorry to have hurt you, but we had to put up a good show."

I felt a surge of joy so powerful it staggered me. This was no trap, it was possible salvation. "My God," I said, "when you took me to the Daimler, I thought you were German."

"I am."

"And the driver, dressed in a German uniform—"

"He's Polish." Peter smiled. "I'm sorry, Mia. That's all I can tell you. We're part of the fight for survival, though I'm afraid there aren't too many of us left. Still, if we can establish a network throughout Poland, an underground—"

I had stopped listening. The driver was wearing an officer's uniform. *Egon's* uniform—I was certain of it. A scream rose at the back of my throat. I heard the sound of the hammer on Egon's head, the look on his face. "You didn't have to kill him," I cried. "Wolf could have stolen his gun and his uniform. But not murder."

"Get hold of yourself," Peter growled. "Listen. They're killing two hundred fifty of us a day. Two hundred fifty! And it'll only get worse. Our only recourse is to fight back, and to do it in any way we can. It might interest you to know that your precious Hildebrand's battalion invaded the ghetto, rounded up hostages, and killed them—but not before raping and torturing two teenagers and a woman in her eighties."

I refused to believe it. "That's impossible."

"Because he seemed so sweet, so courteous? Don't be naive. Be jubilant. The man you lured into Wolf's trap was well known to us. Among other things, he betrayed his girlfriend to the Gestapo when he found out she was one-eighth Jewish."

And what about his wife, Elsa, who died of pneumonia? I couldn't speak.

"Here's how things stand," he said urgently. "We picked you up because the desk clerk at the hotel identified you to the police. They know you by your false name, but they know you. Basically, your life's not worth a zloty to anyone but the *schmalzers*. You're dead if you stay in Warsaw, and we're the only ones who can get you out." His gaze was penetrating; there was no doubting him. "Saving lives is what we do best. That, and preparing those we save."

"Prepare us for what?"

"For war. To rebel against the Nazis and reclaim our country."

It was pathetic. I wondered if their war room was as dingy as this, and if all their uniforms came from corpses. "All you'll end up doing is getting us killed more quickly."

"We're dead already! Don't you see? But we can take ten of them for every one of us."

"We'll still be dead."

"Not everyone. Out of those who flee, as you and Wolf now must, some will make it. Your children will grow up in Palestine."

I turned away in disgust. "So that's it, then. You're Zionists. Well let me tell you, Peter, I had my fill of you in the Baluty. King Chaim, Eldest of the Jews: he was a Zionist, too. Work hard for the German state, he said. Make yourself indispensable. They will send us to the promised land. But what promised land? A fantasy."

He took my hand and forced me to look at him. "It isn't a fantasy if you'll fight for it."

"I haven't got that kind of courage. I thought of jumping from the bridge when I thought the Gestapo had found me."

"What do you think courage is but holding out for an extra quarter of a second? Wolf's told me a lot about you. I know about the cattle car and your father pushing you out. That was an act of courage. As for me, I wasn't so brave when I hid in the root cellar and heard German soldiers tear down the door and assault my own wife while my son screamed in her arms. If I've courage now, it's only because I can't shake the images, the sounds. Without the dream of Jerusalem, there would be nothing at all."

I knew he was right, but I had no such dream, no such hope. All I wanted was to be reunited with my family—and once, just one more time, hear songs and laughter.

"You'd better get going now," Peter said. "A boy will arrive in a moment to lead you to a sewer grating near the ghetto. Head north along the pipe and it will take you to the Eastern Grzybowska gate. Wolf will meet you there. He'll have forged travel permits for both of you. Wait with him and look for a hay truck. Hide under the hay and don't make a sound, either of you, until the driver comes to tell you it's safe. You'll be joining a work gang—farm workers. There will be Germans there, making sure the work goes well, but they won't know you're Jews and they won't harm you. You may have to stay with them for a while—"

"How long?"

"Until we can get you on a steamer going down the Vistula River. It will take you near the Czech border, and from there you can make your way to Switzerland. You'll have to pass through Germany, but it's the safest route. Near the German border, at Lake Constance, there's a nunnery where they'll put you up for a few days." He smiled. "The sisters don't take any shit from the Nazis. They've virtually dared them to close it down—and make the pope an enemy. They've helped us in the past, and if you can get there, they'll see you get to Switzerland." He must have caught the worry on my face. "It's your best chance, believe me."

"And if we're stopped, captured?"

Peter held out his hands, palms up. There was, he indicated, nothing he could do. With a sigh he handed me a piece of paper. "This is the address of the jewelry store in New York where your aunt and uncle live. God willing, sooner or later you'll get to them."

My father had told me about them, the lucky ones who had left before the invasion. I did not ask how Peter had found out about them. But no, I thought. My place is here, my job to rescue my parents, my brother.

There was a knock on the door. "That'll be the boy," the Zionist said. "Go with him and with God."

I reached inside a pocket and drew out the letters I had written to my family and to Jean-Phillipe. "Will you mail these for me?"

He stood with me and took the letters. "Of course. Though there's no saying they'll reach their destinations."

He gave me another piece of paper. "Keep it. You might need it if you reach Switzerland."

I looked at it: an address. "Good-bye," I said, but he did not answer.

"So it's settled then," I said to Wolf. "We'll take the steamer."

We were planting seeds along with at least fifty others in a field God knows how many miles from Warsaw.

"I still think it's too risky," he said, repeating a refrain he had emphasized from the moment we got onto the hay truck. "It's lunacy to sail down the Vistula with forged papers. Out on the water, there's no way to escape. All those hours side by side with *Volkdeutscher* and Poles? It'd be crazy for a Jew to be within ten miles of those boats."

"Which is exactly why we'll go that way. Maybe they won't check as closely."

"Please." He grabbed my hand and searched my eyes. "Don't you

understand? Your German and Polish are perfect. Mine aren't. If anything happens to you and I were left on my own, I wouldn't survive.
There may be troops on that ship. If you excite them, then there's no
telling what will happen."

I realized that outside the ghetto Wolf was frightened. He knew
very little of the outside world. I had traveled, knew the languages,
was more secure. Wolf hated having to depend on me; I had to be
strong.

"And since when is the National Committee so concerned about
young women in the presence of Germans with dishonorable inten-
tions?" I said. "Last week you had no problem encouraging me to get
myself raped."

"How many times do you want me to explain? I've told you why it
was necessary. Besides, all he did was—"

"I know what he did. And you don't regret it, not then and not
now." I smoothed the front of my smock and pulled my babushka
low over my forehead. A car approached and all around us workers
gathered up their spades and pickaxes and stood at attention. No one
stood straighter than Wolf.

An officer sidled up to me and put a hand on my breast. I kept a
dull smile on my face, but I wanted to kill him.

"It's time to pack up," he shouted to the others. "There's another
field to seed before it gets too dark."

I scrambled to the rear of the truck through the other workers.
Only when the truck was under way did I make my way back to
Wolf. Packed in like so much refuse, no one would notice us talking.

Wolf threw a protective arm around me. "You're right," he whispered. "We must take the steamer."

I squeezed his hand in gratitude. "One other thing," he said. "I'm
not sure how to tell you."

"Say it."

"I suggested to Peter that we'd be safer traveling as man and wife.
That's what our papers say, and that's what we must pretend to be."

I looked into the black country night. Through the slats of the truck, I could see soldiers carrying machine guns in the jeeps following us.

"Wolf," I whispered, "I'll do anything I must to survive."

In two weeks, if I lived, I'd be eighteen years old.

CHAPTER 11

$\mathcal{S}$ometime during the night, the Vistula had grown wider and deeper, and the flat plains surrounding us had been transformed into cliffs twenty feet high. From our dingy porthole, I could see murky water that seemed to rise up on the horizon to meet the vermilion sky. I lay propped on one elbow, staring at the dawn light cutting across the river.

The current was rising, making the steamer's propellers growl. The boat rocked until the rise and fall of the banks made me dizzy. At the rate we were moving, we would probably have to spend another day and night aboard the cargo steamer.

Wolf and I were crowded onto a narrow berth thinly padded with a straw mattress. We had spent the night in the deep slumber of exhaustion. As the pale morning light entered our cabin—really, not much more than a storage room, cluttered with boxes, ropes, and other nautical equipment—I felt his hand slide under the covers until it came to rest on my thigh. We were both dressed, but I could feel his heat. I removed his hand and turned my back to him.

Wolf forced me to face him. "Mia," he said, "I love you." His voice was full of pain. "I'm afraid of losing you. I want to feel every part of you. We don't know what lies ahead of us. Whatever happens, I want to remember you."

As I drew closer to him, I felt his hard penis pressed against me.

"Wolf, no. I am a virgin, and this is not the right time or place for us to do this."

Wolf's face in the shadows looked impossibly young. "I would never tell this to anyone, but it doesn't matter now. I have never been with a woman, so I guess I'm a virgin, too."

Maybe the strain of the trip was taking a toll on Wolf. This was not the Wolf I knew before. Outside the ghetto, my bold street fighter was vulnerable—and, I realized, he needed me in so many ways.

I kissed him fully on the mouth. His beard was scratchy, his breath hot as he held me tightly. He was trembling, and when he looked at me naked, he murmured, "Mia, so beautiful." Our quarters were so tight! It was a miracle, but somehow it did happen.

Wolf sat up and gazed at the blood on the sheet, slipped out of bed and got dressed. At the cabin door he turned and looked at me. Were those tears on his cheeks?

"We both have something we'll never forget," I said. I closed my eyes and the music Mozart gave Don Giovanni, by which to seduce the innocent Zerlina, sprang unbidden to my brain.

We entered a region of high plateaus. Above the fiordlike clefts in the bank, twisted oak and beech trees led up to the distant Carpathians.

The day was blazing hot, more like August than late April. I had gone on deck, and beneath my woolen dress, the backs of my knees stuck to the chair I sat on. The air was so thick and stale that the birds had deserted the sky, leaving only wisps of clouds buzzing with a million invisible insects.

We overtook a longboat near the western bank. Teenage boys stripped to the waist strained against long wooden poles in an effort to move it along, their muscles rippling in waves down their backs and into their powerful forearms in a rocking, rhythmical motion. I could sense the power in those muscles, almost feel their sinews tighten.

In the Baluty, I had often stared at the bared chests and stomachs of the workmen, imagining their dreamy eyes admiring me, burning for the sensation of their lips against my shoulders and neck. Where was the maddening mystery of ecstasy now, the electric tenderness?

I could hear the crew cackling as they teased my newlywed husband and traded men's stories of conquests. Their good-natured laughter, particularly Wolf's bleating, grated against me.

I tried to imagine my parents' horror at the shame I had brought upon myself on a steamer churning down the Vistula, but I could not bring their faces to mind. They were as remote as Paradise.

I got up and made my way toward Wolf, who was sitting on a crate surrounded by members of the crew.

"We were just having a little drink, sweetheart," he slurred, patting the top of the crate. "Join us. A celebration of our wedding."

"Get a cup, a cup from the galley for the lady. *Move!*" The first mate's words were addressed to the cabin boy, who raced off to do as instructed, and the crew members burst into laughter. What could be funnier than an embarrassed bride and a drunken groom?

Wolf motioned again for me to sit beside him then turned back to the crowd. "Let's bribe the cook. Thirty zloty for another bottle of his slivovitz. And this one's on the groom, if you'll drink to the health of his bride."

Thirty zloty! Money we'd need for far more important things.

Before I could say anything (not that my protest would have done any good), a German patrol cruiser pulled up beside us. Instantly, we were deserted in the middle of the deck while the crew raced off in a half dozen different directions.

A German officer's request for permission to board was acknowledged; the steamer's captain, resplendent in his white uniform, exited the cockpit. Wolf threw a protective arm around my waist.

I pretended to accept his embrace. "You're drunk," I hissed into his ear. "For God's sake, if he asks us a question, let me do the talking." I led him to the port railing, where the sailors lowered a rope chair down to the officer's launch.

Wolf gripped the rail. Where was the shrewd and arrogant revolutionary now? I wondered. Or the boastful husband? I stared at his profile, half hoping he would turn to me and wink, prepared to hoodwink yet another Gestapo creep out of twenty zloty or a pack of ersatz cigarettes. Instead, he avoided my eyes and clenched his fists. I was afraid his fear would be obvious and give us away, so I gripped his hand with all my strength and tried to smile.

The German and our captain seemed to be acquaintances. They shook hands and jointly inspected the crew. From their dialogue, I gathered that our captain was a smuggler and the officer knew it, but since one spoke Polish and the other German, the nature of their transaction was unclear. Perhaps whatever arrangements existed between the two men had been finalized days earlier.

The German indicated us with a wave of his hand. "And who are these?"

"These are our newlyweds. Stephanie and Johan Pavlovski." Our captain stumbled on the German words and had to repeat them.

"Pleased to meet you," I said in German, curtsying as I offered him my hand.

"The honor is mine, I'm sure, madame." He frowned and stared into Wolf's eyes. "And just who are you—"

"If you please, sir, I must apologize for my husband. He barely speaks German, though he understands it a bit."

"Then he's a Pole. Does that mean he's Jewish?"

"Goodness, no! Would I marry a Jew? Johan's mother—may she rest in peace—was a full-blooded *Volksdeutsch*. From Warta."

"But you speak fluent German, *mein liebchen*. Does that mean you have Aryan parentage?"

I lowered my eyes, making a mental note to adopt a regional dialect next time. My German was too good. "No. They were Poles, too. But I was employed as an au pair for a German manufacturer of optical lenses."

He looked at me, obviously relishing what he saw. "It was not, I trust, running away from your employers that brought you onto my good friend's steamer in the middle of the Vistula?"

"My hand to God, sir." I dug into my cleavage to produce the tiny crucifix I had bought months ago for just such an emergency, and kissed it fervently. "Johan's mother's brother has a farm in Ostrowiec. He always promised Johan that if he ever wished to work there—"

The German shrugged. "Do you think the Russians have left the place standing?"

Wolf and I exchanged wide-eyed glances. *"Weiss nicht',"* I said.

"Weiss nicht'," Wolf echoed, and we both stood silently, waiting for more information. Were the Russians really liberating the southern plain? I wondered. Please God it was true.

"Very well, then. You two may go. Captain Jaslo, I'll direct my cruiser to the western bank and you'll do likewise. Assuming every-thing is in order with the lading bills and your control cards, perhaps you'd care to join me for an evening meal? That is, if the new bride can serve as translator."

"I can assure you, Herr Kapitain, that nothing would give me greater pleasure," our captain stammered.

"I, too, would be honored," I said.

"Then it's settled." He looked at me again. "I'm sure we'll find areas of mutual interest to discuss."

The cruiser docked near orchards of apricots and almonds, and we dined on deck. Against a background chorus of nightingales, with the brackish Vistula slapping against the boat's hull, we listened to the strains of *Eine Kleine Nacht Musik* and ate steak and fresh vegetables as though they were everyday fare. I told myself to save some of the food for Wolf, hide it in a napkin or ask for it outright, but I'm ashamed to admit that I ate it all, steeling myself not to gulp it down, but to be la-dylike, demure. Our captain, however, had no such compunction.

The sound of the violins, distorted as it was through a rudimentary loudspeaker, nevertheless moved me as Mozart always did—passionate and joyous, pregnant. It seemed that everyone around the table—captain, first mate, me, and the Germans themselves—was struggling simply to forget, to sink into the melodies, to flow with the cadences.

To the west, our host told us proudly, Germany was solidifying its control of northern France. I had no trouble imagining the sound of jackboots and the tanks on cobblestones. Soon the army would be in Paris. My lycée would make an excellent headquarters for a German general, perhaps the head of a Panzer division. They could have cognac in the library, hold balls in the auditorium.

And my classmates—what would become of them? When their fathers' factories, offices, and chateaux were taken over, when the artwork, town cars, furniture, and silver were carted away? I knew that there were worse things than sewing buttons on uniforms or selling cigarettes in the black market, yet to my classmates such chores would be unbearable. Meanwhile, I may have been deflowered in the grimy cabin of the steamer, but for the moment—for these few hours—I could be human again, never mind that our host was our arch enemy. There was carp smothered in aspic with horseradish cream, bottles of confiscated pickles and preserves, chestnut pudding and sweet vodka. I sat at the polished and lacquered teak table and ate not only with the officious German officer and our Polish captain, but also with candlelight and Mozart.

Our captain prodded me with his elbow. "Lovely meal, lovely." I translated.

"Surely you'll remain as my guests a little while longer."

"I wish that we could, but we must land at Sandomierz before nightfall tomorrow. So if you"ll excuse me, Kommandant—"

The German's gaze passed from my lips to the twitching mustache of our captain. "Tell him that our fee has gone up. Five thousand zloty will do."

The Polish captain went pale when he understood what was being asked. "But that's as much money as I see in a month. It's impossible. And even if I had the money on board, how could I explain to my superiors?"

"Don't quibble," growled the German. "Polacks don't argue with an officer of the Reich. Particularly when they're smuggling black market liquor and illegally transporting questionable characters on their boats. Refusal to pay is sufficient reason to blast his bilge trap out of the water, or have him shot." He turned to me. "Translate those words *exactly.*"

I delivered the speech. "You must agree," I told the captain. "It's either pay the bribe, or we'll all be killed."

The captain sighed. "Very well. Tell the stinking swine he can have his fucking zloty. If he'd like, I'll shove them up his Führer's ass, one by one."

"The Polish captain is pleased to agree to the terms which you have outlined," I said in German. "In addition, he would like to personally present to you a case of schnapps."

The German grinned. "Either he's a more exceptional fool than the rest of the Polacks, or else you're a very clever girl. And a liar."

"Oh no, sir. I'm can assure you that those were his very words."

"No matter. I accept. Guards: take this besotted ass back to his bursar's office and see to it he doesn't cheat us. Throw him overboard if he gets nasty. I'm sure one of you can count to five thousand. Five thousand. Understand? Yes, I thought so." He turned to me. "And now, my dear, let us share a glass of cognac and listen to more Mozart before I send you back."

I blanched. "But sir, I—"

He laughed. "No, wait. You misunderstand me. I'm not going to force you to fuck me the night after your wedding. What do you think I am, some kind of monster?"

"What the hell did you think you were doing over there?" Wolf slammed the cabin door behind him.

I shrugged. "You, comrade, are drunk."

"Am I? Maybe so. But that doesn't answer my question. *What were you doing on that boat?*"

I glared at him. "What's this, a revolutionary tribunal? Funny, I mistook it for a third-rate berth aboard a decrepit river steamer."

"Sarcasm doesn't become you."

"Very well, then, comrade. I plead guilty to waltzing with Germans, many of them. First the captain, then the first mate. Then some other officer. What's more I ate their food and drank their wine."

"In other words, consorting with the enemy." He paced the tiny cabin. "It's exactly the kind of behavior girls were executed for, back in the ghetto."

"Okay. Execute me. How do you want to do it? Suffocate me? How about strangling? I'm afraid I don't have a proper garrote, but there are some stockings in my valise. I'm sure that you could—"

He slapped me, not caring how much the blow stung. "You loved it, didn't you? All those hands, those stinking German hands pressing against you. When you were dancing with them and they kissed you and slipped their hands over your ass. I'll bet you responded to them."

His pain was so acute that for a moment I softened. "You're being irrational. It was no different than what went on in Three Crosses Square. They buy your cigarettes, they expect a little latitude. You learn to live with it. The German captain slipped a hundred zloty into my camisole. Good pay for a waltz, don't you think?"

"But he's a fucking Nazi, and you enjoyed it. Every minute of it."

"And why shouldn't I? The music and the food and the wine—none of those were Nazi. I didn't choose to be there, I came along as a translator. And if it's any help, I didn't enjoy the dancing that was forced on me." I looked at him with disgust. "How foolish men are.

Do you really think women enjoy being fondled by strangers? Having their buttocks pinched, their breasts brushed 'by accident'?"

He stood silently, wrestling with his feelings like a gladiator.

"Now stop clenching your fists and turn off the lamp," I said. "I'm exhausted."

CHAPTER 12

The icy water of the pond was sweet balm after the washbasin of our cabin where I'd tried to cleanse myself of the taint that had seeped into my pores. By then, not even the catacombs of the dead in Sandomierz, through which we'd made our escape, seemed worse.

I felt Wolf's eyes on me, and I sank deeper into the water. He was yanking off his pants, his shirt already open to the navel.

"Stay out of here," I warned.

He smirked. "You can't be serious."

"I mean it. Wait till I'm clean. And then you'll leave me to myself while you bathe or not, as you choose."

"This is ridiculous!" He leaned over the pool, as though to yank me out. "We've got to keep moving. We're miles from Mielac, our destination for today. As it is, we'll have to travel in daylight, and every minute we lose makes it worse. Come on!"

"Go to hell," I said calmly. "And if you set foot in the water, I'll kill you. Now toss me my comb and stop staring."

He did as ordered, then sulked among the cattails. I slowly worked the comb through my hair inch by inch until it surrendered its cache of mud, lice, and tangles. I felt the chill seeping into my aching left hip and stared down at my scrawny arms and legs. Now that we were safely out of the ghetto and off the steamer, I dared to fantasize that everything would be restored: my family, my music, my body itself—everything that had been taken from me two years before.

Would I ever again sit with Jozef in the drawing room of our house, singing, arguing, listening to music? Would I ever hear Papa's scolding and Mama's words of comfort? Would the memories fade: Litzmannstadt, Nate Kolleck, cigarettes, Egon, Wolf . . . ?

. . . Who was shouting at me. *"For God's sake. Mia!"*

"I'm coming out," I assured him and trudged reluctantly toward him over the muddy bottom of the pool.

Wolf stood on the bank, holding out his shirt for me to use as a towel. But I brushed past him and stepped carefully along the bank to a clearing near a willow tree where I lay in the sunlight, which made the drops of water on my body glisten. Pleasure slowly returned, a feeling so strange that at first I did not recognize it. I allowed my fingertips to roam lightly over my arms and belly, exalting in my own flesh and in life.

A shadow blotted out the sun. Wolf was towering over me, his arms crossed and my camisole crushed in his hands. I sat up angrily.

"Why do you do this to me?" he growled, tossing the crumpled garment at my feet.

"Do what?"

"You're driving me crazy, lying there naked, touching yourself, making me desire you. We have no time for this now. It's dangerous for us to stay here!"

I dressed quickly, feeling ashamed of myself, and rummaged into the kerchief I had left by the pool. "Look. Wolf. I found this nest at the edge of the water." I held it out to him. "There are three eggs in it. Lunch." There was a catch in my voice, and a choking sadness burned into my lungs. "Here," I said, "you can have two."

"Wake up. We've got to get going."

Wolf's hands gently shook my shoulders. We had walked for three or four hours, but then I could go no farther and we lay down together so I could nap. Wolf preferred going at night. There seemed to be an inner clock in him that mandated a particular deadline, though I could see no difference when we got to the border as long as we were not caught along the way.

"It's about a hundred and twenty-five kilometers along the river. We've barely made sixty the past two nights."

I stared at him in astonishment. A hundred twenty-five kilometers? "But I thought the steamer brought us close to the border," I said. "It can't be that much farther."

His expression was grave. "We're not going to the border."

"Not going? What do you mean? I thought the whole plan was to—"

"The whole plan was to get to a safe house. From there, we'll continue the fight. You and me and hundreds like us!"

No! My mind rebelled. I was sick of fighting, sick of running, sick of safe houses that weren't safe and plans that were lies to lead me on. "I'm going to the border no matter what you say." I hit him with balled fists. "I can't take any more . . ."

"Your parents are in Auschwitz," Wolf said without emotion. "Auschwitz is near Kraków. The safe house is near Kraków. From there, you'll be able to get to them."

It was so preposterous, I nearly laughed. Had he gone mad? Why was he lying? "You've got it all wrong. My parents and Jozef are in Treblinka. *Treblinka!* You don't know what you're talking about."

He put his arms around me. "Hush," he said, as though to a child. "When you got that letter from your father, the one he was made to write, he wrote it on the last day he spent at Treblinka. He and your mother both. Peter was able to trace them for me—believe it or not, Mia, I was worried about your family, and so I asked him to find out about them. They were transferred to Auschwitz, another camp, a worse camp, but they were lucky. The others on that train were mostly exterminated." His face reflected his pain. "Your father is a doctor. They need doctors at Auschwitz, not for the Jews but for the Germans, and all the German doctors are at the front."

This was too much information; I couldn't handle it. Questions swarmed through my brain like angry wasps. "Then why was my mother saved?"

He shrugged. "Who knows? Maybe because they knew if she were alive, he wouldn't try anything funny—the wrong medicine, an air bubble in a needle."

"And Jozef?" It was a question I did not want to ask.

"That's the problem. Peter couldn't find out."

The significance struck me so hard it brought tears to my eyes. "That means he's dead. Don't lie to me Wolf. I'm right, aren't I?"

He held me tighter. "Not necessarily. Our sources can only ask so much. Any more, and they endanger everyone. It was only as a special favor to me that Peter found out about your parents. I couldn't ask him to . . ."

"I understand." Any hope was faint, but I clung to it. "When we get to the safe house, perhaps I can find out for myself."

He shook his head. "You can try, but I beg you not to."

Not find out about Jozef? It was like asking a woman dying of thirst to forgo water. I broke free from his embrace.

"There are four or five work camps at Auschwitz," Wolf explained. "Each has perhaps twenty thousand inmates, maybe twice that. The entire area's been declared a Wartheland Camp District. It'll be crawling with German troops as well as the guards—dogs, too. Going there will be like committing suicide."

My anger flared. "I don't understand. You say we're not going to cross the border because we have to go on fighting. I say I don't want to do that. So you tell me I'll be near the camp where my parents are, and maybe my brother, yet you announce I can't even try to contact them. You've lied to me from the start, used our 'marriage' as an excuse to have sex with me—did you cook up those papers? Ask Peter to draw them up so you could fuck me?—and now—" I took a deep breath, fighting for control—"if my family's still alive, I've got to find them. They're everything I have."

He held out his arms. "You have me."

So that's what it was all about. He'd said he loved me, and I couldn't comprehend it. Yet what else but love could have made him act the way he had, not for these few days, but for months? He wanted me, needed me, by his side. And what I wanted or needed did not matter. In all my life, no matter what awful things people had done to me or would do to me, I had never hated anybody as I did Wolf at that moment.

Even looking at him was torture. I turned to run. He caught me by the wrist. "You don't know what direction to go in, where the border is, or where a safe house is. It's hard enough surviving for the two of us together. Without me, you're doomed."

"I don't care!" I screamed. "I'd rather be dead than be with you."

He gave no sign of how much I must have hurt him. "Your only chance of seeing your family again is to stay with me. I'll help you, I promise. We'll go directly to Auschwitz, but you'll have to let me lead you there."

His voice was soft. I knew he was right, knew love of family was more important than hatred of him, and so I nodded mutely. He took his map from his pocket and studied it. "There are railway tracks ten kilometers ahead. If we follow them rather than the river, we'll cut off about fifty kilometers from the journey. It'll be more dangerous, of course. There's better cover by the waterline. But it might be worth the risk." He stared at me until I was forced to look back into his sorrow-filled eyes.

"I don't know," I said. "You decide."

We pushed on through the night and into the next morning. I followed Wolf dumbly, obediently, my mind filled with images of Jean-Phillipe, so at least I could imagine myself being led by a man I loved. Wolf was fierce and determined, devoid of any gentleness. He was angry, too, I knew, and I marched forward steadily, unwilling to give him the satisfaction of any weakness on my part, though my hip was inflamed and pain shot through my leg with every step.

He had opted for following the railroad tracks. The terrain grew hillier. Forests of birch and gnarled spruce grew denser. At his signal, we stopped inside a grove of pines and took turns keeping watch while the other slept. Then, at dusk, we were off again, grateful for the moon that let us find our way around fallen trunks and branches. On and on we walked. It was as though we were the only people alive on the planet.

"How far do you think we are from Kraków?" I asked the next morning.

"Five or ten kilometers. The damned foothills make it hard to judge."

I sighed. "The last time I visited Kraków, I asked my brother where all the Jews had gone. He said they had fled because they didn't like the way they were being treated. But Jozef said he didn't think the anti-Semitism was too bad."

"Did you think to ask why he went to a university where Jews were forced to sit on benches apart from everyone else? Or how he felt about Jews getting beaten senseless by their classmates? That was before the Nazis came, Mia."

"I know. We were somehow immune, I guess. After all, it *was* the Jagellerian University."

"I was tempted to go there, too," Wolf said. "Before the war I dreamt of being a doctor and saving people. A degree from medical school meant a lot to me, but when I saw what was going on, I opted for a Jewish school—until the war broke out. Then the Nazis gathered the faculty into the courtyard and machine-gunned them down."

"So you joined the resistance," I said, warming to him in spite of myself.

"It made no sense to stay in Kraków. To me, it's just one more Nazi outpost on the edge of the Wartheland. According to Peter, it's crawling with German transports. All the Jews have been shipped to Auschwitz. If we're caught there, at best we'll be shipped out, too. And I assure you, it's not the way to find your parents."

"Then let's go straight to Auschwitz."

"And do what?"

"Find them. Rescue them."

"Or be found ourselves—and killed."

"I don't care!" I shouted. "According to you, no matter where we go, we'll be killed. At least I'll be with Mama and Papa."

He nodded. "And I'll be with you."

The simplicity of his words moved me beyond words of my own. There was no talk of a safe house now; he would die with me, for me. My throat constricted so tightly I could barely swallow. The distant sound of a barking dog sent us scrambling through the forest. The trees were dense here, making detection less likely, and Wolf urged me on. By noon, we found a mossy thicket within a cleft in the hills, and here I made him stop. "It's time for you to sleep," I said. "This time first sentry duty is mine. Look at you, you can barely keep your eyes open."

He lay on his back with one knee up, his eyes closed, his breathing regular. Poor Wolf! For all his brains and courage, he lived in a little boy's world of black and white, cowboys and Indians, like the ludicrous American cinema we sometimes saw in Lodz. How comforting to see the world without ambiguity, I thought. Where all Jews were good, all Germans bad, and the two would inevitably fight to the last man standing. Surely in every group of people, there were the good and the bad. What reason would God have to choose us Jews out of all mankind for the special favor that made us so detested by non-Jews? And if He had chosen us, was it for favor or for the suffering he was inflicting on us now? What kind of a God could be so cruel, even if we were to be redeemed in heaven?

Wolf half awakened, and I let him put his head in my lap. Instantly, he fell back asleep. He loved me, he had proven it, but did he really think that I could love him back? Women under siege in wartime, in ghettos, in hiding, selling cigarettes to Nazis on street corners and luring German officers to their death—how could they love?

I let him sleep peacefully in my lap, gathering my courage and strength. By dawn, we would be in the newly resettled Camp District of Auschwitz.

CHAPTER 13

*W*aiting for Wolf in the rain was worse than being stalked by the wolves that had followed us through the foothills of Auschwitz.

I clutched my torn, waterlogged sweater and leaned wearily against an arch beneath a bombed-out railroad bridge. Each set of footsteps above clawed at my senses until I thought I might cry out just to break the tension. Even wolves seemed less threatening than this ghostly village.

The voices I heard above me came not from soldiers heading for their barracks or officers on leave, but from peasants and laborers, their German eerily out of place in this Polish outpost. They had moved in everywhere, Wolf had told me, the churches, shops, cottages, restaurants. Yet the town was not crowded now that it was lacking its Jews.

I heard Wolf's catlike steps on the wet bank and found myself muttering, "Thank God." He slipped in beside me out of the rain and threw himself against the bridge supports, trembling.

"Let me warm you," I offered, taking his icy hands in mine and rubbing them gently. "This is the right place, isn't it? Did you see any signs of the camp?"

"Come," he whispered.

Security towers stood over the landscape like fierce giants. Manned by a guard with a machine gun, each held a searchlight that swept over the terrain, illuminating the dreary scene before us. Beyond two walls of barbed wire, an electrified fence hummed and crackled, occasionally bursting into a flash of purple light as insects impaled themselves against it.

The fence enclosed a small city of stables, concrete storehouses, and large windowless warehouses bathed in a bright incandescent light. In the distance, beneath a belching smokestack, antlike figures hurried in a grotesque ballet.

We crawled closer. On the other side of the fence, a cry rose, lingered, then died away. It was repeated once, then again, the rhythm pronounced: a woman shrieking in agony. I covered my ears, but the unearthly screaming continued. A man laughed. There was another cry, then a gunshot, then silence.

The rain and wind had died down. The thick black smoke from the smokestack formed a cloud over the entire camp, settling in over the watchtowers, making the searchlights seem like dragon's eyes. The smoke burnt our nostrils and eyes, made us gag. Wolf gave a little cough, then jumped up and ran for the hills behind us, his legs pumping through the mud. I followed, his silhouetted form growing smaller, distorted by the smoke until it appeared no more than a swaying branch, jostled by the wind.

I found him at the edge of the wood, rocking on his hands and knees. His head dropped from his neck like that of a marionette with cut strings. He had been sick.

"I'm sorry," he gasped.

"There's no need." I put my hand on his back and he looked up at me gratefully.

"The smoke. My God, the smoke!" His stomach heaved in spasms. "We should never have gone there. I should have known. This afternoon, when I found the place, I saw a prisoner break away from a work crew and try to escape. It was pitiful. He didn't get past the first tower before he was gunned down. Blood was gushing from his wounds but he kept crawling forward, toward the fence. He refused to quit until a guard came up and shot him in the head. A *kommandant* came storming out, furious. He shouted at the other workers, blaming them for inciting the man to escape. He made them stand at attention while he passed among them, hitting them with his stick.

"They seemed to be jealous of the dead man, and I don't blame them. Mia, do you know what that smoke is? What the smell is? It's people burning—it can't be anything else. They're burning people in there, the ones who can't work!"

Papa could work. Mama could work. But what if they got sick? What if the Germans found a better doctor, a better cook? What if for some minor infraction my parents were sent to the crematorium? Oh God, God! I was blind with frustration, sick with sorrow. There was no way to save them, no way to get into the camp and out again. What we had just seen was tangible proof, and rage made me long for vengeance. I understood Wolf now, his single-mindedness, his determination to fight on forever, and I was glad to be his comrade. We would stand and die together.

"We'll do no good here," he said. "The safe house is in a suburb of Krac'ow, a town called Katowice. It's near a café called the Monopol, and if we go there, someone will contact us. Peter said they're expecting us, though we're days behind schedule. Do you think you can walk through the night?"

Walk through the night? If it meant a chance for revenge, I could walk for eternity.

Sometime after midnight, the mountains opened up into wide, fertile plains. Villages sprouted up before us, deceptively peaceful. How many bodies had been burnt at Auschwitz to make room for their new inhabitants? I wondered. Sudeten and Silesian scum? Murderers. Torturers. I hoped hell's fires were hotter and more long-lasting than the ones they had created.

As dawn broke, we slipped into a hayloft at what appeared to be an abandoned farm. Mice chattered about us, gradually growing bolder. The night was cold for April, and the weather seemed to mirror the coldness of the entire world, now dark and alien. When I thought of my parents, horrific images entered my mind that I longed to cast off, but they remained indelible. No matter how many times I told myself that they were needed and would be spared, I saw the clouds of smoke over the camp, and its stench seared my nostrils.

Beyond Wolf there was only a phantasmagoria of transports, Stars of David, barbed wire, searchlights. I reached over and took his hand, easing it underneath my camisole, suddenly eager for his touch. He was awake. I could hear his breath quicken.

Desire flowed from his fingertips. "Please," I whispered. "I need you tonight. Make love to me, Wolf. I want to feel you inside me."

I lifted my hips, threw off my skirt, and tore at his trousers. "Wolf," I murmured, opening myself to receive him. "Just the two of us."

His lips brushed over the surface of my neck and set fire to my skin. I wanted to scream, to bury my fingernails in his back, to pull him closer so that he could be everywhere at once. His fingers caressed my breasts, to be replaced by his mouth as they sought my core.

He entered me and I groaned, rising to meet his thrusts. I had to have all of him, to smother him and be smothered by him. Our bodies locked. Faster and faster we moved against each other, with each other, until there was nothing but desire and motion and consummation.

CHAPTER 14

Café au lait at the Café Monopol. They'd served it with crystalline lumps of pure beet sugar, the best in all of Katowice. With enormous self-restraint, Wolf and I sucked at them, rather than gobble them down. A few middle-aged couples sat beneath huge umbrellas next to our own on the terrace; single women lined the periphery, some sipping coffee, others merely watching the activity at the café.

"You're creating a bit of a stir," I told Wolf, pressing my calf against his under the table. "You're the only man here under forty." I tugged coquettishly at the ribbons hanging from the back of my sun-bonnet, then pulled away from him when I saw he was in no mood for games.

"I know. I feel like we're on display," he said.

We were dressed in clothes provided at the safe house, sundress and bonnet for me, slacks and a white open-neck shirt for Wolf. They had given us a few zloty, enough to buy breakfast and pretend we belonged at the café. Wolf was told to feign an injury, and his limp as we walked to the Metropol would have done Lionel Barrymore proud.

"Stop fidgeting," I warned. "Witold will be here soon. He said it's all arranged, so why don't you relax? Besides, we should order something to eat. I'd like a sandwich."

"Do as you like," he growled, "but this waiting tears at me. I didn't like that Witold fellow, didn't trust him."

"You had no choice. He gave us these clothes, after all, and enough money for a sandwich. *Waiter!*" I searched for one then quickly turned back to Wolf. "A whole slew of Death's Headers just walked in," I hissed. "Stop looking so guilty or you'll get us killed."

I smoothed the pleats of my skirt and dropped my eyes to the folded newspaper beside my coffee. Buried in the bottom corner of the front page was a notice that the United States had closed its German consulates. At last, I thought, something's happening, but why has it taken so long? Two years of German tyranny, not only in Poland, but throughout Eastern Europe. What were the Americans waiting for?

I kept one eye on the soldiers and read the paper with the other. There were three pages of obituaries.

A Requiem Mass for the soul of the deceased will be celebrated tomorrow. Notification of the funeral will take place after the arrival of the dear ashes.

The item plunged me into gloom. "Dear ashes." I recalled the belching smokestacks of Auschwitz and the stench of burning bodies. There would be no obituaries, no ceremonies for those dead.

"Some flowers for Madame?" a voice inquired. "Surely the gentleman—he is her husband, yes?—would like to buy her a rose. These are fresh from my garden." A wizened, bent man stood before us, bearing a few meager roses in a wicker basket.

I tried to wave him away. The soldiers had moved to the bar and, though it was morning were ordering pints of beer. I clutched the knife Witold had given me (Wolf also had one), rage rising in my throat. *The dear ashes.*

"Put down the knife, you imbecile." I jumped involuntarily and did as Wolf bade me. But then I realized the voice was not Wolf's. The flower seller!

"Keep reading the paper," he said. "Yes, that's right. Now, sir, buy her a rose before they get suspicious."

Wolf fumbled in his pocket for some change. He looked like a bird caught beneath a cat's claw.

"Did you say two roses or three?" the vendor asked, leaning over his basket to select them. I noticed how deformed his spine was, forming his foreshortened chest into an S. He handed me the flowers. "We've got to get you out of here," he said, his voice suddenly that of a young man.

"I don't know who you are," I told him, "but I can assure you my husband and I have no reason to fear. We are law-abiding citizens of the Reich. My husband was wounded at the eastern front. Our papers are in order."

"Imbecile," he repeated. "There's no time to waste. A roundup is scheduled in five minutes. You'll be found out and executed, no matter how well forged those papers are. You're strangers here, and the Krauts don't like strangers." He held out his hand to Wolf. "That'll be twenty zloty, mein herr."

Wolf's eyes flashed and he handed over the money. I looked around the café, holding my breath. Soldiers had filled the bar. I watched their dull, complacent faces, listened to their banter. Most of them were already starting to get drunk.

I felt a chill. Something was wrong. Very wrong. I had seen a hundred Nazi roundups in the ghetto, and the thrill of the hunt always showed on the features of the peasant boys, posted to make sure no one would slip away. But where was that energy now? These soldiers were blinking at the sun like country dogs.

I caught a glimpse of a bearded man at a nearby table whose eyes were riveted on us. Behind his sunglasses he was recording the events, shaking his head as if—

I threw down my napkin and leapt up screaming, "Who let you in here anyway, filthy Polish swine? We don't want any of your diseased flowers." I struck at the vendor with my purse. "Waiter! Officers! Would one of you please escort this scum off the terrace?"

The soldiers advanced from the bar, brandishing pistols. Wolf had time to give me one wild, agonized look before I walked huffily from the café, praying he would follow.

"You were betrayed," Witold said. "One more minute and that little crippled *schmalzonick* would have had you. It's remarkable, really, that you got away. Just what tipped you off?"

I shrugged. "We had a lot of contact with *schmalzers* back in Warsaw. I can smell them."

"Speak for yourself." Wolf laughed. "I thought for sure you were committing suicide."

I squeezed his hand affectionately. The events of the morning had disoriented him. Even though I had saved our lives, my action went against his grain. In Wolf's mind, we were still the ZOB of the ghetto. And he was my superior.

"I didn't see that I had a choice. He didn't mention your name, Witold, and that made me suspicious. So did the fact that you seemed not to recognize him—and by the way, thanks for doing nothing to help us."

"I was there to monitor. If I had done anything, I'd have been compromised."

"Then it was just a matter of looking at all those Nazi faces and trying to guess what was happening. Either they were brilliant actors or the soldiers had no idea of the impending raid. And I doubted they were brilliant actors."

"You did just right," Witold said. He turned to my lover. "I'll send your report on Auschwitz to Warsaw with the next courier. Peter will be delighted you've arrived here. We've lost a lot of members." He paused to offer us a plate of mangy cookies. Denied my sandwich, I gobbled one.

"But you can't stay," Witold went on. "We've had word from the Hague advising that it's a good time to get you out of the Wartheland. Right after supper, we'll take you to the Slovakian wilderness. There you'll learn the name of your next contact, and after the next journey, the next contact. Your destination is Switzerland. From there, it's up to you, Wolf, how you get to the Middle East, but once there you'll be told your assignment. And as for you, Mia, you're free to do as you please. You can stay here with us, or we can try to find you a way across the border."

Wolf had never mentioned the Middle East, and I looked at him questioningly. He would not meet my eye. Was this the plan all along? That he would get me to the safe house and then leave me? That he would protect me, but only up to a point? And what was he supposed to do in the Middle East? What kind of assignment awaited him?

The thought of abandonment weakened my knees and I had to sit down. Don't cry, I told myself, but my will had no power. Wolf walked up behind me and put his hand on my shoulder.

"Mia," he told Witold, "comes with me."

Bundled in a massive woolen coat in the backseat of the car, I watched stone walls flash by the headlights. Tiny villages and settlements appeared and disappeared along the rutted roads leading to the Slovakian frontier: Rowien, Michalkowice, Praq.

At the wheel of the Steyr, a stranger in an ill-fitting German uniform traded unfunny dirty jokes in Polish with Wolf. I remembered my husband's behavior with the sailors on the steamer, how angry I had been with him, but now the joking seemed innocent enough, and why shouldn't Wolf have some respite from the tension?

"Don't worry, Mrs.," the driver said. "You won't have any trouble in these woods. Not in the Beskids. We've got them so crawling with the underground that the Nazis have to work with us, just to save their lousy hides. Even gypsies have no worries. You'll see."

Gypsies and Jews. The day they had no worries was the day I'd have arrived in paradise.

Up ahead we could see the red diagonal stripes of the custom's guardhouse, its flimsy barrier no more solid than a toothpick across the road. The truck stopped, then chose that moment to sputter and die. A guard approached, lifting his lantern to inspect our faces.

"Oh it's you, Jerzy. Still running your ferrying service, I see. Who've you got this time?"

Jerzy tried the starter. The gears wouldn't mesh. "Heil Hitler, Karl," he said. "This time I'm transporting the Führer himself."

The guard took a step back, then righted himself. "Very funny."

"Actually, this is Dr. Heller and his wife. He's come all the way from Berlin. I was telling him about your horticultural experiments."

"Fascinating," Wolf said briskly. "In fact, I'm something of a horticulturalist myself."

"Excellent! Perhaps the doctor would like to visit my home. I've been grafting apricots onto—"

"Leave it for our return," Jerzy said. "Right now, we must press on."

"In that case, your paperwork, please."

"I don't have it." Jerzy spoke calmly. Wolf gripped my hand. "Dr. Heller's trip was authorized by Obersturmführer Wolsong of the 323rd Panzer. There was no time for a written order. It's imperative that Dr. Heller and his wife—"

"The new directives from Berlin explicitly state that under no condition can anyone cross the border without a pass."

"The paperwork will be forthcoming," Jerzy said. "You'll receive it tomorrow, the next day at the latest." He reached behind him and handed him a tin the size of a cookie box. "A present from Margot. Go ahead, take it. Apple/plum cake. Nobody makes it like Margot; it'll be a treat such as you haven't experienced for months. Now eat it, and by the time you've finished, the papers will have arrived. In the meantime, we mustn't allow anything to interfere with the doctor's work. He's to report his findings directly to the undersecretary at the Ministry of Health." The engine caught. Jerzy inched the car forward. "Heil Hitler."

"Heil Hitler." Karl made no effort to move away. "What do I tell my relief when he arrives in the morning?"

"I wouldn't tell him anything. And I *certainly* wouldn't share the cake. It's too good for that glutton anyway."

The guard smiled conspiratorially and backed away. In a few seconds, the gate swung up, and we drove through, lumbering down the unpaved Slovakian road.

For a long time, the three of us were silent. Then, finally, Wolf said "Thank you," his voice hoarse. I looked down. Wolf's fingernails had dug into my hand so deeply it was bleeding, but I felt no pain. Rather, I longed to embrace the strange man who had risked his life for us without complaint. How many other lives, I wondered, had he saved?

He reached behind him again and brought out another tin. "It really is good," he said, handing it to me. "Margot knows her way around an oven."

CHAPTER 15

*L*ater that week Wolf and I finally reached the nunnery. I could not believe how peaceful it made me feel. I could have stayed there forever, but I knew that we only had two days before we had to move on. Our final destination was near.

I opened the rickety door of the abbey watchtower and climbed the stairs, being careful not to trip on my nun's habit. It would be my last trip above the ancient walls.

The worn steps felt slippery in my novice's slippers. I imagined thousands of nuns before me creeping up those same steps at sunup to gaze on the mountain panorama of Lake Constance. Switzerland lay across that lake! If we could get there, Wolf and I would be safe. Pressing my forehead against the granite surface of the eyelet window, I watched glistening mountaintops take shape above the mists of morning and closed my eyes against the wonder of it.

The enormous lake was hidden beneath the clouds, but I could hear the songs of birds throughout the valley. Nuns were gathering outside the little cloister below me, slowly parading up the winding abbey road—birds themselves, for they sang as sweetly. At the entrance of the church, they filed in one by one in silence, but soon two hundred voices would weave in and out, crossing melodic lines, pouring forth their hymns to God.

It was music, real music, the first I had heard for months, and oh how I longed to join them. My favorite was the haunting Ockhegon's kyrie, with its odd way of mounting up the tonal scale step by step, leaping an octave and immediately turning back down in a mournful eighth-note figure. Despite the words, there was something cheerful about its flavor, a notion of life without war—or maybe that was what I wanted to hear.

Kyrie eleison. Lord, have mercy. But the God of the Jews was not merciful; He was Elohim, the wrathful one. I Am That I Am. The God of Lodz and Warsaw and Auschwitz. I would sing no songs to Him.

When the first strains of the kyrie rang out, I ran down the steps two at a time, raced across the ancient ramparts of the abbey and down along the stream encircling it, splashing mud onto my habit. At the corner of the stables, I almost collided with the abbess.

"You were supposed to be at matins," the wizened woman said with mock severity.

"I was up in the oriel, Your Grace. Watching the sunrise."

"We're going to miss you, 'Sister Marisa'," the abbess said. "If it were up to the choirmaster, you'd be bolted into place in the pews."

"And I would have to convert," I said. "You yourself said it was the only way to stay on."

The abbess sighed. "Not just convert, but do it sincerely, with the full love of God in your heart. We couldn't take the chance otherwise. To hide a Jew—two Jews—would have us killed if it were discovered."

I shook my head. "I can't love God. I love Wolf for what he has done for me, and my place is with him."

"Of course." She smiled at me fondly. "You must be on your way."

"And I don't know how to thank you," I said, close to tears, "to give us these two days, to risk everything for us through that amount of time—"

She held up a hand. "Be grateful to God, not me." She looked beyond me, toward the water. "There are patrol boats on Lake Constance. You and Wolf must look out for them. The boatman knows about them, of course, but he's an old man and his eyesight's not so good, particularly in the dark."

For Wolf, Switzerland would only be a stopping point. We'd make our way to Saint Gall. Peter had given us an address of a fighter for the cause. Wolf would wait there for his contact to smuggle him into Palestine, where he'd work to build a homeland for Polish Jews once the war was over. But how would that help Jozef or my parents or even Tante Esther? I didn't think they could adjust to a new country.

So I would stay with Wolf until he left and then try to at least discover if my family were still alive. But even if they were, I could not rescue my parents by myself. I could not correspond with them, even tell them of my safety or where I was. Maybe I would be better off in New York, where my aunt and uncle lived, but it seemed as remote and as inaccessible as heaven. I was adrift, and without Wolf by my side, utterly vulnerable, a German Jewish girl from Poland whose only skill, music, was useless in a war-torn world. I lifted the rosewood rosary over my head and offered it to the abbess.

"Keep it," she said. "For good luck. I've brought you some fresh clothes. When you leave tonight, the nuns will give you bread and cheese. There'll be a sharp knife in the package. You can use it to slice bread—or slice Germans. It's too dangerous for Wolf to show himself before dark, so stay with him in his room until someone calls you, and tell him good-bye and good luck for me. Maybe someday, when the war is over, you'll come back here and we can celebrate in the sunlight."

I was too choked to speak and so simply kissed her cheek and turned away so she would not see my tears. She had proved to me that there was still grace in the world, still goodness. But was it only to be found behind walls? When I left, would I ever find it again?

An old ferryman was waiting at his cottage on the shore, bent over a trawling line with a darning needle as we arrived. He gave us a nervous, toothy grin and led us to the dock, where his ramshackle powerboat lay beneath a fishing net. Wolf squatted down to scan the coastline, and I tried to see too, but the lake was dark; there was no sign of other boats. The man gestured for us to crawl on board, then pulled on the netting until it hid Wolf. In sibilant French, he told me to help him bail.

As I leaned over, I felt the stranger's eyes straining to look down my blouse and I glared at him with such disgust that, perhaps ashamed, he looked away and lifted a jug of wine, which he proceeded to drink from with evident gusto. I presumed it was not the first time that evening he had made use of it. He asked me to sit beside him, and in short order I felt his hand on my leg.

Wolf lay oblivious at our feet. I thought about calling out to him in Polish but held myself back. Soon enough, there would be no Wolf to come to my rescue. I would have to learn to stop depending on him. Besides, I knew him well enough to understand that it might be foolhardy to alert him. For all his recourse to reason and logic, he had already demonstrated that any threat to his manhood would unleash an explosion. What would he do now? Shout at the old man, alerting any other boat of our presence? Fight with the old man, stab him with the knife the nuns had given us? Then there would be no one left to guide the boat.

One wrong move and an Italian police *vaporetto* could stop us, and we suspects would dutifully be handed over to the Germans. The boatman's hand traveled to my inner thigh. I held my breath.

Wolf, unbidden, emerged from hiding, shaking his body to rid himself of the net. The boatman's hand returned to his side. With relief, I yanked my skirt down, finding myself in the absurd position of having to hide what had happened from the only man allowed to lift it.

"Look at his eyes," Wolf said in Polish, darting uneasy glances at the expanse of lake surrounding us. "He must have drunk half that jug of wine."

I rose unsteadily. "Yes. Maybe we ought to offer him some bread to keep him sober. Sit next to him and I'll dig it out. Do you want any?"

"God, no! I feel as if the German Army's marching back and forth through my gut." He caught my anxious glance. "It isn't fear—I'm seasick. It's worse than it was aboard that steamer on the Vistula."

It was vodka that had made him sick then, but I didn't argue. He had apologized for his behavior and had done much to redeem himself. He was forgiven. "Look!" I said. "You can make out the lights on the sides of the mountains. Switzerland!"

"You're happy, then?"

"Of course!"

His expression grew sad under the dim light coming from the speedboat cabin. "Funny, I'm not."

"But it means we've escaped. Switzerland's neutral. You can wait there safely for your instructions."

"Yes. But it means the end of us." He swung around to face me. "The time we've spent together has been the happiest of my life. Struggling side by side, even when things were at their worst—I'm in love with you, Mia, and I can't bear the thought of losing you."

I felt a rush of emotion. Not love, surely, and not pity, but maybe a combination or a version of both. He seemed terribly young, terribly forlorn, defenseless. "It's okay that you don't love me," he said. "No, don't protest. For a brief time you were my wife and my lover, and I'll hang on to that joy, loving you, for as long as I live."

"I always wanted a Wolf to be the first," I said, pretending gaiety, and threw my arms around him. "I know you tried to be gentle with me, and tender."

"You could come with me to Palestine. We could have a life there. I would cherish you, make you forget . . ." His voice trailed off; he knew it was a fantasy. I didn't have to talk.

I remembered our first meeting in Three Crosses Square, his bravery, his rage and determination, his protectiveness. He was young, but so complicated. Did he know what he did to me? This man had been God and devil both. How would I feel when we parted?

The engine sputtered, and the boat swung toward shore. I could see a farmer silhouetted against the mountain, watching us with what might have been curiosity or lassitude. I ducked instinctively but Wolf held me firmly. There could be no sign that we did not belong on the boat or had no right to be in Switzerland.

The boat jerked to a halt several yards from shore, accompanied by a string of curses from the fisherman. He shouted directions to Wolf, who looked at him blankly, then grabbed the throttle, pushing it forward and back, rocking us back and forth so violently we slammed up against the bulkhead.

Wolf raced to the stern to see what the trouble was. "The propeller's fouled," he shouted. "I'll try to cut us loose." He tore off his shirt and jumped into the water, holding our knife between his teeth. The water came only to his waist, and I could see him hack at the tallest stalks, sawing back and forth under the water while the fisherman gunned the motor.

"Turn it off!" Wolf cried. "You idiot, you'll cut me to pieces."

The fisherman turned off the engine, yet I could hear another engine, far more powerful and fearsome, approach. A patrol boat. German. Soldiers in uniform stood on its deck.

"Wolf!" I screamed. A burst of gunfire hid all other sound. The fisherman fell silently at my side, as though someone had suddenly chopped off his legs. I watched Wolf try to run, but a bullet pounded into his back, and he threw up his arms, then fell face forward into the water. I jumped in after him, thinking for a lunatic second that I might save him, put my arms around him and pulled him toward shore, taking the knife he still clutched between his teeth. Bullets sliced into the water around me. I felt a stinging in my arm, heard an explosion in my right ear. Blood dripped down my face.

I crawled onto the Swiss soil, dragging Wolf's body with me, struggling for breath. In seconds, the gunfire stopped. Was I safe? Was it over? I gasped for air, but there wasn't enough of it, and I lay still, washed not by the waves but by oblivion.

I was not unconscious for long. A movement behind me startled me, and I raised my head. Wolf's body lay beside me, but I could not tell if he was dead. That sound again. Someone was approaching, his feet making squishy sounds in the sand.

"Don't move," a voice said in German. I lay still. Rough hands turned me on my back and I looked up to see a young soldier staring down at me, his gun pointing at my face. His expression was as amazed as if I had dropped from the sky. He was wearing a uniform. A *German* uniform. Dear God, I was doomed!

"You are my prisoner," he said, his voice trembling. "Under the terms of the Geneva convention, I arrest you as a spy."

It was nonsense, I knew. Switzerland was a neutral country, and I had as much right to be here as he did. But the boy was obviously frightened, and as such doubly dangerous. "Let me stand," I said meekly. "I'll go with you wherever you say. I acknowledge I'm your prisoner, though I've done nothing wrong."

He grunted and motioned me up with his rifle. I stood, my legs almost buckling. "Who's that?" he asked, indicating Wolf.

"My husband. We were taking the ferry across the lake when someone started shooting. German, Swiss—I don't know. He was hit and fell overboard. I dived in after him."

"Is he alive?"

"I don't know." It was a question I did not want answered. Wolf dead? The thought was monstrous.

He kicked Wolf savagely in the ribs. The body moved under the force of the blow but there was no sign of life. "Please," I said. "Let me make sure,"

I started to kneel, but he pulled me up. "I'll do it." He bent over the body, touched Wolf's face hesitantly, as though he were my husband's lover, not I. "Yes, he is dead."

The sight was obscene. With a cry I brought the knife around from behind my back and plunged it with all my strength into the German's back. He spun toward me, his eyes wild with disbelief, and I took a step away. Then he fell face forward, gurgling, blood erupting from his mouth.

I screamed. The soldier had fallen over Wolf's body, and the two lay still, a grotesque sculpture. There was no sound now, from either of them, no sound at all on the beach or the lake save for the caw of birds.

I stared at them, too numb to move, engulfed by horror, terrified, alone. I had an address in Saint Gall, another in New York, a knife, sopping clothes caked in mud and slime, a family imprisoned and for all I knew, dead, and a beloved comrade who was gone. Wolf's dream of Palestine was over and I was alone.

Well, I would make my way to Saint Gall if I could. The night had grown cold. Walking would warm me.

BOOK II

"You must go out more, Aunt Ceena said. "You're pale as alabaster. It's unnatural for girls your age to show no interest in boys, in life."

Aunt Ceena. How good she'd been to me! She and my uncle Martin had met me at the airport, taken me into their Brooklyn home, fed me and clothed me, given me a job with decent wages as a salesgirl in their jewelry company—costume jewelry, not the kind my papa showed me in Lodz—in short, had welcomed me and tried to make me happy.

But I was not happy and did not want to go out. All I could think of was my family whom I'd deserted, and Wolf, who lay dead on the beach at Lake Constance.

In Switzerland, my only wish was survival. I'd found the Abby in Saint Gall and, numb with shock and terror, allowed myself to be persuaded that I could do my family no good by staying in Europe— they were almost surely dead—and that I should travel to America where there was family and the chance for a new life. Transportation through a Jewish relief agency was arranged. Papers were prepared. All I had to do was sign my name and I would be one of the lucky ones, the "saved."

I followed orders. It was as though everything had been prearranged, and I had no power to resist even if I'd wanted to. I drifted through the weeks it took to contact Ceena and Martin, obtain an entry permit,

book a seat on a plane, as though I were smoke, a ghost without substance or weight, blown in any direction the wind took me.

I have only scattered memories from that time. There were
throngs of people at the airport, but my aunt found me, this round,
red-cheeked woman, bedecked in rings and earrings and lockets and
bracelets who threw herself on me like a protective eagle. The ride in
their car to my new home, past shops of every kind and people of all
colors and ages. The searing heat of Ceena's house—I arrived in mid-
July 1941—the bright windows and the paneled walls of my third-
floor bedroom. The mounds of food, meats and vegetables, oranges
and bananas, mine whenever I wanted it. Tap water to drink, bathwa-
ter to bathe in, the sea to swim in—my new family took me there the
first weekend after I arrived.

There were so many sensory experiences—sights, sounds, tastes,
smells—that my brain could not take them all in, and so I sank deeper
into myself, enjoying nothing, not sure that the Mia who was granted
these treasures had anything to do with the Mia who had lured a German officer to his death and slept with the man who killed him, the Mia
for whom a single apple was worth more than all of Papa's diamonds.

Once they saw that their joy at having me as part of their family
was not reciprocated, that food and enthusiasm and comfort and—
yes—love could not rouse me from my despair, Martin and Ceena left
me to myself. I was immensely grateful. They would, I knew, be there
to greet me if I exchanged my old world for the new, but I was not
ready, not sure I would ever be ready. Every night before I went to
sleep, I saw Wolf and the German soldier entangled like lovers in each
other's dead arms.

And there was the problem of language. I had learned some English at the Lycée, and of course Ceena and Martin spoke Polish and
German, but when I went out, or people came into the house, I could
barely make out what they were saying, the talk was so rapid, the pro-
nunciations so unlike anything I had heard before. I insisted that
Ceena and Martin speak only English with me. In fact, that's when
we were most in contact: elementary phrases, broken sentences, mis-

used words (Ceena held back her laughter, but occasionally Martin couldn't stop himself), communication at such an elementary level that there was no way I could express my sorrow, no way my relatives could speak of their disappointment that I was so ungiving, so unthankful.

They were unfailingly kind and considerate, but looking back now it's hard to see what rewards they could have gotten from a lumpen girl who never smiled. I felt bad about it, wanted to show that I was grateful, but that would have required acknowledging that I existed, and I was afraid of that admission. At least outwardly, Martin and Ceena accepted me as I was, and it was really Ceena's prodding me to go out that let me see into their impatience.

"Out?" I said. "Where?"

The possibility that I might do as requested so startled my aunt that it took a few moments for her to reply. "To the Beth Israel Jewish Center in Bensonhurst. It's not far. We'll go tomorrow night. There will be people your own age there, as well as us older folk."

I knew my relatives went there occasionally—it was not the first time Ceena had spoken of it—but I couldn't imagine what it was like. A room full of Jews. The last time I was in such a community, there were walls to imprison us. I had the fleeting thought that we would all be machine-gunned down.

"Very well," I said listlessly.

"Martin," Ceena called, her voice alive with pleasure. "Mia says she'll go with us tomorrow night!"

The Beth Israel Jewish Center reminded me of the hall in Lodz where Papa used to go for his meetings. Balloons hung in clusters like giant grapes from the ceiling, and colorful tablecloths covered the tables that surrounded the dance floor; but the overall effect was featureless and drab, just a giant room with a few dusty windows and people milling around waiting for something to happen.

First, dinner was served, kosher chicken, peas, potatoes, a substance Ceena called "Jell-O," which tasted to me like sweet glue. There must have been twenty tables, each seating eight people, but there were only a few at ours, and many of the others stood empty. If there was anybody "my own age," girls or boys, I didn't see them. The attendees all looked like Martin or Ceena, though nobody wore as much jewelry as my aunt, and no one sat with such self-satisfaction as my uncle.

After the plates were cleared away, five young men arranged themselves on a bandstand at the front of the room. A drummer, a pianist, a bassist, a trumpeter, and a clarinetist. Thanks to a hand-lettered placard proclaiming their presence at the entrance to the hall, I knew they were called the Paulie Giamvalo Quintet—although I had no idea which one was Paulie and no notion of what kind of music they were going to play. Surely, I thought, nothing that would suit my taste, though I confess to a faint curiosity. At least it would be music; I had not heard any (save for the cacophony coming from radios on the Brooklyn streets) since coming to American.

My mind raced back to Lodz and how excited I was when I first took piano lessons. The teacher told my parents that someday I might be a concert pianist. My father was so proud that he bought me the finest piano in Europe, a Bösendorfer. At the lycée in Paris my real love was my music. I loved to play the famous European classic composers like Chopin, Mozart, Schubert, and Beethoven. Even in Brooklyn when I was alone in my bedroom I dreamt of playing in a grand concert hall to a sold-out audience.

The trumpeter walked to the front of the bandstand, and bowed to faint applause. He introduced himself as Paulie G., and then recited names of the rest of the band members. I paid no attention, but my aunt whispered "Catholics" in a surprised voice, and my uncle shrugged. What difference the religion of the musicians as long as they could play?

Paulie announced the first number. "Chattanooga Choo Choo." A few people clapped. To me the title meant nothing; Paulie might just as well have been speaking Greek.

The number began. Unfathomable. A nice rhythm, a tune carried by the piano that to me seemed as alien as its title, more noise than coherence, pleasant enough but not *music.* Paulie sang the song—gibberish—and a few people got up and began dancing. Some of them were good, but most were awkward. I watched them with little interest.

The music stopped and the couples returned to their tables. Paulie stepped forward again. "Begin the Beguine," he said, more gibberish, but Ceena smiled and stood. "This one we can dance to," she said and pulled a reluctant Martin to his feet.

This time the melody sprang full-throated from the clarinet, and I felt gooseflesh rise along my arms and legs as though a sudden cool breeze had swept through the hall. Suddenly I was back in Paris, listening to a different clarinetist, Benny Goodman, letting the exotic music transfix me then as it did now. I had met Jean-Phillipe that night, and though I had declined his invitation to dance, it was the music that drew us together, this strange American music that, it seemed, we alone understood.

How wonderfully this new clarinetist played! I looked up at him and stopped breathing.

He was slim, taller than me, and, I thought, about my age. He stood up straight but let his body weave to the music he made, as though it was part of him, and expressed through the clarinet he carried. He had sharp features, a long nose and thin mouth, and black hair. And his eyes! Dark as his hair, but burning with an intensity easily visible from where I sat, unaccompanied now, near the bandstand. He was totally involved in the music, letting it express him, speak for him, and though his comrades played around him, I knew he was as solitary as I, the music alone his companion.

He looked at me! I could *feel* his gaze as much as see it, and he missed a note and had to struggle to catch up, the only lapse in the purity of his playing. On and on he went, the musicians alongside him picking up on his tempos, his repeats, and all the while our eyes held each other's so that it seemed I, too, a conspirator, was part of the music. The dancers paused and listened, some of them smiling, others seemingly confused, until finally Paulie put a stop to the music with a hand signal and the clarinetist took the instrument from his mouth and grinned at me.

For an instant I was in the grip of something like terror, and then I realized that what had startled me so was the reemergence of life itself, a desire to be here, in this dingy hall, watching middle-aged couples trying to dance and suddenly aware of myself as if I had not previously existed. The sensation was utterly new, and once the terror passed, I welcomed it with such ardor it brought tears to my eyes.

Music's grace and purity, its ability to reach to the furthest limits of emotion, had taken hold of my soul again. I did not have to hide from it, nor deny that it was a fundamental part of my being. In this marvelous America, I could sing if I wished, play if I wished, and no harm would come to me. The only songs in the ghetto were those of lamentation, and even in the nunnery the music was not meant for humans, but for God. This "Begin the Beguine," whatever that meant, was written so that people could dance, so that *I* could dance. One song, a tango (I later learned it was written by an American named Cole Porter), stood at that instant for all the music I had mastered as a girl, and I yearned to push the pianist on the bandstand away so that I could take his place beside the clarinetist.

The band started a new song—so engrossed in my thoughts was I that I did not catch its name—another rhythmic sprint that galvanized the dancers but meant little to me. There was little for the clarinetist to do, and I noticed he was still watching me, still grinning. I can't say I fell in love with him "at first sight"—no, I fell in love with his music. But he was the bearer of it, and for *that* I loved him. I smiled back and held out my arms to show him a connection had been made. When Ceena and Martin returned, they asked me what I was doing. "Just stretching," I said. Yes. Stretching my arms toward the infinite.

The band played three more numbers, then Paulie announced a twenty-minute break.

"I've had enough," Martin said. "Let's go home." It was a command, not a suggestion. Ceena stood.

"I'd like to stay a little longer," I said, "to hear more of the music. There's no need for you to stay with me. I can take the bus home."

"I don't think—" Ceena began, but my uncle elbowed her gently in the ribs. "Of course," he said. "It'll be good for you."

I knew he had sensed my eagerness, and eagerness was something I had never demonstrated before. "Be careful on the way back," Ceena warned.

"I'll be careful," I promised and watched them leave, hand in hand, the remnants of my family.

I went to the ladies' room, feeling a little on edge, hoping that when the band came back there would be another song featuring the clarinet. When I made my way back to my chair—most of the others had stayed and were socializing around the tables—there he was.

He was still sweaty from his playing, and a shock of his hair lay plastered against his forehead, but to me he was the most beautiful boy I had ever seen. His face was remarkably clear, its skin almost translucent, and I could see flecks of gold in the irises of his eyes. He had left his clarinet on his chair on the bandstand, and he kept his hands deep in his trouser pockets, as though he was afraid they'd be ungovernable should he take them out. Close up, he avoided my eyes. I was moved by his shyness.

"I was afraid you wouldn't come back," he said. "That you'd left with the people you were with."

"My uncle and aunt. I live with them, but they let me stay here by myself."

He didn't ask why I wanted to stay, and I offered no explanation. He removed his right hand from his pocket and held it out. "I'm Vinnie Sforza."

I shook it. "Marisa Levy. I'm called Mia."

"Mia." He repeated the word like a lyric.

"I like the way you play," I told him.

He blushed. "I'm glad. I want to be a musician."

"Oh, but you're a musician now!"

"I mean a professional. My parents want me to go to college some-day—they can't afford to send me now—but I think it'd be a waste of time."

"Don't you get paid for playing here?"

He shrugged. "Ten bucks. That's what all of us are paid except Paulie, who gets twenty."

Now he was looking into my eyes and it was I, shy, who turned away. "I think it would be better if you went to music school instead of college," I said. "Though actually I don't think you need lessons." I paused then blurted, "I think you're as good as Benny Goodman."

He laughed, immeasurably pleased. "Actually, Artie Shaw's my hero. I think he's better than Goodman."

Better than Goodman? The idea was transporting. "I've never heard of him. I'd love to hear him play."

"But you've heard Goodman?"

"In Paris. I went twice because I liked it so much."

"Paris." He whistled. "You have an accent but it doesn't sound French."

"It's Polish, really. I was born in Lodz. I went to school in Paris for a year." I shut out the image of Jean-Phillipe.

"And you know about music?"

"Yes. I sing and play the piano—I don't sing very well, but I love to play the piano."

"Really!" The information delighted him. "We're playing 'Star Dust' in the next set."

I laughed. "I don't know the words *or* the music."

"But it's the most famous song ever written."

"Not where I come from. In Europe, the most famous song is 'Lindenbaum.' "

His face fell. "It sounds classical."

"It is. It's by Franz Schubert. But it's very beautiful nonetheless."

He brightened. "One day you must teach it to me."

"If you'll teach me 'Star Dust.' " I was amazed I could be so forward.

He seemed surprised, too. "Really?" It seemed his favorite word.

"Of course," I said quickly. "Music means more to me than anything else in life."

"Me too!" He hopped from one leg to the other in his excitement. I felt like hopping with him.

"We have only this last set to play," he said. "Would you like to go out for a soda with me after we're finished?"

"You mean—a date?" It was a word I had only just learned.

"Exactly." He looked at his wristwatch. "We'll be through playing in forty-five minutes. Eleven o'clock. Afterward, I'll see you home."

"I live in Bensonhurst. It's far."

"I don't care if it's Alaska, not if you let me buy you a soda."

How young he was! How sweet! "A soda would be nice." I had never tasted one.

He turned to the bandstand. His fellow musicians were returning. "Wait for me here. And remember, when I play 'Star Dust,' it's for you."

At Myers Fountain, where the manager, Ida Cohen, knew Vinnie and winked when he asked her to prepare his "finest chocolate soda for Miss Levy," we sat facing each other in a booth, our knees sometimes touching, and talked. The booth was way in back and pretty private, and Ida told Vinnie to watch his manners around such a lovely young lady. Blushing again, he promised that he would.

He told me that he had just graduated from Erasmus Hall High School and now worked at his uncle Gino's fruit and vegetable store under the el on Gravesend Avenue, hauling crates, stacking eggplants, and stocking the ice room from sun up to sun down, when he was free to play his clarinet if the band could get work. His father, a hod carrier, made a pretty good living, which meant Vinnie could keep most of his wages—it was how he could afford such a fine clarinet and how, he boasted, he would be able to take me to hear Artie Shaw.

His mother took care of four other children, two boys and two girls, all of them younger than Vinnie and in various grades in public school. Family situation out of the way, he went on about sports (he loved basketball, a game I had only a vague impression of), about school, where he liked English and history but not math or science or Latin, and about the girls he used to date, none of them worth much in his eyes—he was still waiting for his first "big love" and, from his look, might have found it in me.

All this left me free to be silent. My own history was not one I wished to describe. I was a killer and sometimes felt like a widow, and my experience, I imagined, would not be matched by his in his entire lifetime. Still, I enjoyed his chatter and his intensity. He need not have worked so hard to make a good impression, but I found his attempts at sophistication endearing; had he been more polished, I might never have seen him again.

As it was, I accepted his offer to take me home. Though my relatives lived more than a mile away, we agreed we should walk rather than take the bus, the night being so fine. I could sense as we walked that he wanted to hold my hand or put his arm around my shoulders, and that would have been all right, but he was too shy for action and I did nothing to encourage it.

It was after twelve-thirty when we got to my uncle's house. The light above the entranceway was on, but the windows were dark; evidently Ceena and Martin were not worried enough about me to wait up. I took the key from my purse but did not turn toward the door. Instead we stood awkwardly together.

"May I see you again?" he finally managed.

"I was hoping you'd want to."

"Then meet me at Myers tomorrow at eight. Do you think you could find it again?"

I had no idea. "Easily."

"Good." He looked relieved, as though he had just passed some kind of trial. "Until tomorrow."

Then he was off, followed by my gaze. He looked so young, so newly minted, that I wondered why I had agreed to go out with him again. It was not hard to figure out. He might be innocent, a naif in his manner, but there was maturity in his music. Above that, he was protected, cosseted, optimistic. An American. Maybe he could teach some of that to me.

CHAPTER 17

The Americanization of Mia. What an experience it was! Vinnie started me off on Coney Island, and I was appropriately petrified on the Tornado and the Cyclone, screaming with the rest of the girls while their dates sat beside them stalwart and brave. Vinnie bought me my first hot dog, my first vanilla malted, my first (and only) charm bracelet, adorned with tiny horses and dogs. And he took me to Manhattan, that splendid city within a city, which reminded me of Paris although it wasn't half so beautiful.

The theater became our passion. Neither of us had been before; now we went every week. For ninety cents you could buy standing room tickets, and I remember seeing *Life with Father, Arsenic and Old Lace,* and *My Sister Eileen.* Though I didn't understand most of the jokes—my English wasn't good enough—I laughed at Vinnie's laughter, sharing his pleasure and watching his face as much as the plays, that wonderfully pure and untroubled face which registered emotions with such clarity that I wondered if any feeling of his went unpictured. His feelings toward *me,* expressed in words as well as looks, were the plainest of all: as each day went by, he fell more in love. As for me—well, I wasn't yet in love, but I loved being with him, and I looked forward to the weekends (and occasional week nights) more than anything else in my life. Ceena and Martin knew I was "seeing someone" I had met at the Beth Israel Jewish Center, but because I never brought him home (as, indeed, I never went home with him) they could only imagine him and warn me to "be careful."

One show meant more to us than any of the others. It was called *Pal Joey*, with music by Richard Rodgers, and we both thought it was spectacular. At last we had "new" music to share, music that seemed to have been written with us in mind: "Bewitched, Bothered and Bewildered"—that was Vinnie. "If They Asked Me, I Could Write a Book"—that was me, though I didn't tell him the plot; I had said next to nothing about my past. We got the sheet music, and Vinnie played the songs for me one glorious autumn afternoon while we picnicked in Prospect Park, and later I sang them for him and we dreamed of becoming a vaudeville act—Sforza and Levy, the Music-Makers.

I learned a new term, "make out," and Vinnie and I made out all the time. He had kissed me good night after our second meeting at Myers, and soon after, we kissed and fondled each other anyplace we could. We made out in a car Vinnie had borrowed from a friend; in the park, after dark, hidden behind trees or bushes; blatantly in the street, stopping to kiss and holding each other so closely we looked like one fat person with two rears. Once we went to Grand Central Station and "kissed good-bye," though neither of us were going anywhere. We could have made out at his house or mine, I suppose, but his parents were practicing Catholics and would never have allowed it, and it seemed unfair to Aunt Ceena and Uncle Martin for us to use their house for that purpose.

I loved the taste of his lips, the passion of his tongue, the feel of his hands on my breasts, the command of his fingers inside me, the way his penis pressed against my leg—he seemed always hard—until I brought him relief with my hands. Yet I did not let him make love to me, if love means intercourse. Remembering my first time with Wolf, I wanted to give myself to Vinnie on my terms. He complained, sometimes bitterly, and I assured him he would not have to wait long. That and a "hand job" (how well I was learning English!) left him mollified.

In late September, the classical music season opened, and I noted on a flier posted at Myers that Benny Goodman would be playing the Mozart Clarinet Concerto with the New York Philharmonic. I asked Uncle Martin for the morning off and bought tickets at the box office the moment it opened, orchestra seats befitting the occasion.

I had not said much to Vinnie about classical music, but I missed it and now I would introduce him to it. When I presented the ticket to him, he was unenthusiastic.

"Classical music?"

"Eternal music," I said sharply.

"I'm not sure I'll like it."

"I'm not sure either. We'll have to see." A lot depended on whether or not he did. "But don't worry. It won't bite you."

He grinned. "If it does, I'll bite you back."

"And if you like it—if you really, honestly can say you like it—then . . ."

"Then what?"

I let the question go unanswered.

We went on Sunday afternoon. Carnegie Hall, where neither of us had been before, awed us with its rows of red-cushioned wooden seats and high ceilings, the hush of its audience, the elegant black dresses the women wore. "I could never play here," Vinnie said. "It's an indoor Ebbetts Field." But I could see he was impressed.

The program, all Mozart, opened with his Sinfonia Concertante K. 364, to be followed by the clarinet concerto. The *Jupiter Symphony* would come after the intermission. Having heard recordings of his in Lodz, I knew that Bruno Walter, the conductor, was a Mozart specialist, and the applause that greeted him was heartfelt in a polite sort of way. I had intended to watch Vinnie through the performance to gauge his reaction, but the sounds of Mozart swept through my soul like an elixir of memory, and I was transported back to the time when, for me, music was my life. It felt strange to be sitting there beside this dear boy without hearing Papa's gruff appreciation or my piano teacher's analysis of the melodic structure.

The joyous piece made me sad, and only when it was over did I look at Vinnie, wanting him—futilely, of course; how could he know what was in my heart?—to share my emotion. He was staring at the stage as Walter departed, and I could not tell what he was feeling. But then he took my hand and whispered, "Nice. I like it," and I could not have asked for more.

Walter returned to the stage, leading Goodman, who walked straight-backed and unsmiling to his place by the podium. Vinnie clapped hard enough to bruise his hands, but the rest of the audience was far more restrained. I remembered Paris, where the reception for Goodman was tumultuous, but there were no whistles or yells here, no stamping of feet. Maybe he can only play jazz, I suddenly worried. Maybe he's not fit for Mozart.

Oh, no! With the clarinet's first entrance, playing the main theme that would be the centerpiece for the entire movement, it was obvious that Mozart could not have been better served. Vinnie gave a little gasp and leaned forward, hands clutching the back of the chair in front of him, eyes wide, like a kid watching his first fireworks. Goodman was moving now, swaying to the music like a snake charmer; I expected the ghost of Mozart to rise before him. With each note, Vinnie became more excited and swayed, too, his breaths coinciding with Goodman's, with Mozart's. He was playing along with the musician onstage; I could see him fingering the notes on the back of the chair.

When the piece was finished, Vinnie and I were standing and cheering as if we'd just heard the "King Porter Stomp," and some of the younger members of the audience were shouting with us, much to the surprise of Goodman, who broke his usual impassive demeanor with a smile and a bow in our direction.

We decided that to stay for the second half would be anticlimactic, so we made for the street. "Time for you to bite me," Vinnie said when we were outside.

I had anticipated him—a present I had not mentioned.

"I've reserved us a hotel room," I told him. He glanced at me, unbelieving. I pulled him along. "You didn't think I'd do it in public, did you?"

That first time, he was awkward, fumbling, unsure of himself, and too engrossed in his actions to think of my pleasure. But I was happier in his arms than I'd been with Wolf. Vinnie was more tender and more ardent, and I relished his inexperience, knowing that I was his first lover and could teach him the few things I'd learned.

We were both unashamedly, unambivalently in love. In my eyes, he became even more beautiful; there was not an inch of him I did not admire and adore. I don't know how he felt about the fact that I was not a virgin. Maybe he didn't know, for he never asked and I never mentioned Wolf nor, in fact, did I tell him any more than necessary about the past.

The past had receded. Of course I thought about Lodz and my parents and Jozef, about the days in Warsaw and the killings on the beach. But I was able to push them out of my consciousness and they became flickering memories, like three-dimensional photographs, but remote. My happiness made Ceena and Martin happy, too, and they bought me a secondhand piano the moment I told them I wanted to play again, to sing again.

I introduced them to Vinnie, and though they were concerned about his religion ("But I'm not getting *married*," I told them) he won them over with his openness and obvious love of me. It became customary for Vinnie to arrive at the house around seven, clarinet in hand, and for us to play duets until my aunt and uncle went to bed. We played Rodgers and Porter and Kern, but also Schumann and Brahms. Both of us learned to play Schumann's *Fantasy Pieces* for clarinet and piano, and the music made us one. It was like making love. We "necked" (peculiar word!) in Martin's house, ferocious exercise, but saved true lovemaking for "our" hotel on Fifty-sixth Street where we went on those rare times when we could afford it.

I still remember the first time we went to the hotel—he seemed so shy. He was so nervous he had trouble opening the door, and I had to help him. When we finally entered the room he just stood there not knowing what to do. I then realized how much I loved this young, beautiful, sensitive man who wanted to experience the world as much as I did. I rubbed his back and was able to feel his tension. I was also nervous because I wasn't sure if we were doing the right thing.

When he turned to face me and I saw his smile, I felt relieved. He held me close and kissed me passionately. I felt his full lips and could taste him. Slowly he started to undress me. I wondered how he knew what to do. I became so excited I started to remove my own clothes, but he told me to stop—that he wanted to do it. Finally I stood naked in front of him and I looked at him fully clothed. I then went to him and removed his clothing. I enjoyed this experience and never forgot it. It was so much different from making love in awkward places.

When it was time to leave and we were both dressed he made me take off my clothing again and we made love once more. For such a young man he somehow understood a woman's desire. I thought of Wolf, but I realized conditions were much different for us. Vinnie truly was my first love and he would be with me forever.

I don't mean to imply that music was our only bond. We loved roller-skating, which Vinnie had taught me to do almost as soon as we met, and taking subway rides to the farthest parts of Brooklyn and the Bronx, and going to the movies, and giving each other language lessons (I tutored him in French, which he had taken in high school), and laughing at the eccentricities of passersby, and, and, and—I can't think of anything we *didn't* love as long as we were together.

In late October, Vinnie arrived at the house with more than his usual excitement. "Paulie's landed us a gig," he shouted. "A good one!"

By this time, I knew what a "gig" was. "Where?"

"At the Schlesingers'."

I look at him blankly.

"The Schlesingers'. They own the fancy house at Sea Gate Point."

I knew Sea Gate, a gated community on the ocean.

"They're giving a party," Vinnie went on. "Their daughter heard us play at a mixer and thought we were terrific, so she persuaded her parents to hire us. We're getting a hundred bucks, just for the night."

Enough for two nights at our hotel, I thought, and Vinnie must have had the same idea because he winked at me lasciviously. "You're coming along," he said.

"But I'm not invited."

"So what? They can't turn the clarinetist away at the last moment. We'll tell them you're the singer but you've got laryngitis."

Why not? I thought. It wouldn't do anybody any harm, it would give me a chance to hear Vinnie and the band in a setting different from Knights of Columbus meeting halls or the Beth Israel Jewish Center, and besides, we'd see how the other tenth lived. "I don't have anything to wear," I said.

"Sure you do. The blue dress you wore to Carnegie Hall. Hell, you'll look prettier than anybody else there, anyway."

To Vinnie I would, and that was all that mattered to me. And so it was decided.

You could just see the house from the front gate. A horseshoe gravel driveway led to its front door, and I could see sculptured hedges in the shapes of wild animals, statues of nude males and females, and a tennis court.

Paulie showed the guard our invitation. "Your entrance is to the right of the kitchen," the guard said. "Just before you reach the cabanas."

A young woman was waiting for us at the kitchen door. She was dressed in a long light blue gown cut low at the neck and swirling out just above her feet which were clad in silver shoes. She wore a single diamond at her throat, a gold watch on her left wrist, and a tiara, also of diamonds, adorned her head. Could the diamonds be real? If so, they were worth tens of thousands of dollars.

Paulie gravely shook her hand. She smiled at the rest of us. "I'm Marilyn Schlesinger," she said, as if we couldn't have guessed. "I'm happy you can play for us tonight. Please make yourselves comfortable. You'll be called when it's time to play." While she spoke to us all, she was gazing at Vinnie, obviously attracted. No you don't! I thought, feeling a flash of jealousy. But he was looking at me as always, and I relaxed.

We were taken through the servants' quarters, which lay behind a kitchen larger than Ceena and Martin's ground floor, where at least ten servants were preparing platter after platter of food—turkeys, hams, vegetables, cheeses, clams and oysters on mountains of ice.

All the band members were silent. None of us had seen anything like this before; even Paulie was nonplussed, and his usual arrogance had disappeared behind a curtain of awe.

After about an hour, during which, we supposed, all the food was eaten, a butler appeared to summon the band to work. The guys took their gear into the ballroom, which was lit up like Luna Park (Vinnie had taken me there two weeks ago). A bar stood at the far end, and like the Jewish Center, the center of the floor was ringed by tables, though that's where the similarities stopped. Here were scrubbed and polished people, the men in tuxedos, the women sporting enough décolletage to have satisfied Louis XIV and enough jewelry to have adorned the duchesses at the court of Catherine the Great, and the air smelled of perfumes from Coty and Lanvin. I sat by myself at a table farthest to the right and hoped that no one would ask me to dance. It was not my steps I was worried about—I'm a good dancer—but having to make conversation.

The band opened with their signature "Begin the Beguine," giving Vinnie his chance to show off, but this time I only half-listened. The wealth on display suddenly made me yearn for money, not for myself but to use for the people I had left behind, and it was of the starved and the beaten I was thinking, of the women and their wagons marching to the Baluty.

As soon as the music started the room filled with dancers, most of them moving with ease and grace, a few of the men, obviously tipsy, stumbling on their partners' feet. I noticed Marilyn Schlesinger dancing with a scarecrowlike figure who whirled her around the floor as if she were a mechanical doll. He said something into her ear and she pulled free, scowling. I wondered at their relationship. Lovers? Given her beauty and his gangly homeliness, it seemed unlikely.

Paulie announced the next song, " 'T'aint What You Do," and I looked for Vinnie, but he had disappeared. No, there he was, smiling, bending from the bandstand to talk to Marilyn Schlesinger! A wave of jealousy hit me so hard I had to fight to catch my breath. I was debating whether to approach them when a man's voice behind me said, "Care to dance?"

I turned. A distinguished older man, red cummerbund matching the red carnation in his tuxedo's buttonhole, was holding out his hand toward me. "I'm David Schlesinger," he said. "As your host, I find it unforgivable for a beautiful girl to be sitting alone."

I examined his eyes for a hint of irony, but he was staring at me with intense seriousness. Having no choice, I stood. "Thank you."

He led me toward the dance floor. "Are you one of Marilyn's friends?"

I blushed. "No. I'm Marisa Levy. A friend of one of the band members. He thought it would be all right if I came with them."

Was he taken aback by my name? Was that a slight downward twist of his mouth, as though he had tasted something unpleasant? "Of course! And is that friend the gentleman talking to my daughter?"

"Why, yes—yes he is." I pretended to notice them for the first time.

"Then you have my congratulations. The young man's a fine musician. And handsome, too. Marilyn seems taken with him." He winked at me. "Best watch him carefully, Marisa."

But I couldn't watch them, for Mr. Schlesinger began to dance with me, a practiced but uninspired partner, like a pianist who plays the notes but knows nothing of the nuances. "Follow my lead," he said. "Let's see what mischief they're getting into."

We danced up to them. Vinnie looked at us with bewildered eyes, but Marilyn put her hand on her father's arm to stop our dancing. "This is Vincent Sforza," she said to him. "Say hello. He says he'll come to play at all our balls and festivals."

Vincent. He had never called himself that, even when we first met. What was he pretending to be? One of *them*? I would have laughed, except the threat of Marilyn seemed too serious.

The song finished. "I've got to go play," Vinnie said, obviously relieved to be extricated from a tense situation.

"Of course," Mr. Schlesinger said. "Marilyn, your dance is mine. Very nice to have met you, Miss Levy."

Father and daughter moved off, and I was left standing in front of the entire room, feeling hot and ridiculous.

I went back to my seat and waited for the set to end. As soon as it did, Vinnie came racing to my side. I turned my back to him.

"Ah," he said. "Don't worry about Marilyn. Really, honey. You're my girl, you know that."

I didn't, really. I only knew that I was out of place, that these were the people who, if they had not destroyed my people, had certainly turned from our plight, unseeing. I had never discussed religion with Vinnie, had no idea whether he cared that I was Jewish. But now it mattered to *me,* and I faced him with some resentment.

"Prove it," I said. "Let's get out of here."

He took a step back. "You know I couldn't do that. I have to play until they say the band can go home. Otherwise I don't get paid."

"Then prove it when you're finished."

"How?"

Did I have to spell it out? "Use your imagination."

They played until two o'clock in the morning, number after number until they'd run out of pieces they'd rehearsed and started the old ones over again. Drinks flowed, the dancing got wild, shrieks of laughter filled the ballroom. And all that time I sat at the corner table, feeling abandoned, talking with Vinnie halfheartedly during the breaks, satisfied only that Marilyn Schlesinger was occupied with other guests, other dancers. I was an alien from Three Crosses Square, a girl despised there and ignored here. I was Ceena and Martin's obligation, not their child, and I wondered if they'd even scold me for staying out all night.

At last, at a signal from Marilyn, the ballroom lights flickered, the band played "Good Night Ladies," then packed their instruments, and the guests straggled out. Vinnie raced to my side. Instantly, my self-pity evaporated.

"Let's get out of here," Vinnie said urgently. "I've told Paulie we wouldn't be going back with him."

Before we could move, Mr. Schlesinger was beside us, putting his arm around Vinnie's shoulders while the other held the waist of an aristocratic gray-haired woman, obviously his wife.

"You must come and play for us alone," he said to Vinnie. "Both Mrs. Schlesinger and I would like that."

And Marilyn would, too, I thought, wondering if she had been the instigator of the invitation.

"Sure, sure," Vinnie said, removing himself from Mr. Schlesinger's grasp and shaking his hand instead. He took my hand; I could feel his heat. "But now we must run."

With that, politeness gone, he pulled me away and we raced through the servants' entrance, rushed past the lamp-lit posterns and dying torches, crossed between the pool and the tennis court, found a large enough patch of ground in the forest beyond, and made love as though sex were food and we were starving.

When I got home the next morning, Ceena and Martin were waiting for me, tears in their eyes. They handed me a postcard, dated two months previously, that Peter had sent from Warsaw. There had been no word from Jozef or Papa; presumably this meant that they were still alive. But there was news about Mama. She had died in the camp.

Regret and guilt flooded over me. I had betrayed her! Instead of trying to save her, I had used the underground network for my own selfish ends, my own salvation, and so made it from Switzerland to America without looking back. And I had given a young, treasured boy my love, not the woman who deserved it.

Maybe I could at least make it up to my father and brother. They were still alive, I was sure of it. And if there was some way I could get back to them, I would. Vinnie could wait until after I'd found them, somehow rescued them.

Such fantasies played in my mind like fragments of dreams, and none answered the question: How?

I cried and cried. Vinnie was with me in "our" hotel, but all I did was cry. And at last I told him about my parents, my brother, the Baluty, the ghetto, Wolf. The only things I held back were the murder of Egon and the full nature of my relationshp with Wolf; he wouldn't have understood, and I'm not sure that in this lovely American room with just our unthreatened, well-fed, comfortable selves that I understood either.

"The ghetto's like nothing you can imagine," I told him. "The stench, the disease, the hunger. Always hunger. People have been driven below the level of animals—below even the level of *shaygetz*. Do you know what that means, Vinnie? No? It means lice."

He was looking at me with uncomprehending compassion. "Why do they live there?"

"Because they're not allowed out. The Germans and, yes, their countrymen would kill them if they tried."

"Why? What did they do?"

"Do? They didn't do anything. They're Jews." I spat the word as if it were a curse, hating myself for being a Jew here, sleek and uncaring. While my family, my real family—the tears came again, unchecked.

He put his arms around me and held me until I stopped crying. "Kiss me," I said, and he did, passionately and tenderly, and I let myself be soothed.

Somewhere on the other side of night was Poland.

It didn't matter much that Vinnie couldn't comprehend what was happening to the Jews, or explain why his parents had never invited me to their home, or why Mr. Schlesinger had looked at me with such distaste at the party. What *did* matter was that Vinnie was entirely on my side, that if I was suffering he suffered, that he was there to comfort me about my mother, but he also left me alone in my grief if that's what I wanted.

When I asked him if he minded that I was Jewish, he said, "I don't know what 'Jew' means. I know that you're Mia and that I love you." And oh, in the days that followed, I loved him back—with all my heart and soul, with every inch of my body. Thanks to the Schlesingers' recommendation, Paulie's band was getting more and better-paying work, so that Vinnie began to talk of saving enough money to start his own band—a trio to begin with—or join one of the big bands like Glen Miller's or Tommy Dorsey's as featured clarinetist. We would be married, he assured me, the moment he knew what his future would be. In the meantime, we could go on as we were, totally committed and completely in love.

His adoration took away some portion of the pain of my mother's death. She—and Papa and Jozef too—had become remote to me—much loved figures from a distant past and faraway land. The thought of them gave me so much pain, and yet I loved my new happiness. I became confused. There were times when I thought I would lose my mind. My love and my pain were closely intertwined.

One Sunday afternoon Vinnie came to pick me up so we could go to a matinee at the movies. He was early (no surprise!), so we sat with Martin in the living room while Ceena went to the kitchen to make us coffee. I remember the light in the room, dazzling for winter, and the smell of a cinnamon swirl cake Ceena was heating to go with the coffee. Vinnie, always a little uneasy around my uncle, was talking about the Dodgers' prospects for 1942—they had recently lost a heartbreaking World Series to the hated Yankees—when there was a ring of a telephone, a silence when Ceena picked it up, then a scream from the kitchen. Ceena came racing into the room, eyes wild, her face pale.

"That was Mrs. Landsman. She says the Japanese have attacked us!"

Martin walked to her and put his arm around her trembling body. "Where?"

"Hawaii. A place called Pearl something."

"Hawaii? Are you sure it's not another one of those sightings of German subs?" He clicked on the radio, cursing its static. But the newscaster's voice was clear.

"*. . . Harbor. We repeat. This is not a test. The White House has reported that Japanese warplanes have sunk seven naval vessels at Pearl Harbor, Hawaii, at oh six hundred hours this morning. . . .*"

"My God!" Martin said. "War."

Ceena gave a little cry and turned to face us.

"We'll beat them," Vinnie said. "Don't worry, Mrs. Levy."

I looked at him. His face was flushed, and there was resolution in his posture.

"You don't understand what this means," I said.

He wheeled. "Sure I do. We're going to wipe them off the map. Can you imagine the nerve of them!"

My heart melted in his heat. "No, Vinnie," I said. "It means I'm going back."

CHAPTER 18

I knew that the United States would join the fight in Europe—that my Poland prayers, now sublimated to American love, would be heeded—and that I would have to become part of that fight. If victorious, it meant the salvation of the Jews, the opening of the camps, perhaps even Papa's and Jozef's survival.

Martin allowed me to leave the company, and I took a job in Rockefeller Center as coordinator of wartime information, a high-sounding name for a federal agency that seemed to be in charge of domestic propaganda and recruitment for those men and women who were ineligible for the draft. I translated letters intercepted from non-English-speaking civilians, wrote replies, and sorted through photographs to identify street names, monuments, and institutions around Poznán and Warsaw. The work was colossally boring, but I was happy to contribute and worked for as long as my bosses wanted me. The job was as close as I could come to the war effort. From it, I hoped, I'd find some way to get back to Poland.

I worked late, sometimes past midnight, and stumbled home usually too exhausted to see Vinnie who, when I did see him, looked at me reproachfully. I couldn't blame him.

He would be drafted, of course. Just when, we didn't know, nor was there any way of learning where he would be sent. He could play a musical instrument. Big deal, he said. Glenn Miller was going abroad to raise the troops' morale. What good was a two-bit clarinet player in the face of such competition? No, he would be drafted, sent to the front: cannon fodder.

Inevitably, given the stress on both of us, we began to quarrel. Petty tiffs about spoiled weekends, inattention, places to go, and major fights about my coldness in bed—I was just too tired and distracted to want to make love, and what I wanted was for the man I loved to understand.

One night, he called me at the office to say he had to work and couldn't see me that Saturday.

"Oh? Where will you be playing?"

He paused. Then: "At the Schlesingers'. They're giving a ball to raise money for the war effort."

He did not ask me if I wanted to come along.

"Mia, you there?" a raspy voice crackled through the intercom. "How about making us some coffee? Thornton Wilder is here to go over some new material."

Coffee making. Did I mention that was one of my jobs? I was no good at it, but nobody seemed to care.

"Sure thing, Bob." I stood up, happy at the chance to stretch my back.

Robert Sherwood was reading to a man seated across from him when I walked in. Sherwood was a playwright, I knew, though I'd not seen any of his plays. He and many of his colleagues worked part-time for the Wartime Information office, contributing their time and expertise to the articles we would send to magazines and papers across the country as inspirational reading.

"Now listen to this," Sherwood said. " 'Little Jeremy Paddington is a brave lad. While his father is across the North Sea risking his life to fight the Hun, Jeremy and his mother are doing their share for an Allied victory. Never will the juggernaut of the hobnailed jackboot crush the proud spirit of England's finest—the everyday citizen.' . . . I don't know . . ." His voice trailed off. "What do you think?"

"Honestly?" Wilder asked. He wrote plays, too. Vinnie and I had seen one, *Our Town,* when it played in Brooklyn.

"Of course."

"I think it's a bit heavy-handed."

Sherwood snorted. "It's propaganda, Thornton, not Broadway."

"Shouldn't it at least be addressed to Americans?"

"Yes, yes. I'll change the locale. But I've read so much English tripe I thought it would be easier to copy them in a first draft."

"Fair enough," Wilder said easily. "Give me an hour or two to mull it over, and I'll see if I can improve it." He lit a Lucky Strike cigarette and accepted coffee from me.

I returned to my desk and my stack of letters. What a waste of time, I thought. I'd been promised useful work once I'd gone through the glut of incoming mail, but every day my in-box was piled higher. I pored over photographs of tourists, of dowdy maiden aunts and suspected German collaborators for more than sixty hours a week. The texts were mostly gossip and revenge, amounting to nothing. Then I typed up orange five-by-seven cards, five carbons for each entry, and put them in boxes so "intelligence experts" could look them over. My fingers ached as badly as they had in the Baluty.

Why, if Germany wasted no time in putting conquered Poles to work, was America unable to harness more volunteers, I wondered? Why couldn't someone come in to free me from this tedium? Why couldn't I be assigned interesting work, work that would give me a chance to go home?

The morale of the people working with me could not have been higher, however; I was the only one impatient and depressed. We were fighting the Japs and the Nazis. The government pay wasn't bad. There were no time clocks or supervisors breathing down our necks. We were shoulder to shoulder with such propagandists as Robert Sherwood and Thornton Wilder and Stephen Vincent Benét. Why shouldn't they be happy? They didn't have relatives in the camps.

But this was not the job I'd flirted, pleaded, and fibbed to get. Why had they grilled me about the Jewish resistance in Warsaw if they intended to put me in an office? I'd been interviewed three times, and I'd made it seem that smuggling weapons into the ghetto and assassinating Egon Hildebrand had been my idea. The more preposterous my lies, the more they encouraged me to play a part in the liberation of Auschwitz—an assignment I'd have killed for. In the end, however, they banished me to this rabbit warren of gray cubicles in the Propaganda Division where they needed a Polish secretary.

Above my desk hung a poster of a giant roseate ear beneath a bloody question mark. *Sshhh. The Enemy Is Listening.* I snatched up a ringing telephone wearily. Perhaps the enemy would hear Mr. Sherwood ask me to run down for another pack of Lucky Strikes.

"Mia? It's Vinnie."

I was startled. He rarely called me at work. "Is everything okay?"

"Okay? It's the berries!"

"The what?"

"It means great. Swell. In fact, it couldn't be better. I've just come from a job interview and I've got great news. Have you had lunch?"

"I don't usually go out for lunch. There's too much work."

"Maybe you can let them fight the war for an hour without you."

I couldn't deny that I longed to be in the sunshine with the man I loved. "Meet me in front of the statue of Atlas."

"It's a deal."

I told Mr. Sherwood where I was going and reached into my pocketbook for a compact. The face looking back at me shone with pleasure.

I leaned against the granite wall and looked up at the giant statue of Atlas as he rested on one bent knee straining to lift the world. His burden didn't appear so very heavy, and his face was emotionless and cold. With a wrench of my heart, I imagined how Jozef would have criticized this casting—my brother, the critic.

I pictured him as a prisoner in Auschwitz, gaunt and frail. Had his

blond hair turned gray? Were his smooth hands gnarled and cal-
loused? Even with daily summaries from the European front, Americans didn't care about the fate of the prisoners. Without nightmares
to remind them, they were growing apathetic.

I must stop thinking about him I told myself and from my purse
pulled out a slim biography of Franz Liszt in French, which Vinnie
had given me on Valentine's Day. It would undoubtedly mollify him
if he found me bent over his gift.

I straightened my wool scarf and brushed back unpinned wisps of
hair. My stomach growled, ready for the sweets he invariably brought.

A shadow fell over the pages of my book. Feigning annoyance, I
look up, expecting to see him. But it was an army officer, a captain.
He was tall and slender and his eyes were concealed beneath the
shadow of his cap.

"I see you're reading French. Do you write it, too?"

I glanced for Vinnie in the crowd, but the man blocked my view.
"Yes, I was educated in Paris. Please excuse me. I'm waiting for a
friend."

"I'm afraid that'll have to wait, Miss Levy. I'm Captain Howard.
Bob told me I'd find you here. I've got a cab waiting. Colonel Bickwith is waiting."

Who was this man and who was Colonel Bickwith? "I'm sorry,
captain," I said coldly. "*You're* the one who'll have to wait. Someone is
meeting me here."

He lowered his voice. "Colonel Bickwith wants to know more
about your work in Poland. About what you saw at Auschwitz. And
this isn't the place to discuss it. We need personnel with your expertise in the Foreign Section downtown. We'll get you a limited security
clearance by tomorrow."

Was it really what I wanted, or just a change of venue to do more
paperwork? Probably the latter, though I felt a tingle of anticipation.
Would this be my means to get out? To begin my search for Papa and
Jozef? He held out his arm, but I followed without taking it. In the

passing blur of office workers, I scanned frantically for Vinnie. There was still time for him to appear and me to explain.

"Don't worry," Captain Howard said, holding open the door of a checkered cab. "If he's any kind of an American, he'll understand."

Colonel Bickwith was a tanned, polished man with a no-nonsense manner. He explained that he worked for a division of the Intelligence Department, and his questions were brief but incisive: When had I left Poland? How had I escaped? What was the real name of the man known as Wolf? Where was he now? ("Dead," I replied, fighting back sudden tears.) What had we seen at Auschwitz? Why was I so anxious to do work involving that awful place? Was I prepared to go back to Poland if necessary?

I answered honestly, concealing none of my eagerness, and Bickwith must have been impressed for he told me to report here tomorrow morning and that he would clear my transfer with Sherwood.

I left feeling euphoric and raced for a phone. Vinnie's voice was harsh when he heard my voice.

"Please forgive me," I begged. "Try to understand. It wasn't my fault. You were late and the captain didn't want to wait. He had orders to take me downtown. But oh, Vinnie—wait till you hear—"

"The *captain*? What are you talking about? Where did you go?"

"To a meeting. I'm to do special work."

"How was I supposed to know? You just left me flat." He paused. "Ah, what's the use? I never see you anymore anyway. This fucking war—"

"You mean you don't want to see me?" My arms were suddenly cold.

"Of course I do."

"I'm so afraid I'll lose you!" Yes, afraid. What if I was sent abroad? Much as I wanted it, would I be gone forever? Could he wait?

"You said you had no choice."

"I didn't. And now I'm afraid you'll hate me. I couldn't bear that."

"Are you free tonight?"

"Yes." It might be my last free night. But I wouldn't tell him until I was sure.

"Then meet me at Parkside Avenue. The Circle. Eight o'clock."

Eight o'clock. I said "Yes," but if Bickwith gave me different orders I wouldn't make it. Maybe it wouldn't happen, I reassured myself. What could he possibly have in mind?

Vinnie was waiting when I arrived and threw his arms around me as if he were drowning and I was a life preserver. "Where are we going?" I asked when we untangled our bodies and our mouths.

"To the highest point in Brooklyn."

I knew what he meant: Lookout Mountain in Prospect Park. We had been there often last summer, watching the rowers on Prospect Lake below and listening to the Goldman Band on Sunday afternoons. Tonight, of course, in the middle of a March night, it would be deserted.

"I forgot a blanket, but it's warm," he said. "I thought we'd sit on the hill and talk."

It was in fact chilly, but I didn't care. "I'd like that."

We walked the winding paths to the top in peaceful silence. I never knew anyone who was more comfortable with silence than Vinnie, with all his ebullience and enthusiasm; no one was more respectful of my own. When we got settled, I sat with my arms hugging my knees and let Vinnie massage my shoulders. The lights of Brooklyn twinkled in the distance. They reminded me of the lycée, of concerts and cafés, of long-lost friends.

"You miss the past, don't you?" he asked, sensing my mood.

"The long-lost past. How could I not? It was wonderful for a while. But if I had stayed in Paris, how would I have met you?" I sighed, filled with melancholy. "How does one weigh such things?"

He kissed me on the back of my neck.

"You remind me of myself when I was back there," I said.

"How so?"

"I wanted to be a concert pianist. I was just as ambitious as you are."

"And now?"

"I still want to play, but I don't believe I ever will."

He turned me so that I was facing him and touched my cheeks which were wet with tears. "What's wrong?" he asked.

My heart held a sadness wide as the ocean. "We're so different. You have a safe life, you don't know what it means to suffer, you have parents you go home to if you need them, you have sunlight ahead of you while I have shadows."

From the way he looked at me, I knew he didn't understand. I struggled to find the words "—You're so *American!*"

He laughed. "It's not my fault."

"Oh my darling, it's not a criticism! I love it that you're young, that you're American, that you're *you.*"

He drew me to him and we hugged, my head against his chest, his warmth. "You must never leave me," I whispered. "Never. No matter where I am, even if I'm far away, promise you'll be with me."

"Of course," he said softly. "You're my love, my life. In a little while, when I have money, we'll get married."

A "little while" was too long, I knew, but I did not correct him.

"I've got a job," he said. "In Mr. Schlesinger's company. That's what I was going to tell you at lunch. That's my news. A steady salary. I'll save it all. We can be married by next year!"

"Not next year, no. When the war's over. When I come back."

He held me at arm's length. "Where in the world would you be going?"

"To Europe. To Poland."

"When?" The word was a howl.

"I'm not sure. But soon. It's my new assignment, why I wasn't there at lunch. I've asked for it, begged for it, but now that it's come . . ." I hurled myself back into his arms. "Now that it's come, I don't know if I can stand it!"

He led me to a grove of trees where it was darker and more private. We lay on the grass and kissed again and again while I ran my fingers through his hair and his hands began their familiar exploration. We could not wait to undress but devoured each other, our passion unparalleled, and for the last time we were one.

The following day, Colonel Bickwith told me I was going to England and then Paris. I spoke Polish, German, French, English: invaluable. In Paris, I would become a member of an invisible army, the underground. I was to tell no one I was going. As far as Ceena and Martin and Vinnie were concerned, Colonel Bickwith would tell them I was on a special assignment for the U.S. government.

BOOK III

CHAPTER 19

"*Get up. Quickly!*" a gravelly voice bellowed. I opened my eyes to the blinding light of a bare overhead bulb and tasted bile in my throat. Rough hands tore at my covers, ripped at my nightgown, slapped me awake.

I protested, first in English, then in German, trying to orient myself. The last thing I remembered was walking in a Midlands field toward a meeting with my partners Roger and Poincare, the other two members of our squad of three. Two soldiers in German uniforms had approached—I almost asked them if they wanted to buy cigarettes—and without warning attacked me. One had held me while the other placed an ether-soaked rag over my face, and everything went black. Now I found myself in this foul room, helpless, a prisoner. But who were these soldiers? How did they get past the English patrol? How had they found me? How did they know I was their enemy?

The two soldiers were the ones who awakened me. "Grab your coat and don't try anything," the older one said. "Kurt here would as soon slit you from your cunt to your neck as take you in for interrogation. Understand?"

I nodded and reached for my coat which someone, in an excess of tidiness, had hung from a coatrack in the corner of the room. My change purse lay on a table next to the bed and I picked that up, too, fearful they had opened it. I shuddered at the thought of the cyanide-laden candy coin it contained. It was too late now to take it.

"Move!" the older German said. "Let's see how long it takes before Kurt makes you sing."

My name is Odette LeClerc. Father, Paul, a farmer. Mother, Noe Trinkmann, Alsatian. I'm twenty-one years old, from a village outside Strasbourg. A greengrocer's assistant. I came to England several months ago, looking for work. . . .

That's all I told them, no matter how loudly the older German yelled or how menacing the threats of the younger. They would not know I was working for the British government, or that my code name, chosen by me, was Songbird.

My training in the Midlands had only lasted one week and it was exhausting. Just four of us, and I was the only woman. At first the men looked at me strangely. Here I was—young, slim, and not that strong—but slowly they began to accept me. I had never handled a gun or a knife before and I thought how my parents would react if they saw me. When I first fired a pistol I thought that I had broken my wrist, and when I used a rifle the recoil almost shattered my shoulder. I quickly learned how to use each weapon. I recoiled at using a knife as a weapon, but when I thought about why I was here with my own life in jeopardy, I learned fast. This ancient form of self-defense was exciting, and this is where I excelled.

The interrogation room was dim. Two spotlights were turned on my face as I sat in a straight-backed wooden chair, bound at the wrists and ankles. My temples pounded until I thought my skull would burst. So far they had inflicted no physical pain, and I didn't know how long I could hold out if they did. They knew about Roger and Poincare. Had they too been captured, and had they given me up? Was I resisting for nothing?

"We have an expert in interrogation," the older soldier said. "I'll go get him." His cruel smile indicated how pleased he was at the prospect, and he left the room, closing the door behind him. Kurt, too, seemed anxious for the next level of questioning to begin.

Think of Auschwitz, I told myself. *Think of the Baluty. You can't give in to the Nazis. Not so long as there's still a chance to liberate the camps, to find Papa and Jozef.*

The door creaked open. I averted my eyes, not wanting to see the face of my torturer.

"Splendid, splendid," Colonel Will Johnston's voice said. "Really, quite satisfactory. For a moment there, I thought you'd slip and expose Poincare."

A setup! They were testing me! If my hands had been free at that moment, I'd have torn out Johnston's eyes. I was angry at him, and even angrier at my American recruiters, who had turned me over to their British counterparts, explaining that I could be more effective in their more sophisticated operation.

"I exposed no one," I managed through dry and cracking lips.

"Quite right. Sorry to have doubted you, but we had to make sure."

"Sorry for what? The drugs? For ripping my clothes? For scaring the hell out of me?"

He shrugged. "We had to make certain you wouldn't crack."

"So you drugged me and had me kidnapped by Nazi officers?"

Kurt bowed. "Not quite Nazis. I'm Ted Shaw."

"And I," said the older man, who had come in behind Johnston, "am Maurice Alexander."

They were so obviously pleased with themselves that my anger faded. They were right to test me, I thought. After all, when I finished my training and we were on our own in occupied territory, they needed someone who would be strong if she couldn't get to the cyanide in time.

Johnston dismissed my captors and untied my bonds. "Really," he said, "I *am* sorry. If it's any comfort, we've played the same trick on Roger and Poincare, and they held just as firm as you did."

Good. If we were to work together—

"We've been compromised," Johnston said, pulling up a chair next to mine. "The Germans have broken the code we've used from Paris. Madeleine, who runs a brothel in Paris, is a major source of information. Her clientele are some of the top officers in the German Army. Madeleine's transmitting 'hand' doesn't agree with our files. The Germans have been sending messages to us through her set—misleading messages—maybe for as long as three months."

I felt blood drain from my cheeks. Had Madeleine's set dropped agents into the hands of the Gestapo? "You're sure they captured her code books?" I asked.

"Or else were given them. But not by Madeleine, I'm sure. If she were a traitor, she'd know for sure that we'd catch her."

"Then who? And why are you telling me this now?"

"Because you're going to tell us who. Someone in the French Section is betraying us. By now they may know the names of half the operatives in Operation Sphinx. We've been compromised. Tomorrow night there'll be a Lysander at the airstrip waiting to drop the three of you in France. I'm not privy to where, but it'll be close to Paris."

My heart jolted. "But I haven't finished my wireless training."

"Poincare will do the transmitting. Roger will be the coordinator with other circuits. Your job will be to get information. If you can find out who's betrayed us, fine. But we need information on German weapons and personnel, too. The three of you are authorized to bypass our Paris Section. You'll transmit directly to London."

Poincare. I didn't trust the unctuous little man with his weasel eyes and the accent I couldn't place. And I couldn't tell about Roger. I couldn't tell if he was American or British, but he was almost too competent, too sure of himself. "Do you trust them?" I asked.

"No more than I trust you. Not because I think any of you are traitors, it's just that I'm not sure that you've had enough training. God, I scarcely trust my dog when he's off the leash. And once the Lizzie leaves the tarmac, it's out of my hands. That's why I'm asking you to consider backing out. It's not too late, Odette. And there's no disgrace in it. The Allies have lots of uses for a woman with your language skills. You're no good to us dead. Think about it. I understand that each of us has reasons for fighting the war, but—"

"Not the war. The Nazis. If you knew what they did to my family, to me, you'd be on that plane, too."

"I do know," he said. "And I realize that going to France gets you one step closer to finding out about your family. But you might be asked to do things that will make you sick. It's not like target practice here at the manor. It's easy to kill, Odette. People get used to it. A knife drawn up under the ribs, a severed aorta, a sharpened point between the first vertebra and the skull. It's addictive."

A nice addiction if it meant Nazi ribs and Nazi necks. "What are you afraid of? That I'll be squeamish? I don't think you need worry on that score." True, I couldn't have killed Egon, but he was somebody I knew and liked. Wolf had no hesitation. Now that he was dead, I'd become the female Wolf. "I won't change my mind," I said.

"Well, that's it, then." Johnston placed a large grainy photograph in my hand. An arrogant German looked back at me, one who might have been leaning against the hood of his father's Talbot in the courtyard of the lycée, waiting for one of my classmates. His face bore the finely chiseled effeminate features of the aristocracy, that and a petulant smile. I hated his type at school. I'd have no qualms killing this one.

"His name is Franz Jozef Behrenson. Named for the Austrian emperor," Johnston said. But killing wasn't what Johnston had in mind. "You're going to get very friendly with this man," he said.

I recoiled. "Meaning I'll have to go to bed with him?"

He shrugged.

"Has a meeting been arranged between him and me?"

"No. But he's a man, you're a very attractive woman. You'll figure it out."

"What if he isn't interested?"

"You mean, if he's queer? He isn't, believe me."

"Why him?" I asked.

"Because we need information. Behrenson is military intelligence, stationed in Paris, attached to von Rundstedt's Western Army command. He might lead you to the traitor in our French operation. But more, we need to find out about a new weapon, one Hitler's been saying will annihilate England overnight. Your primary work will be as a courier, to be used by the Resistance as they see fit and to follow their orders. But Behrenson"—he paused—"Behrenson's *our* main objective. You'll have to find the time to seduce him."

I was transfixed by the photograph. By remembering my family, I thought, maybe I can sleep with him. Still, my flesh crawled. "But I know nothing about weapons. Surely there's an engineer . . ." But if this brought me closer to my father and Jozef I could do anything.

"We're not after technical information. Just a location. And names, addresses. We have reason to believe that components of the weapon are being produced in Poland, at a factory near Auschwitz."

Then there could be no question about my acquiescence, and he knew it. "Do you intend to send me there?"

"No, but the Germans might. Berenson might. How you play it is up to you. Just before you leave, you'll be briefed by Captain Czweni-akowski. He'll tell you the best route to Paris and what you're likely to encounter along the way. But from the moment you set down in France, we've never heard of you. Your personnel dossier will be expunged from the section files. You'll not be allowed to write a letter, contact a friend, do *anything* except be Odette LeClerc, German sympathizer who likes good-looking officers."

Johnston seemed to sink into himself, avoiding my eyes, gazing nervously at the picture in my hand. What was he waiting for? Was there something left unsaid? He stood. "Dismissed." He held out his hand. I rose and saluted, then shook his hand.

He pulled me toward him and wrapped his arms around me. "For God's sake take care of yourself," he said, hugging me tightly.

As though he never expects to see me again, I thought. As though he was sending me to my death.

That night, I wrote a long letter to Vinnie, which of course I would not be allowed to send. I wrote it therefore not for him but for me, reminding myself that I was still capable of love and that love existed on the other side of the ocean. I had disappeared from him and could imagine his hurt. Still, maybe he would be waiting when I got back—if the war had not swallowed him as it was most likely to do. I poured out my feelings, expressed what lay deepest in my heart. Vinnie wanted what was possible in a reasonable world: family, music, love. I wanted those things, too, and for a brief moment had had them. He hadn't yet looked into the face of evil or felt the rancid breath of humiliation on his neck. He hadn't seen things that made people pray for death. But I had, and I would extract as much vengeance as I could before death overtook me.

I ended the letter simply: "I love you." Then I went outside and burned it, holding it until the fire singed my fingers.

I pulled my collar tight and took a last sip of hot chocolate. Up ahead lights filled the interior of the cockpit, pinpoints of yellow, green, and red. Outside, where the icy air raced over the wings, it was black.

Shortly, Roger, Poincare, and I would be dropped into the Brie district, there to go off on our various assignments. Visibility, we'd been told, was less than two kilometers.

I gave up scanning for the triangle of flashlight beams that would mark Operation Sphinx's reception committee. Sitting beside me, Roger, our leader, offered a cigarette. When I refused he cupped his hand around a match and lit one for himself. He coughed. "Gaulois. Jesus, they're likely to take your throat out."

"Get used to them," I said. "There are no Benson and Hedges in Paris."

Poincare, our other comrade, knelt in the corner. From the moment we met I did not like him. I felt I couldn't depend on him under any circumstances. He looked like a curled-up snake ready to strike at anyone. He looked treacherous—and must have excelled at garroting.

The engines cut back and the Lysander tilted forward, plunging through the cloud cover. "Drop lights" flashed through the fuselage, and my excitement gave way to terror. I was an excellent parachutist in England, but we were in France and there were dangers everywhere, as Captain Czweniakowski explained during our briefing.

He was Polish, and I had a chance to ask him about the Auschwitz Camp District. His reports were troubling. He knew of the Buna factory, where the new weapon might or might not be produced. He was aware of hidden transmitters, secret storehouses, the movement of German troops in and out of the district. The only thing he did not know was the condition of the Jews inside the camp; he had been unable to answer my questions about how many there were and where they were located. He believed they were kept separated from the other inmates and had been unable to organize any resistance. But he didn't care about the Jews. His concern was to win back his Motherland.

The port door slid open and frigid air hammered the cabin. "Won't be long now," Roger shouted over the din of the propellers. "Wish we could bloody see something."

I started to answer, but my eye caught Henri Poincare, slipping something glistening in the side pocket of his overall.

"Roger, look out! He's got something in his pocket," I cried.

Roger reacted instantly. "What the bloody hell is that?"

Poincare shrugged. "Just a little keepsake." He had a slight sibilance in his speech.

"Keepsake my ass. You trying to get us killed? I didn't trust you before, Poincare, and this doesn't change my mind. You've got two second to produce it before—"

Poincare glared at him. "Bugger off."

Roger lunged at him. In an instant there was a stiletto in Poincare's hand. Roger drew back, the knife a few inches from his jugular.

"Relax," Poincare said. He took the glistening object from his pocket: an antenna wire looped and strung with white beads. "See, it's nothing. A rosary," the little man spat bitterly. "I was scared, all right? Needed comfort. Now get your fucking hand off me and get ready to jump."

Roger studied the beads suspiciously. "Sorry, old man. Can't be too careful. It's my job. No hard feelings." He held out his hand, but Poincare refused to take it.

I was confused by what I'd seen. Something seemed out of joint. But there was no time to reflect on it, for the pilot was making his final approach. Roger squatted by the howling door in the fuselage. *"Now,"* barked a voice, and the jumpmaster tipped Roger headfirst into the airstream.

My turn next, I thought, watching Poincare vanish, my heart fluttering crazily. Why couldn't I make out any lights below? The forest looked too flat, not as I remembered the Brie country from a weekend excursion from the lycée. But it was too late to turn back. A hand pressed against my back, helping me over the last refusal of my muscles to obey my brain's command. Air surged around me. I arched backward, watching the plane shoot upwards and out of sight.

I swung my body around in the darkness. The ground seemed ominously close. I was falling too fast! I pulled the parachute ring and felt a reassuring tug. Above me, canvas spread out between me and the night. I was jerked skyward and I grinned insanely. Then my boots spanked against the earth and I tumbled forward. Earth and sky merged. I tasted mud and sprang up to release the chute.

"Vous avez vue un cheval gris, mademoiselle?" a voice asked from the darkness.

"Non. Le cheval est noir," I answered.

Then, silence.

I assembled my spade and burrowed into the earth, yanking out roots and scanning the blackness for my comrades. They couldn't have gone far, yet I could see or hear nothing. I folded the chute and dropped it into the shallow grave along with my jumpsuit. When I stood, a sharp pain rippled through my right leg—*my good leg!*—but I ignored it and tamped down the earth.

I scanned the misty patch of ground on which I'd landed. A lawn! In the distance, I could make out stands of poplars. I had missed the forest and instead arrived in civilization. Gradually I could make out the silhouette of a massive house. In the stillness, I could hear voices.

Frightened, I crept toward the gurgle of a stream behind a thicket. I plunged my head into the water, and a burst of adrenaline shook me out of my confusion. I washed the dirt from my hands and face, then moved toward the house along the perimeter of a garden. Whoever had greeted me with the password had disappeared. I was on my own.

Voices. Speaking French and German. As I approached a gatepost, I caught sight of black limousines parked around an enormous horse-shoe drive and back toward the sweep of lawn. Lights were burning bright in the house, a touring car spun around the gate, heading in my direction. I dove back into the thicket and held my breath.

The car doors opened and a German soldier's drunken voice boomed out across the lawn. Two other soldiers got out and both walked in my direction. Had they spotted me? Was I to be killed or captured just minutes into my mission?

My fingers tore at the clasp of my purse, and I searched for the cyanide-laden coin, feeling less fear than disappointment. The foot-steps paused, and over the gurgle of the stream I heard the splash of urine in the bushes beside me. "To the glorious Franco-Aryan union," a soldier bellowed.

"To the ass of our hostess," the other said.

"Quiet, idiot," said the first. "What if someone hears us?"

"Then we'll fuck them or shoot them, depending on their sex."

They got back in the car and it lurched toward the front of the house. All went quiet again. I was alone, cowering in the bushes.

Fool, I thought. I should have accepted Johnston's offer and stayed in England. The idea that I was face-to-face once more with Nazis appalled me. They had just as much power; they could destroy me as they had my family; I was crazy to think I could fight them in any way.

I had no idea where I was. Were Roger and Poincare nearby? What if Operation Sphinx had betrayed us to the Gestapo? That someone knew the password meant nothing; it could have been learned through torture. How far was I from Paris? I might be better off hiding in the woods for a few days, then showing up at the emergency safe house in Paris—if I could get there.

One car engine started up and then another. Whatever was going on in the great house was ending. I could smell my own fear. Nerves stretched to the breaking point, I crouched down in the bushes then crawled off to lie down like a wounded animal.

"Vinnie," I whispered, and then again, "Vinnie."

I knew I would never see him again. Mia Levy no longer existed.

CHAPTER 20

$\mathcal{I}$'d already waited too long; the sun was coming up. If we'd been betrayed the Germans would be after me. Obviously, they would be all over the region.

I took a deep breath and bolted for the gate, rushing onto a broad roadway. I could make out lights glinting behind a line of darkened town houses on the deserted street. Clearly, I'd landed in some suburban area in which the great house was the showpiece.

Warily I walked on, straining to make out the sounds of human life. I moved as Wolf had taught me, swiftly, eyes downcast, face turned away from full view. A kiosk sprouted signs in German pointing in a half dozen directions, but before I had a chance to read them, fog lights cast a beam on my face like cat's eyes. I felt a surge of adrenaline; a car pulled over and waited. I bent over, retied my shoe, and scanned the road behind me. The car moved on.

Another set of lights appeared, and a truck went by me with a roar. I started walking again, tamping down hysteria. My destination was the Paris safe house, where I could rejoin the operation, but which way was Paris? A panel truck overtook me, then pulled over. "You there," the driver yelled. I had no choice but to stop for him.

He was a Wehrmacht soldier, but his face was kind. Another truck pulled up behind him, then another and another—a convoy. "We're going to Paris," the driver said. "Want a ride?"

"Thank you very much, sir," I said, climbing into the passenger seat as casually as possible. Soldiers in the back of the truck whistled and cheered. At least there was only one of them in the cab. His arm shot out toward the stick shift beside my thigh, and I jumped. But he was only shifting gears and off we went. He's only a sergeant, I told myself. I'd sold cigarettes to his comrades in Three Crosses Square.

"You speak German?" he asked.

"Only a little, monsieur."

"Then I'll try French. It's a pretty language and I could use the practice." He took in my bruised lips and torn sweater. There was a hint of compassion in his expression, but not the protectiveness I'd been able to rely on as a schoolgirl.

I smiled, crossed my arms under my breasts, and allowed my fingers to play with my hair, pretending shyness. "Have you been in France long?" I asked.

"Not long enough. Paris is a wondrous city, so much to do and see . . . Shit! What's this? Another road check. It's all a man can do to breathe. Every time you piss, you have to do it triplicate . . . No, don't laugh. It's true. Here I am with a beautiful girl in my truck and . . . you'd better duck down when we get to the checkpoint. Hide under my jacket. If they see your bruises, I'll be in trouble."

I dropped under the dashboard and felt the truck stop. "What seems to be the problem, Captain?" the sergeant asked out the window.

"I do not speak German," the guard said. "But you understand French, yes? "

So it was a French checkpoint. I'd half a mind to jump out and throw myself on the guard's mercy, but surely he was a collaborator and I'd be turned over to the Gestapo.

"No, I don't understand, you mealy excuse for a cop. Here are my papers. I've got orders to get to the Hotel de Ville."

"We're looking for—"

"I don't give a shit. We're in a hurry." He vaulted out of his seat and called to the driver behind him. "I've given him the manifest and our orders. I'll give him a minute to clear us. If he doesn't, then we drill him a new asshole. That's right: for attempting to obstruct a military exercise of the Wehrmacht."

The driver's bluster had its effect. The guard stamped the papers and let us through. "It's okay," the sergeant said. "You can come out now."

I edged up carefully and sank back into the cushion. I had avoided detection at the roadblock, but what or who had they been looking for? Me? Roger and Poincare? Was it possible that the wire Poincare used for his rosary was some kind of sending device? I scrunched down in my seat, more frightened than ever.

The truck traveled over cobblestones, and I looked out to see that we were in the outskirts of a city. I saw women in espadrilles and culottes with their hair tied in kerchiefs, bicycling across the intersections. Bobbing faces with neutral smiles swarmed around the truck as we moved along. No hatred of the German presence shone in their eyes. Even the Poles, for all their loathing of the Jews, rarely passed up the opportunity for an impertinent remark, a frown, or a gesture of disgust directed toward the New Masters. But these French were stolid as sheep.

"Where can I drop you?" the driver asked. "Believe me, you're the best thing I'm likely to see in this cab for some time. Tomorrow, we're heading east. Do you understand what that means?"

I nodded. There was fear and resignation in his eyes.

The Eastern Front. I made a mental note to memorize the corps insignia on the truck when I got out, and to count how many trucks there were in the convoy. Information to use in my first transmission.

"Can I see you again tonight?" He reached out to touch my arm. I shied away. "Please. I won't harm you. It's just that I'm lonely and this might be my last chance to see a woman in many months—if ever. I could pick you up at the Eiffel Tower. We'd go to dinner, take in a show. What do you say?"

Paris! Was it possible? Time to get out.

"I'm sorry," I said. "I'm married. You're very kind, but no." I pretended to recognize where I was, although the district was new to me. Neuilly, perhaps, or Courbevoie. Whatever: Paris. "If you could let me off here," I said.

With a look of regret, he stopped the car and I got out, smelling this beloved city once more, mingling with its pedestrians. A moment later, I fumbled in my pocket for one of the Metro tickets I'd been issued, and slipped through the turnstile into the teeming station.

The Metro map was familiar. Porte de Clignancourt, Rivoli, Raspail. Every name brought back memories, street scenes, dates with Jean-Phillipe. Had I really been afraid to ride the Metro alone back then? How long three years seemed! I felt the vestige of that naive girl within me, anxious to be accepted, to seem sophisticated. There was music then, and joy.

The train passed the stop for the Lycée LaCourbe-Jasson. How my classmates would marvel at the changes in me! Celeste with her pride in the voluptuousness of her figure; Janine with her tales of Egypt and Russia; Nanette who lectured us on the techniques of petting.

But "Odette" had not been trained in England and dropped behind enemy lines to go back to brag to her old schoolmates. In all probability, they had all achieved their goals by now, marriages of substance.

I rode for a while longer, trying to decide where to go. It was two days before we were supposed to rendezvous at Juliette's, the safe house, and make contact with Gilbert, our Resistance leader. To arrive early would increase the dangers to everyone. Obviously our carrier plane had strayed off course, landing us too close to Paris, but what did that mean for Roger or Poincare? Had they been captured? Made to talk?

Until I could learn exactly what had happened, it seemed best to stay as far from the safe house as I could.

In the meantime, the thousands of francs I'd brought for the Resistance and the transmitter crystals sewn into the hem of my skirt had to be hidden somewhere. But where? With a rush of pleasure I had my answer: With Jean-Phillipe Cadoux! Given his mother's social prominence, it was probable that the Nazis would not have dared to deport his family.

I could imagine Jean-Phillipe's face when I showed up at his door. If anyone could keep me entertained for a few days it was he. Perhaps there was still an opera. Perhaps he still had tickets.

Perhaps he was no longer home, or married—or maybe he had been killed.

I'd have to buy some clothes before I saw him—a torn skirt and sweater would hardly suffice. I'd get off at the Palais Royale stop and find a store—and eat something, for I realized I was starved. After weeks of horrid tea with horse treacle, maybe French coffee wouldn't taste so bad. And a roll or croissant would be a feast.

By the time I became aware of the young woman beside me, it was too late. Her open hand flew through the air and slammed into my jaw with a stinging slap. "Whore!" she screamed. "I saw you get out of that truck. Did just the driver have you, or all the soldiers in back as well?"

Was she trying to get herself crippled? I could have broken her arm, even killed her, but I realized we both hated the Germans and she did not understand my situation, so I let her go. Around us, the passengers maintained the same smiles their countrymen had displayed in the suburbs.

Paris had grown dangerous. Best not to notice anything.

I emerged into blinding morning sunlight at the Royale station. Swastikas and Reich banners flapped over museum entrances, cafés, and hotel porticos. German directional arrows were everywhere. In their arrogance, the Nazis had left off any French directions from the signs. It wouldn't be long, my trainers said, before I'd recognize them at a glance. Like so many notes on a scale, all this information would be vital to Intelligence.

Ahead a line was forming. As nine o'clock began to toll on church bells from half a dozen steeples, a door flew open and one by one the Parisians in line filed into the shop: servants in starched black dresses, local merchants, businessmen—even a dowager wearing pearl earrings and a moth-eaten fur stole.

The shop was a patisserie, and a gilt sign in the étagère announced the name of the owners and its list of specialty cakes and petits fours. SPECIAL CAKE DAY a sign announced, meaning there was real cake to be had. My stomach growled angrily. Not yet, I told it, reminding myself how long Mia Levy had gone without bread in the Baluty. But my stomach won out, and I joined the line, treating myself to an apricot tart that tasted of France—the best food in the world.

I wandered around the Palais du Louvre, waiting for dress shops to open on the Left Bank and looking for a place to buy a cup of coffee in the meantime. All the aromas of chicory and fresh croissants and ripened cheese were gone, replaced by the acrid smell of acorn coffee. Off in a corner of one *terrasse,* however, a group of German soldiers were hunched over real coffee, fresh bread and butter, and canned meat rations.

They noticed me walking by. "Bonjour, mademoiselle," a voice called. Out of the corner of my eye I saw twin SS lightning bolts on his collar.

"Would you like to join us for breakfast? Real bread, not that sawdust stuff. And butter and cheese. Good coffee."

"Don't pay any attention to him," another SS man hissed in German. "He's just trying to get laid."

"Shut up, idiot! She understands German. Look how red her cheeks are getting."

"Not a chance. I'll show you." He got up and strolled toward me until he blocked my way. I planted the gray French smile on my lips and kept going.

"Fräulein," he urged with a broad sweep of his cap. "I'd like to prove something to my ignorant companions. No! Wait a minute. You're not getting by just yet." He held my arm and escorted me toward the table. "Do you understand me when I tell you how lovely you must look with your petticoat loose and your garter belt around your ankles below your naked ass dancing in front of a mirror?"

It was easy for me to smile noncommitally at the laughing faces around me.

"Do you know what? I'd like to lie with my mouth beneath your cunt while you bounce up and down to a Suppé march. Sound like fun?"

Hardly. I never liked Suppé. *"Bonjour"* I shrugged, backing out of his grasp and smiling at the rest of the officers. I hurried around the corner, walking straight-backed and proud, but when they were out of sight I began to cry. For I was back in Poland, the Germans having every right to say what they wanted, humiliate me at their pleasure, treat me like offal.

No! Odette LeClerc would not cry as Mia had. I was no longer an innocent with no defenses. I reminded myself of my Midlands training, of my skill with a knife and garrote, a rock or a belt. These, not tears, would be my woman's weapons.

When I thought of the German soldier I imagined it was *his* skull I shattered with a stone, *his* eyes I gouged out in the restaurant with a soup spoon. Even as he stood before me, I'd been aware of the point of his ribs I could shatter with a kick, or the beating of his heart I could cut short with a stiletto. If anything, his desire only weakened him, made him more vulnerable. It was almost fun to stand there, picturing the hundred ways I could attack him, all the while betraying no emotion, no sign that I understood.

I would not need Vinnie as my protector, only as my love. For now, there was only survival and revenge. Every piece of information transmitted, every Resistance fighter saved, every bridge destroyed or German officer assassinated, would bring the Allies closer to liberating Auschwitz. Would Vinnie be among them? I was sure he would.

So I vowed to outlast the Germans, to push back the frailty of my soul, the weariness of too many miles traveled, too many countries occupied, too many deaths. Here in Paris I could feel myself reawakening to my mission. I had grown complacent in Brooklyn. Once more my enemy had a face and a body.

I darted into a clothing store and bought a dress and overcoat, holding my breath while the proprietor inspected the serial numbers on my francs for German pinholes or other marks.

The transmitter crystals pressed against my knee, the money belt chafed my raw skin. I would have to leave them at Jean-Phillipe's, if I found him at his old address, until the rendezvous. The woman behind the counter looked up at me, then again perused the list of counterfeit bills. I watched her eyes behind their bifocals freeze halfway down the list, then race back and forth between the sheet and the bills I'd handed her. Finally, she handed me my change.

"Thank you, madame." Her smiled revealed nothing. Had she seen something on that bill? If so, what would her next move be? A call to the Gestapo? A conference with her husband in the back?

My capture would cost the Allies four crystals, a transmitter, and three million francs. I studied a slender pair of shears near the cash drawer. It would be easy to plunge it through her thin cotton sweater into her skin just below her left breast. Then, with a twist . . .

"Is there something else I can help you with?"

"No thank you, madame."

"Good day."

"Good day."

I hurried out to the sidewalk, sweat drenching my neck and back, appalled at my thoughts and my fears. Paranoia attacked me in waves, impairing my judgment and my ability to function, making the act of murder seem sweet. How much more would it have taken to attack the shopkeeper with those scissors?

I went to a *pissoir* and changed into my new dress, leaving my old clothes behind me. Still saddled with my bag and my paranoia, I sped down narrow alleys with my eyes locked on the curb, fearing to look up lest I give myself away. I was alone and things were happening too fast. It was a feeling we had been warned about; they had promised it would pass.

Doubling around the block, I crossed the wide boulevard and headed toward Jean-Phillipe's apartment just off the Place de L'Opera. I paused only once, to gaze at the Hotel Steinfeld where Mama, Papa, and I had stayed five ears earlier when they delivered me to the lycée. The entrance to the hotel had been boarded up; maybe someday it would reopen. In this beautiful city of Paris, no doubt, the Nazi exterminating machine had destroyed most of the Jewish population. Odette LeClerc was not Jewish. Perhaps she could wreak some revenge before she was exterminated, too.

I stood before the dour scrutiny of the concierge at Jean-Phillipe's apartment, trying to exude the sort of confidence I wished I could internalize. Instead, I felt only the crone's impatience, her disdain for my hemline, my cheap dress, my lack of gloves or hat.

Noble by birth, now deprived of everything but her name, Madame Chanier de Taer held fierce sway in her duties as concierge. Five years ago she had denounced me as a slattern, blocking my entrance to the building until Jean-Phillipe had arrived to rescue me. Now the fear she had inculcated rose again.

"I'm here to see Monsieur Cadoux *fils*. My name is . . ." I paused for a moment. "Just tell him an old friend, Marisa, is here."

She did not remember me, or preferred not to, but she dialed Jean-Phillipe's apartment. She said a few indistinguishable words and then unlocked the elevator latch. "Four."

"Thank you," I called out cheerfully and entered the elevator.

Soon I would see him! My friend, my almost-lover, the first "boy" in my life, now replaced by one more precious. The floors slipped by slowly as the cage groaned upward. I remembered the odd tile work of the halls, the wrought iron balconies added in a fit of art nouveau, the windows with leaded glass, the walls of hewn rock with their stippled granite window frames, the skyscape of red tile and slate mansard roofs, and the distant bell towers—all bespoke a distant past.

It was giddying, this sudden surge of the familiar. And there he was! Jean-Phillipe peering down at the rising elevator with his familiar boyish impatience. I inspected his polished black leather Spanish boots—the kind prized by Allied aviators—then a pair of pleated Harris tweed pants, then a leather belt, white shirt, silk scarf around his neck.

He opened the elevator door. "Here you are then!" I expected a hug and readied myself for it, but all I received was a peck on both cheeks in the formal French style. "There've been many surprises in the last four years, but this is the biggest. How good to see you."

He's lying, I thought, and a tendril of fear snaked through my brain before I could deny it.

"Tell me," he asked, "have you missed your big brother?"

"Of course I have," I said. "I couldn't wait to see you again. But you didn't miss me, I'll bet."

He held me at arm's length. "I sent you off a little girl, and look what's happened. Turn around. My God, you've changed. It's been four years since your last letter—from that Polish resort. I thought you'd fallen off the ends of the earth."

I gazed at his anxious face. "You don't seem altogether pleased that I didn't."

"It's not that, Mia. It's just the shock of hearing you were downstairs when I thought I'd lost you forever. You might've called." He opened the apartment door.

"It would have been awkward," I said, stung by his coldness. "But I wanted to see you so much, so I decided to rush over here and surprise you."

"You succeeded. I'm astonished." He bolted the door behind us then disappeared for a moment, returning with a platter of sausage and fruit. It was all I could do to restrain myself from diving into it.

He caught my look. "Don't be polite, Mia. Eat. And tell me how you got back to Paris."

I bit into an apple; nothing had ever tasted so delicious. "We flew in," I said truthfully.

" 'We?' You mean your family's with you?"

"No. I haven't heard from them in almost three years. It's a night-mare in Poland now."

"And yet you managed to make it out. Forgive me, but that doesn't make sense. Who sent you here?"

I recoiled from his interrogation. This wasn't a police station. "No one."

"Then who's 'we'?"

"Please, Jean-Phillipe. I can't tell you any more. Besides, it would only . . ."

"What? Get me in trouble? But how do you expect me to help you if you won't dell me anything. You came here for help, no?"

"I'm alone, but I need a place to stay. Just for a couple of days."

I saw a flicker of revulsion cross his lips. Why? His expression hardened. "Please," I said.

"How many people saw you come into this building? Ten? Fifty?"

"Only the concierge." I knew I was pleading but couldn't help myself.

"Who had ample time to study your face. I don't suppose you understand what this could mean. Harboring you . . ."

"A Jew."

"All right, a Jew. You said it, I didn't. They could kill my family for doing it. Torture them. My mother is an old woman."

"How is she?" I asked, stupidly trying to win him over.

"As I say, old. My father's more or less under house arrest. They raided his apartment just as he was about to flee to the States. His fin-ancier friends kept my parents out of prison, but they're being watched. *I'm* being watched. The Germans despise us only the way a true bourgeoisie despises artists—and the rich. They envy us, so they love us and they hate us. We have to pay black market prices for everything we buy; the Germans think it's a form of patriotism, but I call it blackmail: pay or you die." He faced me squarely. "Have you had enough to eat?"

Without thinking, I'd finished off another apple and a banana. How pathetic I must have seemed to him.

"So you're telling me to leave?"

He paced agitatedly around the room, obviously thinking through his answer. When he spoke again, his tone was kind. "Don't be distressed. I won't leave you stranded. I've got to go out now, and I'll tell the concierge that you're my maid Nanette's new daughter-in-law. Nanette's in the country, visiting relatives for the day; she's sent you to do the housework. Tonight, when she returns, you'll have to go."

He was implacable despite his kindness. "I can't do that, Jean-Phillipe. I'm desperate."

"Just sign yourself into a pension. There's one on the corner. If it's a question of money, I'll pay."

"It's not money. What if they come looking for me?"

"If they do, tell them you're a friend of mine. There's a man I know in German military intelligence, a Colonel Becker. He protects me, he'll protect you."

"No," I said. "I can't leave. My life depends on staying."

He snorted and turned away in disgust. "You were always dramatic."

My anger flared. "Must you be so stupid? I was parachuted into France last night. If the Germans have caught my companions, then the entire Gestapo would be searching for me."

He stopped pacing, and a terrible silence settled over the room. He was a good man; I had loved him and he me. But when he looked at me now it was with loathing. "What happens to me if you're caught here?" he asked.

"Your Colonel Becker will protect you. Isn't that what you just told me? But last I heard my father and brother were inmates at Auschwitz—ever hear of it? Quite probably they're dead. And my mother is certainly dead. If the wind was right, her ashes might have fallen on the Place de L'Opera."

"Damn you for coming here," he snapped. "Why couldn't you have stayed in Poland until the war was over?"

"And how was that to happen?" I asked sarcastically.

"How do you think? The Germans have been waiting for the British to surrender for two years. Now they're tired and impatient.

Any week now, the Germans will deploy a weapon that will make the V-1 look like a toy. Don't give me such an astonished look! Everyone here's heard the rumors. You must have heard them, too. The moment England surrenders, America and Germany will attack Russia and leave France alone. Then we at least will be at peace, and then you and I can go back to the opera."

I was about to ask him more about this new weapon, but his intercom buzzed: the concierge calling from downstairs.

"Your suits have come from the cleaners," she said. "Do you want me to bring them up now, or are you still with that woman?"

"She's just leaving," Jean-Phillipe said. "I'll see her out and bring the suits up myself."

He hung up. "You'll have to go," he said, "at least for a little while. Check back late this afternoon, say four-thirty. Only this time, call. Maybe by then I'll have worked out a plan."

I had my own plan. One of the first things we learned in training was to do the unexpected. Very well. Jean-Phillipe expected me to call in the late afternoon. I would show up unannounced hours earlier. "Come very late or very early, or don't come at all," my instructor said. I would soon see the effect of his advice.

After Jean-Phillipe showed me out, I bought a copy of *Paris-Match* at a news kiosk with an excellent view of his building and pretended to read, all the while scanning the streets. Jean Phillipe went out. Two men entered his building and shortly exited. Jean Phillipe returned in no more than ten minutes, speeding like an overwound toy down the Rue Taitbout and through the front door. In my mind I saw him dashing up the spiral staircase with the antique elevator at its core. He always took the steps.

He would throw his long coat into the corner of his living room, sit, and puzzle out what to do about me. And I would give him a little more time to figure out his answer.

In a watchmaker's étagère, I saw a clock hand sweep through another fifteen minutes. Two-thirty. Why were all the bells of Paris silent? Jean-Phillipe would be furious to see me come back unannounced, but the war, after all, was not being conducted by rules of polite society. Surely now that he had had time to absorb the situation of his old school friend he would understand.

I folded the magazine under my arm and sauntered over to the building. Stepping through the entrance door, I stopped at the concierge's desk and rang the bell. The woman's wrinkled face scowled out at me, astonished, through the curtains behind her desk. She scoured the hallway for signs of life then snatched my wrist and dug her talons into it, pulling me behind the curtain and into the small room where she obviously lived. "My God," she said. "It's you they're looking for. They'll be back in a minute; your friend just returned. Come on now—Gaston, we have company."

"Good, good," a weak voice responded, and I turned to see a thin man lying on a wide, raised bed at the side of the room.

"Gaston, I'm pleased to present you to Mademoiselle . . ." The concierge paused, not knowing my name.

"Mia Levy," I said, fearing to use my assumed name, since Jean-Phillipe knew my real one.

"Indeed," the old lady said. "This is my uncle Gaston, Chevalier de La Toraine-Bressac. My name is Madame Chanier."

His name was almost as long as the arm he extended toward me. "Enchanted, mademoiselle." I took his hand, and the wizened man drew mine to his lips.

"Mademoiselle Levy will be a guest here for a little while."

I had no idea what she meant or why she made the offer, but I was impressed by her urgency, and she seemed to be on my side. It would have been easy for her to have turned me in.

The man grinned with delight and patted the bed next to him.

"You're incorrigible," Madame de Chanier said. "She'll stay *under* the bed, not on it." I stood, undecided. The woman pushed me to the floor. "Now crawl underneath the bed. Do as I say! Quickly! They'll be back any minute to search, I can promise you that. But they won't find you lying beneath the old man."

I slid under the bed and, reaching up, felt the hiding place, which had been carved out of the box spring. With one motion, I slid up a panel to reveal a space like a long, slender coffin.

"Hurry up and pull the panel back in place," the woman called in her harsh, drill sergeant's voice. "I can smell the Fritz a mile away, and they're closer than that. Now I must resume my duties. I'll be back toward evening with dinner. And don't worry about Gaston, Mademoiselle Levy. He's a good boy."

"Mmm-hmm," came the muffled assent from above me.

I curled up in the crate, the ancient bed creaked, and the chevalier hummed to himself, mumbled something, and then began to snore. I fell asleep myself without once thinking of Jean-Phillipe. Exhaustion and fear had caught up with me.

Perhaps an hour later I was awakened by the sound of hobnailed boots outside the door and orders barked by a furious German commander. "Search everything. Every closet and curtain. The entire apartment building. We'll find her. Colonel Becker says she's here."

I stopped breathing. The door opened, Gaston murmured a weary, "What do you want? There's no one here." A man knelt down next to the bed then, finding nothing, stood again.

"Upstairs," the commander barked. "She's here somewhere."

Colonel Becker had told him so. Well then, someone had told Colonel Becker. It was well past the time I would have returned to Jean-Phillipe, and he would have welcomed me in.

My adopted brother, the music-loving companion of my student day, my beloved Jean-Phillppe, had betrayed me.

CHAPTER 21

Three days later, I reluctantly left the safety of Madame de Chanier's apartment, thinking of how I was betrayed by a friend and saved by a woman who seemed to be my enemy. And I thought over and over of Vinnie, who would have died himself before giving me up, just as I would have died for him.

Or would he? Or would I? God knows what war does to one.

But now I was shaken. Fear is a disease that's hard to control; perhaps facing danger head-on, as I surely would when I started my assignment, would eventually inure me to it.

Children were racing back and forth along the Rue Jean Carrier. I dodged a steady flow of bicycles and pedestrians as I headed for the Champ de Mars, where the safe house was located. A boy with a patched soccer ball dribbled past me, staring insolently at my face, and I retreated to the far sidewalk. He was perhaps sixteen or seventeen, about my age when the war first came to Poland. He had the look of a wealthy, well-loved child. These were the people I would be risking my life to liberate. If the Levys hadn't been Jewish, perhaps I'd be wearing that smug smile, too.

The safe house was a nondescript flat in a small building on a busy avenue, the last place one might consider hiding fugitives. Poincare met me at the door, as rumpled and disinterested as ever, though he seemed surprised, not necessarily pleasantly, to see me alive.

"I radioed London that you were captured," he said matter-offactly. "When you didn't show up at any of the detention centers, you were presumed dead. I congratulate you for surviving."

"Where's Roger?" I asked.

"Dead."

No! My friend, my leader. Dead. "How?"

"I slit his throat." Poincare's tone was casual, but he was watching me closely.

My heart leapt in terror. If he had killed Roger, and admitted it, surely he'd kill me. What sort of "safe" house was this? I wanted to run, but I stayed rooted in the doorway, feeling the world go topsy-turvey.

"It was my assignment. Johnston's orders. It was he who betrayed Operation Sphinx the last time he was sent here. He arranged for misinformation to be sent to London."

I didn't believe him. "Why not kill him in England?"

"In England, the Nazis would know we were on to him. Far better to let them think one of them killed him in France by mistake. When he parachuted in." He shrugged. "Actually, I didn't kill him. He was already dead when I got to him. The trees did the job for me."

So he had only been testing me.

"But what if he was innocent?"

"Then an innocent man died. But he wasn't, I assure you." He smiled. "I know you were fond of him, that's why you were suspicious of me in the plane. Lucky you never put it all together or you might have saved his life." He took my arm and led me inside. "Roger was the traitor. He couldn't be trusted. Come, it's time for you to meet Gilbert."

I went with him unwillingly, not knowing whom to believe. Whom to trust, what to think. After Jean-Phillipe, this information was too much to handle.

A thin, almost emaciated man uncurled himself from a couch and stood before me, offering his hand. Our Resistance liaison had a long face, muddy brown hair, and black eyes that had already seen too much. It was difficult to determine his nationality—he was certainly not American or German. A chill emanated from him.

"We have a problem, Odette," he told me. "They know your face—they got your photo from Roger. Our safest bet is to let London go on presuming you're dead; that information will get back to the Germans, I promise you. But you're useless to us as a courier. We can't have you traveling around the country."

Then my trip is useless, I thought. To the English, to the Resistance, and most of all to me.

"I've reassigned you," Gilbert said. "As long as you've come this far, you might as well help out. Besides, Poincare says you're a good soldier."

I let his feeble flattery pass unnoticed. "Reassigned in what way?"

"A way that will still let you concentrate on Will Johnston's objective, Franz Jozef Behrenson."

So Gilbert knew about that! I would have to assume that everybody knew everything and to keep silent at any cost.

"We, of course, aren't all that interested in Behrenson, so while you're looking for him, you'll be doing work for us as well."

Intriguing. I began to regain my spirits. "Where will I be working?"

His eyes flashed. Amusement? "In a brothel."

"What! Impossible."

He raised a hand. "Please. I didn't say you had to become a whore. The brothel's run by Camille de Sevigny, and you'll be sent there as her goddaughter. Madame was in the Resistance, all the while working for that Nazi collaborator, Baron de Tourneau. Seems De Tourneau was so impressed with her work for him, and so blind to the work she did for us, that he had her set up a brothel where he could run his personal chamber of sadism under her roof."

"And Captain Behrenson? He goes to the 'chamber of sadism'?" Sadism seemed to me too much. Already, I was trying to think of ways to back out.

"I doubt it. But the bordello's become the most exclusive in Paris, its girls are famous throughout the city. Captain Behrenson will go there sooner or later; all the German officers do. And when he gets there, you'll be waiting."

Once more I thought of saying no, but Johnston had said Behrenson might lead me to the factory near Auschwitz. Surely I wouldn't have to sleep with him, or anyone else. I would go to the brothel, but not as a prostitute, as a spy. What choice did I have? Walk out of the safe house and into the Paris streets, with no friends and no means of transportation?

"What do you say?" Gilbert asked.

I bowed my head in submission.

"Good. Here's the address."

I pocketed the paper and turned to go.

"Oh, by the way. Don't you have some presents for us from Colonel Johnston?"

I had completely forgotten. With relief, I turned over the money and the wireless equipment.

"Your first and last job as courier," he said. "Did you notice the name of the brothel? It's La Maison aux Camellias. You like music, I'm told. From now on you're La Dame aux Camellias. Or la Traviata, as Giuseppe Verdi called her."

An enormous circular driveway led up to La Maison aux Camellias, which was located inside an ornate grillwork gate. The building was best described as a villa, although it stood in the heart of the city. Ranks of balustraded windows looked out on the front lawn, or, as I soon discovered, on an inner courtyard surrounded by lush gardens.

Gilbert must have told Madame de Sevigny to look out for me, for when I rang she opened the door and greeted me with a languorous superiority. She was a patrician, tense and self-absorbed, a woman, evidently, who had made herself rich through her own resources. I had to remind myself that she was working for Gilbert.

My years at the lycée had familiarized me with such women— many were the mothers of my classmates. As long as I made myself useful and exhibited the proper respect, I would be tolerated. Women like Madame did not take insubordination lightly.

She was perhaps sixty years old, and her hair was dyed a henna shade, often a mistake in a woman of her years. Yet she carried it off brilliantly, looking neither hard nor cheap. She was short and what my mother would call zaftig, a full-figured, sensuous female who, despite her age, radiated sensuality. No wonder De Tourneau was attracted to her.

She gave me a brief tour of the downstairs. The carved medieval stonework, the stained glass lions above the long narrow windows, and the massive arched doorways looked as if they'd been designed to accommodate knights or princes. The inside of the foyer was tiled in black and white, and a white marble stairway spiraled up in twin helixes. A door to a massive kitchen opened off one side; a library and council chamber were on the other. I saw no girls, no customers. Perhaps they were all upstairs, or perhaps they only arrived in the evenings.

Madame de Sevigny lived in a spacious bedroom at the top of the landing—the girls, she told me, had rooms a floor above—and she put me in a tiny anteroom nearby. A bell pull attached to a rope told me it had once been used by the mistress's personal maid. The room was comfortable enough, but I worried that it would only be a matter of time before I'd be sent to work on the third floor. All the while Madame was showing me La Maison, she was appraising me, and I gathered from everything she said that she approved of what she saw.

She introduced me to the other girls and to the staff, always implying that I was someone special. She seemed genuinely friendly, and I found myself liking her. She took my hand and we walked outside.

"This is more than a brothel," Madame said. "La Maison is a refuge for men, women, and even children who need a place to hide, but they can only stay for a few days or the Germans might become suspicious. You must always be alert."

I was wondering who owned the house. Was it Madame?

Madame spoke quietly. "The Baron de Tourneau owned La Maison. I was his mistress for thirty years before he tired of me and discovered other pleasures. It is a beautiful brothel for the wealthy and influential. Now the Germans come to escape and live out their fantasies. La Maison is my house, but on occasion the baron does return."

"Aren't you risking your life?" I asked.

She shrugged in a way I had come to think of as characteristically French. "Aren't you?"

I hadn't really thought about it. My job was to extract as much information as I could, avenge my family if possible (for I was now certain they were all dead), and if I died, better later than sooner for those reasons. As for myself, I didn't care what happened. In death, there is no pain.

Seeing my troubled expression, Madame stopped walking and put her arms around me. "Think of me as your *maman*," she said, "for as long as you are here."

My assignment at La Maison would be a test, of that I was certain. Although Gilbert had spoken of it as a fait accompli, I sensed he was not fully convinced that I could handle it. Useless as a courier now, my value lay in the quality of information I could obtain. If I didn't fit in at La Maison would they send me back to London? I didn't think so but couldn't imagine what else he'd have in store for me. I didn't trust Poincare and hardly knew what to make of Gilbert. They would rely on Madame's judgment, and my success (or failure) in La Maison aux Camelias would seal my fate.

When we reentered La Maison Madame took my hand, and we descended to the lower level.

"Here, my child, is a special room for important guests."

We entered a large, circular room. The lighting was dim, and when my eyes adjusted I could see exactly what this room was used for. There were whips, masks, and equipment I thought belonged in a gymnasium. I would soon learn to master all of the equipment.

Madame said, "This room is almost soundproof. Sometimes our guests make a great deal of noise."

I was chilled by the thought and didn't move.

"Now let me show you another room, but you must never tell any-one because this is the baron's private place, which he built only for himself. He returns, on occasion, and demands his special pleasures."

She walked to the wall and for a moment seemed confused. She finally found a spot and pressed it with her finger. The wall moved and opened to a large room, faintly perfumed and subtly lit, deco-rated with magnificent paintings on damask walls, brocade furniture covers, leather chairs, and a massage table. There was a small stage, and a magnificent grand piano was sitting there. It looked like a great sculpture.

"This is the baron's private chamber. Remember, you must never tell anyone that I showed you this room."

I held on to the Madame's hand. "Why the piano?"

"The baron loves music and he used to play only for himself."

I now knew my place in La Maison. "I would like to work in the circular room if I can play the piano in the baron's private chamber when I am free."

The Madame smiled. "But you must never tell the baron, and we must be careful that he never discovers the truth."

So I was assigned to the circular room. I knew my place and realized that Gilbert had simply lied to me, figuring I wouldn't go if I knew where I was really headed; at least now I had an escape. What tran-spired in that room was not as terrible as I first imagined—apprecia-ble domination, much sadism, relatively routine games, and some marvelous machines. The scene reminded me of a Bosch painting, though I'd seen plenty of deviance back in the Baluty. There I'd disci-plined myself to present an unreadable face to my enemies, and I'd been trained in England to protect myself.

Madame began my apprenticeship with junior officers, whose hunger made them easy to control. They'd work themselves halfway to a frenzy before even entering the circular room. Away from home, beyond restraint, they were bad little boys who craved the forbidden; naughty creatures who could not abide being ignored or denied. I never let them touch me. This perverse contact was so different from my joyous lovemaking with Vinnie that I couldn't think of them both in the same terms.

The more roughly my hands massaged Madame's clients, the more disdainful my demeanor, the more excited they became. And it was not unpleasant to provide what they asked for—a spanking of Eric's bare bottom, a hairbrush applied to the inside of Rutger's thighs as he stood doubled over, his boxer shorts around his ankles. More experienced, and therefore higher level officers requested belts, some with the buckle still attached, or whips, and a few of them begged for chains. I'd graduate to them once Madame felt my apprenticeship was over.

My generous hatred denied my clients nothing, since I did not suffer the fear of hurting them that plagued some of the other girls. I *wanted* to hurt them, and my reputation as a dominatrix grew. I was not shy about pleasing a lonely officer, the more savagely the better.

The baron's special chamber with its piano was my private domain. When I wasn't working I played the piano on the baron's small stage privately. This room was the Baron's private domain, only used by him when he visited. I imagined I was playing for a large audience in Warsaw. My fantasy helped me overcome the many nightmares I had. Even when I was entertaining the enemy I thought of the piano and the music. I stepped into a different world . . . a different time.

One evening I walked into Madame's chambers and she was having cognac with a German officer. I knew he was important because I never saw her entertain in her private quarters. He rose and offered me a seat. I saw Madame smile and the officer said, "I understand that you are Madame's assistant." I wasn't even sure how to answer. He was tall, very handsome, and seemed somewhat shy.

"I hope sometime soon we can have dinner together," he said.

He didn't ask to see me at La Maison.

I said, "Madame would decide when I can have time for myself."

He was holding my hand tightly and we stared at each other. His eyes seemed so sad. He said, "I'm looking forward to our dinner and I hope a long friendship." Then Madame walked him to the door and I found I was still staring at his back. Then Madame turned to me and said, "That is Captain Franz Jozef Behrenson."

A month after I began work at La Maison, I reported back to the safe house—or rather, to Poincare's apartment, where Gilbert directed me when I called. I arrived too early, for Poincare was just escorting out a German officer whose flushed and satisfied face hinted at what he and Poincare had been doing.

"That was Klaus," Poincare told me. "I, too, am in the body-for-information business. Madame de Sevigny says you're doing well." I bristled at his easy familiarity.

We went upstairs to Poincare's one-room apartment. The bed was rumpled, and I saw blood and semen on the sheets. Poincare caught my look.

"I'll make it easy for you, Odette. I enjoy the game as much as Klaus does. He's no use to us in the Resistance, but he keeps me calm. I'd appreciate it if you didn't tell Gilbert."

Gilbert surely knows and is letting the affair go on for his own reasons, I thought, but said nothing.

Poincare lit a cigarette and settled back on the bed. I sat in a chair across from him."You told Gilbert you had information. What is it?"

I hesitated.

"What's the matter?" he asked. "Don't you trust me?"

"Considering that a German officer just crawled out of your bed, why should I?"

He laughed. "Touché. Well, we landed in Paris, *cherie,* and what a fine mess we've made. Thanks to Klaus, the Germans released me after I was picked up, and you were brought here by a German convoy. We're both dirty. In fact, we stink to high heaven. I'll never trust you and vice versa. So why don't you blow back out that front door?"

I considered it. "No. I do have information. I trust Gilbert and he told me to give it to you. I will, but I've got to get out of La Maison, and I need your help. Promise me you will. Believe me, I know that unless I can convince you what I say is true, I'm already dead."

He inhaled, clearly enjoying himself, and blew smoke out his nostrils. "Let's begin with your military intelligence officer, Behrenson."

"Poincare, I was only at the house a few weeks before he arrived. Obviously Madame knew him from some previous visits. The minute we met I knew he was interested. He told me I was nothing like the rest of the girls. He also said we must have dinner soon. Madame made it a point of telling him that I was her new personal assistant, which sounded important."

"I understand that Franz Jozef Behrenson reports to General Blumentritt, the court jester for von Runstedt." He stared at me, his eyes hard. "What did he have to say?"

"Very little. It's probable that Johnston overestimated his importance. He's a lonely soldier, nervous, shy, who maybe likes a little light discipline from time to time."

Poincare glared. "Then you have no information."

"Not from Behrenson. But he introduced me to Commissioner Schmiede from Berlin. Schmiede stopped in on a mission from Albert Speer to smooth the way for *razzias* and enforced labor in Germany. Their production lags are becoming critical, but they can't use the Jews because they're killing them instead. Three thousand Jews die each week just in the munitions plants. You can relay that to London. The work camps are death camps. The smokestacks are crematories. Do you understand the magnitude of what I'm saying?"

I did, of course. It confirmed that Papa and Jozef were dead. Strangely, when I had heard the news and realized its import, I couldn't cry. The numbness that protected me from what was going on in the Baron's Chamber had reached my tear ducts, my soul. Only revenge excited me. Only the meting out of pain.

Poincare gave no indication that my news meant anything. "What else did you learn?"

"The Germans in France are scared. They're worried about the Resistance, particularly since the garrison was ambushed in Clermont. Even the Gestapo officer seemed shaken."

This last sparked his interest. "This officer: what's his name?"

"I'm not sure. Stocky man, balding, hideous ass. Someone called him Hans. Casterdorp, maybe."

"*Westerdorp.* It must have been. You saw him when?"

"Last Friday. But he's been at La Maison before. I'm almost sure he's a regular."

He sat up and leaned toward me. "I need you to find out all about him. What his tastes are in food, in music, in sex. Where he eats lunch, whether he has milk in his coffee. His brand of cigarettes."

"But I've got to leave La Maison!" I cried.

"Why?" he asked quickly. "Has someone betrayed you?"

"No. It's not that. I just hate it there, but I'm safe for as long as I'm in Madame's favor and she in turn is the favorite of Baron de Tourneau."

"Which makes it imperative you stay. Things are getting hot in the North. There'll be other ambushes beyond Clermont. We'll need La Maison more than ever for emergency overnights. Stranded Resistance fighters. Fugitive Jews."

Madness, I thought. "It's too risky. Madame can handle one or two, but no more. The other girls are unreliable."

"We'll work out a system for smuggling them in. The girls will never know."

"But Madame de Sevigny will never permit it."

"She has no choice. Besides, she's on our side, remember. And if she refuses . . ." With a shrug, Poincare drew a finger across his throat.

"But you don't need me there. I tell you, I don't know how much longer I can take it. It's getting worse and worse in La Maison. I'm made to do the heavy stuff now, the unspeakable things. And I'm surrounded by collaborationist prostitutes and German officers. It's getting to me."

"Do you suppose it would be better somewhere else? Forget it. Don't tell me Johnston didn't warn you."

"He did, but he never told me I would be working in a brothel."

"What's the matter? Did you want to follow Behrenson home?"

"Of course not!"

"Fall in love with his Aryan good looks?"

"No more than you are with Klaus," I said hotly. "I'm not a whore!"

He sighed and settled back, propping himself up on an elbow. "Can you think of a better description? As for Klaus, he's a lovely boy. He's been moved from the prison to be a translation clerk for one of the food commissary officers."

"What would Gilbert think of him? Or London?"

"Is that a threat? They all know I'm queer. It makes me valuable. As for Klaus, if I find I'm getting too attached and it starts to impede my judgment, I'll get rid of him."

"It's that simple? You think you can just sleep with the enemy and—"

"I'd say that you'd better get used to that idea. There are worse things than making love to a German, you know. I'm sure you didn't get the information from Schmiede without—"

"I didn't make love to him. We spent the night at arm's length, joined by a riding crop."

He roared. "I must say, you make fine distinctions. But it doesn't matter. The only thing that counts is the information, and Gilbert will be pleased by what you've brought me. I'll tell him tonight."

"Then tell him, too, that I want out. My God, Poincare, you can't imagine what it's like. Every night, riding crops, hangers, bullwhips. Screams that pierce right through your skull. What do you suggest I do about that?"

He was merciless. "I suggest you learn to like them."

"This is the Baron de Tourneau," the voice on the ontercom in the circular room said. "I've much admired your work. Perhaps you can accommodate me tonight."

I was alone in the room, cleaning off a particularly nasty whip when the baron called, and although I was not aware that he had been watching what went on here, it did not surprise me, nor did this call.

"There's a door behind the panel opposite the entrance. Press on the fleur-de-lis design and it will open. Use it when you've dressed as I wish you to." He told me his preferences.

I did as I was ordered—one did not disobey the baron. The door opened into his private chamber.

The baron was a tall, regal man with a high forehead, deep-set brown eyes, an aquiline nose, and a rosy glow to his cheeks, perhaps brought on by too much wine. He looked pleasant enough and he greeted me formally, although I was dressed, as he requested, in black lace garters and was naked under a short silk robe.

"Camille tells me you're a musician," he said.

"I haven't played or sung for a long time."

He smiled and gestured toward the piano. "Do so now."

"But . . ."

"Do so now." This repetition had a faint menace underlying it. I sat on the piano bench and opened the lid. "Brahms," he said.

I played the first movement of the Brahms Third Piano Sonata, with its deceptively simple melody. It was a piece I had learned early; now it brought back the joy of playing—of music—with such force that I almost forgot where I was, what I was wearing, and who the audience was. It calmed me. I lost all fear of the baron. Music was a force with far more power than he.

Perhaps my calm excited him. "No more," he said, and motioned me to stand.

"What does my master require?" I asked in the time-honored tradition of the dominatrix.

"Nothing special this first time. I must get used to the touch of your fingers before I ask you to employ the whip."

He had poured himself a glass of cognac while I was playing, and now he offered me a sip. I tasted it greedily. Its warmth thrilled me.

Slowly, he removed his clothes. He had a fine body for a man of his age, and his penis was thick and long. With a sigh of content, he slipped my robe over my shoulders and let it fall to the floor. He had turned my back to him, the easier to accomplish his task, but now he moved me around to face him and massaged my breasts. His hands were gentle, considerate. I thought of Vinnie's touch, Vinnie's love, and wanted to cry.

He lay down on the massage table with a sigh. I worked his neck muscles, relaxed his shoulders, and massaged out the knots along his spine. When I reached his buttocks I powdered him from a can that lay on the table, making wide slow circles as I spread the talc. He tensed. I ran both hands over the curve of his cheeks until he shuddered, then deftly allowed my fingers to slide into him, sinking deeper until he cried out in ecstasy.

"Very good for a start," he said. "I will tell you when to come back." Then without so much as looking at me, he rose from the table, picked up the glass of cognac, and naked, swallowed it in a gulp.

And so began my relationship with the Baron de Tourneau.

CHAPTER 22

I blew out the candle in my room and lay in the darkness, staring at the streaks of moonlight that glinted through the tears in the blackout shades. Soon, images of the baron, Poincare, and Gilbert vanished, and I fell asleep. In my dream, I was in Brooklyn. Vinnie and I were making love in a field of soft grass. I was happy. *Happy!* But as the lovemaking went on, I grew tired from the exertion and begged Vinnie to stop. Instead, he redoubled his efforts, slamming into me with sadistic pleasure. The grass turned hard; we were on the scrabble outside Auschwitz. There was smoke all around us, but I could see Vinnie's face clearly. He was getting pleasure not from the sex but from the pain he was inflicting. Don't look into his eyes, I told myself, but I couldn't help it, I had to see the monster he had become. He was Egon, dead, taking revenge. He opened his mouth, which was full of sharp teeth, like a jackal, and I knew he was going to bite off my head.

I screamed. Screamed again. Woke. Someone was knocking at my door.

Trembling, I threw a bathrobe over my shoulders and went to open it. There was a girl standing outside, also in nightclothes, barefoot, her black hair disheveled, her eyes gleaming with concern.

"Forgive me," she said. "I was just going back to my room when I heard you screaming."

She was young. "Come in. You look cold."

"Thank you." She entered cautiously, on tiptoes, as though afraid of what she might find.

"I had a bad dream," I told her. "Really, nothing more."

"I was afraid someone was hurting you. One of those pig Nazis come for a second helping."

She sat on a chair by my bed, a slender girl who, when she curled her legs beneath her, reminded me of a picture in one of the books I read as a girl: Heidi, warming herself by a fire. I took one of the blankets from my bed and put it over her, then sat on the side of the bed so that we were facing each other. She was remarkably pretty, I noted, fresher-looking than most of the other girls at La Maison.

"You're new?" I asked. "Have I seen you before?"

"I've been here only two weeks. My name's Sonia."

"Russian?"

"No, French. But my mother was a reader of Dostoyevsky."

"I'm Odette."

"I know. Madame de Sevigny's godchild. The girls resent you for that, think you get special favors, but I don't see what's so good about having to go to the baron's room."

"You know about that?" I said, startled.

"I was in the circular room when you came out, only you didn't notice me."

True. I was only anxious to get to my room. "Then you work in the special room?"

"From the day I arrived." She shuddered. "I'll get used to it, I suppose."

"Yes. I have. But only because I get pleasure from beating them." She was looking at me strangely, perhaps wondering how much she should say. I prompted her. "Do you hate them, too? You called them Nazi pigs."

She shrugged. "Of course I hate them."

"Then why are you here? Why do you sleep with them? A girl like you, so pretty and so young."

"They won't pay you for just standing there," she said with great bitterness.

"That's not what I meant. Why work here at all?"

"It's the fastest way to make the kind of money I need. I have a small house, a beautiful cabin in the Ardennes. I'm saving up enough money to turn it into an inn. A rustic resort. People will flock to it when the war's over. They'll want a peaceful place to forget their troubles. Do you believe me?"

It seemed a fantasy, but I didn't want to hurt her by saying so. "Why shouldn't I?"

"Ricki laughs at me. She says I'm too romantic to be a whore."

"I'm romantic, too," I said, thinking of Vinnie. I remembered the dream. "Or I was."

She was silent a moment. Then: "I like you."

I laughed. "I like you, too."

"No, seriously. You're the only one here with a heart." She paused. "Do you think we can be friends?"

Friends were dangerous. All those I had ever made were gone or dead or had betrayed me. I held out my hand to her. "Of course."

With a smile, she came to me, and we lay on our backs side by side on the bed. "Can I stay with you tonight?" she whispered.

I could hear the need for companionship in her request and suddenly felt that need, too. In the daytime, I would be Odette, the dominatrix. In the private nighttimes, I could, just for a little while, be Mia, and it was Mia who lay next to the troubled girl and breathed deeply until we both fell asleep.

CHAPTER 23

Sonia shifted grumpily, rolling onto her side and burying herself under the covers.

The night had been long for me. The warmth of her body against mine gave me comfort. A sliver of daylight poked through the black-out curtain. Though we were allowed to sleep as long as we liked—our work rarely started before noon, and then only for the "quickies," the junior officers about to be sent to the front; the circular room never opened before 9 P.M.—today I wanted to get to know Sonia better.

When we awoke Sonia went to the window and raised the blind.

"Don't do that!" I said.

"Why not? It's a beautiful morning."

"Because Madame's forbidden it."

"Pah. The old crone's too sensitive."

There was a loud shout from the courtyard. I sat up, pulling on my night robe. Sonia stepped away from the window. I head a car door slam and hobnails tapping like a blind man's cane across the cobblestones. "The Gestapo," I said. Blood pounded in my temples. I ran to the closet and grabbed my change purse, taking out the poison coin and slipping it into my pocket. Mentally, I inventoried the room. Was there any incriminating evidence? No. I'd made it a practice to deliver my notes to Poincare once a week, and nothing had happened since yesterday, the time of our last meeting.

Sonia had crept back to the window and had pulled the blind high enough to look down into the courtyard. "Get away," I hissed. "Go back to bed. Quick!"

"Schutz, Lipsch," a German voice bellowed beneath our window. "Make it fast, before she can get away."

"My God!" Sonia gasped.

"Let them alone and they won't bother us, I promise," I said. "But if you get caught spying on them . . ."

"What are they doing here?"

"I don't know."

But I did. They were looking for a refugee who had arrived the day before. Gilbert had ordered it. Poincare had arranged it, Madame had agreed to it. And the Gestapo knew.

There was a scream, a despairing *Nooo* from downstairs. *"I beg of you. Go ahead. Take me. Do whatever you want with me. But he's only a baby. My poor baby . . ."*

Doors opened upstairs and all along our corridor. Did the girls recognize the crying voice of the new sous-chef's helper? A nervous, antlike woman named Natalie who said nothing, not even when Poincare had brought her in to Madame de Sevigny until she could be smuggled out of Paris.

Natalie was Jewish. She had close-set eyes, a long, thin nose, and her hair was clipped like a prisoner's. She had seemed miserable when she arrived, and I had instinctively avoided her. Now I knew why. She smelled of death.

A baby's shriek gurgled through La Maison, then Natalie's wail. It was silenced by the thud of wood on bone.

"Shit," a German said. "Look at that. No need to take them to headquarters. Let's just leave them here."

All went silent for a moment—then the sound of boots once more in the courtyard, the slamming of a car door, and a car driving away.

Sonia and I looked at each other in horror. Had that thud been the butt of a German rifle crushing Natalie's skull? Had she died holding her baby and had his skull been crushed, too?

Perhaps there would be a stain on the immaculate granite stairs, a bit of hair or flesh to mark the spot of the killings. Who would be assigned to clean it up?

Sonia, weeping, came to me for comfort. I embraced her and we rocked in each other's arms. "There was nothing you could do," I said.

"But the baby. Did they have to kill him?"

"They didn't have to kill either of them. This raid had nothing to do with them personally. It was a warning. To anyone who wanted to use La Maison to shelter refuges." To me, I thought, and once more the urge to get out overwhelmed me. The Gestapo had come again, and I had been lucky again. How long would it be until they caught me and sent me to the concentration camps, which had claimed my family and their neighbors? If the reports were right, the ranks of the camps had swollen to accommodate all of the Jews from the Baluty, despite the fervent Nazism of King Chaim.

What had happened to Nate Kolleck's negatives? I wondered. His hundreds of portraits of the dead and dying? They were documents that might have told the world what was happening to us, the European Jews. To my everlasting shame, I had said nothing about it when I lived in Brooklyn. Yes, Vinnie knew something, but only my story, not the story of my people.

Two more Jewish lives had been extinguished this morning and no one had even tried to protect them. Like rabbits we had burrowed into our lairs, quaking in silence. By this afternoon, no one would speak of the incident. Even for me, it would become just one more nightmare.

The raid had gone quickly; the Germans knew precisely where to look. They had entered by the side door, which evidently had been left unlocked. An ugly certainty rushed through me: Natalie had been betrayed by someone in La Maison.

With this thought came another: I wondered just how much that pretty little inn in the Ardennes meant to my new friend Sonia. Was it a coincidence that just a short time after her arrival Natalie had been found? Odette did not need a friend, I decided. And because she didn't, Mia would have to go without one as well.

In her place, another "friend" resurfaced, one for Odette: Franz Behrenson. In a recent visit, Poincare had chided me about my original report that the officer was a minor figure in German Intelligence. It was what the Gestapo wanted me to think—what the baron wanted me to think—but in fact that attitude simply reflected the power struggle between the Gestapo and German Intelligence; the two were waging a war almost as fierce as the German war against the Allies.

So while my relationship with the baron morphed into something far more baroque than our initial encounter (I came to relish his screams of pain, his pleas for mercy), I spent the bulk of my time with Behrenson and was permitted to leave La Maison on his arm. He liked to show me off around Paris as his mistress—no matter that a few of his officer friends knew that I was also a whore.

Poincare was delighted by the arrangement. Perhaps I would fuck some good secrets out of the intelligence officer.

Franz Behrenson tightened his arm around my waist as we walked toward the blacked-out Hotel Georges V. I nuzzled against him for an instant, then moved away as the fog lights of a Citroën lit up the pavement on the Boulevard d'Alma.

"You'll come upstairs with me for a nightcap?" he asked, though it was a question with only one possible answer.

"As you like."

As we entered the foyer, two Death's Head guards with silver lightning bolts on their collars sprang to attention. Near the front desk, a senior officer was arguing with the concierge.

Behrenson squeezed my arms. "Excuse me," he said and walked to the officer, announced himself with a click of his heels, and lifted his arm in a Heil Hitler salute. Only once before had I seen him so deferential. It had been to Hitler's adjutant, General Jodl.

The officer's features were familiar. I'd seen his face in photographs—perhaps he had more hair then. I allowed my eyes to meet his, then turned to the lift.

Behrenson summoned me back. "Don't be shy, Odette. Come, I want to introduce you to a very important man. Herr Doctor Roos, may I present Odette LeClerc. Odette, Dr. Roos is a leading scientist, working on a rubella vaccine."

A flash of recognition shot through me. Dr. Roos had visited my father's house in Lodz! I was seven or eight years old and had performed Bach and Mozart for him on the piano. I scanned his face for a hint of recognition. If he knew my real name was Levy, I would be dead within twenty-four hours.

"Your reputation precedes you," I murmured, holding out my hand to be kissed. "I've heard a great deal about your work with children. In fact, I carry a reminder, a vaccination on my derriere."

He bowed. "I can think of no more charming honor. Now I insist that both of you join me for a glass of champagne."

I allowed him to slip his arm through mine while Behrenson followed, fuming.

"Did you have to do that?" Behrenson said. "Fall all over Roos?" I was massaging his shoulder muscles, and he lay facedown on the bed so that his words were muffled. "Easy! Are you trying to kill me?"

"Don't be so dramatic," I said, softening my touch. "I've got to massage deeply or you'll be miserable tomorrow. As for Doctor Roos, I couldn't very well refuse his invitation, could I?"

"You wanted to meet him."

"You introduced me!"

He twisted his head to look at me, his face flushed. "Yes. But you deliberately attracted his attention."

I didn't bother to refute him. "It's not my fault if he found me attractive. And if you don't relax, how can I—?"

"You didn't have to accept his invitation."

"Sure. Your mistress insulting one of Germany's most renowned scientists. What a coup for your career. Do you think I found his typhus tales enthralling? Or that I was spellbound by his stories of the different diseases in the camps?"

"You certainly seemed absorbed. Always with the Berliners. The generals and commissioners. You're out to seduce all of them. Laugh at their stupid jokes. Let them drone on about their intrigues with the Führer. Why?"

My fingers froze on his shoulder blades. "I'm just being polite. There's nothing wrong with that."

"Isn't there?" He whirled around and seized my wrists, forcing me back on the hotel bed. "Do you think I don't see how they lust after you?"

"You're not so bad at lust yourself."

"That's not the point," he said, obviously pleased. "Roos tried to put his hand on your thigh under the table, didn't he?"

"Yes."

"And your reaction? Did you spread your legs?"

"I took his hand away."

His rage fed on itself. "How can you pretend to be so innocent? God in heaven, you make me crazy! What will you do if Roos shows up at La Maison with Tourneau if I'm not around? Let him fuck you while you're whipping the baron?"

He tore my blouse open and bit at my breasts while his left hand went between my legs. Involuntarily, I closed them.

"So now you're resisting me?" His eyes were bloodshot with fury. Perhaps I've pushed him too far, I thought.

"You don't have to rape me," I said as gently as I could. "I have a headache. Let me get some aspirin. Then you can make love to me as you wish."

"Not 'as I wish.' I want more from you, passion from you. I know there's passion in you. I've seen it in your eyes. I've seen ecstasy in your face, Odette, when you whip the Baron. Or Schmiede. How could you give it to that pig Schmiede and deny it to me?" He slid a riding crop from under the pillow and handed it to me. "Beat me," he moaned. *"Beat me!"*

I moved the leather up and watched his buttocks tense in antici-pation. He bent over to brace himself against the footboard. For a moment, I felt sorry for him.

"What are you waiting for? I order you to whip me, as you have Schmiede and the baron."

I threw the crop across the room in disgust. "I can't."

"Why not?" he cried. "Please!"

I kissed his back tenderly. "Because I don't hate you enough."

More and more bodies packed into the crude wooden pews until the air was thick with the smell of garlic and stomachs sourly digesting their own flesh. I clung to my aisle seat, ignoring the angry stares and refusing to yield the space beside me occupied by my fur coat. Sullen eyes bored into me, fixed on my clothing: the clean dress, the woolen stockings, the Spanish leather boots. Here, beyond the confines of Paris, the suffering was far worse than I imagined, and I was both well dressed and well fed.

Shivering, I slid my fur-lined gloves into the folds of my coat, recalling the loathsome vegetable soup that had sustained me in the Baluty. Hadn't I earned the right to eat well? Why feel guilty about the clothes and jewelry I accepted from my German admirers? If I was forced to sell myself, why shouldn't I make them pay heavily?

Who among these people, if they knew what I did to earn it, would begrudge me that coat?

A balding figure squeezed into the seat beside me. "It's about time," I hissed. "They were about to stone me for your seat."

Poincare nodded, preoccupied. The organ processional began, and he motioned for me to be quiet while he surveyed the church. To our left, a hulk of a man guarded the door. Was I imagining it or were there men at every exit?

"You heard about the raid at La Maison," I said. There was no question in my voice. "We lost them. Both of them. Does Gilbert know?"

His right hand was buried in his coat pocket. A concealed weapon? Why? He seemed frightened.

"Henri," I whispered, again ignoring his explicit gesture to be quiet. "Why did you want to meet me here? Who sent you?"

A vein throbbed in his forehead. He did not look at me. And knowledge came to me with the clarity of a spring sky: *he was here to kill me.*

The air echoed with the priest's incantation. Poincare dropped to his knees. I followed. Pressing against him, I felt him recoil. Just as I had recoiled from Nate Kolleck in the Baluty.

Perhaps I was already dead.

Seated again, I wrapped an arm around his, refusing to let go. Not even when the congregation stood to go and the candles were snuffed out.

I gazed at the screens lining the altar. I'd seen similar pictures in a church in England, one my trainers pointed out to me, and I knew I was in a Resistance headquarters. A working-class parish on the outskirts of the city where codebooks were delivered and couriers dispatched. Somewhere in the cluster of secret rooms behind the altar there was a transmitter. Poincare would never have risked setting up a meeting here unless he knew I would not be returning.

I watched the last of the parishioners drift out of the rear door of the nave. The Resistance men at the exits held their places, perhaps waiting for a signal.

"You can tell them to leave," I whispered. "I'm not so stupid that I don't understand why you're here. Or smart enough to escape."

I noticed a wry smile; I associated it with his preparing to slit a throat. When the aisles were clear, he motioned me to precede him toward the back of the church. His hand was still buried in his pocket.

"You'll give me a chance, won't you?" I said.

His voice was a monotone. "What are you talking about?"

"I'm accused of something, though I don't know what. I want a chance to defend myself."

"You'll have all the opportunity in the world. The Lysander is taking you back to London tonight."

Back to London? My heart jumped at the thought. But it was a lie, I knew.

We stopped walking, and I turned to face him. "Who in London?"

"I don't know. My orders are to get you to the plane, that's all."

"What have I *done?*"

"It wasn't only the mother and child who were betrayed. Karnak was picked up running the border at Chenonceaux. Emile jumped in a taxi outside La Maison and hasn't been heard from since. Three in the Sphinx circuit were picked up last week and sent to Dachau. And Boar, who would have gone with them, jumped out the window at Gestapo headquarters on the Avenue de Saussaies."

I staggered backward. These names meant nothing to me, but they were allies. The Resistance. "And you think I betrayed them?"

He shrugged.

"So you're sending me off to be executed, is that it? Why? Because you didn't have the stomach for it yourself?"

"Don't be so damned dramatic. It's not safe to have you floating around Paris. I don't know who to believe."

Dared I believe *him?* "Look at me, Poincare. How could I have known about any of them? Gilbert trusted La Maison enough to send me there in the first place. And through you I've reported to him, told him . . ."

I stopped, electrified. "It's Gilbert who's the traitor. Don't you see? Once I'm dead, I'll be the scapegoat and he can go ahead unchecked. I'll bet they offer you Behrenson, though you're probably not as good a fuck. Then *you'll* report back to Gilbert so he can see how much Behrenson knows. No one will wonder why Gilbert personally looks at all the arriving agents, me included, or why he meets with all the Resistance circuit leaders even though London warned him not to. It's so he can manipulate us." I was hoarse with the importance of it. "Why are you looking at me like that? The Germans haven't bought you, too, have they? With your little boyfriend."

"I wish I could believe you," he said gently, leading me past the end of the pews and genuflecting before the baptismal fount.

I grabbed his arm. "Then here's your chance to confirm it. Wire London. Ask them if Mia Levy had parents and a brother in Auschwitz. I'm *Jewish*, Poincare, and my mother—and maybe my whole family—died in the camps. I have more reason than any of you to hate the Nazis. Do you understand what I'm saying?"

I could see him hesitate. "I'm going to walk out the door right now," I said. "You can shoot me in the back if you like. But I'll deny that traitor Gilbert the satisfaction of killing me on the plane."

I took a step forward, sweat pouring through my blouse. The old injury in my hip sent shooting pains up my side. Maybe my arguments meant nothing. Perhaps everything had been resolved long before I entered the church. Did Poincare's silence signify resignation, not agreement?

I paused before the great arched doorway, then turned the handle. I looked back. Poincare stood halfway down the aisle. There was no sign of conciliation in his pinched smile.

I turned again, waiting for the shot, but instead Poincare raced past me, gesturing me to follow. Moving quickly, I slid through the door and saw him running toward the hedge surrounding the church garden. We huddled among the thorn branches. I followed the motion of his hand, pointing to at least three men racing around the grounds.

"They're looking for us," he whispered. "We should have been on our way by now. But don't worry. They're just putting on a show. Soon they'll get tired and say they didn't see us leave."

"Are they Gilbert's men?" I whispered back. I took his silence for assent. "He *did* want me killed, then."

"He's just covering his tracks. London complains about losing too many troops. He selects scapegoats and hands them to London—dead."

The men were on the other side of the garden. I had no fear about asking him questions. "You were going ahead with it. Why?"

"London's jumpy these days. They wanted a demonstration of my loyalty."

"So it was you or me. What made you change your mind? You'll forgive me, but it's not like you to risk your own neck."

"I want Westerdorp."

Yes. I had a vision of the stocky, balding Gestapo officer stripped to the waist, submissive to another of the girls—Erika, I think—while she beat him with a bamboo cane and made him fall to the carpet, begging for more.

"Did you hear what I said, Odette?"

I jerked backward into the thorns.

"I want Westerdorp." He paused. "And Sonia."

"Sonia? Why?"

"Gilbert needed a confederate at La Maison. If it isn't you, it has to be her."

I had suspected Sonia as well. "What do I do about them?" I asked. "Kill them."

No! It was too horrible. Westerdorp, maybe, since I felt nothing but disgust for the man—easy to kill him as kill a rodent. But Sonia. She has been the closest thing I had to a friend, even if a false one. I had joined the Resistance as a spy, not a murderer. I couldn't do it, and told him so.

"Then set them up for me. Westerdorp, at least. You may have to kill Sonia yourself."

Before I could answer, a car door slammed and I could see a limousine speed away. Bicyclists disappeared into the night. Poincare and I were alone, and he was staring at my profile—but not as my German admirers did. There was no warmth in the way he surveyed me, no male interest in his steely eyes.

"To give him to you, I have to go back to La Maison."

"Exactly."

"But what about Gilbert? I can't just walk back in there without his knowing. Why wouldn't he simply assign someone else to kill me?"

"Because I'll hand him a substitute. Persuade him that you're too valuable alive. That London would be all over him if you were to die."

Why couldn't Poincare have thought of this before? I wondered, but let the thought go unspoken. "It's dangerous for me back there," I said. "Even if Gilbert's neutralized, sooner or later the Germans are sure to find out what I've been doing."

"You still have time. You're still under the baron's protection, and Behrenson's so smitten he'd never give you up." He led me to his car, parked behind a row of trees in the back of the church grounds, and we drove away. I hoped it was toward Paris. "Just hold on," he said. "Liberation's coming."

"I know. Behrenson says they're guarding the V-2s west of the city against mortar fire. And in that last communiqué you sent for me, I included a list of minefields and explosive sites. Did you have a chance to look over the fortifications?"

"Every sandbag and bunker. London was gratified."

"Then how could you have thought I was a German collaborator?"

"Because Gilbert put you in the house."

"And now that you know I'm not, why don't they pull me out of France?"

"That's exactly what Gilbert wanted to do."

"Yes, but this time in a Lysander without the Death's Head imprimatur. One Gilbert doesn't arrange—so it has a prayer of making it across the channel."

"What's the hurry?" he asked. "I thought you liked smacking Germans around."

"Very funny. This was supposed to be a quick mission. By now, I should have been killed twice over. I trust no one, Poincare, not even you. I set the Germans up and use them for information. When it's convenient for headquarters, I'm told to kill them. And now you want me to kill Sonia, too. The answer's no."

"We need to be sure the safe house is safe. We can't take a chance."

"It'll be on my head. I'll make sure Sonia has no idea you know about her. Let's watch her in action."

"In order to make sure she's working against us? Very well, Odette, but if it turns out I'm right, you must kill her."

"And if I'm discovered?"

"Songbird disappeared once. She can do it again. I've asked Washington to send us help."

"Washington." I spat the word. "What makes you think the Americans will arrive?"

"They'll come. As reliably as the Paris mail—before the war."

My head pounded. There was no *before the war,* any more than there would be a world after it. How could there be here among the collaborationist French and the Gestapo cells? More than anything else, their existence marked the cruelty of Washington's denial and delay.

Next time Songbird disappeared, I knew, it would be into a grave. I had no illusions left. Someday the war would end, and before that it would be all right to die. To join my parents and my brother, my Polish comrades, and rejoin my ancestors in an unbroken line back to King David.

"I want to send a letter to the States," I said.

The car skidded, and he had to fight to keep it straight on the road. "What are you talking about?"

"You said the Parisian mails were once reliable. I presume yours are now. Well, I want something delivered to America. A personal letter."

"It's out of the question. Do you realize the risks?"

"The risks are mine. The name on the envelope will mean nothing to anybody."

"And the message?"

"As I said, personal. Don't you see? My family's all gone. There's nobody left, except for one person, and it's to him I want to write. I owe him an explanation of how Songbird disappeared, that's all."

The car slowed as he considered. "In return for Westerdorp?"

"Yes."

"And Sonia?"

This hurt. "Yes."

"Is he an American?"

I nodded.

"Then, as he might say, it's a deal."

CHAPTER 24

Most beloved Vinnie,

I am writing to you from Paris, but that's all I can tell you about where I am and what I'm doing. No street name, no description of my work. In fact, I can tell you no facts, only feelings, but it makes me happy to write you about those.

I did not disappear because I stopped loving you. I was literally spirited away, and in many, many ways I'm glad it happened. All I regret, in truth, is leaving you, and each day that regret grows.

My darling, I love you more than a human being has a right to love—so much that it is as much pain as pleasure, so passionately that rather than give it up I would willingly give up my life. You are in the air that I breathe, the food that I eat, my dreams and my fantasies. When my body aches, as it often does these days, I tell myself it aches for you. When I'm hungry, it's hunger for you. When I sleep, you are beside me.

When I sing—and that is rarely, except in my heart—you are my music.

I have no idea if this letter will reach you. Perhaps you will be in the American Army come to liberate France and—presto!—you will liberate me. But more likely we will never see each other again except in our mind's eyes. I am content with that. To have known you and loved you and made love

with you and made music with you is enough for any lifetime, more full of life than any other human could experience
in a hundred years.

I pray that you will live and be happy, that you will find
another love—though not as profound, not as stirring, not as
fulfilling as ours—and in loving her remember me.

As for me, I will remain for as long as my life shall last true
only to you.

Do you remember the Schumann sonata we played
together? I taught you to like Schumann, and now I will tell
you the name of the most beautiful song he ever wrote—"Ich
Grolle Nicht."—"I'm Not Angry."

Do not be angry with me, treasure of my soul, for leaving
you. For I have not left you. I am with you always and will
always be,

Your Mia

CHAPTER 25

". . . so I must say that, well, it was unsettling for me at first," General Westerdorp said. "The constant travel, the irregular hours. So great a change from home. But as an engineer, my services are needed all over the war zones."

"You must miss Vienna terribly," I commiserated. We were sitting on a couch in La Maison's "music room," where Madame de Sevigny had installed a piano.

His great owl eyes were blinking sleepily behind their thick lenses. "Well, naturally, my dear. I have family there, friends. When I was a boy, Vienna was still in her glory. You should have seen us as students, flocking after Franz Josef as he marched through the streets in his magnificent uniform.

"Never, not even in Paris, were there women so elegant. Many were musicians like yourself. Even the simplest girl on the street knew the music of their Papa Haydn, of Mozart, of Beethoven. And of course of Schubert, who makes the Leipziger Wagner sound like an organ grinder. But listen to how I go on like an old fogy. Play me some Mozart, will you? I need to relax a little before we make love."

I walked to the piano, feeling his eyes pass over my bare thighs, woolen socks, and simple lace-up shoes, and lowered myself onto the stool, my crinoline skirt billowing up on a cushion of air before settling around me.

Westerdorp approved of my schoolgirl dress and manner. For him,

I pretended naïveté; awe at his (flimsy) sexual prowess, delight in his endless anecdotes about Viennese life and customs. Like his stuffy bourgeois manners, Westerdorp's docility separated him from the ranks of Gestapo leaders and coarse Berlin administrators who visited me in the confines of Baron de Tourneau's sanctum sanctorum. There was nothing threatening in the old man's behavior, no wellspring of violence to erupt from below the surface of his milky eyes. Yet he was dangerous, I knew, and had once overseen the torture of one of Poincare's comrades for thirty-six straight hours until the man broke.

Westerdorp was a two-drink imbiber, fastidious, regulated. Often after I played for him, he would reminisce about his wife and children. Sometimes he would ask me to sit on his lap like his daughter often did, or dance in my garters, which his daughter did not. Later he would ask for the hairbrush and had me apply its stiff bristles to his powdered and quivering bottom with short, hard strokes. But never in the Baron's Chamber. He had visited me in it once and immediately asked me to go with him to a different room. "They're animals," he said with disgust about his fellow officers, though to me it was only a matter of the smallest degree between his wants and theirs.

We had seen each other frequently once I was able to make myself his "preferred" girl, and despite myself I had come to find him agreeable, certainly much better than the baron and that egoist, Behrenson. Sometimes I found myself wondering if Poincare could possibly have been right about the torture, but then I reminded myself that the man was an officer in the German Army, and all of them were torturers.

I would not mind seeing him dead. And I would not have long to wait.

"Why did you leave Vienna?" I asked as I played Mozart's sonata *Alla Turka*.

"I had no choice," he answered sadly. "Everything was arranged. And then, going to Berlin was quite an honor."

To be made an interrogator for the Reich, I thought. Quite an honor indeed.

"I'm tired this evening," he said when I finished playing. "And I'm off again at dawn tomorrow."

"Where to this time?" I asked.

"Vichy. Forgive me for saying so, but your Marshal Pétain is a worm, surrounded by yes-men of the vilest sort. One cannot pass wind in Vichy without having to file a report. And they know nothing of how to get information from a prisoner. Everyone waits for permission to turn a screw or open a valve. I've become little more than a master plumber, patting heads and spanking bottoms for French cousins of the Third Reich. . . . But I'd rather talk of how lovely you are tonight. Turn on the radio, won't you, and sit beside me."

I snapped on the console and removed my shoes, drawing my feet up under me on the couch and allowing my crinoline to ride up, revealing my thighs. I began to massage his temple and shoulder muscles, feeling excitement kindle within him.

"It's been too long since your last visit," I said.

He nodded, and gradually the pout on his thick lips changed to a smile. "Here. Put your head in my lap. Let me take off your glasses. That's it. Relax." I leaned over him to give him an upside-down look at my brassiere, imagining him a meek professor at my lycée, will-less, helpless in the face of the least demonstration of a woman's sensuality.

I helped him take off his clothes and led him to the table in the center of the room. Again I massaged him.

"You're tense tonight," I chided.

"It's not easy, working for the Reich. There are days when I'd give anything to be back on the faculty of the University of Vienna talking of loftier things than the war. And I miss the parks and the gardens. My wife and children have moved to one of the magnificent apartments right near the Schottenhof, so they get to see the gardens anytime they want. You see, I'm so successful I can give them everything—except a husband and a father."

I massaged him harder, a sudden sadness all but making the work impossible. He had a wife. Children. The normal feelings of millions of middle-class men. I had seen him at the height of his depravity, believed Poincare when he told me about the torture, knew he was my sworn enemy, part of a race determined to eradicate my own, and yet—

With every play of my fingers, I was leading him closer to his death. I could feel Poincare's fury seeping like poison into the cool air of the music room. For a week he'd been frantic, beside himself with worry over the details. And now he waited in a closet standing behind the massage table; he could see Westerdorp, but the German could not see him.

Poincare had thought out every action I was to take, starting now. Even the odd musical selections he had obtained through the French black market, the segue from record to record carefully considered. He was easily capable of simply driving an ice pick into the base of Westerdorp's skull, but in this case—this one case—he wanted the full staging. It did not occur to me to ask him why, because I knew he wouldn't answer.

And now I would become an accomplice to murder. It was either that or face Poincare myself. Kill or be killed, just as the Nazis had made the Jews in the Baluty and Warsaw participants in the crimes against one another.

Run, I wanted to scream. Don't you see death coming for you? I tried to console myself that if I had refused to help, Poincare would have found another way to kill him, and that I was powerless to prevent it. It was the excuse I had used about Egon, though in that case I was an unwitting ally to Wolf.

I removed my silk blouse and crinoline skirt and let them fall to the side of the table. Westerdorp was lying facedown on the table, but I knew the whispering sound excited him. I walked around the massage table, cut the blouse into four strips, and bound his hands and feet to the end rails of the table. "I've got a special treat for you tonight," I told him, and he sighed with pleasure.

Stepping over to the phonograph, I reached for the top recording: the Vienna Boys Choir. "I'll powder you now," I told him and began to sprinkle his ass with talcum.

Poincare came out of the closet soundlessly. He waited for the angelic voices to end "Oh Vaterland, Mein Vaterland," then lifted up the needle and cued the next record: "Un bel dei" from *Madame Butterfly*.

I felt revulsion sweep through Westerdorp's body. "I hate Puccini," he said. "Change the record immediately."

I brought a hairbrush down on his rear, then struck him again with just the right intensity. He tugged on his bonds. "This is disagreeable, Odette. I'm not enjoying it. Let me go this instant."

"I can't do that. Sorry." I put down the hairbrush and backed away toward the far wall.

"What are you talking about? I pay for your services, you do as I say. Is this some sort of joke?"

"Hardly a joke," Poincare said in a calm voice easily discernable above the soprano aria. "Not a joke at all."

I could imagine the shock on Westerdorp's face, the sudden fear. "Who are you?" he gasped.

"You seem unhappy," Poincare said. "Maybe you'd like some Viennese waltzes. There's one here you used to listen to most afternoons. They used to play it when Franz Josef visited, remember?"

So Poincare was an Austrian! Yes, I should have placed the soft lilt in his voice, the slow, heavy vowels in his German. My fear gave way to a terrifying excitement.

"What do you want?" Westerdorp asked. "If it's money, I haven't got any. And I've done nothing. I'm an engineer. I have no political value as a hostage."

"Yes, an engineer." Poincare couldn't keep the triumph from his voice. "And I, too, am an Austrian engineer. I'm surprised you didn't recognize my voice. Perhaps some music from Auschwitz will help you remember. Would you like some Suppé marches?" He changed the record.

"Odette!" Westerdorp cried. "Help me!" He fought to catch his breath. "Why are you doing this to me? What have I ever done to you? I swear to you I have no idea who this man is. I never even visited Auschwitz."

"Nevertheless you're a war criminal. Look at him, Odette. Look how he struggles to get free. This man has seen others struggle the same way, I assure you. And never visited Auschwitz? True." He glared at the helpless German. "But why don't you tell Odette about the special ovens you designed for use there!"

There had been rumors about the ovens. About the incineration of the Jews. Was that how my family had died? "Go on," I said to Poincare. "Let's have him tell us more."

"He's crazy," Westerdorp wailed. "Can't you see that? I don't know what this maniac told you, but it isn't true. I don't know about the ovens. I've never been to Auschwitz. Oh God, don't let my wife and children suffer because of some lunatic who—"

"Lunatic?" Poincare was murderously sane. "Don't you recognize me, Westerdorp? I'm Robert Segal. From the Buna Werke, before it was made into a woman's prison, Birkenau. You designed for it, too, didn't you? And after it was finished, and I was jailed along with so many others, you had us tortured with the very instruments you designed."

He moved in front of Westerdorp's face to give the German a good look. "I was lucky," he went on. "My crimes were sabotage and homosexuality. You can imagine what your underlings did to me, the torture I endured. They taught me that pain will pass. And that death is nothing. Not when you have to kill for a crust of bread or a guard with a machine gun wants some sport and will rip off your balls if you refuse. It was easy to escape. Just several nights of anal intercourse with an SS officer. A small price to pay for this moment. One night we slaughtered a dozen officers. Took their uniforms and stole their Steyr 220. I was sorry then that you weren't among them. But now— it makes the waiting delicious."

"You're wrong!" Westerdorp shouted. "I pleaded with them for you, don't you know that?"

"Sure you did, but I refused to work on the ovens. You didn't. Odette, turn up that waltz. Johann Straus. 'Tales from the Vienna Woods.' Listen to it, Westerdorp. It's as close to Austria as you'll ever be. Good, Odette. Now turn the volume all the way up."

Westerdorp said nothing until the waltz finished. There were tears streaming from his face. I wanted to drink them. They'd be sweeter than champagne. "I just designed what they asked me to. I had no idea why they wanted the pipes and the ventilation. For all I knew they were going to use them to get rid of waste material."

"With Zyklon B gas?"

"Yes. I told you that, even then."

"You lied 'even then,' and you're lying now. I saw those plans. I tried to sabotage them. Two hundred degrees centigrade is all you need for paper and rubbish. Any more and—Do you know what flesh smells like when it's burning? Here, let me show you."

Poincare held his cigarette lighter under Westerdorf's naked foot just long enough for it to blister. Westerdorp's howls of pain and the memory of the stench of Auschwitz made me want to vomit.

"Recognize the smell?" Poincare was enjoying himself. "Every day when it floated over the Buna factory, I thought of you."

"I didn't betray you, Robert. You must believe me."

"But you didn't save me, either."

"How could I? You were sabotaging the drawings. It would have been slitting my own throat. It was no ordinary commission. The Führer himself ordered it."

Even in his pain, he was able to say the words with pride, and with that, whatever shred of pity I might have felt for him disappeared.

"Then you can die for the Führer," Poincare said. "Even so, I can only kill you once, and that makes me angry." He lit a cigarette and jammed it into Westerdorp's back, then lit another. "You know," he said casually when Westerdorp's scream subsided, "Odette didn't believe me when I told her you'd had a friend of mine tortured, but I bet she now believes that you had me tortured as well. Still, I'd like you to tell her it's true." He moved his cigarette close to Westerdorp's ear. "I'm getting impatient. Say it."

"I had no choice. Could I have refused to serve my Führer? I never wanted to—"

Poincare picked up a heavy chain from underneath the massage table and slammed it—it was the baron's favorite—between Westerdorp's spread thighs. I recalled the reports of a rifle fired into the back of a Jew attempting to climb the fence at Auschwitz, and the German's cries were music.

Again and again the chain pounded into Westerdorp's back until it was nothing more than a giant wound. But nothing would satisfy Poincare now. He began punching the gray head with his bare fists.

When he paused to look up, he was staring into the barrel of his own silenced Luger. I had taken it from his belt when he was inflicting the hardest blows. "Out of the way," I ordered, leaving no room for challenge. He looked at me with what seemed to be admiration and moved to the side of the room.

"Can you hear me?" I asked Westerdorp. "It's over. You don't have to worry. We won't hurt you anymore."

I walked around to face him, staring at his bulging eyes. Blood was running out of his mutilated nose.

"I wish my parents and brother were here to tell me what to do," I said, lifting the gun. "Maybe they are." He closed his eyes, but not before I saw his terror.

"Yis'ga'dal v'yoskadash sh'may ra'boo—"

His eyes opened. "You're Jewish," he choked. "Oh, my God—"

I fired.

CHAPTER 26

$\mathcal{T}$hrough the summer of 1944, the pace of my work increased. But I was free each night Franz Behrenson wanted me, which meant each night he was in Paris, though those occasions became less frequent as the danger to the Germans in France, and the threat to the Reich itself, intensified.

During the times he was in Paris, Behrenson spent lavishly on black market meals and black market wines; we went to the finest hotels and the lowest bars, seeking release from his tension and offering me—as his drinking grew heavier and his sexual appetite became more voracious—tidbits of information that would help the enemy he feared.

One night we dined at the Ritz. Behrenson stared at me with furious intensity. His veins pounded visibly beneath the flushed skin of his temples.

"You're quiet tonight," I said. "Have you tasted the white asparagus? They're really succulent, the best . . ."

He gestured my words away, dismissing them and me.

"Waiter!" He clapped his hands imperiously. "More champagne. You understand? Good. Then answer me in German."

He turned back to me. "You think I'm acting crudely, don't you? That I'm just another boorish German oaf . . ."

"I think you've had too much to drink, Franz."

"I intend to have more. And you?"

"I've had quite enough. But you go ahead."

"Nonsense. The evening's just beginning. I don't want to drink alone. And look, you've barely touched your dinner."

"Forgive me. A headache. I'm just not hungry."

A tall, slender man with gilded epaulets appeared at my right and, bowing, kissed my hand. "Good evening, Colonel," I said. "How delightful to see you again. May I present Captain Franz Josef Behrenson. This is Colonel Blasingame."

"Honored," Behrenson grumbled but made no effort to rise. Nor did he hide his fury.

"Do you realize whom you just insulted?" I hissed when the colonel departed.

"Who gives a shit. How do you know him?"

"He came to one of Madame de Sevigny's soirees."

"Fuck fests, you mean. I see. And last night it was the party of Colonel Bechmann, and before that Colonel Schneider. Tell me, Odette: is there any officer in the German high command you haven't fucked?"

He was dangerously angry, dangerously drunk. "You know what I do," I said. "Why are you suddenly so upset?"

"You idiot!" he screamed. "Don't you know?"

I was genuinely bewildered. "No, I don't."

"Damn it, it's because I love you. And you don't love me back."

In his room, I kneaded Franz's taut shoulder muscles and felt their tension slowly diminish. He looked old, beaten, as though the confession of love had drained him of all energy. Behrenson looked up at me and seemed to be measuring his words.

"Odette, when I was a young man I really believed in a new Germany. I loved the military, worked hard, and became a captain. I thought that Hitler could rebuild Germany to what it once was. I met Hitler many times. To me he was like a God. I dreamt of bigger things. I wanted to become part of the New Order. I loved every minute of our victories. When we marched through Poland, Hungary, Belgium, and France—every day was exciting. How important I felt. I even believed we could conquer England. I would lie awake at night dreaming of the excitement of driving through London waving the German flag.

"What happened? I don't know. Did our defeat in Russia change everything? I never thought the United States would enter the war. I knew that once the invasion of Europe by the Allies was successful, it was over for us."

Behrenson started to cry, but I didn't have any pity for him. He was a Nazi. Moreover he had become a petty, bitter man, always poised at the edge of violence, and I was contemptuous of his weaknesses. Stealing secrets from him had become routinely simple. Good God, the fool trusted me, and what kind of man was that?

A frightening man. There was no security in his arms anymore, for he would likely turn on me soon, even as he had turned against his own government. Once he believed in the New Order and the Franco-German alliance. Now he understood that his Führer would leave Paris in ruins and forget about the men he stationed there.

Tonight, however, I would not have to make love to him. The alcohol was making him drift in and out of coherence.

"Relax," I whispered, letting his close-cropped blond head ease back against my breasts. "Darling, you're so tense. You're been like a Lugar with the trigger cocked ever since General von Rundstedt left Paris."

"Not left. He was called away. Gerd von Rundstedt would never flee Paris. Not now, and not a year ago when he realized it was hopeless. The greatest military genius of our era, and the Führer relieves him of his command. Not once, but twice. Wait: you'll see. Hitler will summon him again. And like an obedient hunting dog he'll return. The rest of them aren't fit to lick his boots. His replacement, Von Kluge, is a yes-man. Hitler says he wants an offensive and Von Kluge delivers—with schoolchildren sent to their deaths."

His eyes were bloodshot and he stared at me with his flushed features twisted in anguish. I knew I was walking a tightrope.

"At least he's not here to see it," I offered. "Or to be accused with the rest of the generals in the July twentieth plot. Just think of it—he's away from the Western Front. I wonder why he was called from Paris."

Behrenson was furious. "You make it sound as if his disgrace doesn't matter."

"It doesn't. Not to me. I'd give anything to get out of Paris myself. Just for a day, an afternoon."

"Anything?"

"To be free, yes." Oh, how true it was! My hope rose. Maybe, if I played him right, Behrenson would help me go free.

He grimaced. "So now it's freedom you want? Not caviar or champagne or leather boots, but freedom. From what? From me?"

I flushed. "Freedom from everything. I'm tired of the sawdust bread, the blacked-out buildings, and the endless men—I'm tired of them all except you."

The flattery was useless. "With the city about to be besieged, it's hardly time to take a vacation." He looked at me suspiciously. "Perhaps you had something else on your mind. You *always* have something else on your mind. What is it this time, my love?"

"You're in an ugly mood tonight," I said. "You're cruel, especially since you say you love me. I don't think I should stay here."

"But you will. Because there's something you want. I can see it in your eyes, just like I see everything else in them. So let's save time. What are you after?"

"I told you: freedom. I thought perhaps I could drive out to the countryside."

"And you suppose that with the war closing in on us my driver has nothing better to do than—"

"I don't need your man. Sonia could drive. It would do her good—I've been worried about her. You say yourself that it's only a matter of weeks before the Allies arrive. By then we'll be living like prisoners."

"And where do you intend to go in a Military Intelligence staff car? To the north to meet the Allies? Or what would you two lovelies do when you find yourself surrounded by our own troops who haven't seen a woman—let alone two beautiful maidens from such a distinguished house—since the women they raped on the Eastern Front?"

"Don't be vulgar. We could drive to Sonia's place in the Ardennes. Just for the day. Do you realize how much that would mean to me?"

"It would mean you could sit in the hills untouched, wouldn't it? While Paris goes up in flames."

"I wouldn't desert you. Not after all our months together. Not like that."

"Then how?"

"Why are you asking me these wretched questions, Franz? What's gotten into you?"

"I'll tell you. When I first met you there was something fresh about you. I was deluded into believing you were as innocent as you seemed. And I fell in love with you."

"But you still love me," I cried, as though I wanted it.

"More than ever. That innocent Odette was the one good thing in my life, and it's still there, I know it, even after all the men you've serviced. But when I look for the innocence in your eyes, they seem mercenary. Hungry. I'm not sure for what—it isn't only the jewelry and fine wine. Maybe it's for men, any men. You want their eyes wandering up and down your body, their lips imagining the taste of your cunt. You lure them, tease them, reel them in. Whether we're out in Montmartre or having tea at the Ritz, you won't rest till you've caught their attention—every damn last one of them."

Yes, I wanted men looking at me, but not all men. Just German officers with military secrets to reveal.

"Why are you telling me this now?"

"Because I'm a senior officer. Love you or not, I could have you shot, send you to Fresnes prison, simply remove my protection to see how far you'd get without it. The Gestapo, for instance, would be delighted to tickle my mistress to find if there's a weak link in military intelligence. I know you, Odette, every crack and groan of your body. And what it comes down to is that you're just one more whore, like all the rest."

To have him point out what I already knew was more than I could bear. My open palm flew toward his gloating face. Blocking it with his arm, he sent my fingers crashing into the back of the chair.

He did not let go, and when I looked up his lips were trembling and his smile was ugly. Then he slammed his hand, with mine in it, against the wood.

I felt a brief burning pain, then numbness. I cradled my bruised hand against my breast, then held it out toward Behrenson, letting the damage register in his drunken consciousness. The middle finger was broken.

"Perhaps it will heal," he murmured sullenly.

"Not like it was." I stared at the crooked finger and my eyes filled with tears. A lifetime of training gone numb. It was the thing all pianists feared as much as death. Music was my life, and he had killed it.

"It was an accident. You brought it on yourself." By his tone, I knew he didn't believe it. He had sobered considerably by now, and there was remorse in his manner. He reached in his pocket for a set of keys, which he handed out to me, then drew back.

"What are these?"

"Car keys. To my Talbot. My escape vehicle, but I'll never escape. I'm not a deserter. You're free to leave me now. I won't try to stop you. So take the Talbot. It contains something more precious than gold: gasoline. Enough to get you to the Ardennes, or to the Rhine. Maybe into Free France if you're lucky." He turned a look on me of such hatred I thought my face would burn. "But gas is expensive. You must pay for it."

"How?"

He dropped into the easy chair and let the keys tumble to his lap. "You said you'd do anything to be free. Perhaps you should kneel and beg."

Swallowing bile, I did as ordered. He opened his buttons, pulled down his pants. "Feel my cock for the last time. It's eager for you. Yes: there it is."

I held his penis in my fingers. It grew hard. It was an ugly thing, with its carmine head flushing darker, barely visible about the foreskin.

I gazed at him and watched his eyes narrow with pleasure. He looked like every other German officer in the salon of the brothel, his smile crude, sharklike. "Suck," he ordered.

I couldn't. My throat closed, my stomach rebelled, and I wanted to vomit.

"Suck," he repeated and grabbed my head with his hand and pushed it forward. I surrendered, peeled back the foreskin.

"Don't hate me," he said as I started my work. "It had to end this way. For nearly a year you've tortured me, punished me. Ahhh. I've given you everything I could. I offered you love, pleaded with you to— oh, yes; that's good. I'm through begging. Now . . . you will take me . . . all of me . . . you will have me now . . . You . . . will . . . have . . . me."

His penis rammed against the back of my throat. I felt him shudder, tasted his bitterness. Through a haze of tears, I saw him arch up and he ground harder against my bruised lips. With a groan, he threw his head back and dropped his arms limply at his sides.

I fell backward and lay quiet.

"Forgive me," he whispered. "Forgive me. I'm so sorry. So ashamed. I never meant to . . ." He closed his eyes.

His pistol was in its holster; it had dropped to the floor when he took down his pants. I picked it up and when he opened his eyes I was kneeling before him with his pistol pointed at his groin. I moved the barrel up from his belly to a spot between his eyes, then slowly back down to his shriveled penis.

He whimpered.

Oh, how I wanted to shoot him, and in so doing revenge myself on all those who had murdered my family. How loathsome he looked! Contemptible, shuddering with fear, this man who had unwittingly betrayed his country over and over: I knew his core.

No, I wouldn't shoot. I hoped that maybe someday he would find out what I had made him do, realize how low he had fallen, and then perhaps he'd use a different gun—but his own, his own—to take his life. For me, knowing of his humiliation was preferable to killing him, a sweeter triumph. If I could have killed all Germans, I'd have killed Behrenson, too. But barring that, this way was better.

I stood, leaned over him, and spat it all into his face. He flinched but otherwise made no movement, said nothing. It slid down his face. "Swallowing it would have been like becoming one of you," I told him.

Snatching up the keys, I cast one last look at the crumpled figure in the wing chair. Then I dressed, tucked the weapon into my pocketbook, and left.

CHAPTER 27

"My God!" I gasped, clutching the passenger strap as Sonia lurched the Talbot into oncoming traffic and shot past a mud-spattered troop carrier. "You'll get us killed! It's crazy enough to be on an outing like this with Paris falling apart."

"I'm tired of being behind Germans," Sonia giggled, "or underneath or on top of them."

Her laughter delighted me. Surely Poincare was wrong about her. He had to be! And yet he had not been wrong yet. I caught myself, corrected my thinking. This girl was a traitor.

We veered around a corner and skidded toward a culvert, nearly colliding with a dogcart piled high with clothing.

"But a German paid for that cottage," I said.

"Get it straight, *cherie*. I paid for that cottage. Dearly. No German ever gives anything away."

I adjusted my mirror and glanced backward into the crowd of fleeing Parisians and looting officers. I'd guessed correctly: Franz wasn't going to send the Gestapo after us. Perhaps he even felt guilty about the damage he'd done to my hand. We had left the city behind and were crawling up a steep country road.

"Be careful, won't you," I said. "I think you had too much to drink at lunch. Let's not spoil our one day in the country."

"You just had too little," Sonia answered, winking at me. "Look at you, Odette. A bundle of nerves. We're not being followed, or do you just like Germans stealing from France? Madame gave us the day off, and we're going to my house." She drove in silence for a while, and when she spoke again it was obvious that the house was on her mind. "It's wonderful to think I'll soon be in that house forever. All by myself. Oh, it's taken so long! How many revolting soldiers and kinky bankers have I been through! They're all alike, Germans or Frenchmen, counts or bakers. When it comes to love, all men treat you like a bed toy with holes. Like so much plumbing. And you're supposed to be damn grateful for their come."

I fought back the memory of Franz's groin smashing into my face. "Maybe they're not all like that," I said wearily. Vinnie wasn't like that. Wolf wasn't like that. Sex can be love, I reminded myself, though it was hard to remember.

"You haven't been around long enough to know," Sonia said. "If you live with a man, in no time at all he starts cursing at you to iron his underwear. If he's a Frenchman he mounts you from behind so he doesn't have to look at you. If he's German, it's the garters and the whips."

"But haven't you ever been in love?"

"I thought I was, once. The motherfucker left me when I was five months pregnant."

Amazing! I looked at her closely. She was staring straight ahead without discernible emotion. "And the baby?"

"She died."

"You don't sound very upset."

She shrugged. "I'm not."

"You don't care about the death of babies?"

"Dead's dead."

"What about the baby who died in La Maison. The one who was killed with his mother?"

"They were Jews. I didn't know them."

So it was true! Irrefutably true. Poincare was right. There would be no ambiguity in my actions.

Outside the car, fields of wheat and alfalfa flattened beneath the onslaught of a sudden wind. To the east beyond the wooded high-lands, pine-covered hills twisted along the path of the Meuse.

"We're not far away now," Sonia said happily. "I always know when we're getting closer because of the color of the earth. See the way it's changed? We're going into the slate country. You should have seen the pasturelands before the war. It was like one green carpet along that valley—I swear it. But look! Here's the forest."

An hour later we saw the cottage in the distance through the tree-tops. There was no mistaking it. The mossy roof, the stand of pine trees forming a semicircle around it—even the shadows of the forest were just as Sonia described them.

"Doesn't look like the place for an inn, does it? Well, wait till you see the lake. In the summer it's gorgeous. Not exactly Cannes—but who knows?"

We stopped in the dusty driveway. Sonia vaulted out of the driver's seat and ran to an old hand pump. She swung the handle stubbornly until a trickle of water slid out of the spout. Laughing, she flung the drops on her head and let them slide down her neck to her breasts. How beautiful she was. How *alive*. I could dimly remember feeling like that with Vinnie. And before that, when I was singing or playing the piano. I looked at my bandaged hand and wanted to weep.

Sonia came back to the car and reached in back for the picnic bas-ket. She tugged at my arm. "What are you waiting for? Come on." I stepped out slowly.

"My you're moody today." Sonia threw her arms around my neck and kissed me full on the lips. I gave her a stiff pat on the shoulder. "But I forgive you, just like I forgive all your other little quirks. After all, you got us the car. Now I want to show you the house. This is where I always dreamed I'd return with my lover."

She put her arm around my waist and led me toward the cottage. Like a buoyant child she ran her fingertips along the rough hewn planking, rose up on her tiptoes to place her face against the window-panes. "I'll show you the inside. My grandfather laid the bluestones for the mantel himself."

Inside was a plain room with simple wooden furniture. Steps led upstairs, and there was a small rudimentary kitchen off to the side.

"Here's where I turned my first trick. He was a strapping farm boy—with the tiniest zeezee."

I laughed. "You're so unkind!"

"But it's true. I worshiped him, tiny zeezee or not. He gave me chocolates to play with him. But you know, I really adored him. I'll show you the upstairs."

I followed her up a narrow pine staircase, imagining the scent of oak fire, rabbit stew, mountain air. Was this how it had been for the Poles who occupied our house in Lodz? Had they ever stopped to wonder what became of the bodies curled contentedly under the blankets they now slept beneath? Did they know that Papa and Mama were dead—that Jozef was dead? That Mia was dead? I hoped they choked on the house—that it crumbled under them in protest of our being dislodged.

"Time for dinner," Sonia announced, and we went back outside, took up the picnic basket, and went down a switchback path leading to a stream. We could hear but not see a miniature waterfall as it flowed toward the lake just beyond the rise.

We came to a rocky promontory where the sun's light poured down on thickly piled pine needles. Here Sonia put down the basket, spread out a quilt, and knelt on it. Kicking off her shoes, she patted the spot beside her.

She handed me the champagne, and as I opened it, she slid out of her blouse and thrust her breasts at the afternoon sun. I looked at her blissful face, prettier now without the mascara, lipstick, and bright rouge she wore at La Maison. She was posing for me, arching her back, trying on a pout, fluffing her tangles of red hair. This was the woman Poincare told me to kill. The betrayer of refugees, the traitor to the Resistance, the evil one who did not care that babies died.

We clinked our glasses, drained them, filled them again. I allowed Sonia to remove my bonnet and then, pausing to caress me, slip the blouse from my shoulders. She brushed her lips on my neck, hugging me and pressing toward me until we fell backward, locked in an embrace.

"It's the mountain air. It always does this to me." She laughed. "No, it's because I'm happy here. With you."

She was making love to me! Perfect. It would make it easier for me to do what I had to. I closed my eyes and felt Sonia's hair trace softly over me as the sun beat down on my naked skin.

"Do you remember Natalie?" I asked.

She looked puzzled and shook her head.

"Natalie. The girl with the baby who the Gestapo killed."

She did not answer but rather let her fingers caress my breasts. She sighed.

"Natalie. It seemed to me that morning that you were giving a signal. To the Nazis."

She pulled her hand away and stared at me. "What are you talking about?"

But she *knew*. No one could have heard those screams and not remembered. "It doesn't matter. Come. Do what you were doing. It felt wonderful."

The gentle pressure resumed. I kissed her and slid my left hand between her legs, feeling her wetness. She murmured something unintelligible and closed her eyes. The picnic basket was sitting at the end of the quilt and I reached for it carefully, so as not to distract her.

There it was. The bread knife I had carefully packed before we left. I drew my hand from between her legs, and she pawed at it, wanting it back. I felt her belly beginning to tremble.

"Come, darling," she said. "I can't wait any longer. Please, please and then I'll do the same for you."

For a brief second, then, she opened her eyes to horror. The knife tore through her and she screamed with the force of its blow. Two, three times she bounced with each thrust of the knife, then collapsed on my thighs. "You paid the Germans too much for the house," I sobbed.

Sonia rolled her eyes in agony and began coughing blood. "The house . . . But it was Madame . . . Madame who . . ." And then she seemed to explode from within. Cradled on my blood-drenched lap, she stared upward into the twilight and died.

What did she mean, *It was Madame?* The possibility that I had killed an innocent girl tore at my mind until I could think no more. Acting mechanically, I wrapped her in the quilt and began search for a resting place for her body in the soft forest floor. Three times I had to stop, to turn around and be sick.

A dull moon was rising over the trees when I finally dragged the corpse to its makeshift grave. I threw handfuls of dirt over her figure until her face was no longer visible and recited what little I could recall of the Kaddish—funny, when I had said it so often for the Jewish dead, that I did not remember it all. When I finished, I gathered up Sonia's shoes and blouse and placed them in the grave as well, then covered it all, clothes, body, and memory, with a layer of earth and leaves. Finally, I tore off my blood-splattered clothes and unwrapped a package of clean ones I had hidden in the boot of the Talbot. Numb to the cold, I waded into the icy stream beneath the waterfall and scrubbed away Sonia's blood.

Her words came back to me like an unforgettable melody in a minor key: *it was Madame . . . Madame who . . .* My fingers seemed to burn my skin.

Gasping, I leapt out of the stream and shivered in the night breeze. Then I slid into the woolen sweater and skirt I'd brought and buried the old clothes under a pile of pine needles, not caring that they might be discovered. Who could possibly trace them back to me?

I washed my feet, then squatted by the bank and put on my socks and shoes. I slung the picnic basket on my elbow and began the climb back to Sonia's house and Behrenson's car.

CHAPTER 28

I pushed through the gate of La Maison aux Camillias, the old inflammation in my hip shooting pain with every step.

The trip back from the Ardennes had been brutal. Time and again I'd been forced to stop the car because so many people were fleeing Paris—mostly Germans, thank God—that the roads were too clogged for the Talbot, bucking the tide, to do anything but inch forward. Finally I'd abandoned it and slept in a chicken coop, a barn, and a haystack at night—running across uneven fields while the Germans fled eastward.

In the suburbs, I watched horse and mule carts stream through the Porte de Vincennes, Germans stealing paintings, mirrors, cigars, cognac and jewelry, everything of value they could carry. They moved slowly, nothing like what I was told was the exodus of the Jews from Warsaw at the beginning of the blitzkrieg. These pilgrims looted the caches of the wealthy as they ran, determined to consume as many cigars and liqueurs as their occupation-fattened bodies could accommodate.

As the Allies advanced, the occupying power grew vicious, just as the Aryans had in Poland. I watched them seek out their victims—not Jews, this time, or Resistance fighters or Communists, but any scapegoat they could lay their hands on. Innocent bodies on whom to vent their frustration.

I had the foolscap bearing the signature of the new commander of

Paris, von Choltitz, and the seal of his office as military commander hidden in my brassiere. This had been a bonus gift from Behrenson that he had tucked in the glove compartment—a priceless safe conduct with a blank space for entering names. It might protect me from the retreating Germans, or perhaps from being killed if I had to flee across the lines to join the Allied armies. On the other hand, it could mean instant death; since the twentieth of July, many petty officers and foot soldiers no longer swore allegiance to the generals, not even to Hitler's henchman von Kluge. As for von Choltitz, he was looked on as an executioner, a leveler of cities. His arrival had signaled a death sentence for Paris, just as it had for Rotterdam and Sebastopol and the swath of scorched earth marking his retreat from Russia.

I considered the alibi I'd use with Behrenson—it wouldn't be easy to explain why the car was gone and I was three days late in coming back—and could come up with nothing except a mugging and robbery. By now anyone—a curious neighbor, a German soldier, a child—might have stumbled onto the Talbot with its Military Intelligence decals. After two or three more days, they would also discover the hidden grave.

I'd reached the Metro at Nation just after dawn. Exiting German soldiers surrounded me on the stairway, pressing and pawing at me like ravenous wolves. A moment later, they'd vanished up into the morning, leaving me shaken and furious but unharmed. I paused to adjust my sweater, to brush invisible fingerprints off the pile. *Control.* I had to maintain control.

I rode the Metro to Kleber, then doubled back through the alleys and lanes of Chaillot. I had to avoid a chance meeting with Behrenson before I had time to think of what I'd say to him.

As I slid inside the door of La Maison, excited voices reverberated from inside the kitchen. I peeked inside. Figures were huddled around a radio concealed in a bread box.

"It's just like the last time," Pascal, the sous-chef groaned. "Two days ago they announced the liberation and nothing happened. Bells rang all over Paris, but the Allies never arrived."

"Well, this time they will," a woman unknown to me said.

"Shut up, you fool. Are you trying to get us killed? Madame's godchild just came in, for God's sake. The door's open and . . ."

They stared at me, at the caked dust and grime, the sunken eyes and cheeks. "Someone get her a chair," Martine, the *bonne de chambre,* yelled. "My God, what happened?"

"Sonia and I drove out to the country, to the east. And then . . ."

"So you saw the bastards fleeing? I hope the Allies strafed them into Swiss cheese."

"There weren't any Allies."

"Impossible. It's all over the BBC. Paris has been liberated."

"Think again," I said. "The city's crawling with Germans. They're everywhere, on the streets, in the Metro. I saw officers flee, but not troops. I'm telling you, there are twenty thousand Reich soldiers still in Paris, and not one of the Allies."

"Should we trust a German officer's whore instead of the BBC?" Pascal asked. Why was he so angry, I wondered. Panic began to grip me.

"If you can't trust me," I said, "your own eyes and ears will tell you. The soldiers are all speaking German."

"Then how do you explain the Prefecture of Police?"

"What of it?"

"You mean you haven't heard? It was seized by the Liberation Committee two days ago. The prefect fled. They've taken the town hall at Neuilly as well."

Then it was true. The Allies were coming! "And they've held them?"

"There's a cease-fire declared, so both sides can tend to their wounded."

"Von Choltitz agreed to a cease-fire? It's got to be some sort of trick."

"You sound disappointed." Pascal's voice was sharp, biting. "Can it be that you're ashamed to discover your beloved Nazis aren't invincible?"

"I may have fucked them," I said proudly, "but I hate their guts. You know nothing of real suffering, any of you. Protected here by Madame. But think it through. Don't you understand why Hitler let the SD and the Waffen SS and the Gestapo withdraw? Because the Germans have mined half the city. Every bridge, the Palais du Justice, the Arc de Triomphe. When the Allies reach Paris, they'll be blown to smithereens."

They gathered around me in a circle, unmoved. In some of the faces I read mistrust, in others hatred. "You must believe me! I'm telling the truth." The circle grew tighter, pressing me back against the butcher-block counter. Cutting off any possible escape.

"Listen," I said desperately. "Do you imagine I thrilled to the sound of Prussia's Glorie when the Krauts paraded from the Etoile to the Place de la Concorde? Or the sound of hobnailed boots up and down the steps of the Eiffel Tower? Do you think I liked fucking those swine who called themselves officers?"

"Then why did you do it?" Pascal asked.

"Because . . ." I stopped. I couldn't betray Poincare, couldn't, even at this late day, give the Resistance and my role in it away.

Their eyes grew darker, more dangerous. Martine grasped a meat cleaver.

I pressed against the table surface, my fingers probing blindly until they found the handle of a boning knife.

"Maman," a voice called from the corridor leading to the dining hall. It was Martine's twelve-year-old daughter, Yvonne. At the sound the servants stepped back and I was able to push through.

"Something's wrong with Madame," Yvonne said. "I was just up there combing her hair. She looks terrible, like a ghost. And she's carrying a pistol in her nightgown. It was scary. She kept saying she hoped nothing bad has happened to Sonia, whom she protected throughout the war. Protected her and protected all of us. She said Sonia was stupid, but a good girl. She explained that she was really innocent, that all she wanted was her cabin, which she hoped some-day to make into an inn."

"What did you say?" I could barely get the words out.

"Mademoiselle Odette, is that you? I barely recognized you. Per-haps you can tell Madame what happened to Sonia."

"Repeat what she said about Sonia."

"She said Sonia should be pitied, that her worst sin was stupidity."

And I had killed her, murdered her innocence. Pine needles shifted before my eyes and tumbled onto the shallow grave. I felt the sensation of her body bobbing up with the force of the knife I had thrust into her neck.

Sonia was innocent, and Madame was carrying a gun.

"Why are you all looking at me like that?" I screamed.

Pascal took my arm. "Calm down, Mademoiselle Odette. No one's going to harm you. It's just that we want to know what you did with Sonia."

I had killed an innocent girl. Killed her just as surely as the Ger-mans had killed my family, sacrificed her, as they had been sacrificed, for nothing.

"Excuse me," I said, vomit rising in my throat. "Excuse me. I must . . ."

I shook free of Pascal's hand and fled down the narrow corridor leading to the dining hall. I raced across the foyer and up the winding stair, one hand clutching the worn stone railing while with the other I drew the blade of the boning knife back against the empty air. Let me get there in time, I thought. Please God, let me not be too late.

CHAPTER 29

When I reached Madame de Sevigny her corpse hung from the chandelier like some dadaist mobile. A current of air from the window carried her to the right, the left, then back again—each movement increasing my fury that she had denied me revenge. I fought back an urge to plunge the knife into her lifeless breast. I wanted to stab her once for each of the lives she had taken, especially for Sonia's. I stared at the hanging body and then cut her down.

A thrilling sound came from outside: the pounding of 88-millimeter guns. Either the Allies were attacking the city or the Germans were fighting back against them. Either way it meant the Americans were here. It was only a matter of time before von Choltitz would pronounce Paris's death sentence.

I stared at Madame's limbs as I placed her body on the floor, searching for some hint of evil, some mark of the devil. But there was nothing. A gun protruded from her belt. I snatched it up, wondering why she wore it in her last minutes—perhaps she had been torn between wanting to fight and dying before she could be captured—and hid it in my own belt, between my sweater and skirt.

It was as if everything had been decided in a cosmic game too intricate for any mortal to decipher. Who would live and who would die. Who, like Madame, would sentence strangers to unwarranted deaths. And who, like Sonia, should be chosen to pay for someone else's crimes.

Odette LeClerc had been created to strike back at the Nazis. In some small way she had performed her role—information had been given to Poincare that might have eased the Allies' route to Paris. But she had brought the Nazis pleasure, swine like the baron and Behrenson and Roos, and succeeded only in killing a soft-faced engineer named Westerdorp. And she had killed an innocent girl. Even strangling Hitler himself couldn't make up for that.

"Mademoiselle Odette?" It was Yvonne, coming up the stairs toward Madame's room. I intercepted her, closing the door behind me. "There's a call for you," she said.

Putting my arm around her, I led her back toward the stairs. "A call for me?" Unbelievable. The phone system was still functioning, I noted—but who would call me at La Maison? Surely my German clients were occupied with more important matters.

"Yes, Mademoiselle. A gentleman. An English gentleman. His French was very bad."

Johnston? Impossible. Poincare? His French was impeccable. I knew no one else. "Did he give his name?"

"No, ma'am. But he said it was urgent."

"Very well. I'll take it below stairs."

"If Mademoiselle doesn't need me anymore, I should straighten up Madame's bedroom. It was an awful mess. She'll be angry when she discovers—"

I couldn't let Yvonne see the body—not yet. "Absolutely not," I said. "You are not to disturb her."

"But what if Madame needs me? You know how furious she gets."

"She won't need you. Not this morning, I promise. Go about your other business. Madame will call you when she's ready."

I watched Yvonne step hesitantly down the corridor toward the servants' passage. Her spindly white calves and arms into which she had not yet grown seemed to flail as she walked. She's only twelve, I thought. There was just a hint of womanhood in her hips, a suggestion of fullness in her derriere. She was oblivious to the desolation awaiting her.

I went down the stairs and slipped into the telephone nook. "Hello."

"Am I speaking to Mademoiselle LeClerc?" Not English. American!

"Who is this, please?" I did not doubt that others were listening in. Perhaps Madame's spies. Perhaps the baron's. Or whatever remained of the Gestapo. Perhaps even Poincare.

"Is this Odette LeClerc?" the voice insisted.

Above me, hobnail boots clicked down the stairs as a last pair of hungover German officers zigzagged toward their limousine.

"I'm Odette LeClerc," I whispered.

"Then why not say so? Mademoiselle, this is Bor . . ."

A rumbling from his end made him impossible to hear. "You must speak louder, Monsieur. I can barely hear you."

"Please forgive me. It's the tanks on the pavement. They make a real racket."

"Tanks? Whose tanks?"

"Ours, of course. The Americans'."

The Americans! How close were they? "Where are you calling from?"

"From the Café au Vieux Sanglier, across from the Poste."

"In what town, please."

"Why, in Paris. We're about to take the city. That's why I'm calling. I've been trying for perhaps two hours. I have a message for you."

A message? "You must be mistaken," I said, a germ of hope fluttering into my brain. No. Preposterous. Don't think it. I held my breath, listening for any sound that might betray a phone tap. Obviously, it was a trap. Even back in Rockefeller Plaza I had been warned about such clumsy tricks. "I'm afraid I must hang up."

"Wait. Please. I've had the devil of a time tracking you down. I figured you must be with the Resistance—he couldn't love anyone who wasn't a fighter. I'm in Intelligence. This kid, seems to be a great friend of yours, he's sure smitten, begged and begged me to find out if you were in France. I didn't know how but ran into a fellow calling himself Poincare—can't tell his nationality, French probably. Anyway, he showed us the best route to Paris, seemed to know just where the Germans were and weren't. I mentioned you casually, asked if he'd ever heard of you, and he said he had but didn't know where you were. He suggested I call a man in England, a Colonel Johnston, who told me where I'd find you. Johnston told me your new name. I wouldn't have done this for just anybody, but your friend saved my life when we got into France. I figured I owed him one. He'd have called himself, only he's with the infantry and they're pushing on."

Johnston. The name was magic. Or maybe it was a trap, so subtle I couldn't figure out the meaning of it. "What's this young man's name?"

"Sforza. Vinnie Sforza."

God in Heaven, be a just God. "What does he look like, this Sforza?"

"Tall, Mademoiselle. Dark black hair and lots of it. Otherwise, I don't know. I'm afraid I'm not very good at descriptions. But I don't understand. Surely you know without my having to tell you."

Yes, I knew, the image of him so clear in my brain it was clear beneath my tears. A feeling that had lain dormant inside me for many months—which I did not remember, did not even know existed—rose to my heart and made it sing. "You say this soldier's in Paris?" My voice trembled like my hands.

"Yes. He told me to tell you to doll up. He's coming to see you."

Before shock and joy, shame and exhilaration, guilt and relief had a chance to penetrate, a shell hit La Maison, and it exploded around me.

CHAPTER 30

The name "Vinnie" was all but obliterated by the echo of artillery fire. Dazed, I ran outside, ignoring the cries from inside the damaged La Maison.

It was true. American tanks had entered the city—I could see them rumbling down the avenue. The city would be liberated within hours. What were the Germans waiting for? I wondered. Why hadn't von Choltitz ordered the destruction?

And if the Americans were here, perhaps Vinnie *was* with them, perhaps the anonymous "Bor—" had told the truth and even now my lover, my rescuer, my missing heart was racing toward me. *Be careful, my love. Don't get hurt now. I am here for you, waiting for you, longing for you. Be careful.*

Life was awakening within me. I could almost touch the end of my suffering. Perhaps what was happening now was the vision my father had seen when he pushed me out of the cattle car and commanded: *Live.* I had lived, and now I wanted to hold Vinnie against my body on top of clean sheets and whisper to him of my love. We'd go to Poland. I'd promised Nate Kolleck that I'd let the world know of the hell of the Baluty, and I would keep that promise with Vinnie beside me.

And Papa and Jozef. If this miracle happened today, perhaps another was possible—though I must not ask too much, I told myself; not too much—and they could return to Lodz and start again.

Without a uniform I didn't dare head out to the barricades. No, I would wait in this stone crypt, like Juliet, and awaken to my Romeo's kiss.

"I know what you are," a voice shouted above the music of the "Marseillaise." *"I know about Franz Behrenson."* Desperately, I searched for some hint of warmth or forgiveness, but there was only fury in that voice. *"You're filthy,"* it said. *"A whore."*

Suddenly I was alone on the Brooklyn hillside where Vinnie and I had last made love. I searched for him frantically. Yes, there he was, and I ran to embrace him, but he turned his back and would not look at me. But surely he understood why I couldn't tell him about the hotel in Warsaw where Egon Hildebrand had caressed me and gotten his skull shattered as a result? How could I speak to him about the Baron's Chamber or Franz Behrenson or Sonia, whose eyes were looking at me now with infinite reproach. Where would I have found the words?

A loud crash sat me bolt upright. I staggered to my feet. How long had I been asleep? Why hadn't Vinnie come?

Another shell burst nearby. Where would I be safest? Where could I best wait for him? I don't know what led me to the Baron's Chamber, but there I was. One wall had been blown away, and this room of sadism and delight looked pathetic in the shafts of sunlight. The piano was still there—thank God! I saw my own face in the mirror. My eyebrows were plucked and arched, my eyelids blackened with the residue of kohl. From my uncombed hair to my ragged blouse and skirt I looked like a whore discarded when her usefulness was over.

I went to a secret compartment the baron had let me hew out of the wall and snatched up my jewelry, wrapping the items in a kerchief: a string of pearls from the baron; earrings and a brooch from Franz; a watch from a soldier whose name I'd forgotten—even a simple silver bracelet from Sonia, a monetarily worthless keepsake but the only one that moved me to tears.

The Baron's Chamber was coming alive with screams, like a spectral choir returning to convict me. I was the one who should have been whipped, not my clients. Madame had often let me sit at the piano and play. I remembered the music Poincare had arranged for Westerdorp. Now I would play—damaged finger and all, I would play. Vinnie would hear it and know where I was.

I sat and pounded out a C-major chord, trying to still the screams racing through my brain. What should I play? Ah, the Schumann opus 73 for clarinet and piano. Vincent would hear my part and join me and together we would play as we had on idyllic Sundays long ago. I could not play well; my finger was weak. If I struck the keys forcefully, I could produce notes with an odd, almost syncopated delay. But it was music for Vinnie, and I played with my whole heart. *Oh Vinnie, hear it. Please hear it and remember!"*

Someone pounded on the door. "Who's in there?"

Vinnie? No, the voice was unfamiliar. I walked toward the door, then paused. *The whips.* He mustn't see the whips. I threw them in a corner with the rest of the debris. Evidence accused me from every part of the room: glistening metal and sweat-stained leather, bloodstains in the Persian carpets.

The door pressed inward as I tried to control my right hand, which was numb with pain.

"Just a minute," I called. "I'm—"

With a crash, the door flew open. An American sergeant stood at the door along with a red-eyed Frenchman clutching an ancient rifle in his hands.

"Where's Vincent?" I asked.

"Mademoiselle," the Frenchman said, "the people of Paris accuse you of whoring with the Germans. You will come with us now."

The shock sent electricity into my hands, and I winced with pain. "But that's ridiculous. I'm with the Allies."

The two of them stared at me. "Will you come peaceably?" the sergeant asked.

"But what about Vincent? Don't you understand? I'm waiting for someone. He's coming to see me. I've just received a call from the American Army telling me so."

"Come along," the Frenchman said, pulling at my arm.

Yvonne stood watching at the door. "Tell him about the call," I implored. "You were there when I got it."

She spat in my face.

I stepped back, the kerchief falling from my pocket, the brooch falling to the floor.

"You see!" the Frenchman cried triumphantly. "A gift from the Nazis. Proof of her crimes." He put his face up to mine; I could smell fury on his breath. "And what did you give in return? Not just your body, I'll bet. Perhaps the name of the Free French who disappeared. Good Christ, you're worse than the Bosch!"

"Move," the sergeant ordered. I hung back. His hands exploded against my face. *"Move!"*

I staggered forward, hunched so far over that the stairs seemed to leap at my face. Each step was punctuated by a sharp, stinging pain in my hip.

They paraded me in front of the La Maison staff, but there was no respectful curtsying, no polite words now.

"Help me," I stammered. "Please won't someone tell them I'm innocent?"

One by one they pummeled me, kicking and cursing and tearing at my matted hair.

"Sonia!" I called. "Someone get Sonia."

Sonia was dead. I'd almost forgotten. I clenched my hands, letting my fingernails tear into my palms to drive out the memory. *She was an informer, don't you see? I could never have killed an innocent woman.*

There was a cheer from outside. "Is the crowd gathered?" the sergeant asked.

"Thirty or forty in the courtyard. But Charles says we should take her to—"

"Charles is a horse's ass," the Frenchman said. "He wants us to deliver up our collaborators to de Gaulle. But he can't steal this moment from us. We started the liberation while he was out making speeches behind Allied lines. We paid for this with the blood of our comrades, Maquis blood, Communist blood. The collaborating whores are rightfully ours."

The sergeant shrugged. "They've already fled. Every name on our list except this one here. The others are patriots. They're upstairs now, drinking champagne."

"Well, at least we have one of them. She'll have to do."

They dragged me outside. The noon sun burned down, blinding me. I could hear shouts of derision, epithets, catcalls. I stared out at the sea of angry mouths and flailing arms, and soon I could make out a few faces: Bouvier, the bread baker. The crone from the corner bistro, her flesh swathed in what had been a set of rose damask drapes. "*Vive la France!*" she shouted with the others. "*Vive la France!*"

The men holding me let go, and I collapsed on the steps. The crowd was on me in a second. Features twisted by hatred and hunger, they surged over me in a lava of fury, spitting and kicking and tearing at my clothes.

With exaggerated tenderness, the group's leader wrapped his brawny arms around me and carried me toward a makeshift platform. I tightened my grasp around his neck, ignoring the stabbing pains in my hip, and pressed my breasts against his chest. *You'll save me.* I opened my mouth, letting the fingers of my left hand brush lightly over his neck and he leaned to lower me onto the platform.

His eyes raced up and down over the contours of my body. I looked up at him, arms outstretched. *Yes. Want this body. This mouth. I'll give them to you. You can do whatever you want with me. I'll pleasure you, tear you apart and make you cry out for more. If only, afterward, you'll let me go free.*

He turned to survey the faces of the crowd, then slowly wheeled around and spat into my eye.

The red-eyed Frenchman walked up to me and threw a piece of paper on my chest. "Odette LeClerc. You have been denounced as a traitor, a collaborator with the Germans. In this letter are the details of your associations with the Baron de Tourneau, with Franz Behrenson, and with a dozen lesser Nazis who gave you jewelry, an automobile, countless other gifts. In addition, you are accused of betraying comrades, refugees, members of the Resistance. There can be no refutation of these charges. The proof is absolute." He raised both hands over his head and bowed to the man who had carried me to the platform. "Monsieur Bir, I leave her to you."

"Vive la France," a voice cried from behind me, and the knot surrounding me again picked up the chant. *"Vive la France."*

Bir's massive hands ripped open my shirt and threw it back over my shoulders. Another man grabbed my hair and yanked it back while a woman with a scissors cut it off in large handfuls. I closed my eyes and prayed for death.

Collaborator. Traitor. Spy. It no longer mattered what they called me. I was all those things and worse—the filthiest whore, the lowest cunt, a unique type of vermin defiling their city, their lives.

A shot rang out. Someone screamed, and the crowd stepped back. An American soldier approached. *Vinnie?* I couldn't be sure. Whoever he was, he did not love me, for he grabbed my shoulders roughly and hauled me to my feet, walking me through the crowd to—where? All I knew was that the gravel stung my bare feet. The red-eyed Frenchman stood in front of us, arms raised. "Stop," he shouted. "She's ours."

"Sorry," the soldier said, and he wasn't Vinnie but a stranger with a pale face and sad eyes. "We've orders to take the collaborators, those who might give us valuable information, to headquarters. If I leave her here, you'll kill her."

"What kind of information can you get from a twat?" the Frenchman grumbled, but he stood aside and let us pass.

I let myself go limp against the soldier, embracing him as the savior he was. He half-pulled, half-carried me through the crowd and onto a relatively deserted street where a jeep was waiting.

"Do you know a soldier named Vincent Sforza?" I asked him.

He thought for a moment. "Fellow by that name was with the 101st Airborne," he said. "He was with us, helped take the city. I met him once. Seemed like a nice guy, anxious as all get-out to be in Paris. But he was killed this morning, I think—leastways, that's what I heard. He isn't around here now, I can tell you."

All hope gone. Nothing and no one to live for. I had left my family in a boxcar carrying them to their deaths, and I envied them their annihilation and Vinnie his. The soldier helped me into the jeep and we started off. To headquarters, he said. But weren't all headquarters the same? Hadn't the beasts won after all? What was the difference between this soldier and the Germans, the men I had fucked in vain?

Vinnie was dead. Mia was dead. They could do with Odette what they willed.

"*Vive la France!*" the crowd behind us shouted.

CHAPTER 31

I clutched my bulging net bag in my left hand and with my right
held on to the handrail of the steps leading from the Lodz train station. My left hip throbbed, the old wound as bothersome as ever.

Below me, people were rushing back and forth across the tracks,
drinking coffee out of ceramic mugs, slapping one another on the
back, calling out greetings. I slunk forward, pulling my bandanna
around my close-cropped head, grimacing every time a voice called
out for fear I would be recognized.

Outside the station, there was a sign for the taxi queue, but there
were no taxis. The war had taken more of a toll in Lodz than in Paris.
Cars were still rarities on its bombed-out avenues.

Faces on the street were grim, drawn. There were few children and
fewer men. Filth and decay had settled in. The air was gritty with
brick dust from the shattered buildings, and the streets sparkled with
infinitesimal shards of glass.

Home, I thought, trying the word out in this ugly, barren town. I
had been questioned cursorily by American Army Intelligence, who
let me go once they had contacted Colonel Johnston and found out
who I was. They offered no privileges for the work I'd done, and no
gratitude. I was just one less person they had to worry about, and the
sooner I was out of their offices, the better.

I had no place to go, so I went home.

I trudged through familiar streets. Rubble had taken the place of the café where Jozef and I once had listened to string quartets. The small bakery we used to patronize was, literally, a hole in the ground. At least the German street signs had been taken down and replaced by the old Polish ones.

I walked furtively, afraid I would be identified as a collaborator or a Jewess, though my bandanna hid my head and there were no Jews left in Lodz. Past Walnosci Place I went, up Nowomiejska, on my way to the Baluty. Doctors, lawyers, shopkeepers, housewives once lived here. Where had they gone?

I remembered the clatter of horse-drawn wagons, the Jews with bundles strapped to their bodies, leaving their homes for the ghetto. The streets were finally clear of newspaper-shrouded corpses, there were no more dung wagons, and nowhere did children squat in the mud and shovel it greedily into their mouths.

There was only stillness now. Clouds spread across the sky, casting purple reflections on panes of glass in the windows of vacant houses.

My memories peopled this city of the dead. Here was where the tin pan seller endlessly chanted his singsong advertisement. Farther along was the place where I had seen a man weeping for the first time—there would be many weeping men to follow. I remembered Nate Kolleck talking about a couple who lived there, in the apartment above his, who scandalized the other families by making love with the curtains open. Perhaps they had survived somewhere. Perhaps Nate had also.

I walked up the rickety stairs into the now deserted flat where Nate had shown me his photographs. It had been burned. Nothing remained. Not a sink, a usable plank of wood, a piece of glass. But in the corner something caught a ray of the sun and reflected back its glare. Film cans stacked neatly in the doorway. I picked them up and opened them all carefully. They were filled with charred celluloid. The images and memories Nate had risked his life to preserve had perished in the fire.

And to think that with my shaven head I had been afraid of being mistaken for an Orthodox Jewess! What would a Jew look like to the present inhabitants of Lodz? There were no more Jews in Poland. It was *Judenrein* as Der Füehrer had promised. Purified by fire. Here in the Baluty King Chaim had lost his bid for sainthood.

I knelt on the cobblestones, waiting for phantoms to return, for a voice, any voice, to call out to me in greeting. For a reason to move. Gradually the afternoon wind rose up, kicking the dust about my face. It was an arid, bitter wind, as parched as the emptiness inside me. I had no tears left, no emotion.

In the distance an old woman was singing, the notes falling like the flapping of birds' wings. I could just make out the melody, one of those ghetto songs I had sung for my father:

> *It burns, brothers, it burns*
> *Our little house is on fire*
> *And you're standing with folded arms*
> *While it burns.*

Her voice grew louder, more shrill. She was coming closer, eyeing me as I knelt at the side of the street. She was a witch, deformed and menacing, her crocked finger beckoning me to join her.

> *It burns, brothers, it burns*

With a scream, I pulled myself up and ran. I had to see what had become of our home.

I stood at the gate, watching the lights come on up and down the block. Here, at least, there was life. People lived on this street, even though I would know none of them.

In the front yard, a little girl, about seven or eight, stood with her hands on her hips, staring at me defiantly with fierce blue eyes.

"Who are you?" she asked. "Why are you so dirty?"

I opened the gate and started up the slate path to the house. "My name is Marisa, and I'm dirty because I've been on a long trip and haven't had a chance to wash. What's your name?"

"Junka Kowalska. I live here with my mother and father."

Was this the same family that had taken over the house when we were sent to the ghetto? I couldn't be sure.

"Is your mother home?"

"Yes."

"Do you think she'd allow me to look at your house?"

"No."

I stood without moving, undecided. "It's Friday night, isn't it?"

"Of course it's Friday night. So what?"

I shook my head and looked for the glow of the Sabbath candles in the living room window. For the familiar scowl as Mama called me to hurry in, please, before sundown. The Sabbath was about to begin. There would be prayers, and the ritual blessing of the bread and wine. If only I could be this girl's age again. Then there would be sweet raisin wine for me.

We would be together, all four of us. After dinner, I would sit at the Bechstein and Jozef would stand beside me and I would play while we both sang. As the candles burned we would be in the parlor, rapt in our music, while Mama and Papa sat on the love seat across from the music stand. Papa would smoke his pipe. Mama would listen with the attentiveness she always gave to me and Jozef.

"Junkaaaa," a voice called from a side door. "Junkaaa Kowalskaaa"

"I'm right here, Nanny," the little girl yelled.

"Well, come in this instant. Who's that you're talking to?"

"No one." The little girl raced into the house.

No one.

I waited a moment, then approached and peered through unfamiliar curtains into the interior of the house. There were a man, a woman, and a teenaged girl, evidently Junka's parents and sister, sitting in easy chairs sipping sherry. They looked comfortable, self-assured, as though they belonged in this house—the Levy house. For the Levys were dead, you see, and I, no one, was invisible.

I pushed past privet hedges and lifted myself up to peer into the dining room. A pale blue Chinese rug, an odd teak corner cupboard, Vienna Modern chairs, an ebony table. Nothing of ours. The coldness of the room's elegance tore at my throat. The terrifying pain in my chest shocked me. I had not imagined I had any heart left to break.

I watched as the family moved into the dining room and settled themselves. A sumptuous pot roast was served by an aproned woman, the cook. The father lowered his head for a moment, then lifted his hand and made the sign of the cross. The mother and her two daughters followed. They were a handsome family, dignified, comfortable. As unshakable as Dr. Benjamin Levy and his family had once been.

I pressed my fingernails into my palms and tried to erase the image out of my memory. I closed my eyes and wanted to scream so loud my screams would destroy the salon and dining room and everything in it, people as well as furniture.

Should I rap on the front door, announce myself? My raincoat was filthy, my white socks turned a dirty gray, and my reddened hands clung to an old string sack. The maid wouldn't let me in the door. My door. My family's door. A door forever closed to Jews.

I wanted to go to the prefect of police, return with officers to take possession of my house. I would have Junka and her family thrown out, just as we had been thrown out. It was only fair, only right. The Bechstein, the paintings, the silverware, all that had been stolen from us.

The house—Lodz itself—was suddenly oppressive. I could not stay here. I would once again have to run.

"Where do you want to go, young lady?"

"Away."

"Yes, of course. What's your destination?"

"Anywhere. It doesn't matter."

"Why not go home, then? It's midnight. The next train doesn't leave until morning."

"Where's it going?"

"Budapest."

"I'll go there, then."

"Now look here, miss. What's your name?"

No one. "Look at my travel card. What does it say?"

"It says . . ." The stationmaster paused, running his fingers over the raised official Displaced Persons stamp I had received in Paris—"Mia Levy."

"Ah, but that's wrong, you see. Mia Levy is dead. She died with the rest of her family at Auschwitz. My name is Odette LeClerc, and I want to go to Budapest."

He handed me my ticket and I paid for it. "Where will I stay the night?" I asked.

"You can't stay in the station. It's dangerous. Why don't you stay at a friend's house? Or a relative, maybe."

"Friend? Relative? That's very funny. They're ghosts . . . I had a friend, several of them. But that was before . . . I was bad. Yes, very wicked. They shaved my head because of it. Here, let me show you."

I ripped off my bandanna and showed him my infected scalp. "You see?"

He shuddered involuntarily. "You should get that looked at," he said. "There's a clinic, but I'm afraid it's closed."

"I can't go to a clinic. I'm leaving for Budapest first thing in the morning."

He was growing impatient. "There's a hotel around the corner. Do you have money? You could spend the night there."

"Money?" I reached in my pocket. "I'm rich. Here. Look." I pulled out not zloty, but a roll of blackened celluloid film. I stared at it for a second then began to shriek, tossing it onto the terra-cotta floor and jumping back in fright.

"Miss . . ."

I fainted.

Voices, sirens, screams, bursts of gunfire exploded in my head. I could see Jozef scowling down at me from the roof of the station. Mama was with him, looking also, but her eyes had turned to glass. And Papa—Papa was at my side, pushing me off the bench on which I was lying. Why was he trying to hurt me? Didn't he know how much I loved them all?

"I did everything I could," I told him. "You believe me, don't you? I fought the Nazis in Paris. Fought them by fucking them." My anger was infinite. "You made me a whore. I lasted as long as I could for you. And for Jozef and for Mama. But I wasn't strong enough. I couldn't save you. You're dead. I know that, but I had to try. I never had a chance to say good-bye and now you're pushing me away again. Jozef, please don't be mad. It wasn't my fault. And I almost made it . . . Where's Mia? She's downstairs in the music room. Listen to how beautifully she plays and sings. Yes, Papa, just like a songbird."

I could see her clearly, this young songbird. Such intensity, such single-mindedness in her playing. Oh, and she was beautiful, un-touched, pure behind the protection of the great bay window of her parents' house. She would be a great performer one day, and a fine lady.

I lifted my hand toward the four of them—Mama, Papa, Jozef, Mia. Vinnie was with them now, taller than all of them, his arms so large they could surround the entire family. They beamed back at me, adoring me, telling me it was all right, and my voice rang out like crystal, radiant and full of hope. . . .

When I awoke I was lying on a bench. Someone had covered me with a piece of canvas. The sun was shining through. Did I sleep for days? I felt so rested, but for a moment I didn't know where I was.

A loudspeaker blared, shattering the song. "Six-thrity express to Budapest. Track three."

Weary, every bone aching, but sane now, aware of who I was and where I was going, I headed for the train.

Epilogue

1975

The mirror is a cruel companion when you're fifty-two. I used it only for essentials: face clean, hair combed, teeth brushed, clothes presentable. I avoided it as much as possible. A living corpse disintegrates more slowly than a dead one, but it decays all the same, and I had no desire to assess the damage.

Until this morning.

This morning I stared at myself as though I were a painter and my image a portrait. The hair: better left to fall naturally over the shoulders or tied back in a ponytail? It was black still and though without the luster of youth, still my most striking attribute. Let it fall. The face: what could be done about the too-deep tan, the lines—crevices—etched like paths on a three-dimensional map? A little cold cream, a touch of rouge; these were all I had; they would have to do. The dress, bought on a whim two years ago because a woman had to have something fresh other than shorts and work shirts in her wardrobe even if she only wore it to town meetings: how could I disguise its dowdiness? Ah, the belt gave it a hint of style. Drawn tight it flattened my stomach, slimmer than when I was a girl, given my labors in the field, and made my breasts more prominent. Good breasts still. I remembered his hands on them and felt my face flush.

I must have spent an hour in front of that mirror. There was only so much repair I could manage, and that was accomplished quickly. For the rest of the time I simply let my thoughts drift back to Brooklyn and Vinnie, and listened to the music—faint, sweet, rhythmic, jazzy, tranquil—in my head.

So far away was I that when there was a knock on the door it took me a moment to realize that since the nearest house was half a mile distant, the visitor had come to see *me.*

"Vinnie!" I cried, jumping up with such awkwardness that the chair tumbled behind me and racing the few steps through the living room to the entrance. I was panting as though the run had been much longer, and I waited a second, taking deep breaths, then flung open the door.

Oh, he was beautiful! In all my imaginings, all my longings, I had not conceived the firm set of his jaw, his chiseled cheeks, the same back hair, shorter now but untouched by time, his athlete's body, the strength he exuded even standing still. A mature Vinnie, but most definitely Vinnie, a honed version of his younger self. At first I dared not look at his piercing eyes—it was too dangerous—but with a shiver I conquered fear and glanced at them.

They were smiling, *he* was smiling, and I smiled back, using muscles strange to me.

"Mia," he said softly, and held out his hands.

It was too soon to touch him. "Come in."

He picked up the suitcase he had dropped at his feet and followed me inside. *Was he planning to stay?* I started to tremble. "I didn't hear a car," I told him.

"That's because I parked in the field. I wanted to walk a bit before I saw you. Compose myself."

Then he was nervous, too! The thought calmed me; we were equals. "Would you like coffee? Tea?"

"Coffee, please."

We were both standing. I was aware of how spartan the room looked, simple wooden furniture with a few throw pillows for color, a standing bookshelf, a television set, a secondhand piano, lamps. "Sit down. It'll only take a minute to put it on."

He set down the suitcase. "I'd rather follow you."

Because we had too much to say, we were silent, both searching for a place to begin. I put coffee grounds in the percolator, added water, turned on the stove. All the while I sensed that he was watching me, but what was he seeing? Was he disappointed? Had I aged so terribly while he remained young? Did I match his fantasies as he had exceeded mine? In this brief time, was he able to look inside me to discover that my soul had withered and my heart gone dry? I put the percolator on the stove and stared at the flames, unable to face him.

I felt his hand on my shoulder. "You are as beautiful as I remembered you," he said. "I think of you every day. You inhabit my dreams."

With a cry, I wheeled and buried myself against his body. He caressed the top of my head and I raised my face and we kissed.

It was the first time my lips had met another's in thirty years.

He was married. He told me that right off, as soon as we had settled in the living room with our coffee. His wife was Marilyn Schlesinger, the girl I had been jealous of on that awful day when he played for the "swells." They had a child, a girl named Elizabeth, who was to start at Wellesley College next year. When he got out of the army, he used something called the "G.I. Bill" to finance his way through college, and after that Mr. Schlesinger had gotten him a job with a brokerage firm called Jones & Thompson where he worked in mergers and acquisitions, whatever that was, work he enjoyed, though it was full of tensions and he was often exhausted. It had made him rich. He owned an apartment in New York and a summerhouse in Washington, Connecticut. Now that Elizabeth was leaving home, he hoped to travel more. He had told his wife that he had come to Israel on business, and he figured that while he was here he would call on an associate in Jerusalem to see if they could work together in the future. That part of his plan wasn't set, though. It depended on how long I wanted him with me. He could stay the entire time, or leave this evening—that was my choice. No matter what, he was going back to America in three days.

I received all this without emotion, neither pain for me, nor pleasure for him. I expected nothing else; it was only I who had not been able to go on with life. I enjoyed the land and the changing skies, a glass of wine, vegetables from my garden, and fresh bread from the kibbutz. I liked the warmth of the sun and the cool of the evenings; it even got so I could sleep without dreams. But I had experienced everything by the time I was twenty-two and had no desire for more. Vinnie was among the best parts of that experience; he had known my song.

But surely it had dimmed for him, or was replaced by other music. A marriage. A child. A good job. Comfort, American style. I had never hoped to *live* with him, only to see him again. That he had granted me, we'd kissed and he said I was beautiful. I was content.

As for his staying: I had no answer.

"You know," I said, "you just missed me when the Americans got to Paris."

His expression darkened. "Right. How I wanted to see you! British Intelligence said you were living at a place called La Maison or something-or-other."

"Aux Camellias."

"That's it. Nice name. Anyway, by the time I got there—and I can't tell you how I rushed; it was damn hard moving about—all I saw was a bombed-out building and an angry crowd. I don't know what they were angry about. I saw an Army jeep driving away, and there was a woman in the passenger seat, but that couldn't have been you."

I looked at him closely, trying to tell if there was a question hidden behind his statement. "Why not?"

"The woman had short hair. And yours . . ." He gestured toward me, smiled.

I felt tears spring up. How close we had been. "It wasn't me," I said softly. "Not your Mia."

We were sitting side by side and he leaned over and kissed my cheek. "I've said something that's made you sad."

"Yes."

"I'm sorry."

I stood. "No need. I was just reflecting on what might have been, and it's an empty exercise. Come. I'll show you my property. The apples and vegetables. We'll have them tonight for dinner."

He brightened. "Then I can stay a little while?"

"Of course."

We walked outdoors. The sky was cloudless. The cedar grove was regal in the distance.

"Beautiful," he said.

"I like it."

"You're happy here?"

Happy? Once, with him, I might have known the meaning of the word. I did not answer.

"Are you lonely?"

Lonely people feel their loneliness. "No."

"I'm glad."

We walked hand in hand around my precious acre and I pointed out the special places: a rock where I sometimes read in the afternoons, a tree with morning shade, a rise with its view of Lebanon, the garden, the apple trees. I raved on about them, a sightseeing guide suddenly inspired by her audience and able to see with awakened eyes. He said little, all the time watching me. I was conscious of his look, his breath, the warmth of his body.

"Do you like asparagus?"

He grinned, startled. "Sure."

"I'll pick some for dinner. There are none better in the world."

"Umm."

"We'll have potatoes and a salad. I'm afraid I don't eat meat."

"You used to love it!"

Meat meant blood. "Not anymore. Do you mind?"

"Don't be silly."

We walked back to the house. At the door he said, "Tell me about it."

I felt a chill. Dread. "About what?"

"Your life. You survived the war. What happened?"

My voice broke. "I was lucky."

"Then tell me."

He was leaning toward me, his expression serious, urgent. I felt a key touch the lock of my heart and begin to twist. "Maybe I will. In a while."

We had finished dinner, washed the dishes, and were sitting on the couch, drinking our second bottle of wine. Vinnie had remained in touch with Ceena and Martin, exchanging a holiday card and occasional call, but they knew nothing about the fate of the Levys, and so, hesitantly, he'd asked me. I told him that I never contacted my aunt and uncle. I was trying to forget the past.

"They all died at Auschwitz," I said. "My mother first; remember, I knew about her before I left New York. They kept Papa alive because he was a doctor, but he died of typhus. I was told he developed the typhus germ in the concentration camp and it infected many of the inmates. He felt that dying of typhoid was a more honorable way to die than in the gas chambers. He also prayed every day that the Allied planes would bomb the concentration camps, but that prayer was never answered. The German guards also came down with typhoid, and finally my father died of this disease. Ironically it was the disease he was trying to cure. Jozef—well, he tried to escape. They shot him before he got to the fence."

I felt no anguish telling him. Their deaths—yes, and Wolf's and

Sonia's—contributed to my numbness, and when I found out about Jozef and Papa from the Jewish agency, the news had as much impact as reports of casualties in the Six-Day War: their deaths, too, were distant tragedies. By the time I came to Israel, sent here by the Zionist underground in Budapest toward the end of 1944, I had given up any hope of finding them alive, and confirmation of their fate years later meant little to me. I had already done my grieving.

Vinnie took the temperature of my mood and was solemnly, appropriately sympathetic. No "Poor Mia" or "How awful for you," just an "I'm sorry" and a squeeze of my hand. Soon we went back to our dinner conversation, at once the safest and potentially most dangerous of subjects: Mia and Vinnie in Brooklyn.

It's funny how memory works. Vinnie told me of events—plays we had seen, trips we had taken, secrets we had shared—I had mostly forgotten, while those memories sacred to me were not that important to him. "Oh yes," he said as I told him of a shared cotton candy (my first) early in our relationship. "Didn't it make you sick?" But I hadn't gotten sick—that was weeks later after cheesecake at Junior's. We'd licked cotton candy off each other's faces, laughing, and it led to a kiss so passionate I thought my knees would buckle. For him, that kiss wasn't part of our history. Other kisses were.

It grew late. The sun had gone down hours before, and in those brief times that we stopped talking we had only country noises for company (it was not a night for Arab war games). A pleasant languor overtook me. We were sealed in the little box-house, removed from time, as much in Brooklyn as in Israel, simultaneously young and old, intimates and strangers. Vinnie got up and fetched his suitcase from where he had left it. We hadn't discussed sleeping arrangements, and now I was afraid the subject would come up when I hadn't decided what I wanted. But no.

"I've brought something," he said. "I wasn't sure, didn't know whether you'd be pleased or not. But it seems right."

"What is it?"

"You'll see."

He took out a long box from the suitcase and opened it. Its contents gleamed in the lamplight.

"A clarinet!" I whispered.

"Precisely." He fitted the pieces together, looking at me with an expression of—what? Hope? Expectation?

There was a strange tremor around my heart, the stirring of ancient excitement. "Will you play something for me?"

He laughed. "Not a chance. We play together or I don't play at all."

Together? "But I have no music."

"You have a piano. It's the first thing I noticed when I came in. I've got the music."

He bent over his suitcase and took out a score. I stood, put my hand on his shoulder, looked down at it. "Schumann."

"What else?" he asked. "The *Fantasy Pieces.*"

Those I remembered with a clarity that transported me back to Ceena and Martin's living room, the two of them listening as Vinnie and I played, my hands and his breath merging into the magic of sounds shaped by a master.

"I haven't played in years," I said. "Do you think . . ."

He glanced at me, raised an eyebrow, and I took the score from him and placed it on the piano. I sat down, Vinnie standing at my right side, and raised my hands.

"Now," he said, and we began.

The first of the three *Fantasiestucke* is a passionate song in all but name, its drawn-out melody written with equal attention to both instruments, which ride together like twin ships sailing on a turbulent sea. My piano was slightly out of tune, and the wood of the house made for bad acoustics, so that the clarinet was too bright, but what a difference. The voice of the music sounded in my ear like the voice of all that is beautiful in the world, and it filled my head and blood and heart with warmth. It was too much, *too much.* I felt like a diver plunging precipitously into the depth of that sea, and it was painfully hard to breathe.

Everything I loved about music came back in a rush. My fingers, unused for so long, were supple; my feet on the pedals moved to Schumann's commands as if he were in the room with us, telling us just what pressure was best, just what shading supplied the proper meaning.

From time to time I glanced at Vinnie. He played with his eyes closed, letting the music envelop him, part of that same sea. He was frowning in concentration, but his body swam to the music, and I heard a depth to his playing new to my ears. We were twinned again, partners in our middle age as we were in youth. The Schumann would be brief, I knew, but it opened my ears and let my soul fly free.

The song trails off into a wistful *pianissimo*. Without giving myself time to interpret what was happening inside me, I started the next piece, a gleeful game of hide-and-seek, the piano running away, the clarinet dashing just as fast but no faster to catch up. We took it at a furious pace, showing off for each other, the music laughing for us, and when we finished I threw up my hands.

"That's enough," I said. "Any more and I think I'll die."

He laid his clarinet on the top of the piano, took my hands, and pulled me to my feet. "Ah, we can't have that."

He put his arm around my waist, and I put mine around his. Joined by music and by something more profound than love, we walked together to the bedroom.

We took our time. Naked on the bed, we kissed and kissed and nothing more, letting our mouths join, prelude to our bodies. Then his hands, refined with use, touched me, gently at first—my breasts, my thighs, my core—then more passionately as his hunger rose. "Not too fast," I said. "This is new to me." He slowed, and for a while we simply lay side by side and kissed again, while I searched for desire.

I couldn't find it. I tried to summon up the images of making love with Vinnie that filled my head in Paris while I beat my victims or was fucked by them, but all I was conscious of was the sound of his breath and the too-practiced maneuvers of his tongue. I sat up.

"What's wrong?" Moonlight streaming through the open window danced in his anxious eyes.

"I could be your wife, or any of the others. Any woman."

"No. You're Mia." His protest was weak, and I felt a flash of anger. I started to cry. "It's not the way it was. Not the way I remembered."

"Yes."

He sat up, too, and turned me toward the window so that the moonlight fell full on my face. "I used to do this in the hotel," he said. "Let the light shine on you so I could worship you."

After a long moment, he got up and knelt by the side of the bed. "Lie on your back and put your legs across my shoulders."

From a recess in my heart hidden so deep that only he could have released it, I felt a new rhythm—and an old one. I obeyed him, smiling. "You used to do this at the hotel, too."

"Only with you. It's ours."

He kissed the inside of my calves, letting me feel his lips, his tongue, his breath. Now his bowed head, his black hair, shut out the moonlight, and I reached out to touch him, but he was too far away. The rhythm accelerated. He pulled me closer to him so that his kisses could come close. My nipples hardened. He raised his hands to touch them. I closed my eyes, giving myself over to sensation.

His mouth found what it was looking for. "Oh!" I cried. He brought his hands down, parted my lips, and let his tongue begin its exploration. My legs opened wider, granting him total access. This is pleasure, I thought. This is joy. I had forgotten the feel of them. Both melted into his mouth as I did, and my body shook with a force that brought my head up. "Come to me."

He crawled onto the bed, raised his mouth to mine. I could taste myself on his tongue and moved to repay him, but he had already entered me. I lay back, put my legs around his waist, and gave myself completely over to his urgency. He was fierce with wanting and his need kindled mine into a fire that would not be slaked. I came and came and came, crying out my ecstasy. He would not release me. I thought I could take no more, but he drove me further, letting me realize I had limitless capacity, infinite potential.

His thrusts grew stronger still. I tightened around him. "Yes!" I cried and he cried "Mia!" In freefall, we crashed into one another, rejoined the world, and slept.

The next morning I was up early. I felt like a young schoolgirl again. The sun was shining through my kitchen window and the world felt different. When Vinnie entered the kitchen, coffee was ready and some fresh Jewish bread, which was baked on the kibbutz. He wasn't wearing a shirt because it was warm that morning. He kissed the back of my neck, but I surprised him and swung around and held him tight. He felt so strong.

I decided to show him around the kibbutz and explained to him that a kibbutz is like a very small town where people live and work. I introduced him to some of my neighbors even though I knew they would start talking about me. I never had a male visitor before. They were all very polite. I thought Vinnie would get drunk from all the wine he drank with so many of my neighbors.

Only my good friend Sara, who was a Zionist and came here twenty-five years ago with her husband to live and work on the kibbutz, asked Vinnie where he came from. When he said, "Brooklyn" her eyes lit up. "I'm from Brooklyn, too." For a moment Vinnie was at a loss for words, but for the next hour they had an animated conversation about the many places in Brooklyn they both knew.

I never told anyone that I had lived in New York. To most of the people on the kibbutz I was a complete mystery.

Sara told Vinnie that on rare occasions I played the piano for some of my friends. She said I was great, and Vinnie just smiled.

When we finally returned to my house Vinnie said, "Let's go to Tel Aviv for dinner and maybe we can find a place that has music." I was so excited . . . I called my younger friends and they told me about a wonderful little place that made Eastern food, and served mostly vegetables.

That evening we drove to Tel Aviv. It was the first time in many years that I had dinner in a restaurant. We feasted on each other and the food at the same time.

Toward the end of our dinner a small klezmer band arrived. I explained to Vinnie that a klezmer band plays Eastern music, and I told him that his favorite clarinetist, Benny Goodman, loved klezmer music. Vinnie sat back and listened. He said to me, "Mia, that clarinetist is very good." He got up and walked over to the bandleader. He spoke to him for a few minutes and gave him what appeared to be United States money.

Vinnie was smiling when he returned to our table. The band started playing "Begin the Beguine." "Let's dance to our song," Vinnie said.

"I haven't danced in so many years I don't know what to do."

He took my hand. "Just follow me."

I couldn't believe how easily it all came back to me. . . . I thought I was in another world.

When the music stopped, Vinnie motioned to the bandleader and he played "Begin the Beguine" again.

This time when the music was over I didn't even realize it had stopped. Vinnie and I were standing in the middle of the floor oblivious to everything but each other.

When we finally returned to the table Vinnie said, "Would you like some dessert?"

I took his hand and said, "Let's go back to my house and we will have dessert there."

When we arrived at the house I started upstairs. Vinnie said "No dessert?". . . I smiled and led him upstairs, where our dessert was waiting for us.

We just stared at each other for a minute and he started to undress me very slowly. I decided to help him and he said, "I want to undress you myself."

I smiled. "I remember that first time in our hotel in New York, you undressed me the same way."

Vinnie looked at me and said, "When I'm with you I feel like I am still eighteen years old, and I know that will never change."

When I was standing in front of him naked I said to Vinnie, "You still have all your clothes on—now it's my turn."

That night we made love for hours—we couldn't get enough of each other. It was as if we were trying to get inside of each other and become one.

Finally Vinnie said to me, "I'm tired—let me rest awhile." With that he fell asleep on my chest.

When we awoke in each other's arms the day was cloudy. I started to get up to make breakfast. Vinnie said, "Don't go—stay with me."

"That's funny, I remember you never wanted to leave our hotel room either until the last second, but remember we still have another day here."

I kissed his head and he stood and put his arms around me.

We decided to stay around my home that day and would cook dinner together in the evening. It was so very peaceful.

During the afternoon we were listening to some of my records when he said, "You never told me what you did during the war."

True. I wanted his Mia to be the girl he loved in Brooklyn—the woman he made love to here in Israel. That is who I wanted her to be.

"Nothing dramatic," I told him. "I worked for the OSS mostly translating and interpreting reports. We worked out of La Maison— it was Paris—not New York. Not much different from what I did for Robert Sherwood."

He said nothing, and I wasn't sure what he was thinking.

As we listened to the music he held me very close and said, "I love you Mia. I never would have married if I thought you were alive.

Why didn't you contact me, or at least tell Ceena and Martin where you were?"

He didn't know that I did tell my aunt and uncle, but I didn't want anyone else to know.

"I couldn't see you because the war almost totally destroyed me. I didn't feel alive," I answered truthfully. "You don't love me the way you used to in Brooklyn, but a lot of that love remains. I know this from our last two nights, and I do love you so! You don't know how happy it makes me to be able to say it!"

That evening, after we had dinner together, we held each other very close. Vinnie whispered to me, "Someday I'll come back for you. I don't know when, and I don't know how. But I know we must be together. This cannot be the end."

I said, "I know it isn't."

The next morning while I was packing his bag, he came up behind me and said, "I have a present for you."

It was the score to the music that we had played together so often.

"I will treasure this always."

We walked hand in hand, slowly to the car. When he got in he rolled the window down. I started to lean into the car to kiss him and he turned away from me. I said, "What's wrong?" As he turned to me I saw the tears running down his cheeks. I kissed his tears and then turned away from him.

His voice called my name, but I didn't look back.

I heard the car move away and stood still until the sound disappeared in the distance.

A bird sang. The land was bright with promise.